Raymond Clark was born in a small mining village in the North East of England in 1948 and was one of eight children.

In 1963, much to everyone's shock, as he hated sports and anything physical, he joined the army and enlisted in Newcastle upon Tyne into the Royal Northumberland Fusiliers, later becoming Royal Regiment of Fusiliers.
In 1966, he was sent, along with the regiment, to Aden (now Yemen), where he served for 9 months and where the regiment lost 9 men because of civil unrest.

He saw service in Aden, Northern Ireland (several times), West Berlin, West Germany, Ethiopia, Kenya, Gibraltar, Morocco and Cyprus (UN and UK forces).

One of his most memorable moments was going to Ethiopia with The Regimental Band, meeting Emperor Hailie Selassie and having champagne and caviar with him and his wives at the palace – for a boy from the back streets of County Durham, it was a memory to retain.

He retired from the army in 1988 and worked in the retail, insurance, advertising and charity sectors.

In 2015, he was awarded a British Empire Medal in Her Majesty's birthday honours list for charity work.

His wife, Cynthia, died in Northern Ireland in 2000; his daughter, Jillian, and her husband, Andy, still reside there.

Raymond now resides in Canada.

He is currently the author of three books, two of which are self-published.

To my daughter, Jillian, and her husband, Andy Thompson.

Raymond Clark

GRANDA FRED

AUSTIN MACAULEY PUBLISHERS™

LONDON · CAMBRIDGE · NEW YORK · SHARJAH

A CIP catalogue record for this title is available from the British Library.

ISBN 9781528974479 (Paperback)
ISBN 9781528974493 (ePub e-book)

www.austinmacauley.com

First Published (2020)
Austin Macauley Publishers Ltd
25 Canada Square
Canary Wharf
London
E14 5LQ

I want to thank you all for enduring the nightmare and frustration, especially as far as the most hated and loathed machine on Earth is concerned, for me, MY COMPUTER, my archenemy and the tester of my patience.

A special thank you to my late cousin, Violet Winter and Cheryl Rafuse for their contributions to the picture of Granda Fred.

Penny and Saturday

It was a Saturday morning, and standing at the kitchen sink looking out of the window, Penny could see that there was a good chance of a spot of rain. *But rain never hurts anyone*, she said to herself. *I wonder how that saying ever came about.* Getting back to reality, today was that day again when she had to take the kids to see old Fred and Mary-Ellen. Old Fred, or Granda Fred, was her husband's father and Mary-Ellen was Fred's spinster sister. *So why did her husband never take the kids*, Penny thought. There would be more chance of the moon turning into cheese and even then he would find some excuse to get out of it.

Everyone said that Fred was a cantankerous old bugger and that he had never been the same after having seen service in both World Wars. The first time he had gone away, he'd gone like many other young lads, full of adventure and hope. But then on his return, he was full of disillusionment and hardly ever, like the majority of those who returned, talked about what they had suffered. They just tried to carry on with their lives as best as they could. Then the second war came and they had to go back. The fact that they had to go, they did not dispute. It was the known factor that this time, they each knew what they were letting themselves in for.

Fred had left his childhood sweetheart to go to the first war. Jane was her name. The daughter of the local butcher and lived in a nice semi outside the village. Her father, apparently, was a kind, jovial man, but according to all and sundry, his wife was a social dragon, and if anyone spoke and asked how Janey was, she would rebuke them and tell them that Jane was fine. When Jane had been baptised, her mother had decided that Jane Roberts did not have quite the ring about it, so without consulting with her husband, she had her registered as Jane Wilson-Roberts. Her husband just tolerated her idiosyncrasies and shrugged his shoulders, but the villagers, behind her back of course, would whisper, "Here she comes, Mrs High and Mighty. All fur coat and no knickers. She's no better than us. Do you know, apparently, on a Sunday morning, she insists that they sit on the front row along with others of like standing such as the doctor and other business owners?"

Of course, Mrs Wilson-Roberts knew what they were saying and she also knew that they were only jealous. Plus, it was highly unlikely that her children would catch something off the children of established members of the community. "Could you imagine the sheer embarrassment of having to purchase a 'nit comb'? One has to be seen, my dear," she thought out loud.

Fred and his childhood sweetheart had gone on to have three children, there was Ralph (her husband) and twin girls called Grace and Iris, who were still born. Then, as though that had not been enough, Jane was to die a year later. According to the local gossips, it was at that moment Fred became 'Old Fred' the grumpy, miserable loner, who never talked about his past, the war, the twins or even Jane.

"Penny love," came a shout from the front room, "what are you up to? Are you not going to see Dad today?"

"Don't worry, pet, I'm going. The world won't stop if I'm a few minutes later than normal."

"The kids are getting impatient and the sports will soon be on and you know that they hate that."

She thought to herself, *You aren't really bothered about the kids or your dad. All that concerns you is getting the non-existent winners picked then listening to the pools results in peace.*

"James, George, Claire, get your coats on and make sure that you take something in your satchels to either read or play with, then you won't get bored and start to fight with each other."

"But, Mam, why don't you just take Claire, then me and George can go out and play with the other lads?"

"Just do as you're told, and anyway, Granda Fred only sees you once a week, so it won't hurt you to smile and stop asking me the same question every week, you are going and that's all there is to it. You'll have a lot worse things to do when you grow up and then maybe your grandchildren will moan about going to visit you. In fact, on thinking about it, I wouldn't blame them."

"But he never smiles, and he coughs, and smokes, and blows smoke rings in our faces and he does the other and it stinks."

"And all he does is sit and look at that old tin box of his and won't let us anywhere near it," added George, "and he calls me Georgie Porgie."

"Be quiet, the pair of you. Why can't you be like Claire? Now go and say tara to your dad and give him a kiss. See you later, love, and good luck with the horses," she shouted as they closed the door.

Earlier on, the sky had looked a little downcast, but it appeared now that the sun was trying to break through, so she decided that they would walk. It was only a few miles. The kids did enjoy the walk as they played cowboys and Indians and then they would come to an old stone and metal bridge that crossed a railway line that ran to the pits. They could hear themselves shout and whistle because of the echo, so that kept them busy for a few minutes. Then they passed the allotments where they often stopped for a chat with Dolf, an old friend of Fred's, and sure enough she heard, "Morning, Penny pet, and how are you and the bairns today then?"

"We're all fine and you can guess where we're going, can't you? What about you and the family?"

"Aye, we're canny. Mona is on one of her baking sessions and one of the lads has a trial comin' up for Sunderland Junior team this comin' week."

"That's brilliant news, and if I remember correctly, isn't the other one into Newcastle?"

"Aye, you're right, pet, so you can imagine what it's like in the house when they start. Ah, I took them up to Bedlington Miners picnic, and guess who we saw? We were in the shows on the machines and in came Jackie and Bobby. Ah think, ah was more excited than the lads."

"You're just as bad as them, a kid at heart."

"Why don't you sit yourself down on the bench for a few moments, ah'll take the bairns in to see the rabbits, then we'll pick some flowers and bits of veg for you to take down to Mary-Ellen. Patience of Job has that woman, patience of bloody Job."

Penny thought, *Well, this would add another ten minutes or so to the journey, but it has turned out quite nice and the kids are occupied.*

As Dolf was getting some leeks and potatoes, he said, "If you want, I can always give one of the rabbits the chop and skin it for you, then they'll have some stew mid-week?"

"Thank you, but no thanks. The kids would never sleep, and I can imagine what their school compositions would read like on Monday."

They both laughed.

As she had guessed, ten minutes later, they were on their way with leeks, potatoes, cabbage and swede, a bunch of flowers and the kids a three-penny bit richer each.

Fred and Mary-Ellen lived in a middle terrace which belonged to the coal board and it overlooked a nice green area from the front, and once the kids got there, they loved to play out on the green and feed the old cart horse that was there, Minnie it was called. The back was the same as many other streets in the area. Penny knew that the kids disliked the old dragon that lived next door to Dad, Mrs Legg she was called. Penny wondered if she had been called Mrs Legg since she was born as no one ever mentioned her by anything else. Mrs Legg hated the kids throwing bread out for the birds. She said they dirtied on the washing, even if there was none hung out. She didn't like them bouncing the ball in the backyard as she could hear the banging in her house and she said that she was of a nervous disposition. Her own family were probably too frightened to visit.

The children were already in the house and getting something to eat off Mary-Ellen, when Penny popped her head around the door and said, "Hello, Mary-Ellen, and how is he today? Here are a few things that Dolf sent down for you." She placed the bag on the bench.

"Hello, Penny pet, and you know better than me how he is, sitting there with that tin box on his knee. He keeps saying that it's full of his memories, but I sometimes think that it's like his head, empty. I wish that sometimes he would get himself out and go and see some of his old mates. But no. He could easily pop out for a pint."

Poor Mary-Ellen, Penny thought, *she will probably die a spinster and it's a shame because she has obviously been a fine-looking woman.* Mary-Ellen didn't talk about her past either. It was a case of like brother like sister.

"The trouble is," said Mary-Ellen, "that since the twins died and then Jane, he has never quite come to terms with it. I honestly think that he feels he's somehow to blame. Every Thursday when the local arrives, the first page he goes to is the Birth, Marriages and Death column. The trouble is, being a pitman in a pit area, they've all known each other since they were children. Then they went to war and then back to the pits and then back to war again. It's a wonder any of them survived for him to read about. Plus now he swears he has the dust on his chest and that's what will kill him off. If only he knew that I sometimes think it will be me that kills the old bugger off." They both laughed.

"I often think how lucky Ralph and I are," said Penny, "We have a nice house with inside toilet and bathroom. There's also a garden at the front for the kids. With Ralph being a deputy, it means he rarely actually has to go down the shaft and then there's the added advantage of no dirty baths at home. We can even afford to go for day trips to the coast to Tynemouth, Whitley Bay or Shields, and don't have to wait for the annual pub trip outing. I really do realise exactly how lucky I am."

"It's alright you're saying that, Penny, but you have to remember, pet, that we knew no better, everyone in the street was the same. The pub trip or the pit trip were highlights on the calendar, like the Big Meeting at Durham, for the majority of pitmen and their families. Come rain, hail or snow, you sat on that beach and the kids plodged and collected shells and seaweed. You hired a windbreaker or sometimes a tent and formed a little circle like a wagon train and just got on with it. The men took off their jackets and rolled up their trouser legs and went and kicked water at the kids. Some of the bairns didn't have costumes and tucked their skirts into those hairy blue knickers that we wore. The kids slept well on the bus on the way back and parents had a sing-song. Then, of course, you had to remember when you got home, to put the seaweed out on a nail and if it was damp in the morning you knew the day was going to be a bit miserable. I mean, of course, if the bloody stuff was wet it was obvious it was going to be a wet day. Old wives' tales, eh?" Again they laughed, and Penny thought, *She really has quite a sense of humour.*

"Do you fancy a cup of tea, love? I have some Ringtons in?"

"That would be lovely," said Penny, "in the meantime, I shall pop in and see Fred."

"Good luck," Mary-Ellen said.

Opening the door, she said, "Morning, Dad, who's died this week then? I was talking to Dolf on the way down and he sent his regards and wishes that he could get you interested in the Leek show this year. He also sent some veg and flowers down and said that if you want a stew anytime he'll give one of the rabbits the chop for you."

Fred did not answer her straight away. He was thinking that Ralph had found himself a good one. She was kind, pleasant, a good mother and a bonny lass. *A lot of the qualities that Jane had,* he thought.

"Aye, lass, I'm fine, what has she been saying about me," nodding his head in the direction of the kitchen, "I was just thinking to myself what a bonny lass you are."

Feigning shock and looking suitably embarrassed, Penny said, "Well, thank you, kindly sir, you make me blush," mimicking someone from high society. "I'm flattered."

"Tell me, how are the bairns? Is Claire still being a tomboy? What about Georgie Porgie? He really needs to be toughened up and you need to stop mollycoddling him, let him get into fights. If you don't, he'll have a hard time when he gets older, you know that yourself. He'll end up being called names. You mark my words. James, on the other hand is a real lad."

"Strange you saying that about George, Dad, because he's the one who is insisting that when he's old enough he'll join the army as either a cook or a bandsman."

"Well, now that is a turn up for the books. I would have put good money on anything but that happening. I mean he's afraid of his own shadow that one and hates team stuff. I dare say he won't last, though, even if they take him. You know that yourself if you're honest. He would sooner stop in and play with toys."

Sighing, Penny said, "Well, he'll probably grow out of it and next week want to be a brain surgeon."

"Now that's something he has got. He is bright and may even end up at Grammar school, aye, be prepared for that to happen and he'll soon change his mind about the army as a job."

"I'll go and get you a pot of tea and a couple of biscuits. Ginger snap and custard cream, all right for you?"

"Aye, that'll do fine, pet."

Bringing the tea and biscuits, she said, "May-Ellen wants to know what you fancy for tea? I brought a homemade corned beef pie and a mince and onion one, or do you fancy chips from Pyles?"

"Thinking about it, a piece of mince and onion with some chips and mushy peas and a little brown sauce would be grand."

Penny went to the door and shouted, "James, I need you to go to the chip shop." He enjoyed going to the chip shop as there would be old newspapers to take and she always gave him a couple of small bottles of either dandelion and burdock or cream soda for bringing the papers. He also liked to listen to the gossip although the majority of times it didn't mean a thing to him.

When he got back to the house, the table was set for them, all except Granda, who always ate by himself.

After the meal, the kids were told to pop in and have their chat with Granda, and amidst much face pulling, they went and shouted, "Hello, Granda Fred," in unison and then sat down for their usual weekly grilling of what they had done at school etc.

James, as usual, was the first to speak and said, "Well, there's a new family moved in the street and they have a car, a Vauxhall, I think it is called."

"But they don't go anywhere in it," piped in George, "they just seem to clean it and tell us to clear off when we go anywhere near it. And last week, there was a wedding in another street, one of our schoolteachers, so we all went to the house and watched her come out and then her da did the hoy out of the money from the car window."

"I got five pence halfpenny, George got three pence but we had to give Claire something or she would have cried, so we gave her a penny each."

"My, my little, my little millionaires, are we? I can see who I'm going to have to borrow off for the gee-gees this week, eh?"

"Granda," said James, "can we ask you a question?"

"Aye, of course, you can. Don't know until I hear what it is if I'll be able answer it though."

"Every time we come," chipped in George, "You are sitting with that tin box on your knee. What's in it?"

There was a silent pause while Fred looked at them slowly in turn and then finally said, "Boys, this is not just an ordinary tin box. This is my memories tin. As I get older, I start and forget things and there are many things that I do not want to forget and there are maybe things that I want to forget. But we must keep all of our memories, the good and the bad, each helps us to be the person that we've become over the years. Remember, I once was your age, I wasn't born old Granda Fred, you know. We have to have the bad and the good in our lives. I never liked getting the belt off my da or a smack with wet hands off me ma, but they made sure that whatever I'd done to deserve it, then I never did it again. So, I did learn lessons from bad things. You will discover soon enough that life isn't all cowboys and Indians, goodies and baddies, football or knocky-nine-doors. One day you'll have responsibilities, a family, a job, a home, but you need those memories to help you see things from a view that you'd perhaps forgotten about."

"Granda Fred," interrupted George, "can you please show us something out of your memory box?"

James looked at him angrily. *How many times has Ma told us not to ask or even touch the tin without permission?* he thought. *There'll be hell to pay now.*

"The box. Would you really like to see something out of the box?" he said.

They looked at him in awe, he wasn't angry. "Are there really secrets in there, Granda?" asked George.

"If I start to show and tell you about them, then you mustn't tell your ma and da. Is that understood? It's our secret. And certainly don't tell your fuddy-duddy Aunt Mary-Ellen or she'll think that I've gone soft in the head. Is that understood?"

"Cross our hearts and hope to die," they both echoed.

Just as Granda Fred was about to open his box of secrets, the door opened and Penny stuck her head around and said, "Right, boys, that's enough of pestering Granda, we have to be on our way home and get your dad his tea and see if the pools have come up."

"But, Mam, that's not fair, Granda Fred was just going to tell us his…" said George.

"I thought we had made an agreement. There'll always be next time."

Penny was stunned. *They actually want to stay?* she thought to herself.

"Your ma's right, boys, it's time for you to be on your way, and no fighting on the way back and watch that railway line."

"Can we do it next week then, Granda Fred?" said George.

Granda Fred looked at them in a conspiratorial way, winked and said, "Aye, but remember what we agreed?"

"Yes, Granda Fred," they both said and gave him a kiss, and as they did so, he slipped them a tanner each and said, "Sh…"

As they said their goodbyes to Mary-Ellen, Penny said, "I don't know what's been going on in there but Fred's in a good mood. Bye."

Mary-Ellen replied, smiling, "That's good. Makes life easier for me so I won't complain. Now give my love to Ralph, and you three," she said, looking at the kids, "behave yourselves, okay."

A Strange Week for Penny

Penny could not believe it but she was actually sick and tired of hearing the boys talk about going to Granda Fred's again.

"What do you think about it, Ralph?"

"What do I think about what, love?"

"Will you listen? I'm on about the boys and your father. All of a sudden they don't want to go out and play with their friends but want to go and see your dad again."

"Why worry, love. They're now wanting to do what you are always on at them about. Stop fretting yourself. Some people are never content," he said and sighed.

"Mmmmm, I suppose you're right."

"As usual, my love," she heard from behind the newspaper and playfully threw the tea towel at him.

Looking at him, she thought it was strange how her mother had never liked him, probably because he didn't have his own business and was content to work in the pits. She just didn't understand that a deputy was like a shift manager, someone with the energy and enthusiasm to work his way up. He didn't want the increased worries of having his own business. She suddenly remembered something and said, "Ralph, have you remembered that there are some shelves to put up in the boys' room and it would be nice if you could box the bath in."

"You'd be better off asking Vera's hubby if he has time and give him a few bobs, you know I'm useless at woodwork."

"Not that useless to put up a greenhouse, a shed, rabbit hutches and a coop for the hens down the garden. And you seem to have an affinity for collecting wood, especially when it's just lying around the pit yard."

"That's different, love. I've told you before, there's no skill to any of that but shelves are different and boxing the bath in, you need all kinds of tools for those jobs. Anyway, must go down and feed the hens and change the bedding in the hutches. See you later."

*

The week was the same as normal, except for the kids. They kept pestering her about Granda Fred's and it was as she thought, they had written about him in their composition on the Monday. The teacher had written 'good story and Granda Fred sounds a very interesting man'. Monday was washing day, woe

16

betide her if she attempted to do it on a Sunday or hang anything out on the line. Ralph, like all men, said Sunday was a day of rest, even if the weather was good for drying. Then tea would be the normal fry up from Sunday leftovers. The ironing was for Tuesday and she hated it but it was one of life's requirements, now if she could get someone to do that for her, then life would be bliss.

Friday came and Ralph was late home from work and they'd all had their meal and the kids were in the bath with their boats. What a mess there would be when she went up. They'll have thrown water at each other and there'll be water all over the floor.

"Will you two behave yourself up there, or you'll be in trouble when your dad gets in." *Fat lot of good that threat does*, she thought and looked at the clock, it was just after 7 and she wondered about Ralph.

She was brought back to reality with a shout, "Mum, James has thrown soapy water in my eyes and it's stinging."

"I haven't. It was him. He started it."

"Right, you two, I'm coming up and irrespective of who started it I know who is going to finish it and there had better not be a mess either."

When she got up to the bathroom, she could not believe the mess. The towel was in the bath, there was water on the floor and George was rubbing his eyes crying and making a scene.

Once dried and the bathroom tidied, she put them into bed with the normal warning and a good night kiss and then she heard the front door open and Ralph shouted, "It's only me, love, sorry I'm late but it's been a bloody damn awful day."

Strange, Ralph certainly doesn't normally swear, there must be something wrong. Closing the bedroom door, she went downstairs drying her hands, as she did so and there was Ralph having a whiskey.

Looking at him, she could see that he wasn't his normal self, his shirt was dirty and the collar undone plus he looked exhausted. "What's up, love? What's happened? Are you alright?"

"There was an accident down one of the seams today, a couple of men were trapped and injured by a fall. It was just about 30 minutes before shift change and the alarm sounded at the top of the shaft and the clock man rang me to say there had been a fall but he didn't know as yet what had happened. I went over and put some overalls on and a couple of us went down and it was dark, dusty and wet. The air was really choking with the coal dust and it settled after a while and then we made our way along and met some of the men and they were pulling Gowlands' young lad away from the fall and he appeared to have injured his leg."

"Oh, poor lad," Penny interrupted. "Is he going to be alright?"

"Aye, they got him to the top and an ambulance was waiting, it appears as though his leg is broken but he's in Shotley now and his dad has been told."

"You said that there were a couple of injuries, is the other person alright?"

"Aye. Well, I hope so. We managed to dig him free but from what we could initially see it looked like there was a fracture to one arm with some bone sticking out and his breathing was pretty erratic. He was in quite a state of shock. Only 19, a young lad, poor bugger. Believe it or not, he was a grandson of Mrs Legg, the Mrs Legg next door to Dad."

"No. Really? I didn't think there were any relatives, she never talks about them."

"He's working at the pit to get extra money to go to college, he wants to study law and he knows that neither his family nor his gran can afford to help him."

"Is he going to be alright then?"

"He'll be fine, a few weeks or months off work will help him recover and he'll be able to study. I am going to speak to the union rep tomorrow and see if there is anything we can do with his tuition costs on a compassionate basis. Dolfy used to do all that stuff free in his spare time, but there is a new union rep, Embleton, I think, aye, that's right, a Gordon Embleton. In the meantime, any chance of a hot bath and another drink then I'll be down for some tea."

"Well, if I see Dolf tomorrow on our way down to see your dad, I'll ask if he has any advice, eh?"

"You can do but you can guarantee he'll know all about it already, these things go on the tom-tom quicker than lightning, plus I don't want to upset the new union rep by appearing to go behind his back. It might also be worth taking a bunch of flowers or even plus one of your homemade pies to Mrs Legg."

Tin Box Day

"Ma, will we be going soon?" James said.

"Mam, can we take some sugared almonds for Granda Fred and get Aunt Mary-Ellen something soft because of her false teeth," chirped in George.

Ma, Ma was all she had heard this last few days. *Sometimes I wish I'd never been a mother, life was a lot more peaceful and easier,* Penny thought. *No one ever told you that you stopped being a name when you have kids, and just become known as 'Ma'.*

Turning to Ralph as he was getting dressed to go out to see people after yesterday's accident, she said, "I don't know which is best, them fighting because they want to go, or them fighting because they don't want to go?"

He gave her a peck on the cheek and said, "Never happy, typical woman," and smiled as he dodged her playful slap, "I'll see you later, love."

*

"Granda Fred, Granda Fred," they shouted in unison as they ran past Mary-Ellen, dropping the satchels in the corridor, "have you got your box ready?"

"Calm down, boys, calm down. I can't do with all that excitement. And what did I tell you about mentioning the box? Eh? What did I say?"

"I haven't said anything to anybody, cross my heart and hope to die," said James.

"Aye, okay then, I believe you, thousands wouldn't. Come in and sit down quietly."

The box was on top of an old cracket that had been in the family for donks years and he himself had used it as a fort for his tin soldiers when he was a kid.

"Right, pass me that box then, Jimmy lad."

They sat wide-eyed as the first thing he pulled out was another small box and took the contents out which consisted of three bird's eggs wrapped in an old hanky.

George was the first to speak, "Granda, did you collect bird's eggs when you were little? Cos we got into trouble from the parkie and then Dad found out and we got into trouble again."

"I had a friend called Sam who was about your age and we played together, when we weren't collecting slack for the fire. We used to go up the park and

19

there wasn't swings and things like there are now, but there was a bandstand, tennis courts and a bowling green that the old men used. There was also a wooded area at the edge of the football pitch. We used to go there picking bilberries in the summer, but from spring, it was also a great time to go bird-nesting. Of course, neither of us knew how to blow an egg and we wasted a lot and I even swallowed one, shell an' all. Sam's brother had a book telling you about different birds, where they lived, and what their eggs were like, so we used to use that. The ones that you see there are a starling, a thrush and a sparrow. I was a bit on the small side, so Sam did the climbing up and passed them down to me. Everything seemed to be going alright until Sam was startled by a pigeon flying towards him. He fell out of the tree, tore his school shorts, and as he lay there at my feet, I was laughing because he had fallen on some of the eggs and the others were in my jacket pocket smashed and what a mess they made. We knew we would be in trouble when we got home, but, all of a sudden, there appeared the park keeper and the groundsman who had heard the noise we were making."

"God, no," said James.

"I'll have none of that language in this house. Do you hear me, lad?

"Yes, Granda. Sorry, Granda."

"Well, the park keeper lived two streets away from me ma and da, so he took us both by the collar and walked us home. If you had seen my da's face when he knocked at the back door. He had just come in from shift and was as black as coal, he just took off his pit belt and said a thank you and a sorry to the keeper and shutting the door smacked me five times with his belt. Poor Sam watched on horrified as he thought he might get the same. Dad looked at him and told him to get himself home and tell his da that he would be around later to see him."

"Did it hurt?" said George.

"Of course, it hurt, idiot," said James.

"That same belt is hanging right there on the door even now."

They both looked at each other and then at the belt, suddenly terrified.

"He then sent me to bed and told me that I wasn't coming down for tea and told me that it would be a long time before I was playing out with Sam. Needless to say, I lay on the bed and pulled the clippy mat on top of me and cried. I could hear me ma saying that she would take me a bite to eat up later but Da said, 'No, you won't he has got to learn.'

"She said, 'I bet you did it when you were a bairn.' Aye, that's as maybe but I never did it again."

The boys were stunned by this revelation, their granda pinching bird's eggs and keeping them.

"I look at those eggs, lads, and I remember learning that it was wrong to interfere with nature, those birds had as much right to life as me and you. It was a hard lesson to learn and that is why they are in my memory box. I still see Sam now and again and we have had a laugh over it. He told me that he had got the same belting when his da found out. Two things I learnt extra from it was, firstly, if you are going to do it, do not be greedy, there is no need for you to empty the nest, and secondly," lowering his voice and making sure he had their attention, "don't get caught."

"Wow, Granda, wait until we tell Ma."

"No, what is said in this room is our secret, alright?"

"Granda, what is that funny thin-shaped brass thing with the hole in it?"

Fred looked up at the clock and wondered if he had time to tell them about it before they had to make their way back home. "That," he said, "is a very important thing to a pitman. It can also be a thing of sadness. It is what is known as a tally or token. All pitmen, no matter what colliery they belong to, have them. Before you get into the lift at the shaft entrance you have to hand yours in to the 'tallyman' at the lift entrance and he records it against your name. If anything happens down there, an accident or an explosion," he paused, thinking about last night's incident, "when the men come up, they collected their tally and this way they could have another record of who was still down there. Everyone had to match their own tally, you could not hand it in for your workmate. This one belonged to my own da. Boys went down the pits early in those days and they were wage earners. They were used in a variety of ways, bearing in mind their size. They were handy for getting access to small areas and they often helped out with the pit ponies. Those ponies hardly ever saw the light of day. Aye, poor little buggers, they had to go down there. The men ate their bait and drank down there amongst all the coal dust, and if they wanted the toilet, then they just found a little space and did what they had to there and then." He watched them pull faces at the thought of it. "The times were similar to now in that no one owned their house, they were owned by the pits, who were often owned by people that did not even live in the area, or even in the county for that matter. They were the landed gentry, and when you saw them, they were all in their finery and you doffed your cap like a good little boy. People like the Marquess of Londonderry, the Bowes-Lyons, etc., etc. Aye they all made a pretty penny. Nearly, everyone in the street had someone working in the pits, some had all their menfolk including the lads, some as young as 12. There was one day and it started out like any other, the men off to work, younger kids off to school, housewives either doing the door step or hanging washing out on lines hanging across the street. Then all of a sudden, there was an almighty explosion. I was not much older than you two and I was in the playground at school and we all heard it. The teacher got us all in the class and tried to occupy us. Women and men left what they were doing and ran to the pit yard. Over 126 men and boys were killed that day, they were able to keep a record because of those tallies. Some of the families lost husbands, dads and sons. Do you know what the pit owners did? Families, when they got their pay packets at the end of the week, found that the wages of their loved ones had been stopped a day's pay because they had not finished their shifts. Then, because the houses belonged to the pit, the family was forced to leave, the house went with the job. It is a true story and one which many miners still feel grieved about. There had been 126 men and boys killed that day out of 168 that had gone down that morning and 2 of them were still unaccounted for when the day was finished. They had been coming up in the cage a few at a time and families were all waiting in the yard to see if their man or son was amongst them. Sam and his ma were there, and she was holding tightly onto young Sam while waiting for her husband and other son or to see if there was any news of them. Me and me ma went down as dad was on that shift and his tally was still at the top so we knew he had not been brought up yet. Women were in pinnies and slippers and some had their hair in curlers with a hairnet on, others brought mugs of tea and blankets. It was late in the afternoon when everything calmed down and da was one of the last ones up. By which time Ma was a wreck, totally worn out but the look on her face when she saw dad was fantastic, you could see that she loved him. The families of the dead were not treated well by the owners of the pits, as I have already said, some were told to leave without any warning, after all their houses were needed for new workers. My friend Sam's brother was alright but his father was one of the missing two that were unaccounted for."

"Did they close the pit down then, Granda," asked James.

"Close it down? Nae, such luck. That would have meant men out of work and no money coming in for the owners. No, they closed that seam and worked on others. It was about 24 years later when men were working on another seam that they broke through and found the other two bodies, one of whom was Sam's dad. They had died only yards away from where the others had been rescued. That crucifix there," picking a black cross with Jesus on it and showing it to the lads, "belonged to Sam's dad and his ma gave it to me as a memento of a friend. The other tally there is mine, everything's the same except for the number and name. That type of treatment to families wouldn't happen today because of people like your da who speak out for the pitman. And he does it free. Bit of a hero is your da. The only thing is don't tell him, as he would think that his own da had gone soft in the head. Remember my pal Sam? Well. As I said, his da was one of them that lost their lives that day."

The boys had fallen silent and were deep in thoughts and then George spoke, "Do we have to go down the pit, Granda Fred?"

"Well, there isn't a lot of choice for work here is there? There is the steel works up at Consett or the ball bearing factory at the 'Plain'. Of course, if you are really clever and can get to the grammar school, then there is work out there. But getting to grammar is a difficult thing, lads. You have exams to pass to get there and then there's a uniform."

The door creaked open and Penny stuck her head in without disturbing them, then went back to the kitchen and said to Mary-Ellen, "You won't believe it, there is total silence in there. Go and have a look at the three of them."

When Mary-Ellen came back, she said, "I think he's giving them his version of history and I hope that they don't become too upset by it as they may have nightmares tonight. I know that no matter how hard you try to block it out, you always end up worrying about your family and friends going down there."

Penny could see that Mary-Ellen was miles away in her own thoughts and then she thought of Ralph last night and how upset he had been. Apparently, Fred had only been nine when it happened, February the 16th, 1909, and the pit buzzer had gone, signalling a return to their shift.

"You're probably the same as any other pit wife, love, you learn to live your life around the pit buzzer, indicating change of shifts, dinner etc. It is like having another alarm clock in the house."

Penny smiled and said, "What drives me mad is this habit pitmen have of always having the clocks 30 minutes faster than the actual time."

"You know what men are like, love, they're not capable of thinking for themselves and need that clock faster than it is and then they know that when they look at it, they still have another half hour to get ready. Daft."

"I think that I'd better go and rescue him as he'll be ready for his usual pot of tea in a few minutes, won't he?" said Penny.

"Right, boys," she said, opening the door, "Time for going home."

"Aw, Ma," said James.

"Do we have to? Granda Fred is brilliant!" said George.

"There's always another day, and besides, I think Granda Fred needs a break."

"Aye, lass, that I do. But they've been good bairns today and I look forward to them coming down next week, if I'm spared till then that is."

"You'll outlive us all, Dad, unless Mary-Ellen decides to poison you, of course," said Penny.

George got up and ran into the kitchen and grabbing Mary-Ellen's pinny said, "You're not going to poison Granda Fred, are you?"

"Whoever put that daft idea into your head, pet? Poison him? No. Mind you, there are times when I could gladly throttle him though. All women say that about the man of the house, so don't worry yourself, he'll still be here next week when you come down." She gave his hair a ruffle. *Childhood innocence,* she thought. *Bless. The old bugger will outlive us all that is for certain.*

Why Can't We Visit?

On the way home, Claire was her usual self, pushing her dolls pushchair with her little black doll in and she was chatting away to it. The boys, well, they were in a strange mood, very quiet and very secretive. James had even been pestering her for them to go back to Granda Fred's tomorrow, Sunday.

"Mam, can we please?"

"No, tomorrow is Sunday and you have Sunday school in the afternoon, then we always have a look to the park as a family. Why the sudden interest in going to Granda Fred's anyway?"

"He tells great stories and did you know he even got the belt off his dad for bird nesting?" George said.

"Be quiet, big gob. We promised."

"Promised what," said Penny, stopping for a moment to look at the pair of them, "what have you promised?"

"Nothing really but we're pleased that we don't go bird nesting. I wouldn't want the belt," James said quickly and slyly tripped George up, making him cry.

"Will the pair of you behave or I'll give you both something to cry for," said Penny at the end of her tether. The boys ran straight into the house and said, "Da, do we have to go down the pit when we're older? Could we be killed if we do, and if we're killed, will Ma be kicked out of the house?"

"Whoa, slow down and where've you got all these ideas from? No need to ask. Well, you don't have to go down the pits, but you must stick in and do your homework, learn your arithmetic, your spelling, your English. You could be like Mrs Sowden's two daughters, one went to New Zealand to teach and the other is still at College in Durham.

"Her son has a good job working for the government in Newcastle, so there is hope, lads, but it's up to you. Anyway, George, I thought that you were wanting to go and join the army and be a cook or a bandsman? Have you changed your mind again? When I was your age, I was going to be an engine driver but I didn't get the chance, my education had not been that brilliant. You'll probably change your mind a few times before your time for leaving school comes around. Young lads are now aiming a bit higher. As for being killed, well, you can be killed in any job, a bus driver, a train driver, anything, there's always the risk of the unknown. You needn't worry about the house either at the moment. We're in a nice home with a decent job and we're saving for our own and then no one can kick us out. Do stop worrying. If we worried about everything, we would never get anything done, would we? Who knows what's in store for us? All each of us can do is to do our best both, for ourselves and for others, and look out for your family and friends. Yes, they're good general rules to go by. Now off with the pair of you."

Penny looked at Ralph and said, "Well, that was very profound, wasn't it?"

"I know. I must be getting more political, the next thing I'll be standing for the council or even the allotment association," he said and laughed. "Actually, Penny, I have been thinking –"

Penny interrupted, "Political and thinking. Both coming from you. My God, what will happen next?"

"Seriously though when we think of George, we've both agreed that he's not the rough and tumble type like James. But we do know that he's interested in music. So why not encourage him and then we can see if it is just a phase?"

"What are you suggesting then?" Penny asked.

"One of the men at work's dad has died recently, so his mother has moved into one of the retired miners' cottages. She has an old piano that she wants to get rid of for a couple of quid. So, I suggested to him that we'd be willing to have it for George. Then he can get some piano lessons and see how things go."

"What about the other two, though? Won't they feel left out?"

"What do you mean left out? James has cubs that he goes to, he also gets to see local football teams play. As for Claire, well, she's not interested in anything at the moment except her dolls. What do you think?"

"I suppose it's a good idea, but he'd have to be told that if he wants it, then we're not going to waste money on lessons if he's not going to commit himself. Yes, let's try it. Do you want to speak to him or is it going to be me?"

"No, we'll both do it before we all go down to see Dad."

"I note that you said before 'we' go and see Dad. Is that the 'royal we' or is that the one that excludes you?"

*

Morning came and Ralph was up earlier than his shift as he still had paperwork to complete after the accident and said to Penny, "Shall we have a quick chat with George before he goes down to Da's?"

"I'll give him a shout," said Penny, "George, come downstairs a moment we want to speak to you."

"What have you done now, George?" said James.

George just shrugged his shoulders and went downstairs and saw both his mam and dad waiting, and said, "I haven't done anything wrong. Honest."

"We know you haven't, not this time anyway," said Ralph. "No, we wanted to ask you about music because you're interested in it. If, and it is a big 'if', we were to get a piano, would you want to learn to play it?"

"A piano for me? Where would you put it?"

"Never mind where we would put it. That's our problem. We just don't want to waste money if you're not interested."

"I am, I am, yes, please," he said, shouting.

25

"Right then, get back upstairs and finish getting ready."

He ran upstairs, and said to James, "I'm getting a piano. *Nah-nah-nah-nah*." He said in a sing-a-long voice.

"Don't talk rubbish. You can't play one."

"I am, so there, smartie pants."

"You'll be a proper cissy then, as only girls play the piano," said James, not going to let go that easy. "And you'll have to stay in and practise instead of going out and playing. You'll end up playing all those horrible hymns from Sunday school. Soppy. Yugh."

James spoke to his mother as they went downstairs and said, "When we get in tonight, can we go up the bogs and get some ball bearings from the tip?"

Penny said, "I don't see why not as long as you put your old stuff on and Claire's not going with you."

"Good," whispered George.

"What was that you said?"

"Nothing, Mum."

"Mmmm."

She thought about Claire with the pair of them, they made her life a merry hell, although she was a bit of a tom girl, she still liked playing with her dolls. But when they played cowboys and Indians, she was always the one captured by the Indians and tied up to something. Or at other times, they'd fill her pockets with worms and creepy crawlies but when questioned it was always a case of 'it wasn't me, Ma'. Obviously, there was someone else in the house that she was not aware of.

When they got back, they changed and went up to the tip, a lot of steam was still rising from where the lorry from the ball bearing factory had emptied its load and they gathered quite a few of different sizes, enough to use as marbles or cannon shot.

George said, "I wonder why they don't make square ones?"

"You are gormless. If they were square, they wouldn't be called balls, would they, you idiot? Who ever heard of square balls? You can see you don't play footie that much. Come on, we'd better get home and washed or there'll be trouble."

"You're late," they heard from the kitchen as they tried to sneak in. "Wash, tea and homework and then the blanket show."

*

Penny was sitting by herself with some toast being made and the smell was mouth-watering and then the peace was shattered. All three of them came downstairs at the same time and dressed. Dressed in a fashion.

"Where on earth do you think the three of you are going and dressed like that?"

"It's Saturday and we're ready for Granda Fred's," said George.

"With your pyjamas still underneath your clothes? Upstairs now. Wash, teeth cleaned and dressed properly. Then breakfast. You're not going anywhere yet. Plus, there's someone important that you've all forgotten about since you became interested in Granda Fred. What about Bob? He still needs taking out for a walk." *God, I despair sometimes. Kids. Who would have them?* Until a few weeks ago, Bob was spoilt. They were always playing with him and taking him out for walks.

"I'm sorry, boys. And you, James, are old enough to know that dogs do not look after themselves. Go and take this cup of tea to your dad and then, without fighting, get washed and dressed and out with the dog. And don't make a noise because Mr Keebles has not long been in from work and will be in bed."

Mrs Keebles was all right but he always complained about the lads except, of course, when he wanted them to go to the shop for him. He waited until they got back from the shop and then gave them two empty bottles for giving the message which they then had to take back up to the shop they had just been to and collect three pence a bottle back which they then spent on sweets.

An hour later and they were ready again but today they had no toys with them but Claire, on the other hand, had two dolls this time.

"I'm taking Holly with Wilma this time and I've told her that if she behaves, she can come and feed Minnie with us."

The boys were wearing their balaclavas which had been knit by their Aunty Jane, Dad's sister, which meant that they intended to play highwayman on the way and waylay them for ransom, which normally meant that the ransom payment would be a gobstopper each. If not, then they were Robin Hood which always produced another row as Claire used to say she was Princess Maid Marian, George would then call her stupid because Maid Marian was not a princess, she was just a bonny woman and Claire was definitely not that he would tell her and then the tears would start. *I hope that George takes to the piano,* Penny thought, *because I hated the violin which Mother, of course, insisted that anyone who was anyone wanted to play. Screech, screech, screech and she used to show me off or tell people how well her Penelope was doing, but then she would be doing well as she had a natural ability. I am sure people avoided Mother on purpose.*

The kids were finally ready and Bob had been out for a walk and she popped in to see Ralph and said, "Do you fancy some cooked ham tonight? Mr Harris had some nice in yesterday and I'll get a couple of slices of tongue and corned beef as well."

"That'll be fine, love, and give Dad and Mary-Ellen my love, will you? See you later. And if you pass the bakers, a nice Peach Melba would finish off tea grand."

"My goodness, you've been listening today, what's up? It is normally a case of whatever. Anyway we're off now, so see you later."

Sure enough the boys went on ahead and hid behind some blackberry bushes that were growing wild and jumped out at them.

"Oh, my goodness," exclaimed Penny, feigning shock.

"Don't worry, Wilma and Holly, my mum will take care of these horrible, nasty highwaymen? Everything will be all right," said Claire to the two dolls.

"Please, take these, it is all I have. We are just poor travellers going to visit elderly family. Please. Spare us."

The highwaymen took the sweets and galloped off.

Claire said, "Mum. Wilma and Holly don't seem to get on that well together. Wilma says that Holly's hair is nicer than hers, but I've told her that she has nicer eyes, they are a very deep colour."

"What you must tell her is that God made us all different in our own little ways. It can be our hair, our eyes, our skin. But if we were all the same, wouldn't life be boring and complicated. Plus can you imagine if every boy was like your brothers?"

"Yugh. No, thank you. We wouldn't like that, would we?" she said to her dolls.

Isn't life amazing when you're a child, full of innocence, thought Penny. *I suppose even Mary-Ellen had that innocence. She had an advantage, I suppose, in that she didn't realise that she was poor because everyone else was the same. They all lead very similar lives, work, some play, made their own entertainment, hardly ever went anywhere except maybe to the local pub.* Penny had noticed that Mary-Ellen liked a glass of Mackeson Stout, a thick black-looking drink, 'purely medicinal' as said by Mary-Ellen.

The boys ran straight into the house and threw their coats and balaclavas in a pile on the floor.

"Wait there, you two little imps," said Mary-Ellen. "Where on earth do you think you are? You know where coats belong, so just go and do it now please," she said very sternly, stopping them in their tracks.

"Well done, Mary-Ellen," said Penny. "That put the fear of God in them. They're not used to that type of talk from you. And you two, you haven't said hello yet or given a kiss."

James did as he was told but hated it because Mary-Ellen had a mole with hairs growing out of it near her mouth and she always stunk of snuff.

Having done what they considered was their duty, they ran into see Granda Fred.

"Hello, my laddos, and how are you today? And what have you been up to this week?"

James said, "Well, we had to write a composition with no more than 500 words about our grandmas and grandas so now you're famous."

"Famous, am I indeed? I hate to think what you said about me. And you, Georgie, what did you get up to?"

"We did a lot of singing this week and it was about things that were from this area. We learnt about a worm that grew a lot and ate sheep and bairns and a knight came and killed it. Then about a woman called Cushie Butterfield who liked her beer."

"Well, the worm, so the legend says, wrapped itself around Penshaw Hill near Chester-le-Street and there are a lot of different versions of Cushie Butterfield, but apparently, she was a big lass."

While they were getting themselves comfortable, James ran out and got them a glass of pop and Granda Fred a pot of tea.

"Remember last week we were talking about the pit disaster, well, before we carry on, I'll tell you a little about the house we lived in. Like all the others it was owned by the pit and consisted of a backyard, a kitchen that was also you're eating area and a sitting room or main room. In that room was a large black metal fireplace and that's where you also did all your cooking. Then upstairs were two bedrooms, plus what was called a box room, which was just big enough for a single bed. There was a fire in each of the bigger rooms but they were never used. Couldn't afford to light them. The rooms were freezing, and in the winter, you scraped the ice off the inside. To keep warm, we put big homemade clippy mats which Dad made from old clothes cut up, on the beds. In the bed, we would have a firebrick which had been heated in the oven and wrapped in a bit of old sheet or something. Bathroom, there was none, at least with no bath, there was just a sink, for a bath we brought a big tin one in that hung on the yard, and a toilet, which was outside. You would have had a fit, especially you, George. The toilet, or netty, to give it the local name had no water to flush it and you used the newspaper that was hanging by string on the back of the door. The toilet seat was always cold on your bum and you had to take a candle in to see, so you never stopped longer than required. Ashes were put on the toilet. But, and I am very proud of this, me ma used to keep it like a little palace, they all did. Every week she was out there on her knees scrubbing the back door step and cleaning the hearth out. She used to go for walks and pick some wild flowers or bits of blossom to put in a jug to brighten the place up. The only thing they would not have in the house was May Blossom from the Hawthorn as they considered it unlucky. No, we had little but there was pride in the home. The allotments that the men had did a lot of feeding us, especially with potatoes and veg. Like all kids, we didn't like Brussels sprouts but there was always homemade broth and bread on the go and this lasted for several days. The people were proud of their houses and the thought of losing them was frightening. After that explosion, me da was not himself for a long time, in fact if I am truthful, he was never himself again. He had suffered a lot that day, the loss of friends, or marras, as they called their pals. Da was poorly but he still managed to get to work although you could see that it took it out of him. He kept saying to me, 'Freddie lad, I want you to do your best at school and try and get your exams and especially your writing and sums correct and then you can maybe get to the grammar. Then you won't have to go down there.' Well, I was doing well at school and it looked as though I was going to go to the grammar and then Da took really ill and I was actually old enough to go down the pit. Ma had no choice but to send me. We never told Da as it would have broken his heart. My first day was terrible but I was not alone as there were quite a few starting that day, it was a September day, cold, wet and the sky was still dark and the dawn was not really awake. I did not realise that when I came out again that day nothing would have changed. The sky was still dark, it would still be cold and it would still be raining. The only thing different was that I was filthy, tired, and hungry and every bone in my body was aching. I could have cried. I think the rest of the lads were feeling the same, but no one would give in. One of the older men said, 'Don't let yourself get down, it does, and will get better. There'll be a pay packet at the end of the week and you'll suddenly feel like a man.' I turned around and said to one of the others, 'I don't think that I'll see the end of the week.'

"I don't know where they found the energy from but he laughed and said, 'You'll have to survive or they'll dock some money off your pay.' At that even I laughed."

"But, Granda," said George, "Did you not get back to school at all ever and finish your exams?"

"Back to school? Nae, lad. School. That was a thing of the past. I kept reading and writing on the table at home, learning my time tables off by heart when I wasn't busy doing something else, but as for school, well, the next time I saw anything that looked like a class was when I joined the army. But I did become used to it and life got a bit better and the pay packet got better and I was able to go out to the village hall and have a dance and look at the girls. That was one of the first times I saw your gran, bonny lass she was, but looked well out of my class. Aye, don't let anyone tell you that they were the good old days. Because they weren't. What made it look as though they were was the fact that we didn't know any different. We still had fun, but all the hard times that we suffered, other people were suffering the same things. Yes, we knew there were big houses and some people went to church in a nice pony and trap. We just accepted all that. We had been born different and it seemed as though that is what it was meant to be like. You felt good in yourself if the local big-wig remembered your name and spoke and asked how the family were. There were also a lot of nuns around then at the local catholic school and you often saw them out but they looked such frightening creatures and you always watched your P&Qs when they were around. If you were a Catholic, then they always seemed to know what you had been up to and if you had been to mass or not."

"Granda," George said, "You know Minnie, the old horse in the field, would she have been a pit pony?"

"No, lad, she was too big to be a pony. She would have been a carthorse with the local co-op. The ponies were probably no bigger than the donkeys that you see at the seaside. They were nice little things but they had a worse life than us, but then again, like us, they didn't know anything else and many of them died down there or were sent to the knacker's yard and –"

George interrupted and said, "Granda, what's a knacker's yard?"

"That, young lad, is a good question. I sometimes think that's where I'll end up."

"If you do, will we still be able to come and see you, and why would you end up in a yard? I don't understand."

30

"You will one day, Son. It is just another of those daft sayings that you learn as you get older."

"There is such a lot to learn though as you grow up, isn't there? I'll have to tell teacher about that on Monday when we write our compositions."

"No, I wouldn't bother about that, as he being a teacher he may have never heard of it. They are clever people, you know. That's why they are teachers." *Hope that keeps them quiet on that one*, he thought.

"Then, apart from Ma worrying about me, your aunt Mary-Ellen was to be sent in to service. She had been picked to go to Windsor and live and work for posh people. She had been offered a place as a scullery maid. She would get paid, have her room and bed and food plus she would get holidays when she could come home. We had no idea where Windsor was, all we knew is that the King and Queen had a castle there."

"So she was going to live with the King and Queen and be guarded by soldiers then?" asked George.

"Well, not quite, although she might get to see them. It was a strange day when she left. She got the bus to Durham all by herself and had a label tied to her coat. Ma had done her some sandwiches, corned beef and brown sauce, I think, and some tomato and egg ones for the journey. At Durham, she had to get on a bus that would take her all the way and had never been away from home. It was nearly a year until we saw her and she had grown and full of stories. Her uniform was paid for from money from her pay. She also had to write home every week and send some money home for her family. She got about twenty-six pounds a year, which was a fortune then."

"Did she meet the King and Queen at all?"

"She met a Duchess, the Duchess of Athlone and also the Queen who was encouraging all her staff to make a collection for the poor. They all had to give a penny and she had to take it in a bag on a tray and curtsey. She was also given a present of a linen handkerchief by the Duchess, it wasn't new, but she was told she could keep it. But enough of her. When we could, we would still find time to have a game of football. We also had to go the pit heap over there and collect slack which was used to bank up the fire on a night. Although we were working down the pit, we were still classed as kids, and one day, one of my pals had got hold of a woodbine and we all thought that we would have a puff each. I was sick, really sick and then a man came along the path and asked what we were up to. My pal dropped the lit fag in his pocket and it caught fire. He ran to the pond and the man said, 'That'll teach you for telling porkies.'"

"Did you have a girlfriend then, Granda Fred?" said George, "James has one, her name is Violet."

"Don't believe him. I don't have a soppy girlfriend."

"Oh, yes, you do. I saw you blowing her a kiss the other day."

"I'll kill you, you little pig."

"Where on earth did you hear language like that? You do not call each other names and pig is not a very nice word, it's a dirty creature. I want no more of

31

that behaviour or language or you'll get the belt off me and there will be no six pence this week for you both."

Just at that moment Penny stuck her head around the door and said, "Are they being a nuisance, Dad? If so, they can come out here and take Claire to see the horse."

"That might be a good idea, pet, and, Georgie, you had better stop winding James up and, James, you are old enough to know better and should be setting an example instead of behaving like a softie. Now shake hands, the pair of you. Now. Be off with you and behave yourselves."

Penny said to Mary-Ellen as they were on their way out, "Don't quite know what's going in there today, but they've come out very subdued and with their tails between their legs. Anyway, we'll see you next weekend if not before."

The boys were sulking all the way home and Claire was chattering away to Wilma and Holly. She looked at the lads and thought to herself, *They are so different.* George was chubby, prone to going in the huff and was very clingy and not that keen on sports and games. James, the complete opposite, the muckier he could get the better. Always untidy, the hair, socks neither up nor down and had the tendency to look like a future thug in the making. Typical little lad everyone said. Whereas he wanted to be a famous footballer like Stanley Matthews, George still had this fancy for the army, heaven help him. Thank goodness for Claire. She wanted to be a nurse and was always putting bandages on the dolls and taking her dad's temperature. He had the patience of Job with her.

Fred and Mary-Ellen

Fred and Mary-Ellen were having one of those rare moments where they sat down and chatted about life. She'd made some homemade gingerbread and Fred was having his with a thick covering of butter and a mug of tea. Mary-Ellen settled for a nice China cup and a piece of gingerbread.

"Strange, isn't it?" he said. "When you look and listen to the bairns, how all of our lives are entwined, and then you think that whilst our lives were similar to Ralph's, and his is similar to theirs, yet how different they are at the same time."

"Well, it's a good thing that things are so different, isn't it? You wouldn't want them having to face the same things that both you and Ralph did, would you? I mean, the pressure isn't on them to have to go down the pit. As for Claire, she doesn't have to worry about going into service."

"Did it do you any harm though? Going into service I mean?"

"In many ways, it did, and, in many ways, it didn't. I saw life at first-hand how the other half lived. It was impressive for a while that I was part of it. It even showed me that the poor were not all alike, there was still a rank system between them, and I think it was worse than amongst those upstairs. They understood the rank system, but downstairs did not, after all, they all originally thought they were the same until they got promoted. Me, a scullery maid. I wasn't even allowed to sit and have my meal at the same time as them. Then, when you did eat, it was normally food that they had not wanted. But I did have a bed to myself, a toilet and the place was warm, and if I do admit it, you did feel special working there. The sight of all those soldiers coming and going and doing guard duties at the castle. There were some right bobby dazzlers if I say so myself. They could certainly turn anyone's eye. But we only got one afternoon off, sometimes a Sunday after church and it was only once every two weeks. A couple of us would save some food and sometimes cook, if she was in a good mood, would let us take some sandwiches and have picnic in the park. You could watch all the nannies pushing their charges around. The gentlemen walking with young ladies. It was so different from up here. In fact, you could forget up here quite easily, but you did get homesick and missed family, even you, if I am honest. It was also nice not to worry about the pits, the strange thing is that apart from one other girl, the rest of them who were there hadn't the faintest idea what it was like for a family who worked in the pits. The majority were country girls and they found the life in a city strange and busy, whereas we found it exciting."

"It's when I look at young Ralphy and Georgie porgie that I worry," said Fred.

"I wish you wouldn't call him young Ralphy, you know that James hates that name, and as for George, he doesn't like people think that he looks like a nursery rhyme."

"Well, they'll have to get used to worse than that as they grow older, especially George, if he doesn't get some of that sissyness knocked out of him. If Penny's mother had been alive, she would probably have him learning some of the shopping trade and certainly would not be encouraging him to think about the army."

"Aye, she was a funny 'un, alright. I remember once, a young couple used to come in the shop and Jane's da always put an extra ounce on for them and then she found out that they were from the local gypsy site. Well, she blew a gasket and proceeded to get the carbolic soap out and set about cleaning everything. And she was a good Christian woman. Humph, I think not."

"Mary, do you ever wonder what life would have been like if your William hadn't been killed in the war?"

"He was not killed. He was listed as missing in action and there is a big difference," she replied.

"There is no bloody difference, woman. It is over thirty years now. Is he still missing?"

"Fred, there is no need or call for you be so, so, so, bloody blunt about it. What's done is done and I can never change that."

"Yes, but do you never regret not falling in love again and having children to look after and having your own life?"

"Don't you think that I have enough to do now anyway, looking after you? Plus, all your old boxes of stuff cluttering the place up? Plus, if we had had children there is every possibility that I may have lost him or her in the last war." If the truth was known, she had often thought about William. She had thought of that one night of sheer magical sexual bliss that they had shared before he went off to war with his friends. She often looked in the mirror in the hall and thought how time had treated her. Sometimes, she was that young, naive girl at Windsor, infatuated with the soldiers, other times she was the young lady with a glint in her eye, thinking of William. Then other times, she saw an old grumpy, hair-netted old spinster that life had passed by. But lately, and she hadn't told Fred, that someone had commented on her eyes and how they must have glinted with devilment when she was younger. She felt a flush coming to her face at the thought of it, *Me and old Mr Laverick.*

"Those boxes aren't clutter, everything in them has memories and a use. Anyway, look how useful they are being at the moment, the boys are fascinated by their contents, and it is giving them living history lessons. It's good for them to know where they came from and the type of life we had. We want to try and encourage them that there is life out there and to improve themselves. I am not ashamed of where I came from or of what I went through, but if we can teach them that there is more in the world than pits and war, then that is a good thing."

"But Fred, in many ways, it could all happen again. You had your war which affected you and our lives. They said that there would never be another and what happened, there was. That affected you and your son. What guarantee do we have that we won't see another?"

"We can't guarantee anything, pet, except that once we're born, we will die. Anything else is out of our hands. All we can do is hope. Aye, all we can do is hope, pet."

Grandma Jane (To-Be)

It was that time of the week again, Saturday, and the weather was looking the same way as Penny felt. If she did not know better, she would have sworn down that she was pregnant, God, that would have the neighbours talking. Should she go today, or in fact, could she even be bothered? No. The kids were looking forward to it and she enjoyed the chat with Mary-Ellen. *I am sure that in his own way even Dad enjoys the lads going down.* Ralph must've had a winner during the week because he even gave her a couple of shilling to get ice creams when the van came around the street and he sent Dad an ounce of baccy. *Must have been two winners,* she thought, smiling to herself. The boys were in their normal form. They stood near some puddles until Claire got near and then they jumped in them and ran off and, of course, the tears were rolling, mainly because Claire's two 'children' had got wet.

"You two, when we get home your dad will hear about this and woe betide you both, and Claire, it's only water so stop making a scene." The rain had stopped, and the lads went off and picked some wild flowers for Mary-Ellen and they passed the time of day with Dolf in the allotment but did not linger as he was loaded with cold. Two workmen at the old brickworks shouted out, "Going to turn into a canny afternoon, pet."

She smiled and returned their greetings.

As they approached the street, she noticed that the front curtains of the house two doors up from dad were closed. That could only mean one thing. Someone had died. "Right, you lot. I want you to behave and be quiet today. If you're going to play ball, do so in the field and not in the street. Do you understand?"

She had wasted her breath as they had not even heard her and ran straight into the house, gave Mary-Ellen the flowers and went into see Fred.

"Granda Fred," started George already, "how did you meet Grandma, and did you have any other girl friends?"

"Well, now you ask, I did have other girlfriends. I was like your film stars of today, but I did not have them at the same time as I was going out with your grandma. God forbid, I would have been hung, drawn and quartered. No. One woman is enough for any man at one time, at least if he values his life anyway. I had an eye for the girls but they did not seem to have the eye for me. It was at the church hall where you met any girls, or, if you were older, at the Palaise dance hall. Dancing is something that your ma should be making you learn, the girls love it and if you keep sticking in with your music, George, girls seem to have a fascination for musicians. There were four lasses that used to go together,

Anne, brother of the Dodd's, lads, and those were lads you had to watch. Always up to no good. Then there was Edna, who lived nearby, Lillian who lived near the school and, of course, your grandma. Your Grandma Jane was the daughter of the local butcher and would have been considered out of my league. Well, certainly in her mother's eyes anyway. And there was also a girl called Violet, a real little madam. When there was a dance, the lads used to dare each other to ask someone for a dance as we stood with our backs to one wall, the girls with their backs to the other and the group, if there was one, in the middle. Of course, there were always fights with some of the lads belonging to gangs and they tried to show off to the girls. If you went and asked a lass to dance and they said no, then your pals would fall about laughing, but this night, your grandma came up and said, 'Well, are you going to ask me to dance or do I have to ask you.' The lads' faces were a treat. I told her that I could not dance and she said, 'I know.' I had never been that close to a girl before and… well, you will find out one day yourself. I am not sure who was the most embarrassed. I thought that I was in heaven. We left the hall at the end of the night and the lads were all winking and nudging me, saying, 'Well. Did you?' Come on, you can tell us.' From that moment on, we managed, accidentally, on purpose to bump into each other often. Then on my sixteenth birthday, she said, 'I have a present for you. But you will have to close your eyes.' I did and she gave me a kiss on my cheek."

"Yugh, how disgusting!" said George. "Fancy being kissed by some horrible sloppy girl. I think that James has had a kiss as well."

"I have not," said James, rather sharply, in a way that implied that he had. *He will either be boasting soon or not telling anyone,* Fred thought.

"George, one day, I know, you will look back on that remark and think that you were daft. Well, at least I hope that you will. As I said, we kept seeing each other as often as we dared because if the dragon found out, there would be hell to pay. Jane's mother was a reincarnation of the devil himself. Her name was Rosalind and woe betide anyone who even thought, let alone attempted to call her Rose. In her eyes, if you did not sit in the front two pews at church and go to evening service, then you were a no one. She had even decided that she would be known as Mrs Rosalind Wilson-Roberts, as she had added her maiden name to her married name which made her think that she was even posher."

"So did you marry her then?" asked James

"Not then, but we eventually did, and that was a story. I told you that we had been seeing each other very discreetly so that the dragon would not get to know. We went to the park one afternoon and were seen by a 'good-intentioned neighbour' who happened to be passing the bench that we were sitting on near the bandstand and holding hands. 'Good afternoon, Jane. I didn't realise that you came here,' she said so sarcastically. 'I must have missed your mother. Is she looking at the flower beds?'

"'Good afternoon, Mrs Harm. I think that she may be having a scone in the pavilion.' Of course, the neighbour knew that that was a blatant lie and hurried on. Unbeknown to us though, she did bump into Jane's mother later in the day and said, 'Hello, Rosalind. I'm sorry that I missed you at the park earlier today, but I asked Jane and her young man to pass on my regards to you.'

"'I am sorry about that, but you will agree that the park was busy today and I needed to sit in the shade, but maybe next time.' The neighbour smiled and nodded her head as a farewell, knowing full well that she had done the damage."

"So, what did the she-devil do, Granda? Mam says that the devil weaves all kind of nasty magic."

"Your mam is right there, lad. I never saw Jane again for about three years after that. She had been sent away to a relative who lived at the seaside and then to a private school near Newcastle. My mother was now older, more middle-aged really but Da had gone to work one morning and suffered chest pains and died from a heart attack. Although Ma could keep the house because I was working at the pit, she decided that she would apply for a retired miner's bungalow up near the park. Up near where you go bilberry picking with your da. It was a nice little place, two bedrooms, a kitchen, living room, garden at the front which also had a section for vegetables. There was even a washroom with bath. The house looked onto the football field at the park and the vicar's house was at the end of the row, quite a large house and garden it was. There was a road of sorts running through the wood and there was a milestone post there telling you how many miles it was to Newcastle and to London. The old men used to tell us that the ghost of Dick Turpin was sometimes seen there."

"Wow. Did you ever see Dick Turpin then?"

"Not then, lad, but I have met many a man doing highway robbery since and before you say anything – don't ask. It is just another of those daft things that adults say. When you are your age you say to yourself that you are never going to be daft like your mam and dad but, believe me, you end up doing and saying the exact same things that they did."

A Marriage Proposal and the King's Shilling

"Anyway, as I was saying, it was another three years before I saw your Grandma Jane and I had been seeing a lass called Edna, but a girl called Anne was always attached to her which was a pain. Jane had come back from her time away and we met at the church hall again. We were by now older, and all the lads talked about nothing else but girls, we all bragged, of course, about what we had been up to, but if the truth was known, we were all still cherry boys."

"Granda Fred," said George, *I know what is coming now*, Fred thought. "What are cherry boys and what's a cherry?"

"Ah, I suppose that I should not have used that expression, but a cherry boy is a young man who has still not been familiar with a young lady." Before George could ask again, Fred continued, "Yes, now, where was I? That's right, Jane had just come back and we were now three years older, but the other thing we all talked about was Germany. We had heard of it, of course, and we knew it was over the water, but no one had been there. Well, for some reason or other, a king had been murdered. Germany was talking about a war. We knew that if there was a war our king was going to be fighting his German cousin, The Kaiser, which seemed strange to us. Whenever we went in the house or down the pit, it was the main topic of conversation, and our families were gathered around the wireless listening to the BBC. An important announcement was going to be made and we all sat and listened. The prime minister and the King said that we were now at war with Germany. The government wanted young men to join up and fight to save their families. Some people were exempt from joining up, the sick, shortsighted, those with bad chests. Ship builders, miners, steel workers were not being accepted because their jobs were considered essential to the war. Naturally, we discussed it among ourselves, and believe it or not, we thought that it would be exciting."

"Well, did you see Grandma Jane again then?" asked James, "And were you familiar with her?"

"Aye, James. I did see her again, and again, and again. We talked about the war and whether I should go as it wasn't good seeing other men go and you stay at home. We had also discovered that we loved each other, in fact, we discovered that we loved each other a lot and not seeing each other every day made that love stronger. I had some money saved. My ma had moved into the retirement home and your Aunt Mary-Ellen had returned back from service in Windsor and was now working as an invoice clerk in Woolworths in Newcastle and her prospects looked good. She was even able to bring odds and ends home on a night from the small counter that had biscuits, cake and cheese on it. Jane looked at me and said, 'Fred, I know that you and the lads will all end up going and fighting, but I wish you wouldn't, as you are needed in the pit.' I told her that other people would do the pit jobs but that our country needed us. I then had a brain wave, which for me is quite unusual," he said and laughed at his own joke. "I thought why don't I ask Jane to marry me?"

"Bloody hell, Granda –"

"What did you say? What did you say? How many times have you been told not to swear? How many?"

"Sorry, Granda Fred, but I just wondered what the she-devil would say if she found out you were going to marry her daughter?"

"So, I said to Jane, 'Well, why don't we get married before I go off to war?' Total silence there was and I thought that I had well and truly messed things up. She suddenly grabbed me and said, 'Yes, Yes and Yes. But what about Mam and Dad, especially Mam, she will go crazy?'

"'That's easy. We don't tell them yet.'

"'What do you mean? We won't tell them yet.'

"'Exactly what I said. There is no need to tell them. I have been saving up and anyway one of the lads has already done it. You can go to Scotland to a place called Gretna Green and get married over an anvil. It is legal and we could go from Newcastle to Carlisle by train, then a bus to Gretna Green. All we need is the two of us and two witnesses. They could be anyone that happens to be there at the time. Stay overnight in the B&B there, come home and carry on living as we do now until we tell them. What do you say?'

"'What do I say? What do I say?' she repeated, 'I'll tell you what I say. Yes, yes and yes,' and hugged me tightly. 'Can you imagine my mother? Dad will be champion, but Mother. Her daughter marrying a pitman who is intending to join the army as a common soldier. She might have minded less if you were going to join as an officer.'

"'Aye, pet, I can imagine your ma. God, can I? There are a lot of things to sort out, and as I have said me and the lads are very serious about joining up and thought that if we all went together to enlist that we may be able to join the same outfit. Probably either the Durham's or the Fusiliers.'"

"Is it that easy to get married then, Granda?"

"Normally, it takes a lot of arranging because a woman wants to look her best and have bridesmaids and a church and a nice tea laid on in the hall for friends and relatives to come. But sometimes, things can be done quicker and without so much fuss. But first, we had to see about joining up. We all got the bus to the town and there, outside the big co-op, was a tent, a band playing and loudspeakers and men queuing up to sign on. There were posters everywhere and people clapping and cheering. It was more like a day 'out at The Hoppings' than anything else. The atmosphere was fantastic. Outside the tent, there were a couple of men in uniform, an officer with a peaked cap and shiny boots. Someone who looked a bit fierce with a big handlebar moustache with a stick under his arm. There was also a table where someone else was taking names and a load of men, fat, thin, tall, short, dirty, in suits, posh, and all smiling. You could hear their towns and they were from places like Consett, Durham, Hexham, Morpeth, Newcastle and even some places that I have never heard of. The man was shouting, 'Come on, lads, don't let your mates fight for you, fight for your own family. The King needs you. Come and collect the King's shilling.'

"When you got into the tent, there were different lines and you stood in front of another table and had to take your shirt off and drop your trousers. Someone measured you and weighed you, checked your eyesight and looked at your teeth and then someone held your bits in their hand and asked you to cough. One bloke nearly punched the man that had touched him and he said, 'You can pack that in, I'm not having any of that.' Then the man with big stick popped his head in the tent and yelled, 'You, you cissy. Shut up and do what you're told, if he wants to hold them or even play with them, you let him, you understand? You're not in bloody Sunday school now with your mother mollycoddling you. You are nearly in the army, but on looking at you, I don't think that we're that desperate yet.' Everybody laughed at that, and he yelled again, 'Who the hell gave you lot permission to laugh? You laugh when I tell you to laugh. I decide what is and what is not funny, not you. Do you understand?' There was no answer, and he continued, 'Do you bloody understand, you stupid idiots.'"

"'Yes, sir,' was the loud combined reply.

"'Once you have signed that form there in front of you, you will have no such thing as a mother. I will be your mother, your father, your bed partner. Now isn't that a pleasant thought?'

"He heard one of the men mutter 'aye'.

"'What did you say?' singling a man standing there in his singlet and a pair of long johns.

"'Aye, Sgt,' said the man with a look of trepidation on his face.

"'Well, lad, you got 5 out of 10,' the lad smiled. 'What you're smiling for I don't know. That means you only got half of the reply correct. From now on, you will always reply either "Yes, Sgt", or if an officer is on parade, it is "Yes, sir", do you all understand?'

"As one, we all shouted, 'Yes, Sgt.'

"'Now you, you long skinny streak of shit get down and do 20 press-ups now, and the rest of you close your mouths or you'll be joining him. When you have all finished in here, follow the corporal into the next tent where you will find an officer waiting to talk to you as a group which will happen in exactly 15 minutes, not a minute earlier or a minute less and you stand without talking.'

"We were all gathered together, nearly 100 of us. Along with the Sgt, there was an officer and a corporal who looked just as evil as the Sgt. I whispered to Spelk, who was next to me, 'If all of the soldiers are like those two, why not send them and they can beat Jerry before we get there?'

"'Silence in the ranks. Officer on parade, Sah,' he shouted and saluted at the young captain.

"'Gentlemen, today you have answered the call of the nation. You have answered the call of His Majesty. You have decided that it is your duty to take up arms and defend everything that is near and dear to you. Your family. Your country. Your king. The people of these islands are depending on you, and I am sure that you will do each and every one of them proud. It will not be like playing soldiers at school or on the fields near your homes. It will be for real. Some of you will be killed. You will have to kill others. Remember that this war has not been created by England. It has been created by Germany and her allies. Even the King and his family are personally affected in that their relatives will be fighting opposite them. I want you all now to raise your right hand and looking at the pull-down screen to read the oath of allegiance. To God, King and Country.' We all read and felt very special and proud that we had been picked to fight for our country.

"'Right, men, remember there is an officer on parade. Stand to attention. Permission to carry on, Sah?' the Sgt said.

"'Carry on, Sgt. Thank you.'

"'Right, you horrible shower, stand at ease and relax. You are now under my maternal care. I will look after your welfare, your training, even wipe those tears from your eyes when you miss your mass. You will go from snotty nosed lads to men. Fighting men. Men not afraid of their own shadow. Men who will lay down their lives if required for their pals and country. When we have finished in here, you form lines in alphabetical order at the tables marked and you then collect some money from the officer and corporal at each table. You then report to the central station in two weeks' time, that is 14 days for the thick among you. You will then be taking by lorry to your training destination, which, because it is wartime, will remain confidential until you get there. You now have 14 days to get everything out of your system, shag as many women, or sheep, if that is your preference. Say all your goodbyes. In two weeks' time, your life will change, forever. Fall out.'"

Back Home and the Wedding

"The gang of us, well, four of us actually sat on the bus home chattering and making comments about the Sgt and how we thought that maybe he was really a nice soft guy.

"'You are joking,' said Spelk. 'Did you hear what he said about being our bedfellow? The man's a stark raving nutter. Then he said that if we were into sheep, get it all done before we go back.'

"'Yeah, but he then said, if you had been listening, cloth ears,' said Snotty, 'that when we get wherever it is we're going that there'll be no women but plenty of sheep for those interested.'

"'Aye, maybe it is sheep you're interested in after all, Spelk. Plus we haven't seen you trying to chat up any girls or is it the Sgt that is interesting you,' said Chalky and we all laughed except for Spelk. 'Ah, hadaway and shite, the lot of yous.'

"The first thing ah did was to go home and tell me ma and Mary-Ellen but neither jumped for joy, I think that deep down they were both pleased that I was going to do my bit but, at the same time, were concerned."

"But what about Grandma Jane? Did you not tell her?"

"Aye, I went for a walk and we had arranged to accidentally bump into each other at the park, near the bandstand. When I got there, she was there waiting and ran to me and we kissed like two young lovers."

"What did she say?"

"I said, 'Well, pet, I am a soldier now. Your boyfriend is a soldier but doesn't know what regiment or anything until we have done our training. We go in two weeks' time, so how about I arrange the wedding for next Wednesday?'

"'Fred, you really are something else, aren't you? Springing all these surprises on a totally innocent young lady. Suggesting marriage. Whatever next? What will my 'mata and pata' think? You really are a soft romantic at heart.'

"'Bugger your 'mata and pata' or even your ma and da for that matter, we are getting married and going to be Mr and Mrs Frederick Hardy. You are going to become the wife of a soldier in the King's service.'

"'I hope that I get to play with your weapon then, Frederick Hardy,' she said quite cheekily.'"

"But you wouldn't have let her really touch your gun, Granda, would you. I mean that would be dangerous, wouldn't it?"

"Of course, you're right, lad. That would be silly and dangerous. No, we were just being silly giddy young people. Touch my weapon indeed. Never."

"So how did you both get away from your parents? Did you tell lies? Because you tell us that we haven't to do that?"

"Well, they weren't really lies, they were just little fibs, like we all tell from time to time. I told Mary-Ellen that I was going to stay for a few days with a friend from Hexham and Jane told her mother that she was going on a bus excursion to Hexham to see the Abbey and stay over with a girlfriend that she had met at private school. We met on the bus to Newcastle, but with both of us getting on at different stops and then sat in separate seats but near enough to chat so we didn't bring attention to ourselves. It really was exciting and then we got the train at the central station to Carlisle. There were other people in the compartment and one of them smoked a pipe and the smell was horrible and the window was stuck so we decided to try and make him feel guilty and I started to cough."

"Did it work, Granda?"

"No, it didn't. Instead he turned around and said, 'You should get a linctus for that cough, lad, 'cos if lies on your chest it could be death of you.' Jane hid her smile behind her hand, and she said, 'The gentleman's correct, Fred. You really must go and see the doctor about it as we do not want you with long-term problems now, do we?'

"'Sensible young lady you have there, if you don't mind me saying so. Yes, not many as sensible as that, certainly not.'

"We eventually got to Carlisle and then had to wait for the bus to Gretna Village. There was another couple on the bus and we got talking and we agreed that we would be their witnesses and they would be ours. He was in uniform and was going off to the front in a few days' time, so they had decided not to wait until he got back but do it now. I forget their surname but I think that they were called John and Ethel and were from Manchester, so they had come a long way to get wed. Unlike us, their parents knew, and although they had given their blessing, they weren't too happy as they had wanted to have a proper wedding with everyone there. Lovely little village it was, and the wedding place was nice and I managed to buy some flowers for Jane which I decided to share with John, so they could have some flowers also. Why buy two bunches when one would do. They had a little brownie camera so were able to take pictures of us all and they said they would send them on as soon as they had been developed. We really had a laugh and then we went for a drink and a bite to eat, nothing special but the café lady made it all look and feel special. That night we stayed in a lovely little hotel nearby as the new Mr and Mrs Hardy. Then next morning after breakfast, we headed off back home as Mr Hardy and Miss Jane Wilson. Here is a picture of us at the anvil and this one has John and his wife on it."

"Granda, you looked very smart in your suit and Grandma Jane looks like a film star from the black and white pictures."

"I'll tell you a wee tale about the suit. Because I was joining up, I never got to get a new one from the co-op, just didn't have time. So I went into the wardrobe and got one of my da's old suits. It fit me and it looked champion and no one was any the wiser."

"So you didn't live with Grandma then?"

"No, lad, we had decided that until we had to tell them we would wait. We would be a bit older and then they could do nothing about it except tut and moan. To be honest, it was quite funny pretending that you were single when you bumped into her mother and knowing at the same time that you were husband and wife. We had many a laugh at that. Only one of the lads knew, I told Spelk and he was able to help us out and see each other now and again. It was a bit like being a spy I suppose. I saw her the night before I had to leave and we had a cuddle and a kiss and a few tears, not me mind, it was your Grandma Jane that cried. No way was I going to cry, men don't."

The door opened and Penny said, "Hello, Dad. They have been quiet today." Looking at them, she said, "I hope that you haven't worn Granda out?"

"No, they've been fine and it was a pleasure to have someone listening to me instead of Mary-Ellen saying I was senile and rabbiting on. Get yourself out, she keeps saying."

"Well, you should, there's nothing to stop you, and you know it wouldn't hurt you. I'm sure that Sam and Dolph would enjoy having an excuse for getting out of the house. Anyway, boys, say your goodbyes and then take Claire over the field to say goodbye to Minnie before we go. Bye, Dad, and see you next week unless…"

"I know, unless you see me earlier," and they both laughed.

A Welcome from the Sgt

"The day had finally arrived. There was me, Spelk, Chalky and Snotty, along with about nearly a hundred other lads all at the Central station in Newcastle at the start of a new adventure. My old friend Sam had come to see us all off as he had been turned down because he was too small. Poor soul, it really upset him. Anyway, they had told him that as he was a pitman, he was more use where he was than at war. It didn't make him feel any better though, but he accepted that what he would be doing was, at least something useful for the war. We were all saying our goodbyes to loved ones, friends and then we heard that voice again, yes, it was him, the Sgt.

"'Right, you horrible lot, you have had your fun and said your goodbyes. It is now time to turn you into men and make you a fighting force that will frighten those Jerries and make sure they don't reach these shores. Now fall in in three ranks. Make sure you have got your suitcases. We shall have a short march to the cattle market where we shall meet the trucks and off we go. Right listen in. Attention. By the left quick march, left, right, left, right.

"'Your bloody right foot follows your left, you piece of shit. Left, right, left, right. Swing that free arm and look proud. We'll soon be there and looking at the lot of you the first thing that you'll do is to get your bloody haircut.'

"I looked at Spelk and said, 'I've just had mine done and paid a bob.'

"'Nobody said you could talk, concentrate on marching, left, right, left, right. Listen in. Company halt.' Some of the lads carried on and bumped into those in front.

"'For those too thick to know what halt means, it means you have to stop. And stop that laughing because I can assure you that where you are going, there will not be time to laugh, and you'll be too busy wishing that you had stopped at home with your mammies. What free time you have, you will find that you are too tired to laugh, all you will want to do is sleep and I can also tell you that sleep is another thing that is going to be in short supply. You have to learn to stay awake and alert, after all Jerries won't stop attacking because you haven't caught up with your beauty sleep. And just looking quickly at you now, you all need some beauty sleep because you've got to be the ugliest bunch of men that I have encountered for a long time. Now climb onto those trucks and we'll be off.'

"When we climbed on board there was about 30 of us plus our cases, some of the lorries had covered fabric roofs and others were open to the elements. As we drove through the town and out into the countryside people stopped and waved and wished us good luck and others just went about their normal everyday business.

"'I've just had my bloody haircut,' said one.

"'And me,' said another, 'and if God Almighty thinks that I am going to have another one, he's got another thing coming and I'll tell him. You mark my words.'

"'You're all talk, mate. I for one am not going to start off on the wrong foot with him. Remember he said that he was going be our mata and pata.'

"'Heaven help us all,' said a voice from the front of the lorry.

"'It seemed that we had been on the road for about three hours or more, we had passed towns and villages and just came across the odd farmhouse and there were lots of sheep and cows around. The land just got more and more desolate and bleak.'

"Chalky said, 'I think that I have been up here before and I am sure that we're up in Northumberland in the country rather than the coast. Probably somewhere like Otterburn.'

"'Where the hell is Otterburn?' said Spelk. 'I bet it is miles away from the nearest pub and I have brought my pulling clothes.' Everybody laughed. But there is always one wise guy in a crowd and he shouted, 'The only thing you'll be pulling up here is yourself, mate,' and more laughter followed but by then it was starting to drizzle and the sky was looking very gloomy."

"Was it a real army lorry, Granda, and did it have any guns on it?" asked George.

"Well, there was a soldier in uniform at the back of the lorry with a rifle, but I don't know if it was loaded or not, but every lorry had one. In the front was the driver in uniform and either an officer, a sgt or a corporal alongside them. Then all of a sudden, we pulled up outside of this camp with lots of huts, soldiers on guard, some soldiers with dogs walking around the outside and all looking very official. We moved off again and stopped a few minutes later on this hard gravel area. The shout came, 'Right, you shower, get down, put your cases in a pile over there beside the corporal and fall in on the square.'

"At this stage, I was starting to think what the hell have I let myself in for, but deep down, I knew that what I had volunteered for was the right thing. We were formed up in three ranks again and told to listen out for our names. When they were shouted out, we then had to go and stand by a couple of designated soldiers, there was a lance corporal, he had one stripe on his arm and then a corporal, he had two strips. When your name was called, you had to shout 'Sir' and join your NCO as they were called."

"What's an NCO, Granda?" asked James.

"These were some of the things that we had to learn and there were loads of them. An NCO was a Non-Commissioned-Officer which meant that he wasn't a posh officer like a captain or something like that. In fact, we learnt that really, he wasn't an officer anyway, he was just some bloke like me and the rest of the lads who had behaved or was good at his job and then been promoted. It sounded good and terrifying at the time though. To us lot he was either a mini God or a mini devil, and we soon found out which he was. It was normally the mini devil. What was even funnier was that one day several of us, including me, would end up mini devils. Funny that, isn't it?"

"Then what happened? Were you bullied?"

"As I said, our names were called out alphabetically so that meant the Spelk (Harris), Woody (Hall), Snotty (Jones) and me were all together. We found out later that Chippy (Wood) and Chalky (White) had also been put together. We stood there in a group of 32 we had counted and waited to see what happened next and then… 'Right, you lot, be quiet and listen in. My name is Corporal Smith and you will call me exactly that from now on. I am not your friend. I am not your mother or father. I am one of the men that has got to turn you shower of shit into men. I am also your hut NCO. I shall be living in the same accommodation as you. In a few minutes, I will take you to your hut. Firstly, though there are several things that you need to learn fast and one of them you should have already learnt because that is who you are from now on. Every time you speak to me, the Sgt, the Company Sgt Major, the Regimental Sgt Major or an Officer, you will give your number and name. You will start doing that immediately, so for those of you that have forgotten or not read it on your documentation that you got when you signed up, you had better start and believe in the Almighty, because if you don't believe in him now, then you will by the time that we are finished with you. Right, fall in in three ranks and come to attention when I come to you and tell me your number, name, your previous occupation and where you come from.'

"Needless to say that the majority of us, me included, had forgotten our numbers and were each ordered to do 20 press-ups and then run around this square with our arms up in the air shouting out our number, if you could remember it and name, then come back to the corporal and say it. If you had been lucky and remembered it, then you were told to crouch down and remain in that position until the whole 32 of you had completed the task. We were still there nearly an hour later, but when we looked later on, one or two of the other groups were still at it. Poor buggers.

"We marched off and did not head to the wooden huts that we were to be accommodated in but to another set of inter-connecting huts, same colour but there was a name saying 'Quartermasters stores' and inside were a couple of soldiers and another NCO who was filling paperwork out and you had to give your number and name again. You were told to sign at the bottom. You didn't get a copy and as yet we had no idea what we had just signed for. You then went to another section and in front of you was your pile – a horrible mattress, two sheets, one feather pillow and one pillowcase and four hairy blankets – told to pick it up and wait outside. It was bloody hilarious and daft. Trying to carry it all by yourself. The more we laughed, the more we got told off by our corporal Smith."

"Wouldn't they let you use the lorries that you had come in to move all of the kit that you had, Granda?" asked James innocently.

"No, James, we were in the army now and had to learn to do things the hard way.

"Then Corporal Smith told us to follow him and we ended up outside a wooden hut marked B1, this was to be our home for however long. The door was open and inside it was freezing, and there were 16 bunk beds plus some metal lockers battered and damaged, plus a large room at the rear of the hut. B1 had a stove in the middle, but there didn't seem to be any coal or wood. We all picked our beds. I went for a bottom bed and Spelk got the one above me. We were just about to start and introduce ourselves to each other and have a woodbine when Corporal Smith made himself known again.

"'Right, you lot, stop giggling and chattering like virginal schoolgirls. Put your bedding down on your bed and form up in threes outside. Yesterday, not tomorrow. Move it.' So now we headed off yet again in the direction of the Quarter Masters Stores, but this time to a section marked 'Equipment'. It was the same as last time, a queue, and two people getting kit and putting it on a counter in front of you and someone with another piece of paper to sign. No one asked sizes or anything like that, they looked at you and said either small, medium or large. I bet they still did that in your dad's time. To be honest, if you ever get to join up, Georgie, I dare say they will still be doing it. There were swimming trunks, underwear, hairy shirts, PE kit, boots, a battledress uniform that was also hairy and lots of other miscellaneous stuff, and again we had to carry it all back to the hut.

"'Right, dump it on your beds and outside in ten minutes in running kit.'

"'Ten minutes,' said Spelk, 'ten bloody minutes, how the hell are we going to do that?'

"'Well, if you shut up and sort out the stuff, we'll all do it quicker,' said someone else. Ten minutes later, we were outside the hut, all dressed and ready except for one person who said, 'Corporal Smith, sir. I have only had time to get one of my sandshoes, I couldn't find the other, Corporal.'

"'In that case, you have my sympathy, but if you are too damn idle to manage what everyone else can do, then you'll just have to run like that, won't you?'

"'But, Corporal Smith, what about my feet?'

"'What about your feet, lad, you have two now and you'll have two when we finish, and I am sure that next time you will remember the other sandshoe. Now shut up all of you and listen in. We shall be marching and then running, and when I say break into double time, you then run in step. Quick march, left, right, left right.'

"This went on for over an hour and then we turned up at an assault course, there were ropes, swing bridges, ponds, mud and more mud. No one moaned, we didn't dare for what might happen to us. It was nearly three hours later when we returned to the hut. No one was talking, we did not have the energy.

"'Right,' said Corporal Smith, 'that will do for starters. You are a bunch of Nancy boys. You go get your showers and then there is evening meal 30 minutes after. You then will have about two hours to sort all your kit out and lights will be out at 9pm. Tomorrow morning, you will be shown how to lay your kit out the correct way. You also have to remember to go to the stores and get your cases before they close and looking at my watch, that is in about 45 minutes. Fall out.'

"Spelk said, 'Bloody hell, does he think I have some kind of rocket up my arse?'

"'Well, mate, if you don't have one up there now, I think that you had better learn to get one up there or I think we shall all suffer. Remember he told us that a hut is only as strong as its weakest person,' shouted someone from the other end of the room.

"Bloody hell, there's no hot water as we turned the taps on all that came out was bloody ice-cold water, plus there were no cubicles, just a row of showers, sinks and toilets. We also did not realise that we, every day, would have to clean the whole place. Needless to say having a shower did not take long."

"But what about your gun, Granda? When did you get that? Did you kill anyone with it?" asked George.

"Don't be stupid, you idiot. Of course, he killed someone with it, that's what happens in wars. Doesn't it Granda?" replied James.

"I would have wanted a gun straight away and then I could have shot that corporal," voiced George.

"You couldn't shoot anybody. You're too soft," said James and pushed George then gave him a sly kick.

"What on earth have I said to you two before? Behave or else. Am I talking to myself?" he said as they continued to fight.

"Penny," he shouted, "I think that it's time for these two rascals to go home, they seem to have had enough for today."

"Sorry, Dad, we'll be on our way shortly, but I know what will calm them down. They can go and see Aunt Mary-Ellen and help her to wind some knitting wool, that'll stop their arms from fighting."

"But, Mum, it wasn't me," said George, "it was him."

"I am not bothered who it was or was not, you'll both help."

Fred sat and watched them leave the room and stared at the picture of him and Jane. *She really was a bonny lass*, he thought, *and she had the pick of the lads, but picked me.* He kissed a finger then placed on the lips of Jane on the photograph, *If only life had been different, pet, and you could have seen the grand kids, you would have laughed at their antics and probably spoilt them at the same time. Little Claire has a look of you but, unfortunately, she also has a look of Penny's mother. It's be hoped she grows out of that before she gets much older,* and laughed to himself.

Ralph, Penny and the 'Familiar' Word

When they got home, the boys ran straight in to see their dad who was busy watching the results and checking his coupon.

"A bloody home win," they heard him say. "Why the hell for once in your life can't you just draw?"

He was startled by the kids, and knowing he wasn't going to win a six-figure sum, or any other figure, he put the paper down.

"Yes, and what are you two up to and after and don't say sweets because I know your secret about Granda normally giving you some money, I have my spies everywhere."

"But how can you know that? It is supposed to be a secret. Unless it's big gob here," George said, looking at James.

"And I know that you normally get midget gems from Mary-Ellen."

They looked at each other wondering who the 'tell-tale tit' was.

"It was you, wasn't it," said James to George and pushed him so that he fell on the floor.

"You," said Ralph, slapping James on the leg, "behave. And you," looking at George, "stop being such a cry-baby, he didn't push you that hard. So whatever it is you're after, the answer is no. Go and wash your hands and then help your mam to set the table."

The pair of them stood there looking a little crestfallen and James rubbing his bare leg.

"Now, I said, not tomorrow," he shouted at them. "What's the old bugger being saying to them today that they are so wound up?"

Penny had been lost in her own thoughts thinking about the kids and their futures, she had a little money saved, well, quite a lot really, from money that her dad had left and then there was several bits and pieces of jewellery that her mother had left which one day would be good for Claire. The money would help the family all around. "Sorry. What was that you said, love?"

"I was just wondering what Da had been talking to them about today?"

"I've no idea. They were a bit quiet on the way back. I think he had told them off."

Just then James came in and said, "Mam? Were you and Dad ever familiar before you got married?"

She nearly dropped the cup she was holding and said, "Were we what?"

"Familiar with each other," James innocently repeated.

"Where on earth did you get that expression from?"

"Granda Fred," he answered, "he told us that he and Grandma Jane got familiar with each other before they got married but he didn't tell us what he meant and then he said that they had run away to get married."

"He did, did he?" said Penny, "Your dad and I knew each other from childhood, he used to come in the shop that my dad had. We were on speaking terms with each other, but there was always someone around. Your grandma Roberts did not want me to be friendly with your dad."

"Why?" James asked.

"Because your dad and his family were all pitmen and my mother thought that they weren't or never would be good for her daughter. She felt that a vicar, a teacher, or a businessman would be more suitable for me, anyone but a pitman."

"I heard Dad call her a stuck-up cow one day. What did he mean by that? How can a cow be stuck up?"

"I think that I shall have to speak your dad," said Penny, trying not to laugh. He had probably said it after one of her very brief visits after we had got the semi.

"Da," said George, "were you in the same war as Granda?"

"What, me in the same war? Just how old do you think I am? No, that's not quite true. I wasn't in the First War with him, but we were both in the Second one. Not side by side but we were in it together."

Then James decided to add his pennyworth, "Da, were you ever familiar with Mam before you were married like what Granda Fred and Grandma Jane were?"

"Penny," shouted Ralph, "Do you know what he's talking about? And, more to the point, do you know anything about what he's been talking to them about? I shall have to go and see him and have a word with him or stop them going over there for a few weeks."

"Ah, Da, don't do that please," said James, "he teaches us –"

Interrupting him and very quickly losing his temper, Ralph said, "Have you never been told that it is rude and bad manners to listen into people's conversations and not to speak until you are spoken to? Well? Have you?"

They looked at each other very sheepishly. James was going to say something but suddenly thought better of it.

"And after tea, you can get yourselves upstairs, washed and ready for bed and no toys for a week. In fact, for the next week apart from school, you will not be playing out, there is homework to do and you can both help your ma."

Penny looked at their faces and thought if best not to interfere as Ralph was exercising his power as man of the house.

Ralph's Visit to Granda Fred

Sure enough when the weekend came around, Penny was surprised to see Ralph up and around early. He wasn't even studying the form for the horses and was sitting putting his shoes on.

"You off out, pet, the paper lad will be here soon."

"Ahm, off to see me da about whatever he has been filling their heads with. I'm amazed that you and Mary-Ellen haven't picked anything up."

"All we know is that he is talking to them about his memory box, including the pit, the pit accident and, I think about Grandma Jane."

"It's alreet asking," she knew he was annoyed and getting himself worked up as the accent was stronger. "But talking about people getting familiar is bound to make the lads curious, and then we'll end up with dads banging on our door telling us that their daughter is pregnant and our lads are to blame."

"Ralph, you know that your dad is not that daft, not with everything that happened with him and your mam, I'm sure."

"No, Penny, I have to go and see him and clear the air. Either he or Mary-Ellen will stop speaking and go in the huff for a couple of weeks, but at least if that happens then the kids may have forgotten it all by then."

"You know something, Ralph Hardy. I sometimes think that you and your da were in the same wars. And remember, if you can go that far back, of course, that you were a nosey kid and an even worse teenager."

She slammed the door shut and took the three kids off for a walk despite him saying that they could not go out. They went over the bogs, watched a coal train pass and waved to the driver, who hooted his whistle and waved at them. They walked on to a village called Old Kyo which consisted of a couple of pubs and a school and one shop cum post office. Popping into the shop, she bought them a two-penny homemade pineapple lolly each.

They returned the same way they came, and it ended up with them pushing Claire into a gorse bush. When they got to the top of the hill, they sat on some old large stones which had once belonged to a very large old house which had been burnt down many, many years ago. This was a world that Jane knew and one that she wouldn't want to change. She had had the opportunity to move to a 'posher school' after the Newcastle one but she had managed with a lot of sulking and a lot of arguing that it wasn't for her. She learnt more about geography from the labels of exotic fruit tins. Yes, I suppose that mother would have been correct and that she would have met a 'well-positioned' young man as her mother would say but Ralph was well positioned enough, and they were comfortable. No, she was happier than the Queen of Sheeba.

At the same moment, Ralph was on his way to see Fred but was waylaid by Dolf and he had asked where the missus and kids were today.

Ralph thought Dolf a decent bloke, in fact his brother Ted and sister Anne were also good sorts and seemed a close family. Dolf had done a lot to help miners get compensation when they were injured, and Tot worked at the Steel works and also had an allotment. Anne lived at a place called Catchgate.

"They're all out for a walk together, so I thought that I would take the chance to pop down and see Da. He always tells Penny that he might as well not have a son."

"Aye, well we all think that about our families, I remember my mother saying to me that a daughter is a daughter all her life but that as son is a son until he finds a wife, and I think that that is true. And he thinks the world of you and the family, but you know what us blokes are like. We can't go around telling other men, even if they are our sons, that we like them, can we?"

"Aye, ah kna but I don't want the bairns getting their heads full of nonsense. Anyway, what about you? Did you go to the dogs on Friday night? I managed to get myself a winner 'The Youngan' owned by old Jack Walker over at Craghead. I must admit that I had always thought that he had stood more chance of winning if he'd run his missus instead of the dog." They laughed and Dolf said, "Aye, there's not that much difference to look at, is there?"

Dolf went and picked some veg and a bunch of wallflowers for Ralph to take over. "Before I forget, what's this I hear about Mary-Ellen setting her cap at old Laverick?"

"Well, I never," said Ralph, "she has kept that quiet, not even a word to Penny. Isn't he the widow with three lads and a lass? I think one joined the army and moved away and the daughter lives somewhere else as well?"

"Aye, that's the one. Anyway, give them both my regards and tell ya da I'll pop over myself and see him one day."

"Well, well, Mary-Ellen and old Laverick." *Well, I never*, thought Ralph.

He knocked at the back door as no one ever went to the front door, and Mary-Ellen answered, wiping her hands on her pinney.

"My good God. We had better watch that the roof doesn't collapse," she said, "come in, pet, and I don't stand on formality in this house, especially when I live with old grumpy." Giving him a kiss and a hug, she continued, "How are you, Ralph? And the rest of the family?"

"We're all fine, Mary-Ellen, just thought I'd come have a chat with Dad. They'll probably not be down today as I think Penny was going to take them up the park to clear her head she said. No, I think she is maybe coming down with something and was going to pop in the chemist and get herself a tonic or something."

"Well, you know where to find him. I'll put the kettle on and bring you a pot of tea and some homemade cake. Go on through. And make sure that you tell her to look after herself and not put everyone else first."

When he opened the door, he noticed that his dad was sitting in the normal place and was either staring out at the fields or having a sly nap, pipe in his hands.

His dad had heard him come in and turning around, said, "Bloody hell. Miracles do happen then. I haven't won the pools you know and you're too old for pocket money. So, what brings my busy son down to see his lonely old da?"

Ralph took a seat opposite and said, "It's nice to see you, Da, and I am fine, thank you for asking. I'm not going to beat about the bush, but I have been wondering what you have been telling the lads?"

"We are just reminiscing, or at least I am anyway, plus they are learning a little bit of history. They were amazed when I told them about the pit disaster and that because me da was ill and then died, I had had to go down the pit."

"That's alright but what is this about you and me ma being familiar with each other and before they got married? I knew what it meant but James is at that age, and they both have inquisitive minds and what do I tell them?"

"Aye, I remember saying that to them and they asked questions. I remember thinking that when I was halfway through the sentence and stopped saying what I was going to say and told them that one day when they were older, they would understand. I certainly wasn't trying to blacken anyone's memory, especially your ma's. They were looking at the wedding pictures and just got curious and wanted to know more about your ma. Then they wanted to know how I had joined the army. I wouldn't dream about telling them about sex. They'll probably learn about it the same way as I did, from the lads. I remember trying to talk to you about it when you were courting Penny but gave up in the end."

"Do you know I remember that day, and at the time, I thought that this was embarrassing for both of us, because like all lads that age I thought, daft old bugger, I know all about it. All I was concerned about was being picked for the captain's position on the football team and there was you trying to talk about birds and bees."

"Are you going to talk to them, especially young Ralphy before he gets much older?"

"I think that there is plenty time yet, he hasn't started pinching my Old Spice yet and washing himself voluntarily," he said, and they both laughed at a preconceived picture.

"Anyway, now that you have had your moan, when are they down next?"

"If Penny is feeling a bit better and more on form, they might have a look down tomorrow afternoon and take the afternoon off from Sunday school."

"You used to hate it, and if both Mrs Wanless and Mrs Armstrong were going to take it, you played nick and went up the bogs with one the Kelly lads if I remember."

"But if you knew that then why you never said anything?"

"Why should have I? I hated Sunday school as well and used to do the same thing. Learning the catechism like a bloody parrot, arranging white blocks of wood pretending that they were houses in the desert and then having to sing hymns. Then practising nativity plays and especially getting that 'nice little parting in your hair'. My ma, your nanna, used to tell everyone, 'You should see them when they go to church, they look like real little angels.' How embarrassing it all was. And all the women went, 'Ahhhh, isn't it nice.' You felt like being sick." And they both laughed.

"That's all well and good, Da, but for heaven's sake, whatever you do, don't tell them that or life will never be worth living again."

They were laughing when Mary-Ellen popped her head in and brought them some buns and a pot of tea each. "So, I can see that you have kissed and made up. Like a couple of bairns, in fact, you're worse than the bairns, they don't know any better. They have more sense than the two of you combined."

"So," said Fred, ignoring Mary-Ellen, "who do you fancy in the Derby this weekend? The Toon or Sunderland?"

"I fancy the Toon but I am putting them down for a draw on the coupon. I still keep trying to get Penny to go to the matches, but she says that she prefers cricket, it's calmer and more ladylike she says."

"When they say that what they really mean is that it is the whites that attract women, they have seen enough clarts at home from their kids and husbands. I remember my ma often wondering how she was going to get football strips clean, but she always did."

"With us, it is James that gets everything filthy, George is another story. He seems to prefer it when it is a kick about with no rules, any number on a team. Whereas for the other one, it is more of a way of life to him. Did George tell you that we are getting a second-hand piano? It is one of those that have sticky out candle sticks on the front. It was still pricy though, £5 we gave. So I only hope that he takes to that, anything will be better than that recorder."

"Aye, he told me all about it and that a woman from Church was going to give him lessons which must be a couple of bobs?"

"Half a Crown an hour. Then there will be sheet music to buy. But if he sticks in, it will be worth it. He keeps saying he wants to join the army as a bandsman, well, if that is the case it may help him. After all I remember that bandsmen didn't do much on the physical side and did not even see a weapon."

"In all seriousness, Ralph lad, don't you think that he needs some toughening up? He is a canny bairn, but the army?"

"We are hoping that it is a phase and he will grow out of it. I remember when I joined up, I know that it was under different circumstances, but they soon knocked out any namby-pambiness out of us, and it certainly toughened me. Even though I had been working down the pit if still does not prepare you for army life. I hated that bloody drill Sgt, I remember that."

Fred started to laugh and said, "I hated mine as well and the little corporal. But now that I look back, they had to make us tough and quick. They had to, I suppose. I just hope that the two of us having been in wars that the kids never have to suffer the same, and that, in fact, there will be no more wars. Why the hell can't governments listen to people? Mary-Ellen always says that they, women, should run the world as they have common sense."

"I think that the Germans have learnt their lesson now though, Da. If anything, it will probably be the Russians or the yellow people, there are millions of them and they can afford to lose some. I mean look what the Russians did to their own Royal Family. I just hope that if there is another one, we don't have to rely on the French or Italians. They watch who is winning and then change sides. Then again that is maybe not a bad system as they have not come out of the last one too badly, and we'll be dead before we pay all that war debt back to America."

"That's right, lad. The French and Italians, mmmm."

"I'll be off, and it was great having a bit of a natter and to see that all is well. I'll pop in and see Mary-Ellen before I go. Take care."

When he went into the kitchen, Mary-Ellen was just putting some buns into a bag for him to take home with him. He said, "Now, Mary-Ellen. What's this I hear about you and old Laverick? Who is setting their cap at who? You'll be taking that beret and hairnet off and wearing lipstick next time I see you."

Blushing and trying to hide her face, she said, "Where on earth have you heard such useless tittle tattle."

"It's the talk of the pitman. They even have a syndicate taking bets as to when the wedding will be or if you will have to get married."

"Away with you, you cheeky bugger, and remember to show respect for your elders. I am too old for all that hanky-panky lark."

Not to give up too easily, Ralph said, "Does me da know that he might have to give you away or even that there is something going on? You still have a glint and sparkle in your eye I can see it." He said as he tweaked her cheek making her blush again.

She playfully smacked his face with a wet cloth and said, "Away with you and there are some bits and pieces to take home with you. Now get yourself away."

When he had gone, she thought of old Laverick, *After all, they both deserve some company as for the other, humph, the Mills and Boon books will provide all that excitement,* and smiled to herself.

*

When Ralph got home, Penny and kids were back from their walk and the boys were upstairs playing.

"How did you get on with your dad," asked a very miffed Penny, still harbouring a little anger at their argument before he went out.

"I can see and understand what he was trying to tell them, and he realised, too late, that he was going down the wrong route so added 'getting familiar' instead. He had been talking about him and me ma walking out together. It was funny though," he said, looking at Penny, "can you imagine if he had said the sex word?" and laughed, "Our lives would have been hell."

"Mine would, you mean. You would have made some excuse to get out and left it all to me. We just have to hope that if they have a composition to write this next week, they don't mention any of that or the teacher will be sending for us to have a chat with. What would be even funnier is if they started asking their friends about it, and they, in turn, asked their parents. Could you imagine? There would many deaths caused by shock and indignation in your papers column the following week."

"Oh, by the way, I mentioned to Da that if you were feeling more up to things tomorrow that you might keep them off Sunday school and have a look down there for a change," then picked up the paper and switched the results on.

A Sunday Visit

Penny was in the kitchen preparing the Sunday dinner, this week they were having a nice piece of Lamb and Yorkshire and veg. She had set George on topping and tailing some goosegogs they would have for afters with some custard, James was in the garden picking some mint and Claire just seemed to be making a mess in general. Normal routine for a Sunday, Ralph was at the local and would come back after they had eaten and get his out of the oven. He would probably bring back a couple of bottles of beer and lemonade so they could have a shandy. The kids would go to Sunday school after they'd eaten, but this week, and she had not told them yet, they were going down to see Fred and have tea down there.

"Can we go to the park after dinner, Ma?" said James.

"Not today, lads, we're going to Granda's after dinner for a change as you did not get there yesterday."

"Whoopy," shouted George.

"Right, straight after dinner, you two can put your Sunday best on and wash your necks and behind the ears, otherwise you shall be able to grow potatoes there. Claire, I shall see to your hair before we go out." She had come home this week with nits and Penny knew she hated both the nit comb and the shampoo.

Dinner came and went and everything and everybody was washed, tidied and Ralph's meal left in the oven on a low heat. She shut the door and left the key in its usual place, under the plant pot at the side of the back door.

"Now, boys," she said, looking at each of them in turn, I want no daft questions today and just take everything Granda says with a pinch of salt. Do you both understand?"

"We think so, Mam, but we're not sure about the salt," said George.

Penny thought to herself, *there are days when I could murder them. I wonder if I would get away with it in court though.*

They ran in and gave Mary-Ellen some chocolate and carried straight on through to Fred and gave him a bar of Bourneville.

"Ah. Who told you that this was my favourite? Nice and dark. Right, where were we? Ah that's right, I had got married and was away training."

"Was training exciting?" asked James.

"Exciting? Mmmm. Not exactly the word I would use for it. It was more like tiring, different and hard work. By the time we had been there, we could easily have murdered all the corporals and Sgts and I think that we would have got away with it in court. They really were so and so. Apart from the canteen, cold showers, a beer in a hut run by some local women volunteers, there was nothing else to do. The local village was out of bounds, well, out of bounds to us that is. The Officers still managed to get out and the Sgts had their own little place for a drink. There was a rumour going around that we were coming to the end of our training but when we tried to find out anything, we had no luck. We also thought that everyone with a foreign sounding name was a spy, so when we were on guard duty, we kept shouting for the guard commander and he had to come out and check their identities. There was one young lad who happened to be Dutch, but his name sounded very German and Spelk took an instant dislike to him because of that. He kept winding him up and calling him spy until one day the lad had had enough and just turned around and punched him. Of course, we were cheering, and this brought attention to the fight and all of a sudden two Regimental policemen stepped in and stopped it. The Sgt appeared and there was all hell to pay. Spelk was taken to the medical hut and then put in the barrack guardroom cell, this was followed closely by the Dutch lad. What is strange, after that they became great friends, and Spelk would not have a word said against him. He still called him names though, but this time it was more of a joke and the Dutchman accepted his nickname, which was tulip. That was because the tulip was the national flower of Holland. The next week or so was one continuous round of inspections of kit, rifles and then to the orderly room for more form completing, but this time we had to complete will forms in case of anything happening to us. It was at this moment that I had to tell the army that I was now married. It would also mean that if anything was to happen to me that your grandma would get a pension. You have no idea how much paperwork there is to do in the army. We also then had a padre's hour, and if you were Protestant you went to one place in camp and the Catholics went to another. If you were chapel or any other denomination, then you just were sent to the Church of England one. Everybody kind of liked the sessions as it was sometimes an excuse to have forty winks, but woe betide you if you were caught. Then one Thursday morning, the rumours were rife that we were moving out on the following Monday. By lunchtime, there had been no announcement, but then at about 1400hrs, every squad was marched to the parade ground. We were brought to attention by the RSM who then handed over the parade to the adjutant and the other officers marched on in front of their respective squads. Then the adjutant handed over to the commanding officer, and his dog, when they arrived. The Commanding Officer told the RSM to stand the parade at ease and easy. When you were standing easy, you could relax but not talk or move.

"Then the CO began to talk. 'Good afternoon, chaps. You men have been here for several months now. Everything that you have been doing may, to you, seem to be pointless, but all the drill, all the spit and polish have contributed to the men that you are today. Training to become soldiers. You have had inspection after inspection, drill upon drill parade. You have learnt how to handle and strip your weapons blindfolded, some of you have been trained on other weapons and had medical training. You have been taught how to become men and how to look after yourself and your fellow soldiers. Some of you have probably felt like murdering your corporals and sgts" – there was a faint murmur at that remark – "but the work that they have done is first class, and in front of me now, I see a fine body of men. In front of me now, I can see men that are not the same men that stood on this parade ground in front of me several months ago. I now see real men, proud men, real soldiers. Men who His Majesty would offer his hand to. We, gentlemen, we have now been given the chance to prove our worth. We have now been selected to go and fight the Germans.' There was a huge cheer went up until you heard, 'Who the hell has given any of you permission to cheer? You will stand still and listen. You will cheer when I tell you and not until then. Sah.'

"'Thank you, Sgt Major. As I was saying, men, it is now our turn to go and fight and defend everything that our country stands for. You will be going somewhere, and it will not be easy work, and mark my words, some of you will not return. The enemy may be strong, but they lack the leadership that you have. As you are aware the war has now been going on for over a year, it has not been the pushover that everyone thought. There have been losses and gains on both sides. But there is one thing that enemy have not encountered as yet, and that is the sheer guts and determination of the men from the North East of England. Proud men. Strong men. Loyal men. Brave men. Because of that strength, that loyalty and that bravery, the enemy will not know what has hit them.' There was a cheer again and yet again the RSM shouted, 'Listen in everybody. Battalion,' and we all straightened up, 'Battalion attention,' and we all came to attention. 'All of you and I mean officers included will remain at attention until I say otherwise. The commanding officer will now carry on, and I would advise each and every one of you to listen. The commanding officer is not standing out here for his own benefit. Listen in. Sah,' he shouted again.

"'His Majesty, the King and his family send their greetings to each and every one of you and to your families their best wishes and gratitude. When you fall out from here, your company commanders will speak to each of their companies. Good luck, men. RSM.'

"The RSM yelled the order, 'Remove headdress,' and to a man headdress was removed. Three cheers for the commanding officer, *hip hip hurray, hip hip hurray, hip hip hurray.* 'Replace headdress. Company commanders fall out and company Sgts take charge of your companies.'

"Our Sgts marched us back to our respective company lines and handed over to the company commander who stood us all at ease and easy.

"'Men, I am proud to have been your company commander and very proud as to how you have turned into a fine company of fighting men. As the commanding officer said, it is now our turn to go and fight for everything that we all love dear, our king, our country and our families. I have great news and the honour of telling you that on Monday morning at 0900hrs we shall be leaving here and going to war. After I have finished with you, I shall hand over to your company Sgt and further details will be given then. In the meantime, I wish you all good speed, God bless and good luck. Thank you, Sgt.'

"'Company, company attention. Sah,' he shouted and saluted. 'Right, you wankers. I am only going to tell you once. Everyone is proud of what you have all achieved, you have been turned into a bunch of fighting men and I must confess that I am surprised. At 1800hrs, there will be transport waiting on the parade ground which will take you all into Newcastle and from there you can go home. You will be picked up again at the central station on Sunday at 1200hrs. Before you go make sure that all your kit is put away and securely locked up, your huts are tidy. Go home and say your goodbyes to your families, friends etc. and do all the shagging that you have to because where you are going there will be little opportunity for that. Good luck, have a good few days, and by the way, before I forget, well done. Now bugger off out of my sight.' There was a loud cheer from everyone, and we all ran to our huts to get started packing. Needless to say, that we were all going to go home in uniform, if nothing else it may get us a free pint at our locals.

"You probably won't understand this yet, but it was strange going home to a wife that did not live with you but with her parents who thought you weren't married."

"What happened then when you did go to war, Granda? How many Germans did you kill?" asked George.

"Were people lining the streets to welcome you like we see on the pictures?" asked James.

"My, my, you certainly want to know a lot and ask a lot of questions, I dare bet that you are not like this at school."

"Well, our George wants to join the army, so who is he going to have to kill?" What are the medals in the box for? Were you a hero? One of our friends at school says that his da must have been a coward because he had not been in the war, he had carried on working in the pits he said. Is that true? Was he a coward?"

Fred looked at them sadly and thought, *Films in the local flea pit on a Saturday morning glorify wars. They don't show the dirt, the suffering, the lice, the rats, the tears, the missing limbs, the bodies lying mangled over barbed wire. They don't show the bodies of horses that once grazed in green fields. Yes, there were people waving, flags flying and bands playing, but there was more of the other. Do I tell them that the politicians said that it would be over in six months? Or that the American President labelled the war as the war to end all wars.*

"Right, lads, I need a snooze to catch up my beauty sleep which I desperately need, so, until next weekend look after yourselves and your sister, and don't pick on her either. I shall pop in the kitchen and see your ma."

"Hello, Dad. What's up?"

"Nothing, pet, nothing at all. I am fine. I just hope that the pair of you are alright with me talking to the lads about the past."

"We are fine. It is when it comes to you talking, well, you know, about personal things, we worry. James is now at that age when his mind and body are having conflicts, if you know what I mean, and he is already starting to notice things."

"Aye, boys will be boys, pet. Next week we are going to talk about the war and there wasn't much time for personal things, so they won't come into it. So diffent fret yourself, pet. No, diffent fret."

"That's as well as maybe, Dad, but don't you overdo things either and I know that you'll be thinking of some things that people do not want to remember or hear about war. I know that Ralph even clams up about talking about the second one and his involvement. I think that it must be terrible for someone to relate to one war but, like you, there must be hundreds who can relate to two. It must be one thing going off to war as an innocent young man not knowing what awaits, but to go off as you did and knowing what awaits must have been pretty horrific. If politicians, sitting in their plush Palace of Westminster, could even start to think what it must be like for the man in the street, they might think twice. After all it is politicians and governments who start wars not the ordinary man."

"It's never going to change, pet, boys will be boys, girls will be girls, men will be men and woman will be women, that's the rule of the system. It is fear that often makes the hero. They think they know what they are doing, but often it is a combination of fear and gut reaction."

"They really enjoy coming down, and while they are listening, they are learning. It is probably better than their history lesson at school, learning about the Normans. I'll be off now and might even try and get the prodigal son down again."

Laughing, he said, "The roof nearly collapsing once already this week is enough shock for the system, don't you think? Take care, pet."

Fred's War

James and George were in their usual position and had a glass of pop and some biscuits ready.

"As I said last time, we were given time off to go home and spend some time with our families, and then come the Sunday, no one was late at Newcastle. As we climbed on the lorries, everyone was chattering about what they had and had not done. Then it was back to our huts which smelt damp and cold. Beds had to be made, someone went and collected some coal and scrounged round for some firewood.

"Monday morning the bugle call went at 0600hrs with the corporal coming in and shouting, 'Welcome back. Breakfast in 30 minutes then bedding returned to the stores at 0800. Rifles and kit ready for moving out at 0930hrs. You're off to war.'

"'Do you know where we shall be leaving from, Corporal?"

"'Yes, that is an easy one to answer and it is not confidential. Here, you idiot. Where did you expect to leave from? You'll soon find out. Now get a move on.' 0930hrs and everyone was on the parade ground and lining the ground were rows and rows of lorries to take us to our first destination. As we drove through the countryside and then ventured into civilisation, there were waves and cheers from the locals on their way to work and school. Wolf whistles were obviously part of the activity. Then once again, we pulled up at Newcastle station. So that was to be our starting point and by train. Special troop trains. Officers travelled first class, with their batmen in adjacent compartments. One of our group, Chalky White, that had originally set out with us all had been picked as a batman for one of the young baby lieutenants. The officer was Rupert somebody Robinson, I think that his father was some titled big wig with an estate outside of Morpeth somewhere. He was, or should have been just addressed the same as any other officer 'Sir', but Chalkie had decided to see how far up his arse he could get without turning brown and called him Sir Rupert which boosted his ego to no end. Plus, Chalkie had been made an acting unpaid lance corporal. There were eight of us to a compartment, but some of the carriages were not split into compartments so I suppose we were lucky. No sooner were we settled than a trolley came along the platform providing mugs of hot tea. The journey took quite a while and we travelled right down the country, station names had been removed, so unless people recognised where we were, it was hard to come to any conclusion. After the normal round of woodbines, some card playing, some of the lads started writing letters.

"Spelk said to Snotty, 'You bloody big Nancy. Writing already. You've only just left your mother.'

"'Bugger off and mind your own business,' he replied.

"The train pulled up at a station in the middle of the night, but it was a hive of activity and waiting for us was hot tea and something to eat but we were not allowed to leave the station area. There were military police all over the place, and they weren't putting up with any nonsense from anybody. One guy tried to get passed them but no way, they just manhandled him back and threatened him with the guardroom. About an hour later, we were back on lorries again and taking to a tented waiting area it was called and assigned tents and made ourselves comfortable. It wasn't until the bugle sounded in the morning that we discovered that we were not alone. There appeared to be thousands of tents as far as the eye could see. We all formed up in our companies and were inspected, kit checked and stood down. This happened several times during the next few days, but we had noticed that the Jocks who had been the nearest to us had gone. It was no use asking anybody anything because you didn't get told anything. Kit was checked and rechecked again and again. New wills were written and then word came down the line that we were moving out at 0600hrs the following morning and told to get some sleep. None of us tried to show any nerves but I knew that if they were like me then they were nervous. It suddenly hit you that you were going into the unknown. We had been told that we could keep some personal possessions like photos but not too much personal information. Diaries were not allowed, and at about 2200hrs, some corporal came around gathering items to be left behind. They did not want the Jerries coming into possession of anything that may be of use to them, maps, any details whatsoever that would be of use to intelligence. According to Chalkie, the officers seemed to be exempt these things as his Sir Rupert had a writing desk, a small travelling one and some nice glasses and a decanter. My luxury was some toilet paper which I am sure would not last long as my bowels could not settle.

"We sat talking about the last time we had been home and Spelk was looking a bit down, so I said, 'What's up, Spelk? You look like the cat that has lost the cream.'

"'I suppose I have at that. I am bloody jealous of the lads that are staying behind and going down the pit.'

"'You're jealous of those poor buggers. Are you mad?'

"'Just put it like this. We're away and they are staying. Conclusion is that they will be screwing the arse off everything going, probably even the pit ponies at that.'

"'We don't know that, and we have to trust our girlfriends and wives,' I said. 'You trust your lass, don't you?'

"'It doesn't matter whether I trust her not, she's already dumped me and found herself a pitman, a deputy at that. A trollop, that's what she is. A bloody trollop.'

"We all looked at each other and we weren't quite sure what to say to that. Poor bloke, and him not even out of the country.

"'She's not a trollop really, Spelk, and you know that. She's young and will be worried about everything. Her da and two brothers are away already and the other one is just coming up to that age and then she would have had you to worry about. Anyway, you remember Barbara Allen?' I said.

"'You mean that blond lass down at the chip shop?' said Spelk.

"'No, you daft bugger, not that Barbara Allen. I mean the one in the song that we all learnt at school. She lived in Scarlet Town or somewhere, and she went to see her dying partner on his deathbed and she said to him, young man you're dying. Now she was a heartless trollop.' We all laughed at that and even Spelk raised a smile and said, 'I suppose you're right. She wasn't a bad lass. Too young for me anyway,' ensuring he did not lose face.

"A short while later, Chalkie came to see us as he had been looking after his 'Sir Rupert' and some other officers in a larger tent. They had got him to get some glasses and a bottle of the finest whiskey so, at the same time, he managed to acquire a couple of bottles of beer for us. Anyway, he told us a story that he had overheard which went something like this.

"1st Officer: 'The training went well, don't you think?'

"Sir Rupert: 'Yes, but you as you know we all had to rifle training under that stupid oaf of a corporal. He had the audacity to tell me, me of all people, that I could not hold a rifle correctly and then added or focus on a target correctly. Me, who has been shooting and using guns on my father's estate since I was a youngster. He did say sir after he had reprimanded me. I mean what experience had he had working down a pit or something ghastly similar. Bloody fool. How the hell are we supposed to win wars with arseholes like that? I mean, I ask you, how the hell are we?'

"1st Officer: 'Then?'

"Sir Rupert: 'I said right, Corporal, thank you for your advice and I shall just forget you reprimanded me. He replied that he'd already forgotten the incident, but he would remember it when writing up his weapon report, as he was required to do, for the commanding officer. The audacity of the man. If it was at home, I'd have the wretch sacked. He then saluted me and walked off. Cheeky blighter.' The other officers laughed and said that he couldn't let him get away with that, but still laughed.

"'We cannot pick who we have to go to war with any more than we pick who we go to war against.'

"'My father said that he wished that he had been young enough to go and fight for King and Country. I know that the family will be having fundraising events on the estate to help the war effort. I just hope that it's not all over by the time we get there. We don't know if the Kaiser will see sense and realise that relatives shouldn't fight each other. At least not in a bloody war.'

"When Chalkie told us the story, we thought that it was hilarious, a corporal telling an officer off. One of the lads, Tulip, I think, said, 'Trouble is that half of the buggers haven't even started to shave yet and will still expect us poor sods to wipe their arses for them.'

66

"Chalkie said, 'Well, I know that you lot think that I am a brown-arser but I draw the limits at wiping it.' We all laughed at him and drank our beers. We had to keep our noise down or either the orderly Sgt or the patrolling military police would be here, and then that would cause trouble for everyone. They would want to know where the beer had come from especially.'

"'Right,' I said, 'let's try and get some shut eye as that bloody bugler will be waking us before we know it, and we don't know what tomorrow has in store for us.'

"'Hey, I am the lance corporal around here and I give the orders,' said Spelk.

"'Bugger off then, Lance Corporal, and let us get some sleep,' Tulip shouted.

"As we settled, we could hear someone playing a lament on a harmonica and each became lost in their own thoughts. Strange isn't it but when the Jocks did it on the bagpipes, we complained, but somehow the mouth organ was different. We were worried about our families, worried as to what it would be like at the front when the guns were firing. But the tent gradually began to fill with the sounds of men snoring and talking in their sleep. Me, I kept thinking of Jane. Married Jane. Unknown married Jane. How would she cope being married and no one knowing that she was?

"I fell asleep thinking about her and just as the dream was getting interesting, the bugle sounded.

"'Come on, you lazy lot, out of your pits. Washed and breakfasted and ready for inspection with all your kit in two hours,' shouted the Sgt.

"'Come on, you heard him,' echoed our illustrious corporal.

"We were all on parade exactly as required and our kit was all inspected, letters that had been written were handed in to the orderly corporal. There was the normal procedure, brought to attention for everybody under the sun until finally about an hour later, the commanding officer turned up.

"'Right men, the day has finally arrived. The day that we have all been waiting for. It is the beginning of the end for the enemy. Listen to your platoon commanders and their instructions carefully. We shall soon be leaving the luxury of the tent and marching down through the town and into the dock area. There will be a lot of activity there with other units and equipment waiting their turn to board the ships. Remember you are representatives of your Regiment and you will be receiving instructions from people from other units and the Royal Navy, so just do as you are told. I wish you God speed and good luck.'

"As we marched through the town, there were people lining the streets and waving flags and cheering. Some of us were lucky to get kisses. I kept thinking that whoever was making flags that they must be making a fortune. As we came around the final bend and saw the docks, we were all stunned. There were boats of all sizes. Men from all Regiments and people handing out mugs of tea. There were also a lot of ambulances and they were being fully used by people being offloaded from some of the ships. We stopped just inside the dockyard and watched the events. None of the men coming ashore looked happy, they were tired, dirty, and dissolute and the number of the injured kept being brought ashore was horrendous. It certainly brought each of us back down to earth with a bang. We just looked at each other.

"'All right, you lot, stop gawping. They look worse than they probably are, some of them will be patched up and sent on a bit of leave and then back to carry on where they left off. Some of the other poor buggers will have to convalesce for a longer period. But look at them and tell yourselves that you are going to ensure that you do not end up in that condition. They are all brave lads who have been and done what you are about to do. They have done a lot of the hard work already and softened up the Jerries for you.'

"The boat that we got on was already packed with other troops and equipment and there were even donkeys and horses. There were also plenty of medics on board and their equipment. There was even a mobile canteen. I also noted that there were preachers and ministers of other denominations going around and talking to the men. Rosary beads were on show a plenty and, like me, there were many holding their wallets and looking at loved ones. I looked at the St Christopher that Jane had given me. St Christopher, the patron Saint of travellers.

"'Hello, my son,' a voice said, bringing me back to reality, 'would you like to talk or pray?'

"'No, thank you, Father, no prayers for me. I'm not one for all that fuss and palaver. Save it for those that believe.'

"'Is there any particular reason that you don't believe?' said the priest again.

"'Well, I'm kinda' confused by it all. If there is someone up there, why then did he let it all start in the first place. Surely, he could have stopped it?'

"'That theory is a good one, but we must remember that God does not make us chose good over bad or bad over good. It is man that makes that choice. He gave us the ability to see right from wrong and the choice is ours.'

"'That's all well and good, Father, but it's those buggers in their palaces, who should not who have made these choices. Me and the rest of us here are literally here to carry out those instructions.'

"Woody chipped in and said, 'Plus whose side is he on. You say we are fighting for right, but surely, the other side are also being told that at the same time? And if they are being told the same rubbish, then how does he work out whose actual side he is on and who will win? Or does he just like to see a good fight?'

"'As you can see, Father, we all have admiration and respect for you and what you stand for, but we see the world in a very cynical manner.'

"'I do understand, men,' said the Father, "but I'll remember you all in my prayers and I assure you that both myself and the Lord will be at your sides to guide and comfort you. If you ever need to see me, even for a few minutes to moan then please feel free.'

"'I wonder if he is as scared as me?' said Spelk. 'My bowels are playing up, and from the smell, I am not sure if it is too late or not.'

"'We aren't interested in your bloody bowel movements and if you feel like that you had better go and check.'

"We all laughed at that and tried to settle down for the crossing, which was starting to be rough. The only boat I had been on, in fact, I would think that the only boat that the majority of us had been on was either the Shields ferry or the rowing boat on the park pond at Shields. We tried to get some kip using our tin helmets as pillows but what with the boat rocking, somebody praying out loud and Spelk farting it was an impossible task. We could hear in the distance noise, noise like I have never heard before. There were lots of loud explosions. The sun was trying to break through the low-hanging clouds that seemed to match how we were feeling. Everything had a dull grey sort of look about it. There were no flag waving cheering crowds with beautiful girls waiting to kiss us. No bands playing rousing music. As we disembarked, the navy lads shouted a variety of things, they were wishing us good luck, telling us to give jerry one for them, one even said sarcastically that we needn't worry about the Mrs as they would look after them for us. We were to go to the grouping area behind the front lines by train or should I say cattle trucks. The trucks were roofless, and we could see columns and columns of people carrying whatever they could, bedding, chairs, suitcases, a horse and cart packed with furniture and children stuck on top. The effect it had on us was two-fold in that we thought about those poor people bombed out of their homes and it made you sad, but at the same time, it helped to give you more anger to fight the Germans. We also saw ambulances with their red crosses visible plus walking wounded, and from what we saw, gone was the bull. The spit and polish, in many cases gone was any sign of any equipment but they still managed a wave and shout good luck and give them what for lads. Spelk suddenly spoke up and said, 'I know I am scared, and I'm not frightened to admit it, but when I see those poor buggers there, it makes my blood boil. Can you imagine if the Jerries ever get to England, it would be our families trailing along roads like this. No, seeing that has made me more determined than ever to give them what for.'

"'Aye,' replied Woody, 'those sods sitting on their arses back in London should be here seeing what it's all about. They should be ashamed that it has ever come to this. What's even worse is the fact, and we know it will be true, is that some toffee-nosed mummy boy and their daddy will be making a fortune out of all the misery. You can be certain they will not be providing guns and ammunition for nothing. No, they may give a donation or something to some welfare fund, but their pockets' will be well and truly lined. They'll probably even get a knighthood for their loyal contribution.'

"The train pulled to a stop and a voice shouted, 'Right, lads, off you get and fall in by companies.'

"Spelk said, 'Well, we're obviously not at the front, this is a railway siding and there are more tents.'

"'That man must have been to college,' said Woody, laughing. "Of course, it's not the front, any imbecile can see that.'

"Our favourite Sgt got us all together and said, 'As you can see, this is the regrouping area. Our troops come back here for a break and a rest and try and catch up on some beauty sleep and that is what you have to do now. Once you have had something to eat, ensure all your kit is clean, weapons oiled, then try and get some shut eye and relax. The noise you can hear is the front line and is about six miles away, so listen to that noise and think what it will be like when you are closer. Your company commanders will be issuing instructions later and all NCO's report to me once we fall out for further instructions.'

"We got our mess tins and went and got a mug of tea and some food, which looked like a corned beef stew of kinds. Some of the men already resting had been up at the front and had the look of zombies, their eyes looked as if they had sunk into their heads, there was a strange silence from them and not a lot of banter. Just looking around it appeared that we were running short of men, had the Germans got some secret weapon that was causing this shortage or were they in the same situation back in their re-grouping area? As we were eating, one lad stopped as he approached us and said, 'Dinna fret, lads, you'll get used to the noise and if it helps you, today is fairly quiet, must be the Kaiser's birthday as they are not throwing everything at us. Some nights the sky is like Hogmanay in Glasgow,' he moved on, laughing.

"'I think he was taking the piss and winding us up,' said Spelk.

"'Well, if he was, then it worked,' added Woody.

"We settled down and as the sun was setting it could have been a day out at the coast. Then the rain came. It poured and poured, the ground becoming one quagmire of clarts with your boots getting stuck in it and the shelter was virtually non-existent. There were tents as I have already mentioned plus a medical compound, an officers' area, an area for Senior NCO's as well as a basic cookhouse area. We'd found some shelter in a very small hut beside the rail line and some blokes were sleeping under the trucks. The shelling was still going on, but not one of the old sweats moved a muscle, apparently, they considered themselves safe here.

"Spelk, as normal was the first to speak, 'And we thought that stupid Jock was taking the piss and trying to wind us up!'

"Someone threw something at him and said, 'Spelk, why not give it a rest and let us all try and get some rest?' Each of us in our own way was trying to make light of everything but we all knew that deep down inside we were all shitting it."

"Granda Fred," George said, interrupting his thoughts, "you mustn't have been scared like the others because you have some medals in your box."

"Aye, Georgie lad. There are medals there but I didn't have any then, and believe me, I was like the rest of them, I was also scared. It is nothing to be ashamed of being scared. We all handle fear in different ways," he said, looking at them.

"What was strange was that at that exact moment the jock that had been winding us up came passed the hut, and as the door was hanging off, he popped his head in and said, 'Never mind, lads, if you're alive this time tomorrow you'll be veterans,' and then buggered off again with a smile on his face. Next morning, there was some hot food and plenty of hot sugared tea and word went around that in an hour's time, we would be off. No sign of any vehicles to take us anywhere either. We marched, or rather walked one after another through a series of trenches, passing men smoking, some leaning with their rifles against the soil wall, some running passed us delivering messages backwards and forward. Then all of a sudden, a man fell or rather slid down the soil wall and ended up in a heap in front of us, he had been shot in the head by a sniper. It was our first sighting of a dead soldier. No one moved, then two stretcher bearers came along and took him away. Us, we just carried on as though nothing had happened. A shout came along the line telling us to keep our heads down, as if we needed to be told, Spelk's head was that low he was nearly licking his boots. Then we encountered another officer and salutes and handshakes were exchanged, and we were informed that we had arrived at our sector. Our Rupert said, "Right, chaps, we are now at our sector and we will shortly be attacking the enemy. When the advance is given, we climb over the top using those ladders or anything else at hand, and keeping our heads down, we make our way through the barbed wire and take Jerries' lines. Tonight, there will be a barrage fired hoping to cut the wire and to give us cover by forcing them to keep their heads from looking over the top of their trenches. There will be a briefing at 1800hrs for all Sgts and NCO's and we will be going over at 0100hrs, so get some tea and some shut eye if you can. Well done, chaps, and good luck.'

"Our Sgt then spoke to us and said, 'You heard the officer. This is it. This is what you have been working towards since you took the King's shilling. There will be smoke cover and hopefully the barbed wire will have been cut before we go over. Remember, you will not be playing at soldiers, they are real men with real weapons facing you, not cardboard cut-outs on the range back home. Their intention is to kill you and stop you killing them. They will also be scared. The one big difference between them and you is that I know what you are like, they don't. I know that you are evil sadistic bastards and love a good punch up. When we go over, there will be no turning back, no stopping for your mate, there will be other people looking after them. Your sole purpose is to take that position.'

"We all looked at each other with a thousand questions on our minds, then one voice piped up and said, 'But, Sgt –'

"'There are no buts, lads. If you stop to look after someone then that is two less and not one less. You will recognise the medics; they are everywhere and are identifiable by their armbands with the Red Cross on them. Whether those armbands will protect them or not is not our concern. I am now going to give you positions and you will have noticed there is a form of periscope that you can use to keep an eye on the enemy. If you feel the urge to poke your head up, then make sure when you come back down, that it is still attached to the rest of you. Okay?'

"'Yes, Sgt,' we all seemed to say.

"'The whole battalion will be getting into line and the bombardment will start shortly and then your turn will come.'

"Spelk, as usual, was the first to speak. 'As your lance corporal, I want you to remember what the Sgt said, this is not a game anymore. The one thing he didn't mention though was this bloody weather. The ground will be as clarty as hell, and running in it is going to be difficult. Make sure that your equipment is secure and that your laces are tight.'

"Woody said, 'Howay, Spelk, how does it feel to be a lance corporal now and then? If you come out of this alive you could end up a general. It'll be strange though not getting hell from our mothers for having clarty feet.'

"Everyone laughed and memories of home suddenly came to the fore.

"'Another thing,' said Spelk, 'if I do go down, you'd better nor pinch anything out of my pockets. I know how much is in there.'

"'Well, if it is same as when it's your round in the pub, then the answer to that will be nothing,' Woody replied.

"'Ah, bugger off and remember, I am a lance corporal,' was Spelk's reply.

"As it got dark and the rain was still throwing it down, some men came forward and started to climb up the ladders and crawled through the mud towards the wire. Some had cutters, others spades and they were followed by men to give them cover. Everything was quiet and I am sure that we actually stopped breathing because there was not a sound. Then all hell broke loose, the sky lit up with shells exploding, dirt was thrown in the air and the other side were firing flares which also lit everything up, it was like bonfire night without the spuds. We could see some of the men had fallen on the wire and just lay there helpless while others were carrying on trying to make things easier for when we went over. There were shouts and cries from the injured and dying, some were shouting for help. We looked at the sergeant and he looked at us and shook his head. That was probably one of the worst things, listening to men crying out for help and not doing anything."

Pausing in his story, Fred looked at the boys and saw that they were transfixed and in a world of their own, they still had some pop left in their glasses.

"We were ordered to give some covering fire to enable those that could, to get back. What a strange feeling that was. We had fired our weapons. I don't know if we had killed anyone. We saw some men coming back but they were few and far between, some were wounded and you could see the blood on their uniforms, despite the mud. Well. This is it, I thought. This is war. Nothing like the films. It was dirty, wet and bloody. Where were the victorious sounding bugles and the heroes? This was what we had joined up for. It was so far away from our real lives and certainly not as glamorous as the posters lead you to believe at the recruiting tents. They portrayed men coming back from the front the same as they went. Smart, kit shining and smiling. Yes, we had had our christening and in a few hours' time we would run over the same bodies that we had seen fall. Those bodies that only a short while ago were the same as us, living. I wondered where that bloody priest was and what he would have to say about it all now."

Fred paused, a sign of a tear in the corner of his eye and slowly but positively, closed the tin box and his thoughts.

Looking down at the lads, he said, "Right. I think that's it for this week, time for you two to be on your way home, and remember it's school tomorrow."

Both George and Ralph had been silent, and their eyes showed that they had been reliving their granda's experience as though it were theirs. Fred looked at them as they stood and said their goodbyes and thought that tomorrow, weather permitting, he might have a walk up the allotments and see Dolf and put the world to rights.

A Peaceful Life

Working at the sink, Penny turned to her husband and said, "Have you noticed how behaved the boys are these days?"

Ralph put down his paper and picking up his mug of tea replied, "Ah have, love. If I'm honest, it's a nice change and they are doing their homework. I dread to think what it will be like at the next parent's night, what with their compositions about Dad."

"Well, it won't be a problem for you, will it? When have you ever gone to one of them?"

"Do you think that Claire is getting her nose pushed out of things at Dad's?" Ralph said.

"No, to be honest, I don't think that she actually notices most of the time. Mary-Ellen and her are often at work baking, and she seems to enjoy that. But you know how small your da's scullery is and you can imagine the mess. Plus, Mary-Ellen lets her play with that old jewellery box that plays *Swan Lake* in its own fashion. I think the ballet dancer on it has seen better days, a bit like me."

"Talking of ballet dancers, do you remember that phase she went through wanting to be a ballet dancer?"

"Yes and looking all over for shoes for her and it lasted all of three weeks and the shoes ended up in the church jumble sale."

"Well," said Ralph, looking at the clock, "enough small talk, it's getting near that time again, another day another dollar."

"Daft saying that really, isn't it?" said Penny. "Why say dollar and not pound?"

"Just another saying I suppose."

"Your bait-box is ready and eat what's there instead of swapping with the others."

"Swapping a sandwich is fine, love, but I wouldn't swap you."

"Smooth talker," said Penny. *That's nice,* she thought to herself, *but I'm not telling him.*

Ralph gave her a kiss as he was leaving and said, "Anyway, Geordie Milburn says that you make a better corn beef pie than his missus."

Penny sat down with a cup of tea and thought that they really had quite a happy life, and everybody seemed to get on. *Well, not taking into account my mother,* she thought. *But when you look at her and then think about what Jane's mother must have been like.* Apparently, it was said that because she was a businessman's wife and sat in the front row at church, she considered herself some sort of distant relative to Queen Mary. How on earth had Jane ever coped and kept quiet about the wedding whilst Fred was away fighting? The secret must have worn heavily on her shoulders, but yet at the same time, there must have been something very naughty about it. Imagine, your parents not knowing you were married.

Ralph off to work, the kids in the bath, a cup of tea and a ginger snap, what more could you want?

"Ma, he's pumping in the bath and it smells, and he's trying to drown me."
Peace shattered, she thought.
I'll be the one doing the drowning if you haven't washed yourselves properly. And there had better not be a mess otherwise your da will get to know tomorrow when he gets in."
Because of Ralph's job, he had a bigger house than some of the neighbours and the boys shared a room and Claire had her own which was nice, and it was kept tidier than theirs. One of the men over the road had two bedrooms and a small box room and there seemed to hundreds of them, well, not exactly, there were seven of them but he was a proud man. He wouldn't even let the kids have free school dinners because he didn't want people to know he was poor but nearly everyone was in the same situation. Still, his wife managed to keep them clothed and fed and Penny was able to pass a few hand-me-ons over which seemed to be gratefully received. They never seemed to be able to go anywhere for a holiday but really enjoyed the pub trip and the local Sunday school one. Sandwiches were made and we all hired tents and windshields, then put them up on the sand irrespective of the weather. The kids were going to get wet, so what was the problem. His wife had been in service somewhere when she was younger.
"Ma, tell him to stop."
"Right, you pair, that's it," she said, storming up the stairs.

Over the Top

"'Right, lads, prepare yourself,' shouted one of the officers. 'Remember what you have been told, no stopping for anything or anyone. Listen to any orders from your sergeants and good luck to you all.'

"The barrage had been going for well over an hour and the smoke screen was now starting to have effect.

"'Must be smoking some pretty powerful woodbines,' said Woody, laughing.

"'Stop messing about, you lot, and listen for the order,' our favourite sergeant said.

"Some of the lads were kissing rosaries, looking at pictures, rubbing rabbit's foot and crossing themselves. The officers had their pistols drawn and everyone was now ready to meet the enemy.

"'Over the top, lads, and at them. Show them what you are made of.'

"The noise was deafening, people were shouting and cheering, but no sooner had some made it to the top and they were falling back short. I was running and next to me was a young officer that I didn't recognise, he shouted and then fell. There was an explosion a few feet away and blokes seemed to be flying through the air. When one landed, he had a leg missing. Chalkie hesitated and went to bend down but someone grabbed his collar and pushed him forward. 'Don't worry about him, the medics will see to him.'

"Progress was slow, and it seemed as though we had been out in that hell for hours. Our feet were getting stuck in the mud, men were being shot and falling face down. Then we came across the barbed wire and it was strange, there were men hanging from it like some sort of home-made Christmas decoration. We tried to jump over it, but it was useless, we ending up stepping on bodies, it was bloody awful. We could see the enemy trenches only feet away and even German helmets. The noise was still going on all around, but all of a sudden, we heard someone shout, 'Down, everyone down, and try and take cover.' I dropped into a bomb hole and straight into the arms of a dead soldier. I was sick. An NCO said, 'Get a grip, lad, pick up your rifle and cover me. If you see anything move whatsoever then bloody shoot it. Do you understand? I said do you understand?'

"'Yes,' I replied, picking up my weapon and giving myself a shake, 'I understand and am fine now.'

"'That's the spirit, lad, don't let the bastards beat you.'

"All around me men were using bodies as shields. I thought to myself we were never taught that on training.

"Another shout, 'Right, lads, grenades, after three, then up and at them.'

"It seemed to work as momentarily they stopped firing at us and we charged forward. I thought that I saw Chalkie falling or he had jumped into a trench, I wasn't sure. The next thing I knew was that I was face to face with a German. Neither of us moved, I think we were as shocked as each other. He looked about the same age. Then he was lying at my feet. I had killed my first German and I was not even aware I had done it.

"'Well done, lad. It was either him or you. It was as well that you had your wits about you.'

"What appeared to be hours, in fact it felt like days later the firing stopped and we had captured a trench. There were about 100 German prisoners and a few of our blokes were used to take them back to the rear lines for interrogation. They looked so pitiful and crestfallen, what were they thinking? I suppose they were lucky really as that would probably be the end of the war for them. We set about making the trench acceptable, gathering bodies and helping with the wounded. Spelk, of course, was helping himself to souvenirs, something to flog back home and something to make his stories more elaborate to his future grandkids no doubt.

"Meanwhile, one of our corporals had done a roll call to see who was missing or killed. I was pleased to see that Chalkie was not among the dead or missing, he came up and told me he had killed at least twenty, or so he said.

"Woody was listening and said, 'That's good then. All we need is another couple of dozen like you on our side and we can all go home tomorrow.'

"We all laughed but Chalkie was having none of it and was already looking forward to meeting the King and getting the Victoria Cross that he felt he so rightly deserved.

"We were all brought back to the real world when the Corporal said, 'Right, lads, pile their weapons and kit up until they are collected and no stealing. Remember they may be our enemy, but they are still people. If you find any identity tags, then hand them into the sergeant.'"

"Granda Fred," said James, "If you had won the battle, why didn't you come home then?"

"I wish that it had been that easy, Son. We had won the battle, yes, but we had not won the war. Little did we know then that we were still a long way from that happening. The trench that we had fought for and won, guess what? We lost it the next day. What was the whole bloody point of it? That seemed to happen on a regular basis, and it became like a game of snakes and ladders, up one minute and down the next. Can you imagine going for a walk and taking one step forward and then two back? Try it the next time that you are walking down here. Several weeks later, we actually moved onto the next trench and we liberated some bottles of French wine that the German officers had probably stolen from some chateau. We decided that it was going to be stolen again, but this time by us. We all packed a bottle each into our kit and then Spelk decided that he should give the Rupert a couple of bottles and the Sergeant. We moaned at the time but in the end, it made it easier for us to have a drink and forget all the carnage and waste of life. It was sheer heaven. Then about six months after we had arrived, there was a delivery of post, yes, six months. We each listened eagerly for our names being called out and those that were lucky went into a quiet spot to be alone with their thoughts and tears. One or two of the lads got what were called 'dear Johns' which were letters from girlfriends who, for one reason or another, were now dumping their former sweethearts. Of course, sometimes the name was called out, but no one answered because they had been killed. That always brought the calling of names to a stop, for only a couple of seconds though. I was reading mine and suddenly stopped and re-read the paragraph and then re-read it yet again. 'I'm pregnant,' I shouted out. 'I'm pregnant.'

"'I always thought there was something fishy about you,' said Chalkie.

"'What?' I said. 'No, it's not me that's pregnant, you daft bugger, but Jane, my wife.'

"'Well. We would never have guessed that, would we? Have you checked the dates? Are you sure it's yours and not one of those stay-at-home pit boys?' Woody shouted. 'Anyway, congratulations, mate, and now we can really celebrate.'

"'Wait a minute, you said your wife. What bloody wife? You're not even married.'

"'I am, I mean we are. We got married on that two weeks off we had and went up to Gretna Green but never told our parents. You know that Jane's mother would have gone crackers, her daughter with a common soldier!'

"'She's going to have to tell them now, isn't she? Or they will think she has been playing away. I bet that you are secretly pleased that you aren't there. Poor lass. The gossips will be in full gear and your mother-in-law'll be ringing up the Ministry of Defence complaining that you had taken advantage of her Jane. You mark my words; you'll be getting called into the commanding officer's tent.'

"'Do you reckon?'

"'Fred, relax. He's only winding you up and you are biting. Well done, mate.'

"'Anyway, there is nothing the CO can do as the army are already aware that we're married. I completed all the relevant paperwork when we were down south waiting to leave England.'

"'Bit of a sly bugger on the side, aren't you? What other secrets have you got that you haven't mentioned? Do you do that secret handshake thing that the free what me call its do?'

"'No. I am not a freemason, and if I was, it's no bloody business of yours, and if you don't shut up, you'll get a secret handshake alright.'

"'Calm down, the lot of you. Enjoy the peace that we have at the moment, and open another bottle of that wine,' said Spelk, our illustrious lance corporal. 'I had better go and see if our Rupert wants anything before, we settle for the night, so keep the noise down, we don't want to share this with any of the others.'

"'Before we left Blighty, we had even discussed about having kids in the future and had decided the first boy would be called Ralph, then a girl would be Claire. It just shows what a virile young stud I am.'

"'Yeah, okay. Dream on,' Woody said."

Back Home

Jane had known, or rather assumed that she was pregnant after Fred had been away for four months, she had missed her period and had also been feeling sick on a morning. Fortunately, she thought, she wasn't as yet showing any outward physical signs of pregnancy but she knew she soon would. She had been watching other pregnant women and some appeared to be the size of a barrel.

"Are you ailing for something, our Jane?" her mother called when she saw how pale Jane looked.

"No. I'm fine, Mother. Honestly, there's nothing to concern yourself with. It'll just be some bug I've picked up somewhere. I'll pop into the pharmacy and get myself a tonic."

"All the same, dear, I think I'll call into the doctor's surgery and make an appointment for you with Dr Fox. I have to go to the Church Flower Meeting first, they don't seem to be able to make any sort of decision about anything without me there. Just because there's a war on, we mustn't let standards drop. There are plenty of wild alternatives we can use for decorating the church. We have to use our initiative now the government have decreed that gardens are for food. Nature will ensure that everything is still nice."

For heaven's sake, Mother, Jane thought, but didn't say, *Life is more than about flowers in a church.*

"Yes, Mother, you are right, nature is a wondrous thing and I'm sure the minister and the congregation will enjoy bringing nature into the church."

"I shall be coming with you to the doctor's, and no arguments. I am not having them fobbing you off as there is definitely something not quite right with you. Anyone with an ounce of common sense can see that. Take it easy and have a nice cup of tea and a lie down. Bye for now and see you later, love."

Do I own up now or should I talk to Dad and get him on my side? He'll be busy in the shop at the moment. Even though meat was now rationed I'm sure a lot of the older and regular customers come in just for the chat and see if there are any bones available for making some broth. He was a bit of a flirt was dad, innocent, but the old dears loved it. If it made them smile for the rest of the day and made them feel special, then it was a good thing. She looked at the clock and saw that the time was approaching where he would probably stop, if there was no one in, for a cup of tea and a custard cream. Putting her coat on and wrapping her floral scarf, which had been a present that mother had bought her from Fenwick's, around her shoulders, she headed for the shop.

On arrival she noted that there were only two customers in and they were having a good old chin-wag with her dad. There was Mrs Harm, whose son was away fighting in Africa, and he asked, "Hello, Mrs H, and how is that fine lad of yours? Have you heard from him at all?"

"He was never a great writer, terrible with his compositions at school. The teacher always wrote in his book 'could do better' but he wasn't interested in writing, sooner be out playing. No, we have had two, they came together, and one had some grains of sand in. We could not learn much from the letters as they had been censored and despite holding them up to the light, we still couldn't make anything of interest out. He did say that it was hot, and he had been burnt by the sun. I mean, burnt by the sun, he's supposed to fighting not sunbathing."

Mrs Kane joined in and added, "Well, I heard, although I don't know how true it is 'cos I haven't spoken to her myself, you know. That one of the Kelly lads had been listed as missing in action. I mean, what does that really mean?"

"I am not sure if I would prefer to know that they had been killed or not. After all, if they have been killed then at least you know one way or the other, whereas missing in action could mean anything," Mrs H added.

"Ah, hello, love," Dad said as I came to the counter, "we were just talking about the lads at the front."

"Yes," Mrs Kane said. "What about that nice young lad that you were once seeing before you had to go away?" she said with a little hint of mischief.

"I'll just pop in the back and put the kettle on for your cup of tea, Dad," turning to the two women, Jane said, "It was nice seeing you both again and give my love to the family when you write."

When the two women had gone, her father turned the sign around, and it now said closed, and said, "They are two old gossips and don't let them get to you, pet."

"Dad, please sit down, there is something I want to talk to you about."

"Is it about Fred? I know that you were secretly still seeing him before he went away. Your mother had not the faintest idea and I thought I am not going to tell her. I thought that Fred was a decent enough lad. So, what is so important that you have some to see your dad at the shop then?"

"Dad," Jane said and burst into tears.

"There, there, lass, things cannot be that bad that you're driven to tears. Have a drink of your tea and start at the beginning. I am all ears."

"What about the shop though, if anyone wants something?"

"Bugger the shop, pet, if it's important and they want something they'll come back. It's not as if there is another butcher in the village, is it?"

Jane laughed and said, "I have never heard you swear."

"Aye, well, there's probably a lot that you don't know about your old dad, pet. Now, what's this all about?"

"Mother goes mad when I tell her though."

"Let me worry about your mother. Now tell me."

"Well, you guessed right I had been seeing Fred. We meet up again when I came back home, and we met on a regular basis in the park or at the palais or at the village hall dances. There is no need to worry we didn't do anything improper. But we did gradually fall in love and we were like two children, it was a marvellous feeling and I knew that I couldn't tell you both about it. Mother would have been beside herself with shame. You know what she's like. Her daughter and a pitman. The scandal."

"Mmmmmmmm," was all her father murmured.

"We really did love each other and then the war came along and Fred and the others all went and enlisted. Despite being in the pit, he felt that he wanted to go and do his bit for us all. He asked me to marry him."

"Mmmmmmmmm," was all she heard again.

"Dad, did you hear me? He asked me to marry him."

"I heard you loud and clear, pet. He asked you to marry him."

"Aren't you angry at all?"

"Why should I be angry? Two young people in love. I hope that you said yes?"

"Do you really mean that, Dad? Really?"

"The lad is not the brightest person in the world. But he is honest. He comes from a good, decent family. He has cared for his mother since his father died and provided for them. It shows that he is a man of good character. It shows how rich he is not in a monetary sort of way but where it really counts, his heart. What position he holds in your mother idea of society is really totally irrelevant to me. Your mother is a snob, always has been and always will be. Probably one of her traits that I find both frustrating and endearing, although don't tell her I said so. If there were more men like Fred, then life would be a finer and a safer place. So, having said that, what was your answer?"

"I think that I said yes, if not once then a million times, yes, yes, yes."

"Then I suppose is the next question is what are the pair of you going to do about it?"

"We have already done it. We ran away to Gretna Green when he was on his last leave and got married over the anvil. When we got back home, we lived as a single couple but managed to meet up now and again."

"Well, I'll be blowed," said her father, "my daughter married and I have a son-in-law. I am so happy for you, pet, I really am."

"There is something else. I believe that I am pregnant. About four month I think."

"A married daughter, a son-in-law and a grandchild all in one afternoon. I am shocked, stunned, amazed and delighted. Are the army aware that you are married, and does he know that you are pregnant?"

"Firstly, the army are aware and only one of his mates knows about the marriage, as we thought if others knew, then it would soon be common knowledge. As for him knowing about the baby, I have written to him, but as the post is so erratic, I don't know if he has received it yet. But the real problem is Mother."

"I can definitely say that I am over the moon for you both, well, for all three of you, in fact. As for your mother…"

The shop bell rang, and her dad said, "Better go and open up but don't run away, we'll sort things out."

"Hello, Mrs Robinson, don't tell me you're after more tongue, your husband tells everybody that you have plenty of that but I'm sure he's only joking."

"Aye, well, he deserves getting a piece of my tongue now and then. As much as we tolerate and moan about each other we're like everyone else, we'd be lost without them. Better the devil you know than the one you don't, eh, don't you think?"

He recognised a veiled hint at his beloved there but just smiled and said, "You're right there. Where would we be without each other? We'd just have to moan and talk about someone else and none of us would ever dream of doing that, would we Mrs Robinson? There, I've put a little extra on and there are also a couple of bones for some broth with my compliments and it was nice chatting again."

After Mrs Robinson left, Jane said, "What do think Mother will say?"

"Oh, she'll huff and puff for a while. She'll make out that the world has come to an end and that she'll be on the front page of the local paper. Then there'll be the gossip. Actually, I am quite looking forward to it, it will be better than going to see a play at the Theatre Royal. Seriously though, you yourself know that she will make a scene. She won't blame you, of course, it will be Fred and then me. We shall do it together, pet. Secretly, she will be delighted and will be the first to tell everyone and don't be shocked if there is an announcement in the births, marriage and dispatched column. You will be mentioned in two and me in one," he said, laughing.

"Oh, Dad, why can't everyone have a dad like you? You will get on famously with Fred."

"The only thing about everyone having a dad like me is they might end up with a mother like yours," they laughed and cuddled each other.

"Mind you she will probably drive you mad with all the mollycoddling that she'll do, and the other thing is that you must tell Fred's mum before the tom-toms tell her. You wouldn't want that, would you? In fact, thinking about it, why don't you go around there now and tell her, that way she will certainly not hear it from anyone else. You can take her a piece of nice beef and tell her to not to worry about the coupons, she's nearly family now. You have to bear in mind that your mother is no different from mother's the world over. You'll probably be the same one day. They want to see their children do well and better themselves, have a good husband or wife and then have children. We are always going to have a society based on class, there will always be those that have and those that haven't, but this war is hitting all families, irrespective of their status in life. You just have to read the columns of fatalities and you can see the landed gentry are up there with everyone else, in front of many in fact. Your mother, through her church work, comes into contact with people who have lost their homes that are begging to feed their children. She doesn't want that for you or anyone else, that's why she appears overprotective. Rest assured, pet, that we are, and will be delighted with everything. Let her have her minute of tutting and self-righteousness. Get yourself around to your mother-in-law's, give her the news, and I am sure that we can open that bottle that is kept for purely medicinal purposes after dinner."

When she got home, her mother was already back from her church meeting and said, "Where've you been? You were supposed to be having a lie down. Anyway, put the kettle on while I start and get dinner ready. I have also made told the doctor's receptionist that we shall pop in tomorrow morning sometime."

"I felt a little better and thought that a brisk walk in the fresh air would do me the world of good. You always say that fresh air never killed anyone. I also popped into the shop and had a cup of tea with Dad. Mrs Harm and Mrs Robinson were there, and I think the other one was Mrs Kane."

"Well, with that lot in, your father will certainly have had his ear bent and they are such gossips, you know. I just don't know how they find everything out or indeed have the time. Me, I can never seem to find the time for idle chatter, and that Mrs Harm, always flirting with someone. She says it's all fun, but I doubt that very much, I think she is desperate to take up with someone. Now that rationing is on, she'll be after anyone with an allotment. She's shameless that one, mark my words."

Jane thought, *It is a good job that her mother doesn't gossip. She's priceless really and she doesn't even realise that she's doing it.*

"Mother, it is all harmless fun, people need a laugh now and then, especially now."

I hate to think what she'll be like tonight. Dad thought that after a few tuts all would be quiet on the western front.

Just then the door opened and Dad shouted, "Hello, the loves of my life," walking into the kitchen and giving them both a peck on the cheek, "I've brought a bit of brisket in for a change, what do you think, love?"

"I hear you have been encouraging that, that… Woman again. You know that she is after setting her cap at anybody who encourages her."

"But, my love, I am not anybody and she knows that she would have you to handle anyway and I don't think she is that suicidal."

"Just go and get yourself washed and out of those smelly clothes, then we can settle, have dinner, then listen to the wireless. Off with you."

He looked at Jane and gave her a wink.

"I don't know, he's very cheerful tonight, don't you think? Was he like that when you were in the shop? If I didn't know better, I'd say he had an itch in his pants."

"Mother," Jane said embarrassingly. "Anyway, she is a different class of woman to you, after all, it is obvious to all that she lacks your finesse and style."

"Do you think so, dear? That is very sweet of you to say so," her mother replied, feeling very flattered. "Well, you know yourself I am not one to look down on others, but you either have breeding or you don't. It's not something you can buy at Fenwick's. Yes, one is born with it. You have it, but that is understandable, of course. It is that breeding that will bring you a nice young man one day, you wait and see."

It's as though she had been a fly on the wall when I was talking to dad. Maybe they are right after all and she is a she-devil, Jane thought.

The dinner was enjoyable, although Jane did not eat a great deal, but her mother put that down to her feeling under the weather. Conversation went well, but if anyone had asked Jane, she wouldn't have been able to tell what had been said in the least.

Her mother said, "And, apart from those awful women coming into the shop, how has your day been, love?" Before he answered, she carried on, "I helped organise a fund-raising event for those people whose husbands and children are away fighting. You never know when they may need something in an emergency."

"I think that is a marvellous idea, love, and you can count on me and the other businesses to make a contribution either in money or in kind. Shall we go into the other room, and I think that Jane wants to talk to us about something that is on her mind. That is if I have been reading the signs correctly," her father said, pretending he knew nothing about it.

When they were sitting comfortably, Jane started to talk and told them, including her father who already knew, everything that had happened and what the current situation was. There was silence, not the reaction that Jane had envisaged from her mother at all.

"Mother, did you hear what I have just said? Mother."

"Yes, my dear, of course, I did. I'm not quite senile yet, you know."

"Well, what do you have to say? Dad, what do you think?"

Her mother replied, "Naturally, my dear, I am disappointed in some ways and I am shocked to say the least. In fact, I am a little lost for words and…"

Jane's dad interrupted his wife and said, "Did I hear correctly? You are lost for words? That has to be a first."

"You can stop laughing at me and I do not hear you saying anything about this whole situation?"

"I have listened and I understand what they have done and why they have done it, but it would have been nice to have a bit of a do for everyone, but I am pleased for them, and I think it's about time the bottle was opened, don't you?"

"My dear," her mother said, "I am delighted for you and your young man, what did you say his name was? I remember, Fred. Yes, I am really pleased for you and Fred, or is it Frederick? It's also a shock about the baby, yes, a shock but a pleasant one. I shall have start knitting, now what colour do you think?"

"I have been terrified of telling you both as I was unsure as to how you would react to suddenly having a son-in-law and becoming grandparents."

"I think I may get the shop sign changed and add '& Son'. What do you think, love?"

"It is strange. When you said you wanted to talk to us, I felt that you were going to tell us that you were with child, and I thought, before I knew the facts, of course, oh my god, she is going to have a bastard. I really did. I thought about it after you told me that you had been sick and was feeling queasy. I am pleased though that everything is now out in the open and I am looking forward to meeting my son-in-law. I think I shall give a strong lecture on deceit when we meet. Yes, I think it's my turn to do the teasing."

Jane and her dad looked at each other with a smile and a sigh of relief that the deed was now over and done with.

Going into the kitchen, Jane could still her mother whispering, "Well, I'll be. Getting married and us not having an inkling about it. Well, I'll be. That is certainly a turn up for the books. We have to stand by her and look after her and the baby until the dad comes home. I bet he will be surprised when he gets his letter. And they only slept together one night. Mmmmm. Jane." She shouted, "You must start and wear your wedding ring now, in fact, come and let us see it. You must also tell your mother-in-law about everything and take a bunch of flowers over when you go. I suppose that, as we are nearly related now, that I should make a social call or invite his mother here for a meal."

"Now, don't start taking charge, love. Guidance and help are what Jane will need and you are the best person for that. Guidance and not being in charge. She is still our daughter, but we missed her growing up and becoming a woman."

"I understand, dear. You know me. I shall be the height of discretion as per normal. Discretion is my middle name as well you are aware," she reiterated.

"Of course, my love."

The weeks went by and they grew into months and the time for the birth was approaching. "I think that it must be a boy," her mother said, "from the way it is lying and how you are carrying yourself. Have to notify the midwife and get everything ready, just in case."

"I'm not bothered whether it is a boy or girl as long as everything is alright."

Her father had heard some gossip in the shop queue one day, one of the women saying, "Pregnant, they say she is married, but, convenient if you ask me."

"Well, no one did ask you and I would appreciate it if you took your slander some other place," said Jane's father.

Storming out of the shop, she stopped, turned and said, "Well, I know where I'm not wanted. Speaking to customers in such a manner, especially in these times, I shall take my custom elsewhere."

As she left the shop, slamming the door of course, he thought, *I shall not go bankrupt because I have lost a weekly sale of half a pound of peas pudding and a pound of dripping.*

The Baby

"Mother, come quick, come quick," Jane shouted from the bathroom.

"What is it, love," her mother said as she came upstairs.

"It's the baby. I think it's going to come early. The pains are terrible, and my water has broken."

"Let's get you back into the bedroom. Your dad is still here so he can go for the midwife. When did your pains start? How long ago?"

"I'm not sure, I thought that it was just wind but… oh, please let everything be alright. Bloody hell, Mother."

"Try and relax, dear, and breathe gently, the midwife will soon be here," her mother said, looking at the clock on the mantel.

About twenty minutes later, they heard the front door open and close and coming up the stairs was Nurse Wilkinson, or Wilkie as everyone called her. She was a familiar face around the area. The kids all thought that she carried babies in her big bag that she always had with her.

"Good morning, Mrs Roberts, Mrs Hardy. Now, dear, I would like you to try and relax. When did the pain start and how often are the contractions?"

"About half an hour ago and the contractions appear to be every three minutes or so," said Mrs Roberts.

"That's fine but I would prefer it if your daughter could answer my questions, Mrs Roberts, it will help to keep her focused," Wilkie said, looking at Jane's mother. "If you could ensure that we have plenty of hot water and clean towels please."

From the bottom of the stairs came a shout, "Can I do anything to help?"

"Yes, get yourself off to work and open up the shop. Your admirers will be waiting."

"But…"

"No buts, Mr Roberts," said Wilkie, "Your wife is right. There's nothing that you can do here apart from get in the way, and if the baby is as big as the bump, you will probably hear it in the shop."

"Agh," screamed Jane.

"That's good. Deep breaths, dear."

"Should I call into Fred's and let his mother know?"

"That would be a good idea," said Wilkie. "It is good for both sets of grandparents to be involved especially as Mr Hardy is away fighting. We don't want his family to feel left out. Do we, Mrs Roberts?"

"Wilkie is right, love, and tell her the front door will be off the latch in case we don't hear her."

"Agh," shouted Jane again. "Do something and stop talking as though, agh, I'm not here."

The front door closed and Wilkie said, "It won't be long now, dear. Raise your knees, that's grand. Take a deep breath, and when I say push, you push. You understand?"

"Of course, I bloody understand. Do you think I'm bloody thick? Agh, never again," she said.

Wilkie and Mrs Roberts looked at each other and smiled that knowing mother's smile at each other. *Jane's language was quite mild in comparison to some delivering mothers,* Wilkie thought to herself.

"Now, dear, push and keep pushing. That's it. Take a breath, a long deep one and then push again."

"Aghhhhhhhh," Jane yelled, "bloody Jesus, aghhhhh."

"That's good, keep pushing and you will soon be a proud mother."

"Mother, where is Fred?" shouted Jane.

"Don't worry about Fred, pet. Concentrate on yourself for now and the baby. Listen to Wilkie and all will be well," her mother said, moping Jane's brow with a lukewarm damp cloth.

"You're doing just fine. Won't be long now, pet."

*

Her father popped in and told Fred's mother, who quickly put on her coat. Grabbed her bag and off she went. He then went to the shop and decided for once to close up. He wrote a sign which said 'Closed due to urgent war work'. Laughing to himself, he thought, *Well, it is true in a kind of way. Having a child is making a contribution to the war effort.* Of course, being Saturday, there were several customers always turned up early, even before he opened to see if there were any choicy pieces of meat. With rationing on it was even more important to get in a queue early.

Mrs Kane was there with another lady and looking at him pitting up the sign said, "Does that mean you will not be opening today at all? And should you be putting up a sign like that even? We are always being reminded of spies. And what would they make of it? A butcher contributing to emergency war work?"

"Come in, the pair of you, and I will sort you both out, but leave the sign as it is. With a little luck," he said, touching his nose to indicate a secret, "I shall probably be able to open up later this afternoon if they, the powers to be, let me." *That will give them something to talk about. By the time that information gets back to me this afternoon, I shall either have had a meeting with Churchill or the King*, he smiled to himself.

Mrs Kane and her friend looked at each, raised their shoulders and eyebrows and both at the same time said, "Mmmmmm."

"Very intriguing," said Mrs Kane. "Your secret is safe with us. Well, you know, Mr Roberts, anything to help the war effort is to be applauded, but you must remember that not everyone is as honest and secretive as us, isn't that right, dear?" she said, looking at her friend.

He thought that he shouldn't really have encouraged them, but he couldn't resist it. His wife would be angry when she would hear about it, but they would have a laugh later on.

When he got back to the house, Fred's mother had arrived and all he could hear were screams coming from upstairs and decided maybe he shouldn't have come home early and he put the kettle on. *I'm sure that they would all love a cuppa.* Just as he filled the kettle, he heard a different sound. *It was a baby, yes, I am sure*, he thought. *It is a baby.* He started to run upstairs and his wife popped her head out of the room and said, "You can just wait there a moment or two and allow a woman to get herself decent, Granddad."

He sat on the top stair waiting and in that brief moment thought about the war. *There was no sense in all that carnage, the loss of young lives, who knows what future scientist, or academic or doctor would be lost to mankind and the devastation it brings to young families like his daughter. Why on earth does it have to happen? They sit there in their ivory palaces in Berlin, London and anywhere else, but they are not aware of the effect their decisions have on ordinary people.*

"Right, Granda George, you can come in now. They are both ready for you."

Stopping in the doorway to the bedroom, he looked and saw not his little girl but a grown, married woman with a new future in her arms. Going up to the bed, he gave his daughter a kiss and then picked up the baby. A boy, how fantastic. "Congratulations, my princess, he's a bonny-looking young man. Congratulations to both the Grannies also. Who is going to be called what? I can see you as Nanna, my love, how about it?"

"I'll Nanna you. Nanna indeed. No, I think Grandma Roberts will suit me fine."

"In that case, I shall be plain old Nanna," said Fred's mother, "to me, my mother's mum was always Nanna and I thought the world of her, a real Nanna she was."

"What about names for the baby then," said Wilkie, "or do you feel you have not had time to even think about it?"

"No, when Fred and I talked, and children came up we kind of liked the name Ralph and maybe a middle name also. Do you think that they will let Fred come home on leave, Dad?"

"I very much doubt it, love, but you will have to notify the military as they will need to know for his records. I think that if they let men come home when their wives had a baby, the country would probably be over-run with children. Anyway, if I remember correctly, he is better out of it. All those sleepless nights, dirty nappies and teething, no, he is definitely better off away."

"What do you know about teething, or sleepless nights, or dirty nappies? You were a typical man. That was all a woman's job according to you, and I even remember that you had the cheek to say to someone that you had done all the hard work, the rest was up to the missus."

"And before you think about asking Mother, he is not having a double-barrelled name, one in the family is enough."

"I think that it is nice to have something different," she looked at Fred's mother and said, "I mean you have such a sweet name, Maude, isn't it? Queen Victoria named one of her children Maud, old-fashioned but sweet."

God, I could kill Mother sometimes. I don't know if she actually knows that what she says is condescending or not, poor Mrs Hardy. "Actually, Mother, I am pleased that you like Maud as a name because that is one of the names that we had talked about if the baby had been a girl. Now that I know you like it, I shall write and tell Fred and he shall be over the moon when we have a baby girl."

Mrs Hardy looked at Jane and gave her a conspiratorial wink as Mrs Roberts went down to put the kettle on.

"Don't bother with the kettle, love. Let's finish that bottle that we opened last night and wet baby Ralph's head and welcome him into the world and hope that it is a better one for him."

Fred and Mary-Ellen

Penny and the boys had gone home, dishes washed, and Mary-Ellen and Fred were passing the time of day after having listened to Educated Archie on the wireless.

"It's amazing how interested the boys are becoming in the past, and your telling of it must be very good as you hardly hear a peep out of them when they are in here with you. Penny often says that she could do with you up there to keep the peace. I often wonder if you have murdered them or something sinister as there is no sound except for when they want some pop and a cup of tea for you."

"It is good for them to know, love. I am sure that they are not taught about the war at school. It is all about William the Conqueror and The Battle of Hastings and all that boring old stuff. They learn about William Tell and Robin Hood, neither of which is really true and they play war games on the green. They tug each other and they come alive. If only it was that easy. But what is the point of telling them all about it if the same thing then happens again. Bloody Hitler, jumped up Corporal, must be something about corporals because I think that Napoleon was a French version of one."

"Yes, I know that the American President said that the First war was the war to end all wars and there was peace for a while. But think of all the things we have seen and done, we have been a part of history ourselves and the boys will become part of history in their own ways. We have no idea what contribution they are going to make to the world. You never know they could end up prime minister or something else important."

"When have you ever heard of a prime minister having an outside netty and going to Greenland infant school? Come on woman, when have you?"

"You are just being silly now, Fred Hardy. You know what I mean."

"Yes, I do know what you mean but we have to be real and unless a miracle happens, they will probably stay here. Claire will probably end up as a clerk somewhere in the town. Although James can think of nothing but football at the moment, he would have to be really talented to be spotted and picked. As for George, well, what can I say? He wants to join the army, now be honest with me, can you possibly see it. They'll need to toughen him up a lot more otherwise he may end up on the other team and that would bring all kinds of complications. It would be nudge, nudge from the other blokes and he'd be bachelor George, never got married, not interested, never seemed to have time, always doing something else, always helping others and time just seemed to pass him by. Mind there was that girl from the next village that he took a shine to, but nothing ever came of that. That is how conversations about young George will happen and insinuations implied but never said."

"Oh, Fred, you don't think he's like that, do you? I mean it's probably just a phase he's going through. If you look at things in that kind of text, then James is likely to end up a mass murderer the way he pulls insects to pieces and enjoys dissecting newts etc. No, I think that you're wrong and that it's all something he'll grow out of."

"I hope so, love, for his sake. Being that way inclined he could end up in jail and the army certainly wouldn't tolerate that kind of hanky-panky, that's for sure."

"Look at all the good things that have happened though. Think of the working class. Children do not have to go down the mines now or be sent away into service, there is even welfare to help people. Yes, we have been through two wars but good has come out of it all. People are still hard up and housewives still have stuff on tick at the corner shop, but they are not really poor are they. When I say poor, I mean poor like our parents were. There are no workhouses, orphanages are few and far between. You don't see many beggars, in fact, I can't recall the last one I saw at all. People think that they are poor because they see others with something and wonder why they don't have it and the result is that they steal to get what they want without working for it. Bring back the birch I say."

"There you go praising everything about life now and suddenly announce you want to turn the clock back and see the return of the birch, bit drastic, if I say so myself. You need to make your mind up, woman."

"I hope that schools will one day teach them though."

"The thing is teachers and schools want an easy life and there is too much influence coming here from America, the music, the din, the way they talk and dress. But I still strongly believe that as long as they still do their reading, writing and arithmetic, they will have the groundings for a secure job."

"Mmmm, I suppose," she said, "but life keeps changing."

"Yes, but part of the trouble is that men up here are still bloody dinosaurs, they don't realise that things are changing and have to got to look forward. The pits and steel won't last forever and even the shipyards are not as strong as they used to be. We still relish in this Andy Capp image."

"That may be the case, but Penny is certainly no flop, she is content and is looking for the best for the kids."

"Well, she's no different to any other mother, is she, but you wouldn't know what it is being a mother."

"I'll have you know, Fred Hardy, that whilst I have had no children of my own, which is not my fault, I have been more than a mother to you, Fred bloody Hardy."

"Of course, it is your fault. Who else's fault is it, woman? You are the one who wouldn't accept that her lover wasn't coming home from the war. I mean, missing in action and still nothing heard since 1917. Come on, admit it." He looked up and she was crying. "I'm sorry, I didn't mean to say those things. They were pretty hurtful and I know that you hoped beyond hope that he would still turn up or that you would hear something."

"No, it is me. All those years, waiting and for what? Nothing. A miracle that was never going to happen. Anyway, you go on about the men up here being dinosaurs. What about you? Your life could have been a lot different, no, probably if you had gone into Jane's father's business when you came back from the war. He did hint at it often enough. But you were too proud to take full advantage of the hint. Your own son was the same as you, pig-headed, and it doesn't take a grammar school education to work out where he got it from, does it now?"

"Our Ralph is a man of principals and a keen union man, helping others get superannuation and other entitlements from the coal-board."

"I suppose really it is none of my business, they are happy and not wanting for anything, so what else can anyone ask for? They are certainly a lot better off than we were, the kids are always tidy and clean, there's is always food on the table and there always seems to be money to spare at the end of the week. I wonder what it would have been like for them if Ralph had gone into Penny's dad business. Strange that, isn't it?"

"What's strange?"

"Well, both you and Ralph marrying girls whose fathers had shops, very middle class, don't you think? I often wonder, out of curiosity, of course, what the outcome of her father's will was? They never did say, as there must have been a few bobs."

"No, they didn't say, and it is no business of ours either. If they had wanted to tell us then they would. And don't you go asking them either."

"Me? What do you think I am?"

"Don't give me that innocent voice of yours. I know that it is killing you to know."

"It is nice that the kids each have their own Post Office Savings Account, they take sixpence in every Monday and they get a stamp to stick in a book, the school started it up for them, it's a good idea. They also manage to get time away, Bridlington, I think was the last trip. Could you imagine when we were little, we thought going on the bus to Chester-Le-Street go the paddling pool with some tomato sauce sandwiches was sheer decadence," she said, smiling.

"Now there's something we haven't had for a long time, a sauce sandwich."

"Anyway, I must get on, the work won't get done by itself, or anyone else in this house for that matter."

When Mary-Ellen left the room, Fred got to thinking about the front again and he recalled something that neither he nor his mates would forget…

*

Snotty Edwards said, "Do you remember that kid who we took the piss out of from one of the other companies, you know the one who looked as though his balls had not dropped yet and we thought that he hadn't even started to shave yet?"

"Aye. What about him?"

"He has been in the thick of it the same as us, but I heard the senior ranks talking about him the other day. All hush hush, apparently, well, it appears that he has been arrested for cowardness in the face of the enemy."

"I'll be beggared. Are you sure that's right? Don't want to be spreading that around, especially if it's not true. He seems a canny lad, as we say, a bit wet behind the ears but a decent enough kid all the same."

"It appears that yesterday when all went over the top, he refused and threw his rifle on the ground and then the best bit, he hit the Sgt Major."

"Bloody hell, he punched the Sgt Major. Good on him. I've wanted to do that for some time now."

"It's true," Spelk said, "I heard our Rupert talking about it to the Adjutant. He is to face a field court martial. Because of the whole confidentiality of it, I didn't say anything, but it seems to be out of the bag now."

The next couple of days went on as normal, up and over and back again. We tried to get Chalkie and Spelk to keep their noses to the ground and see what they could find out.

That night we were sitting in our little home from home dugouts having a fag when Chalkie came in and said, "He's well and truly locked up and there are a couple of lads form Head Quarter Company guarding him. He's allowed no contact with anyone other than the subaltern who is going to represent him. The word is that they seem to think it's an open and shut case of cowardice. It appears that he joined up underage also."

"So, the poor kid, brave poor kid. He's still a bairn and he's been here fighting. I call that being as hero, not a coward," said Spelk.

"I bet if that bloody priest is anywhere near, he will be offering him prayers and spiritual guidance, telling him the Lord is looking over him. The Lord should have not let him come here in the first f*****g place."

All of a sudden, it appeared that the Jerries had woken up and wanted to brighten up our night. There were shells exploding, dirt flying everywhere, screams and shouts intermingled, and then there were the fireworks lightening up the evening skies highlighting the stars.

"I'll tell you what," said Woody, "If I knew then what I know now I wouldn't have been so keen to join up, especially voluntary."

Two days later, the court martial took place in the field, they managed to get some brigadiers and generals to come to the front, which in itself was a bit of a novelty. The standard joke amongst all the men was that the generals would probably get a medal for bravery. The conclusion was a forgone one, and the verdict was guilty.

We were discussing it and I said, "I wonder what the punishment will be, after all the poor kid is still underage."

Spelk replied, "On the grapevine, he has been sentenced to death by firing squad."

"That's all wrong. The kid wasn't a coward and he doesn't deserve that. Poor bugger. His parents will be devastated, and the gossips will have a field day. Some bloody wanker of a general who never has to face what that kid faced calls him a coward and says he must be shot. I bet that this is his first time at the front without half of the army wiping his arse. I would love to give him a piece of my mind."

"What good would that do? It would get you into trouble, wouldn't do the kid any good either."

"It would make me feel a hell lot better though."

There was total silence then, each of us lost in our own thoughts and one or two had a very watery look about their eyes. We looked at Spelk as he was our eyes and ears amongst the officers.

There was a cough and Spelk spoke up again, "What I am about to say is at the moment confidential, but tomorrow morning the whole company will be told by their company commanders." Pausing and looking at each of us, Spelk said, "They have decided that they are going to draw names for the firing squad. Every company will be represented except his. So that means that one of us may be involved."

There was silence again, no one said a thing.

"Rumour has it that only one weapon will have a live around which means that no one will ever know if they were the executioner or not."

"If that is the case what happens if the person that unknowingly has the round then decides, either accidentally or deliberately, to miss the target?"

"Can we refuse?"

"You would be charged with disobeying a lawful order probably. So, I don't think so, but I am sure that they will tell you tomorrow."

*

It was 0900hrs and we watched as the Company Sgt Major approached our lines and I thought, *Oh God, no. One of us has been picked.*

No one moved but all eyes focused on the Sgt Major and he said, "As you know, there has been a court martial concerning a case of cowardice and punishment has to be carried out today." Another bloody pause and a piece of paper was looked at and he said, "Wood. Report to the orderly officer at 1000hrs and smarten yourself up." he added in a strange, forced sort of way. Not unlike the Sgt Major at all.

That was all he said, "Wood, report to the orderly officer at 1000hrs and smarten yourself up." It appears that you even have to have spit and polish to kill one of your own men. We all looked at Woody but strangely no one said a word. My heart went out to him. Spelk went over and just touched his arm. Woody was sitting there transfixed. I had never seen him so quiet and solemn. *He'll never be the same again*, I thought. I was pleased though that it was him and not me. Was that selfish? Yes, it was, but for once I was pleased to be selfish.

Death by Firing Squad

0950hrs arrived and Woody, looking very crestfallen, picked up his Lee Enfield and looking at us, shrugged his shoulders and off he went.

What could we say to him? What could we do about it? Nothing, absolutely f*****g nothing.

The day passed in a strange surreal sort of way, there were the normal messenger's running backwards and forwards, the sergeant yelling at us to try and keep the place organised and to keep our spirits up. *Strange when you think about it, if you are going to a funeral back in the real world and it is a nice day, you say, 'Well at least it's a nice day for it', or if it's raining, some bright spark says, 'It isn't rain, it's God crying and shedding tears' all eventualities are covered.* Well, the weather today was dry and sunny but it certainly wasn't a nice day for it. *Maybe God isn't interested in the poor lad, I must ask the padre the next time I see him why, if there is a God, wasn't he crying?* Nothing was happening and it was normally during moments of tranquillity like this that you would sit and re-read your letters or write another to the family. But what would you be able to say about today? More to the point, what would they let you say about today? Anyway, what was normal about today? Even when the food came around, there appeared to be no appetite to eat. Each of us was lost in his thoughts and in a different place. *That young kid could have been anyone of us. None of us know when that breaking point, if it comes, will come. I remember when I froze on my first day. What if some officer had seen me? Would he have thought that I was a coward? Then there was the incident... why am I putting myself through hell even remembering things like that? Breaking point also came to officers but you never ever heard of them being shot for cowardice. No, an officer cannot be seen to be a coward. He would have been sent home to recuperate... F......g life....*

Spelk broke the silence and said, "You realise that the poor kid could be any of us?" saying out loud exactly what we had all been thinking.

Chalkie looked at him and, with a bitter anger in his voice which was fairly rare coming from him, said, "Spelk, we know it could. I'm just thinking of things that have happened to me that could have brought me to the same result. I'm also sure that others are thinking the same. At this moment, I'm thinking and thanking God that it isn't me about to be shot. I'm thinking of his family also. I don't know what they say to them in a telegram. 'Killed in Action' or 'Shot for being a coward'? He's also probably thinking of them right now. He's probably still a cherry boy, never having loved or felt a woman. I hope that he wasn't a complete cherry boy and had at least had a wank… I also hope that he is religious though, and believes in the here-after, and if he is, that he can forgive those that have made this decision. Those that are going to carry it out and, importantly, that he can forgive God. Think about Woody. My heart and thoughts are also with him, poor sod, he'll have to live with this for the rest of his life. Now, if you've nothing sensible to say, then shut the f**k up."

The atmosphere was very tense, and it was made worse by the fact that Woody hadn't come back either.

"Hey, Sgt. When will Woody be back? He's been gone a fair while now?"

"Woody'll be back tomorrow morning sometime, anyway, stop worrying about him and worry about those Jerries, they've been too quiet this morning."

"Aye, well, maybe they sense that there's something not right today, something unfair. Maybe they even think that justice in their army, our army, any f*****g army, is only for certain people. What do you think, Sgt?"

"What I think is totally irrelevant and is between me and the man upstairs. Justice has been done by the powers to be and everything else will happen accordingly," he said, and he walked on.

"I notice that he didn't say that justice had been carried out. I wonder if, like us, he thinks that it's all wrong?"

"I suppose we'll never know. Poor Woody if he has to go through all of these emotions all day. We're going to have to be very tactful, and that includes you Spelk, when he comes back. He'll probably be a gibbering wreck."

It's strange when you're sitting there in the comfort of your own home and think back about things like this and especially when history tells different facts. Out of all the men that were killed for, what they call cowardice, only one was an officer. There had been others apparently that had deserted their posts because of the stress but they were sent home or to the rear. They even received Royal Pardons. It appeared that there had been discrepancies on the charges. Discrepancies be buggared. It was more like that there was one rule for them and one for us and I have just been going on to Mary-Ellen that there was a lot of good came out of the wars, such as equality mmmmmmm.

Next morning, another sunny day and, it had been a quiet night with neither side doing anything major. There was the odd skirmish when someone went over to do something with the wire or when you were stupid or daft enough to pop your head over the top to see what was happening. I think it was a way to ensure that no one got a good nights' sleep.

It was about 1100hrs, and all of a sudden Woody appeared. He was an awful sight, despite having washed and shaved, he looked as if he had been out for a night on the brown ale. He even looked as though he'd aged overnight.

"Don't, please don't ask me anything," he said. "If there's a brew going with a bit of something in, that would be nice. Cheers." He sat down lost in his own little world.

We caught him looking over at us, but his eyes were distant, I think he was looking but not seeing.

Spelk said to Chalkie, "I think he wants to talk, but how do we encourage him?"

"I think that we've just got to let him go at his own pace. It's a pity old Sitting Bull was not with us as he would've got him talking."

"You mean that he would have driven him mad and would've talked just to shut Sitting Bull up. Actually, when you think about it, he is quite a miss. All that mumbo jumbo he used to come out with saying he was a descendent of the great man himself. I mean, who has ever heard of a Geordie Red Indian taking scalps?"

"You've obviously not been to some of the pubs I've been to in places like Byker and Wallsend on a weekend. The buggers there made Andy and Floe look very up market. The birds there were even frightened to try and get the cream from the milk on the doorstep on the morning. Ah'm tellin' ya' those buggers would have made short work of the Germans."

"Hadaway and shite, ya daft sod, ah've seen them in action at the Newcastle, Sunderland match, soft as shite. The Sunderland lads made mince-meat of them."

I sat there listening to them and thought, *Well Sitting Bull may not be with us but just the mention of his name has made everyone forget for one slight moment. I wonder what's happening to him these days? Went away on some special course, got himself promoted twice, and the last I heard was that he was in Africa as a sergeant. Not bad going, considering Woody and Chalkie used to wind him up something rotten and said he was as thick as pig shit. Aye, he has the last laugh on us lot.*

*

We'd all had a bite to eat when Woody spoke up.

"It was terrible you know. Something that I can never tell folks at home. They would just never understand. Terrible."

"Take your time, Woody, and if you want to stop or can't carry on then don't. It is your business, we're just being bloody nosey, especially Spelk, you know what he's like."

"No. I'm fine really. Last night the padre came to see him and a couple of military police took over the guard duty from the lads. They brought him whatever he wanted to eat but he wasted the majority, apparently, he just picked at it. Anyway, who the hell would want to eat, knowing that it would be the last that they would have on this earth. The police gave him some rum and there was plenty of beer. It was funny, 'cos the kid said that he wasn't old enough to drink but that the law said that he was old enough to be killed. Anyway, he decided to have one and then that led to another and soon he was well away and singing. We could hear him from where we were. We were also given some drink, but not enough to make us forget our task ahead. He was singing *Cushie Butterfield*, then he attempted *Blaydon Races*. He even tried to get the police joining in with him on the chorus. Then, silence, all of a sudden everything went quiet. We looked at each other, and each of us were secretly hoping that a reprieve had come or even that he had choked on his sick. But no, he was only having a riddle and then burst into song again. You had to smile though. About 1am he fell asleep and we all tried to get some shut eye. At 6 o'clock, we were woken up and told to get washed and smarten up. Any bugger would have thought we were about to get inspected by the King himself. There were twelve of us in the firing squad. Some I knew but no one was in the mood for any socialising. We marched out in single file, no band playing, no flags, no cheers, just silence. Our weapons were already in place for us and loaded. I suppose that was so we couldn't tamper with anything. Strange really to think that when he'd left home and the shores of home, there had probably been bands, crowds, flags etc., but now, nothing, not a f*****g thing. Not a f*****g thing."

"What would have happened if the lot of you had just refused?"

"That scenario had already been given to us. We would have been arrested, someone else would have been picked to take our place and then we would be facing similar circumstances.

"Anyway, they brought the kid out. He looked as though he was still drunk from the night before. They had blindfolded him, so he was unable to see us. Then they secured him to a stake with rope. He really was trussed up, as though he could go any bloody where. It was so stupid, so sad and so damn futile. What a waste of a young lad's life. The padre came out and did what they do, blessed the soul and said that the Lord would be waiting with open forgiven arms. The kid couldn't answer at all. He was just there. His head bowed. Then to top it all, they placed a white square of fabric over his heart. Really, that's what they did. Remember when you'd a drink and wanted to show off at the Hoppings, and you tried your hand at shooting to win some lass a prize? Well, it was like that, except this time there was no fucking prize except a bullet and a place in hell or heaven. There were no orders given. The officer held up in the air a white hanky and the signal to shoot came when he dropped it."

There was a pause. Woody's voice was quite low, and you could tell he was fighting back tears, his Adam's apple swallowing quickly.

"You don't have to carry on, Woody pal."

"Yes, I do. I want you all to know. Then maybe one day we can get a wrong put right. I have to share it with someone because none of the twelve spoke about it. All of a sudden, twelve rifles went off as one. There was no other sound. Apart from some birds screeching as we disturbed their peace. Can you imagine, not a sound? The officer went up with his pistol out of his holster. If he hadn't been dead, then it was his duty to finish him off with a bullet to the head, a 'coup de grace' or something posh they call it. Anyway, he was certified dead. We laid our weapons down and this time there was an order. The first one during all of that, and it was quick march... There was some rum waiting for us and the padre came and said that we had carried out our duty well and that the lad was now at peace with his maker. How the hell did he know? It was pure lip service to make us feel better. I have never hated a man, or God as much as I did at that moment

98

and I was this near," indicating a gap between his fingers of about quarter of an inch, "to sending the padre to meet his maker. How could he be so fucking detached? How could he be a man of God? Then the company commander came in, shook the padre's hand and smiling said, 'Come on, we'll go and have a drink. It must have been awful for you.' Bloody awful for the padre. Bloody awful for the fucking padre! He never said that it had been bloody awful for us or the young soldier and what about his family? Who was going to be there to comfort them when they told them that their son was shot for being a coward? Who? No bugger, that's who. Is the padre going to be there to comfort them? Is God? Poor sods."

Each of us was looking at Woody wondering what to say. He never normally swore and always told everyone that if they had to resort to swearing it showed they had no knowledge of the English language. Poor Woody, at that exact moment, his knowledge must have been non-existent. There were tears in many of our eyes and a lot of anger also. I went across and did something that I don't think I'd ever done before, or since. I gave Woody a cuddle and he just cried. He was inconsolable. The sergeant came in and was about to say something and then thought better of it. It was quiet even for the Germans. You felt that they must have known what had taken place and had decided to show a little respect for a fellow soldier, who through his willingness to fight for King and Country actually found himself being shot for it. Too young to drink, too young to vote, yet old enough to kill and be killed, what an irony. To come through all he had and to be killed by your own side and not the enemy. What an ending. *It will live with me forever and I don't think that I can tell the boys about it. It would break their hearts; I know that at the time it did mine. As for Woody, the subject never came up again and no one else mentioned it to him. I think that somehow or other he had found a tiny corner of his brain that he could lock and throw away the key. Maybe one day, in the distant future the subject will come up and kids or their kids will learn from history books. I think that this is one piece of history that I shall not be telling them...*

A Letter to Fred

Saturday morning again, and the lads came arrived at their granda's earlier than Penny and Claire, as they had run on ahead because Claire was playing up and wanted a wee, so Penny had to take her behind some bushes which she didn't like because of the spiders.

Fred continued with the story exactly where he had left off the previous time...

"The post had been brought to our trench by an orderly and I had six letters, trying to get them all in date order was sometimes a problem you know because they were all read by someone else before we got them, and things crossed out in case the information could be of use to the enemy if they were found.

"Your grandma told me that she had seen some soldiers in the village, one of them, was a lad called Ian Metcalfe who had known me from school. Well, he had lost a leg in Africa. He was now at home awaiting discharge but still seemed to be positive about everything. Some organisation had got him a desk job at the pit and there was a rumour that he was going to get some kind of medal. He'd also sent his regards to me and hoped to have a pint when I got back home.

"I remember looking at the letters and wanting to write straight back and tell her about things here but, how could I? We couldn't talk about where we were anyway, or even where we had been. To tell you the truth, we never knew where we were half the time."

"Granda, did they ever tell you where you were?" said George innocently.

"Yes and no, Son. If I'm honest, I sometimes wondered if they themselves knew where the hell we were anyway. We were kept up to date with what was happening in the world. We knew that the Germans had invaded and occupied Belgium, France, Luxembourg and Holland and there appeared to be no stopping them. We sometimes passed villages which had obviously been nice little villages or towns, but they were now in ruins, the fields weren't looked after, food was pretty scarce too. As for knowing where we were, that trench we had been fighting for and won and then lost, well, we won again and this time we kept it. At times we didn't know whether we were coming or going. I can only say that it was like winning a football cup, except, that is, for the fact that it had cost lives, and pretty pointless it often seemed at times. We then get good news; we were on the move. We left the trench, the rats and the mud. It was strange really, although the weather had been reasonable and we hadn't had any rain for about a week the trench was still clarty, it was everywhere, it got everywhere, you had great difficulty getting your uniforms clean, but clean they had to be. After all you couldn't be killed in clarty uniforms now, could you? We now had some Canadian soldiers on our left flank. Poor buggers, there had been a lot of new recruits in their outfit and they really weren't ready for war. The Germans attacked their position and used what was called mustard gas which was devastating, and they suffered horribly. Although they lost a lot of men and officers, they had shown tremendous bravery, but what a way to die. We were all sorry but at the same time pleased that we had not had that unleashed on us.

"We passed many a body and every now and then we would stop and have a smoke. I am ashamed to say that I stole from those poor lads, French, Canadian, German and British."

"But, Granda, why? That really is naughty, isn't it?"

"Aye, lad. It's naughty as you say. But those men had stuff on them that was going to be of no use to them, but of plenty use to me, to us. There was baccie, rations, chocolate and all kinds of goodies that had been sent from loved ones back at home. Spelk never lost the opportunity to take an odd German medal or dagger or two though. We sometimes found letters on them that they had written to send home so we would keep hold of them and hand them in whenever we got the chance. I said to Spelk, 'Where the hell are you going to get rid of the stuff you keep nicking?'

"'Fred, the trouble with you is that you have no imagination. You've been to the quayside in Newcastle on a Sunday morning, haven't you? You could flog anything there, including the missus. If anyone was daft enough to have her.'

"'You know that we're not supposed to be taking stuff.'

"'You're not telling me that the likes of Rupert and them are not picking stuff up, officer's binos and daggers. They're bound to be. I'm also sure that Jerry will be taking watches and any cash they find, I'm certain.'

"'I have no problems about taking rations and tabs, but robbing the dead, like you are, is different, it's obscene. I only hope that if I kick it then some other poor sod picks up my tabs. You need them out here. After all, they're no use to a dead man, are they?'

"As we marched along, it was more like a tired walk really, Woody said, 'Have you noticed how all the new baby officers make our Rupert look like a seasoned old soldier? They say that the turnover of the lieutenants is quite fast, but I suppose that, as they are normally the first over the top, they are the most likely to be hit. I think there'll be a lot of country estates without someone to inherit them when this lot is over.'

"Because our Rupert appeared to have the luck of the devil, we decided, unofficially, to adopt him as our mascot. We thought it would be a good idea to keep ourselves near him. Stupid really. It was just luck ninety-nine times out of a hundred. We often met a few of our troops escorting German prisoners back to the front and they looked just as fed up as we often were. Today was no different. They were lucky, those Jerries, they were going in the opposite direction to the fighting. When we stopped for a tab and a break, there were a couple of dead

German soldiers propped up against a wall. One of them had in his hand a picture. We looked at it and it must have been his wife and a small child about one year old, there was a kiss on the back of it. We looked at it, then put it back in his hand and realised that he was no different from any of us. His wife and child looked like our wives and children, they didn't have horns or fanged teeth. They were just like you and me, normal people.

"I looked at Woody and said, 'Look, he has a young wife and kid. That could be me.'

"'First, Fred, let's get your English correct, he 'had' a young wife and kid. You need to stop thinking like that and putting yourself in his place. Thinking like that will only cause you to lose concentration and then you'll relax and then it'll be you sitting there. Yes, he'll have had a mother, a father, a home but you have to think, and tell yourself that it is one less bastard that is trying to kill you.'

"'That is as may be, but he is someone's man, and he was just doing a job the same as us. He was fighting for his country, his family and his Kaiser.'

"'Yes, but him and his Kaiser started the bloody war. Think of all those innocent people he has probably killed, burnt out of their homes while his missus and the like are sitting safe and sound in Germany, but not for long, I hope. No, I have no sympathy for him or his family, as I say, they should've thought about the consequences before they started.'

"'We're all just numbers being moved around on charts in offices in London, Berlin, Paris. They don't think 'where shall we put Fred Hardy today' do they? It's some general saying that this position and that position has to be held at all costs and then they go off to some plush safe place in London and have a drink. They move people around as though they were chess pieces, take for example Wellington, what's he do? Gets loads of men killed. Comes home, gets a title, land, pension and the nations gratitude. What does the cannon fodder get? A medal if he's lucky.'

"'Bloody hell, Fred Roberts. I didn't think that you thought and felt like that. Some people would say that you were a defeatist or a communist or even an objector.

"'No. That's one thing I'm not. I mean, supporting Sunderland I can hardly be a defeatist, can't afford to be,' I said and they all laughed. 'It's just seeing all the waste, of land, of lives and for some, of hope, has kinda' made me a realist. I sometimes think when we are on the move, like now, look at the surroundings and see what should be there. Flowers, trees, birds, children playing, crops, animals. Where are they? That is the sheer waste. Is that the way we want a world to bring our kids up in?'

"'Have you noticed we seem to have been marching away from the shelling, things are definitely a lot quieter than they were.'

"'Maybe we're getting a rest?'

"'Lance Corporal Spelk,' Woody started shouting, 'Lance Corporal Spelk, sir, permission to speak, sir.'

"Spelk was just ignoring him as he knew he was just taking the mickey. It was all good fun. But you could guarantee that any minute now Spelk would lose his patience and then the temper would start.

"'I say,' putting on an accentuated posh voice, Woody continued, 'I need to ask a…'"

"Spelk went over and grabbed him by the collar and said, 'Keep this up and you won't be able to ask a question.'

"'My goodness, doesn't she get all het up? Must be that time of month.'

"'Right, that's it, you're on a charge.'

"'You're putting me on a charge after having threatened me, on active service, in front of plenty of witnesses? I think not, Corporal.'

"Chalkie piped up and said, 'Enough is enough, Woody. There were no witnesses here to hear you being threatened by a non-commissioned officer, were there, lads?'

"Chalkie looked at everyone and we all shook our heads to agree with him.

"'The trouble is, mate, that you just never know when to stop. You got your rise, and it even created a little laugh and lightened up the moment, but then you should have seen how the land was lying and left it. If our Lance corporal wants to make a charge against you, then you deserve it.'

"Spelk looked at everyone and he realised that he had overreacted and that he must set an example. 'Right, let's forget it and everyone get on with what they're doing.'

"'Come on, Spelk,' said Chalkie, now the situation had been defused, 'What's the score? What is the big secret and where are we going?'

"Spelk thought he would get a little of his own back and replied, 'Sorry, men. I'm only a lance corporal. It's only when you reach the dizzy heights of full corporal that you get to know the secrets.'

"'I'll bloody secrets you lot in a minute,' came the dulcet tones behind us. It was our sergeant. 'In another mile or so, we shall be digging in for a large offensive and will wait to be reinforced by troops from Canada and France, if there are any French still fighting on our side,' he said with a little snigger. 'Now when we get there, I want sentries posted, a toilet dug and then some tea on the go. Right?' So, that had answered all out questions. I would be able to settle down sometime later today and finish, or should I say start a letter to your grandma. I took out of my breast pocket a couple of small pictures, one of us at Gretna Green and one of Jane and the bairn, your dad."

George said, "It's strange really."

"What is?" said James.

"Thinking that our da was once a baby and you, our Granda, was his da."

"What's strange about it, idiot?" said James. "Did you think he had been born old or something weird?"

"Right, you two, that's enough. I fancy a bit of a shut eye anyway so off you go."

They waited and looked at their granda expectedly, but there was no sixpence forthcoming today. They looked at each other, pulled faces and stormed off, banging the door behind them. Fred smiled to himself and thought, *The little buggers have got used to that tanner every week, let them stew. Can't take anything for granted.* He then looked at the two pictures he had just been talking to them about. *I had even got bollocked for stopping and looking at them,* he thought. It had been worth it though as they were the only things keeping him going and making all this waste, well, worthwhile in a strange sort of way. The fact that knowing what you were doing would bring peace to one side or the other. I would love to see the padres from each side meet and discuss who had right on their side and whose side God was on. That would make for a good play or sketch at the theatre, wouldn't it? They could call it 'Whose side are you on anyway, God?'.

He carried on thinking about the silly chit chat they used to have, for instance, when they were getting to the point where they were to dig in and they came across some blokes making their way back to the rear, 'Sound like Jocks.'

'Good luck, lads. We're on our way home. You're welcome to it.'

'Home,' said Woody, 'Bloody Jocks are all talk and all wind, like those damn bagpipes they say they play. They can't have been playing them out here or the Germans would have buggered off anywhere for some peace.'

I said, 'Must admit being a little envious of them though, wish I could fit in their kit-bags.'

'You, fit in their kit bag? You're the only sod that seems to have put on weight out of us all. You even look pregnant. Has someone been having a go at you and you haven't let on? Must be enjoying it on the sly then.'

It was my turn to get the mickey taken out of me now. Oh well, someone else is getting a rest then.

'Probably one of those miracle misconception things that Mary had,' said Woody.

'Idiot, it is conception, not misconception and stop blaspheming.'

'Aye, I often think that lad Joseph must have been a thick mackam putting up with and accepting a story like that. Come on. I mean misconception, a miracle.'

'All I can say is that it was a miracle the other bloke didn't end up with a black eye or worse.'

'Well, if it had been two blokes from Sunderland, they would have to resort to handbags at dawn. That's right, Fred?'

'If you're implying that one of them was me, when did I come from Sunderland?'

Spelk said, 'You lot stop all the blaspheming otherwise we'll go to hell?'

'Go to hell? Look around. I think that we are already there. It can't be much worse than this, can it? Oh my God. Worse than this? Anyway, since when did you go all holy rollerish? I remember you being caught having some kind of competition with someone else which involved your shorts being down and being caught in the vestry by the priest. Two questions. One – who won? And two – how many hail Marys did you have to do? Sorry, there were three questions – was he a good looker, the priest that is?"

That story caused great laughter and we never knew if it had been true or not 'cos poor Spelk went off in the sulked to see his Rupert. They were the stories that made everything bearable and, if you could find some kind of normality, even if only for a few minutes, then it was a few minutes well spent.

I often meant to ask Spelk about it though. Interesting.

Another Saturday Morning

It was a strange sort of morning. I didn't know what it was. Couldn't put my finger on it. Mary-Ellen said that it was just me being old. Yes, I know I put two odd socks on this morning, but I reasoned that I had another pair like them in the drawer, so what was the harm? Of course, when I told her that must be obeyed, she'd told me that she was going to get me certified and put in the local nut house. I still couldn't work out what it was about today though. All right my socks were an issue, the paper lad was late, and there were the usual bills in the post. Had I forgotten someone's birthday or anniversary? So, what if I had, that was normally Mary-Ellen's job, too difficult for a man to trust to do, she would say.

"Well, aren't you going to make a comment then?" she shouted from the kitchen.

Hells bells. It must be hers that I have missed. No, that falls near Grand National Day. Had she had her hair done and I hadn't noticed? No, too early in the day.

"Nothing to say sister, dear," I shouted.

"Then there must be something wrong with you. Calling me dear and no comment, what is making this year any different?"

This must be pretty serious if I comment every year. Perhaps I am going looney. I shall have to admit defeat and ask her.

Just as I was about to shout to her, in she walked with a cup of tea and some toast on a tray and a card and present of a box of fifty Capstan cigarettes.

"Ah, pet, I didn't want you to make a fuss this year, after all, it is another year nearer the box, isn't it? But thank you anyway."

"If I'd known that you hadn't wanted me to make a fuss then I wish that you'd said something, and I wouldn't. Anyway, make sure you tidy yourself up and have a shave as the bairns and Penny will be down later and you'll have to remember that you forgot and act surprised. The bairns seem to like that."

"It's sure to be sugared almonds, a bottle of port and some cheese. What's the bet?"

"Do you know something, Fredrick Hardy? You can be an ungrateful old bugger at times. You'll probably get a mini allotment hamper with some Old Spice off Dolf when they pass, he never ever forgets, and you haven't had the decency to pop up there now and again. I wonder if Old Spice keeps? You have about three lots in the top drawer. I wonder who we can give it to?"

"What about the next church jumble sale or the school raffle?"

"Okay, Brains of Britain. What if Penny won it? She would give it to Ralph and then guess where the next port of call for it would be? Have you worked out the answer yet? No? No wonder the army never made you an officer."

About thirty minutes passed and then Mary-Ellen shouted, "Get prepared, I think I can hear the lads. They're making enough noise to waken the dead and remember…"

"I know. Don't keep on. Act surprised."

"Granda, Granda," they shouted in unison. "Happy birthday to you, happy birthday to you, squashed tomatoes and stew, Happy Birthday to you."

"Birthday! Well, I'll be blessed. I had forgotten all about it and your Aunt Mary-Ellen never mentioned it. In fact, I'll have to ask her where my present is."

"You'll never guess what we've got you? Come on, guess."

"Come on, tell me. Is it a young woman with plenty of money? Or is it just a young woman?"

"Granda, stop being silly. We got you some sugared almonds and some chocolate. Mum got you a bottle of something or other."

"Did you hear that Mary-Ellen? Sugared almonds and a bottle of something. Well, thanks a lot lads, and you, Penny pet. They'll keep me quiet while I get drunk on the port."

"You're welcome, Dad, and happy birthday from us, and Dolf sent some veg and a bottle of Old Spice, which was quite kind of him, don't you think?"

"It is, love, he never forgets. I think we'll open the sweets and have a couple while we reminisce, eh, lads? What do you think? As I was telling you last week we were going to settle in somewhere else whilst waiting for more troops and it seemed to be in a decent area, but one that had seen a lot of activity. The terrain had changed, it was more wooded, quite dense really, a bit like the one up the park, there were also broken down and destroyed vehicles. But the other thing that there was, can you guess?"

"A trench," said young James.

"That's right, lad, another trench. Do you know, each one looks exactly like the last one, no matter which side had used it, or dug it. When we saw the trench, I thought about the allotments at home and said to the lads. Could you imagine what size leeks you could grow in this thing back home?

"Ah, well, there's a point. We aren't talking about home though, are we? Or leeks or tatties? The one thing that no doubt we'll have are plenty of pets again, that's if you can call rats pets. They are worse than the Jerries, they manage to get everywhere.

"The last lot that had occupied this place had been Jocks and taffs and their officers would be holding debriefing meetings with our officers and senior NCO's, then those words of wisdom would be passed down through our corporals which would make Spelk feel good."

"Granda, you keep talking about Spelk being a lance corporal, was he important then?"

"You know something, lad? He had been promoted, which is good because you end up getting more pay, you do get to know more stuff than the ordinary soldier but there is responsibility that goes with it. So, if the men you were in charge of did something wrong, it could be you that got into trouble for not keeping an eye on them or telling them the right thing. He was on the first step of importance. So, to answer your question, yes, he was important in a sort of way. But and this is a big but, we would never dream of telling him as he would then think that he was Napoleon. You do know that he was a French equivalent to a corporal, don't you? No, why should you? History in schools has probably not reached that stage yet and probably never will. Now, where was I? Ah, yes, we were talking about the new location and what happens.

"Woody said, 'Maybe our own Mr wonderful will condescend to give us details later?'

"'Leave him be,' said Chalkie, 'Poor soul he's taken enough stick off us today. If we keep on, it's liable to turn into something nasty, with someone getting hurt, and it'll probably lose him his stripe.'

"The next morning the company commanders spoke to each of their respective companies and told us all what had been happening. 'You will no doubt have noticed that over the last twenty-four hours there has been one of our planes circling the area. It has been gathering information about troop movements, sighting the local terrain and villages etc. Those pictures have been studied and decisions will and have been made at general level. The reason that you are often not told is not because you are of no importance, but actually the opposite. Without you, none of our objectives would ever be achieved...'

"'What he really means,' whispered Woody, 'is without you as cannon fodder nothing would happen. It is you poor buggars who will suffer and die, and not some poxy general at the rear. That's what he really means.'

"'Wood. Shut it, and see me afterwards,' said one of the NCO's.

"'What did I tell you?' I said. 'Always got to be the one who makes a comment, now you're in the shit.'

"'We will be advancing tomorrow and there will be a rear party covering our forward movements, the trenches will still be occupied, and the platoons involved will be informed by their Sgt Majors. The following will also parade outside by position at 1500hrs today.' A list of names was called out and then we heard, Lance Corporal Wood, Ptes Hardy and White.

"There is nothing worse in the army than knowing you have to parade outside someone's office at whatever time or another. You never know if you're in trouble or not and you always start to think the worst, what have I done? Who did I not salute? Etc. etc.

"Our sergeant came and talked to us, 'Apparently, when we go over, there is to be another four battalions at least so you can be assured it's going to be a big one. Some of you will be tasked to do various operations during the assault. You will get to know who and what in the next twenty-four hours. Make sure, as normal, everything in working order, oiled and cleaned. If you have any post to go out get that done, as it will be leaving this location in two hours. Keep some food inside of you, and if you are not designated for any duties, then try and get your head down as God only knows when you will. As always, lads, no matter what happens, you keep going. No matter if it is your sleeping pal that goes down, there will be someone to see to him, you just keep going unless you are told otherwise. Because of our numbers, don't think that's going to be a doddle, as rest assured, we shall be met by force. As normal, there are likely to be trip wires, barbed wire and be prepared for gas.'

"'Well, everything but dancing girls,' someone said.

"'Forget the dancing girls, we have Spelk here, and if he plays his cards right, I could get used to him,' someone piped up.

"Here they go again, winding him up and poor Spelk, he always bites. The thing is he had brought all this teasing on himself. I remember one day we were in training; it was wet and freezing outside and not much warmer in the hut. We had all come in and the stove was out. Spelk had wanted to know whose turn it was to have got the wood and coals. Of course, no one answered, so he started getting all irate. Someone had said that it must be his time of month, then he really lost his temper and stormed out. Since then they had teased him and told him he was a girl's blouse. They all knew though that in a tight spot they could depend on him, quite a butch bloke was our Spelk, although we would never tell him. We all knew exactly where his breaking point was and made sure we didn't cross it. The only thing was that he didn't know exactly where it was. Funny bugger, but someone you wanted nearby.

"'Just been told that there should be some post from home later this afternoon,' Spelk said. 'More socks and knitted balaclavas no doubt. The powers to be said that even the Queen had been sending knitted items for us, but I can't personally see her sitting doing 'pearl one, knit one, can you?'

"'Well, if she is, I suppose the King will be standing there rolling balls of wool in his uniform, and medals of course.'

"'If we keep up advancing the way we are, then it won't be long until we're knocking at the Kaiser's door. Only hope they wait until I'm there,' said Spelk.

"'I am sure that they'll wait until our favourite Lance Corporal is there,' said Chalkie.

"'On another note, don't forget that some of you have to see various people later on and don't be late.'

"'I hate this business where they tell you to report somewhere hours before you have to as you always think that you've done something wrong and trouble is brewing.'

"'Well, let's face it, no one ever gets a pat on the back but you can guarantee that someone will notice the minute you cock something up. They always bloody do. Sod's law, that's what it is. Sod's law.'

"'As they say, lads, 'now it's fair in love and war,' said Spelk.

"'You can say that again, but don't; Woody chipped in, 'look at all those Dear John letters that the lads have been getting. All because the lasses can't do without, and it's all down to those bloody skiving miners. Mine has run off with a black Canadian.'

"'You never said anything about that to any of us, did you?'

"'What? And have you lot taking the piss and talking about him being black and having a big John Thomas? No, thank you. I'll suffer in silence.'

"With the post came some newspapers and it was odd reading about the war and what we had achieved, mind you there was never really anything about our losses. We read that some nurse had been executed by the Jerries, the bastards. Also, a politician had said that the machine gun was not an effective weapon. He needs to be on the receiving end of one, dumb sod.

"'It appears that the South is getting hit a lot now but remember at the beginning it was places like Hartlepool, Whitby and Redcar that were being targeted by the big guns of the German Navy. Quite a few killed there if I remember.'

"'Aye,' said someone.

"'It says here that Turkey is now on the side of the Germans. How old is this bloody paper? We've known that for ages?'

"'They'll not cause much damage, bloody pox ridden camel shaggers,' Woody said very elegantly.

"Me, I kept thinking about home and about Jane and baby Ralph. I hoped that the Germans would not bother with the North East much, despite the Steel, Coal and Shipbuilding industries. Jane had said that Mary-Ellen had got herself a young man, well he can't have been that young because he was apparently a Sergeant in the Durham's. According to the letter he had been to: deleted, deleted and deleted and had been mentioned in some despatch or other. So, he must have done something brave and heroic. Good on Mary-Ellen, pleased she's got herself someone.

"'Guess what? You'll never guess,' said Spelk panting. 'You know that mobile canteen thing that turned up with those women on? Well, I was around the back having a Johnny riddle and could hear the two lasses talking. They were talking about washing and keeping clean in the circumstances.'

"'God, that's exciting.'

"'No, listen. One of them said to the other, that she uses the three F's method of prioritising.'

"'What the hell is the three Fs method when we're at home then?'

"'Face, Feet and Fanny. She didn't want to be smelling like some fish market. Did she?'

"We all laughed and raised our eyebrows but of course Woody had to say something.

'I wonder if she needs any help with her cleanliness routine?' and scratched his bollocks.

"'Dream on,' nearly everyone replied.

"'Right you lot that have been delegated to go somewhere go and do it. The rest of you get some rest and if you are on lookout then make sure you do it. 'Cos if I wake up with my bleedin' throat cut by the tin helmets over there, woe betide whoever was on duty, I'll have their balls on a string and use them for conkers.'

"'He might find it's me slitting his bloody throat and not a German,' said Chippy very quietly, 'and who would know any different?'

"I sat there on a couple of bricks and some old hessian and thought that despite everything they really are a great bunch of mates. We have been quite lucky compared to many other companies, they have lost officers and some of their NCOs and it does affect moral, but touch wood. I picked up the photo of your gran and dad again and giving them a kiss put it back in my breast pocket along with that of the German soldier that I'd picked up. I suppose that their officers also write to families telling them that they died in heroic circumstances the same as ours did?"

I was brought back to the real world with someone shaking and grabbing my arm and me shouting, "Get off, you German bastard." It was young James grabbing my arm and saying, "Granda, Granda Fred, are you all right?"

Both the lads were frightened by my sudden lapse of concentration and I had been momentarily transported back to the trenches.

"Aye, lads, I am fine. Just for a moment there, I forgot where I was. Often do that when your Aunt Mary-Ellen wants me to do something, it's nice and convenient."

Penny came running in thinking there was something up and said, "Is everything okay? I heard the lads shout. Are you all right?"

"I'm fine, pet. Really. I just went into a daze but I think we'll call it a day and they can go and say their taras to her that must be obeyed. Right, lads, off you go and they have probably never heard their granda curse like that before so I'm sorry for that, pet."

"Right, boys, coats and you too, Claire, coat and don't forget the doll, then say your goodbyes. I'll bake and bring some mince and onion pies down for you next week for a change."

"I'll look forward to that, pet. Take care and tell that son of mine I was asking after him."

After they had left, Mary-Ellen went in to see Fred and said, "Do you think that you ought to be telling the bairns everything? I don't want you getting upset again and frightening them."

"I look at them and, especially young George, who is wanting to join up and I think, in fact I hope, that there'll never ever be another one. Look at us, and your boyfriend, whom you never talk about, and then our Ralph. We've all been involved in wars that were never supposed to happen and we have all been affected in different ways. I just hope that those two wee lads will never become part of a series. The war ruined me and I'm sure that our Ralph puts on a brave face as he never talks about his experiences. It would help him if he did, I know that talking to the lads is helping me. I mean, when you think he was a prisoner of war with the bloody Japs for three years, and we now know that those buggers were far worse than any German ever was. Who is going to be next, the Arabs, the yellow people or the Russians with all their power. If you think of some of the countries that we helped save from someone else, they are still ruled by someone else. What a waste of time. Was it all worth it in the end? Was it?"

"Fred, you can't take the issues of the world on your shoulders, there are people in London, Washington, Paris, Rome, Moscow who are paid to do that, not you."

"No, pet, you're wrong there. Those sods are parasites. They put everything back on the man in the street. There is no justice for the man in the street. War will always make rich men richer and poor men poorer. It was so easy when we were kids, we never knew anything else. We were all poor. Now we can see how others live and we want a taste of it. Take you for example, you were sent to Windsor when you were still a kid to work in service and I remember you telling me a tale of how you had to collect coppers from other staff members to give to some Duchess so she could make a donation to the poor. Who bloody got it? You were poor, did you get it? Did your mother? Then, there were times that when you were scullery maid your meal was sometimes leftovers from upstairs."

God, he's on form today, thought Mary-Ellen. "Well, if I'm honest being in service didn't really do me any harm. I would never have been further than Durham if I had stayed here. Plus I did see London and Windsor."

"But what did you come back with to help you and Ma? A head square with a picture of Windsor Castle on that now covers the pedestal and a silk handkerchief that the Duchess of Athlone gave you as a thank you, and where is that now, eh? I ask you, where is it now?"

"Right. Enough. If you've upset yourself, don't start taking it out on me or you can sing for your supper. You can be such a grumpy old thing at times, heaven only knows how poor Jane put up with you all those long years?"

"What's for supper anyway?"

"It was going to be Pease Pudding, some ham from the shank, pickled onions, some stotty. That's what it was going to be," she said, and she stormed, off slamming the door behind her.

Fred thought to himself, *She'll get over it, she always does.* But it was a shame she had wasted her life, looking after Ma and now me, and then all the time thinking that her betrothed would come back. He'd been listed as missing in action and nothing had happened to prove otherwise, but she never gave herself to any other man, not even a twinkle to interest somebody and yet, deep down she was still a bonny woman. How many of them like her were out there he wondered? In many ways those that had received telegrams telling them their loved ones were killed had been better off, at least they'd had something final. Every time that bodies were unearthed in Belgium, France and Holland, women all over the country hoped. *I wonder if these rumours about old Laverick setting his cap at her have any truth in them? Think I'll see if she fancies a walk up the fells see if there are any bilberries out? Mary-Ellen...*

Bilberrying and More

Mary-Ellen hadn't been keen on the walk up the fells, especially as she was still sulking with her brother, but once there, she started to enjoy herself. It was a long time since she'd done it and memories came flooding back and said, "Do you remember when Da used to bring us here and if we dropped the billycan that we were filling, there was hell to pay?"

"Aye, and it still takes ages to get enough for a couple of pies, but they are worth the work and they're free. I could never get Ralph out up here unless he brought that kite that I'd made for him, didn't have the patience to pick them."

"But have you noticed, we are the only ones up, it was the same when the blackberries were out, people don't seem to realise that nature is quite generous, either that or they are too lazy."

"More like the fact that they are too lazy," said Mary-Ellen.

"Sometimes I think that they have lost a little something in life, I'm not harping back for the good old days, because we both know, they weren't good old days. I just think that sometimes we are being too protective of them and mollycoddling them too much. After all, there were always dangers when they were out playing, what with old quarries, open cast sites and remember the old tin war shelters we used as gang huts. I remember we were in the Black Hand gang, with a horrible old couch from the tip. The Black Hand gang be buggered."

"I think on the way home I'll pop in the shop and get some pop for the other Black Hand gang coming down tomorrow, I'll also make a couple of pies and have them with some evaporated milk."

*

"Hi, Granda Fred," he heard the shouting from the back door. "Hello, Aunt Mary-Ellen," they shouted as they passed the kitchen. Then the peace was shattered as they came in the room.

"Right, and how are you two this week? And, Ralphy, haven't you got your eleven plus coming up the week or so? And what about my little soldier boy? How are you?"

"My exams are in two weeks and I hate the arithmetic part of it all. We've had the mock exam and the teacher says that I have to concentrate more but he said that my pass mark was okay."

"Well, whether you like arithmetic or not is totally irrelevant. It is part of your life and always will be. You have to get the marks to ensure that you go up to grammar school. Plus, just because your teacher said that your marks in the mock exam were acceptable don't take it all for granted. The atmosphere in a real exam is different. I always remembered that I hated them walking around the classroom and the noise of the clock ticking away. Concentrate, laddie, just concentrate."

"But, Granda, if I do get to the grammar, I'm going to have to get proper uniform and a cap, and the rest of them will probably be posh."

"You are as posh as the next. Just because someone has been born into more money doesn't mean that they are any better than you. Remember that. They may have had different experiences than you, but they are no different and many a time they take stuff for granted. Your ma and da have worked hard for what you have got and done their best by the three of you and never forget that. Now, where were we up to last week?"

"You were waiting to go into see the boss and wondered if you were going to get into trouble because you might've done something wrong," said George.

"That's right I was. What a surprise we both got when we went in. It tuned out that we were being promoted to Lance Corporal and we found out that Spelk was being promoted to a full corporal, so he would still be higher than us. Because of people being wounded and evacuated and others being killed promotions were bound to happen. Some men were even promoted from Sgt to become an officer…

"We were standing in front of the Commanding Officer and we just wanted to congratulate each other, but the boss said, 'Right. It has been decided that tonight the pair of you will be part of a team along with your Sgt Major that will have the special task of going over the top, capturing and bringing back a German for interrogation purposes. Under no circumstances is he to be harmed. Understand?'

"'Yes, sir,' we both answered and saluted then marched out.

"'Now we're out of there, congratulations, mate,' said Woody.

"'And you,' I said. 'Capture a German just like that he said. Why the hell doesn't he go and do it himself if it's that easy?'

"'Getting back to the promotions, can you imagine what Corporal Spelk is going to be like? Unbearable. H's bad enough as it is now. Probably demand his own batman now.'

"When we got back and were ready to tell everybody our news, they all knew.

"'How the hell did you all know?'

"'Our new corporal told us.'

"'You big-mouthed bastard,' said Woody.

"'Now, now, lance corporals. Remember you cannot behave like ordinary soldiers now. You have to rise above it. And remember, not to let the power go to your heads, take a leaf out of my book. Learn from me.'

"I'm sorry. Did you say learn from me? What will we learn from you, Corporal? How to be a knobhead?'

"'Seriously though, I want to wish you both all the best and congratulations, couldn't have happened to two nicer blokes.'

"'Is he taking the piss or is he being serious?'

"Night drew in and the two of us joined the Sgt Major, while at the same time, several others were going out to try and cut barbed wire ready for the attack that would happen in a few days' time.

"As we crawled on our stomachs towards the wire, we could see at an angle a spot which was manned, and it appeared to be only manned by three men. We were lucky that the section of the wire that we had come across had already been cut, probably from a previous bombardment. We looked at each other and waited for the nod to come from the Sgt Major. You could virtually smell them. They were not being too observant, the smell of coffee was tantalising, there was laughter and then one of them poked his head up and then went for a piss. The nod came and we just jumped. I went for the one taking a leek and because he was so conveniently or inconveniently occupied, depending on how you looked at it, he was practically defenceless and therefore an easy target, no flies on this lad. The other two used their knives, and there was no noise whatsoever. One of them had pulled a gun but had been stopped before he could use it and he lay dead with a knife sticking out of his stomach. It had all been so easy. The reality of war was brought home to you, but it was strange in that you were there, you were part of it but if you could detach yourself from the blood, the death, the cries then it became easier and, I am ashamed to say, I was finding it easier. They'd been caught totally unawares. That had been the easy part, getting him back to our own lines without being seen and before their silence was noted by their own side would be something else. Getting him back was going to be a problem as he certainly didn't want to come either quietly or peacefully, so we had to hit him and hit him hard to knock him out. We dragged him back literally and believe you me it wasn't an easy job, the bugger felt a ton weight, but we managed it without getting into any scraps or stirring a hornet's nest up on the way."

The Prisoner

"As we had caught him, we got the job of looking after him overnight, so we thought that we should try our own hand at interrogating. I opened some tabs and offered them to the German soldier, and he looked at them at them and then all of a sudden he said, 'English tabs, far better than the French and certainly better than the German. Thank you,' and took one.

"You could have heard a pin drop, everyone looked and there were mouths wide open, everyone just staring at this bloody English-speaking German.

"I was the first to speak and said, 'Where the hell did you learn to speak English?'

"'In your country long before the war. My brother and I went over for work, he met a girl and they married, I stayed there with them until it looked like war was inevitable and then came back to Germany. He stayed there with his wife so I don't know if I will be fighting him or if he will be in a prison as an enemy person. I even have a nephew and niece there somewhere.'

"I passed the bloke a bottle of wine that he had acquired, and he drank it greedily.

"'So, whereabouts did you go to find work?'

"'It was hard at first because of the English accent, it was really weird, some of it sounded quite German, but it was in the North of the country at a place called Hartlepool and we got jobs on the docks there. It was cold, a little like the north of Germany, but the people, once they accepted you, were friendly and liked to get drunk.'

"'Hartlepool, you say. Bloody Hartlepool, the monkey hangers. The majority of us here are from the North East, places like Newcastle, Durham, Conset, Sunderland.'

"'That's enough,' said Spelk. 'Too much information."

"'So, you decided to go back to your country and bomb and kill the people that had taken you in? Bloody hypocrite,' said Woody.

"'Well, what would you have done if it had been the other way around. Of course, you would go back to your own country, after all it is your home and your family were there.'

"'Aye, ah suppose you're right.'

"'Be buggered, it's quite a turn up for the books. A German Monkey Hanger.'

"'Anyway, what's your name?'

"'I am Kurt and my home is now in Hamburg. I have a wife and a small daughter,' showing them a family snap, 'and this is my brother Wilhelm and his wife Anna-Marie and their children Roy and June. It was taken on a weekend trip to Whitley Bay.'

"'Whitley Bay be buggered. Of all places. A German prisoner with family on holiday at Whitley Bay.'

"'Is be buggered all you can say? He'll be thinking you're the monkey hanger.'

"'Be buggered, Whitley Bay though, of all the places. Ah mean, Whitley Bay.'"

Fred looked at the bairns watching and listening to him and said, "You know, we sat all night talking to him about his family and home and about his time in England. He turned out to be no different from us, just another pawn in a game of chess to be moved around a board by the powers to be. He told us his brother had changed their surname as having a German name would not be popular. He said, 'Do you know something, lads, looking at the kids, if the powers to be realised that everyone in this war was someone's son, husband, or father and were the same as them then maybe wars would never happen.'"

"What happened to Kurt then, Granda?" said George.

"The next morning, we handed Kurt over to the intelligence people, gave him some English fags, even got his address for after the war. He gave us the last address he had for his brother and sister-in-law in Hartlepool and we said our goodbyes. He was a canny lad, just doing his job like the rest of us, one advantage he had was that he would probably see England before we did.

"Anyway, getting back to the story. I'd received a letter from your grandma telling me all about the birth and how Ralph was doing and how all the parents were discussing what they wanted to be known as. She had also bumped into a couple of lads on leave from France and they told her about the weather and the people but anything else that she tried to find out appeared to have been erased from the memories. Too painful one of them had told her and it was all such a mess, destruction everywhere. She said that letters were censored and bits either cut out or blackened so no information was ever let out in case it fell into enemy hands.

"That afternoon the orders were handed down the line from the Division HQ that an attack by the heavy guns of the artillery would commence the following day and would continue non-stop for 48 hours. The idea was that it would hit their defences and their moral and make an attack by us lot easier. No doubt there would thousands involved and the French would be doing something similar at their end.

"You have never heard anything like the noise when it started. There was nowhere to go to hide from it. They tried to counteract the activity but it was pretty futile. The noise though. We tried to cover ourselves with anything we could to drown it out but it was there. Someone said that it was like being at home listening to his missus going on and on at him but even joking only made you stop worrying for a couple of seconds. We were cowering and then someone

117

said, 'Look. Over there. The bloody cooks are still at it preparing something to eat for us. Bloody true heroes. I only hope that when medals are being given out that some bugger remembers them.'

"'Aye, they do a grand job but have you seen who are coming up the lines – the bloody do-gooders, the clergy. They are like parasites. I suppose they'll be wanting us to confess our sins. I only wish that I had some to confess since the last time he asked. I haven't even had the time to play with myself let alone anything else.'

"'If that's the case,' said Woody, "do you lot make something up to keep him and his boss happy?'

"'Piss off, you heathen. God knows what we have been up to, so we don't have to make anything up.'

"'Well, excuse me, but if that is the case why does the priest want you to tell him? Or does he just want to hear a dirty story so he can go and play with himself. Pervert.'

"'Right. That's it. When this is over, we are going to sort this all out. You'll never get to heaven and will rot in hell.'

"'Look around you. If we are not rotten in hell now, then what do you call this? Eh?'

"'Come on. Think about it. Woody's got a point. If this isn't hell, then what is?'

"Spelk couldn't resist getting involved and said, 'Will you lot shut it and save your energy for what lies ahead. As for God, let him do the worrying for all of us. He can decide as to what hell is and what it isn't. He can also decide who is going there and who isn't but all I'll say is that no doubt I shall see some of you buggers there.'

"It broke the tension and we all laughed, and everyone was back to normal, all internal bickering forgotten about.

"Then suddenly, the time was here, and our Rupert shouted, 'Right, lads. One minute to go and over we go. Remember, you stop for nothing and no one.'

"I looked around and there were men everywhere, more than I had even seen and every one of them ready to go and die for King and Country. Amid all of the activity, we heard the shout and a bugle sounding and over we went, yelling and shouting to frighten the enemy. Some that went over came back quicker than the time it had taken them to get out of the trench, they had been shot, but we just carried on. We ran over men, stood on them and even hid behind their bodies to protect ourselves. Men were being thrown in the air by explosions, and it looked as though the enemy had not been weakened by the last forty-eight hours in any way. A piece of a man went flying past me. *God, if you haven't found where hell is yet, then look around you.* There were cries coming from men who were injured, a stretcher party were just returning back to our lines with someone when they were shot and fell, the poor soldier still lying on the stretched unattended and crying. You could hear him shouting for God and his mother. What good either were going to do him at that moment I do not know? On and on we went, it felt like miles, but it was just a couple of bloody trenches and victory we were

118

told was ours. Victory. Some bloody victory. Over 20000 men and boys killed for what? A couple of bloody trenches. No doubt some bloody big wig in London was praising the heroic victory that had been achieved. They did not have to sit down and write to families to tell them that their loved one would not be coming home. Looking around we tried to see who, if anyone was lost from our own little group. Everyone, or nearly everyone, seemed to be accounted for, a couple of small injuries here and there but all intact otherwise. Then someone said, 'What about Spelk? Haven't seen him and if he was around, we would have heard him telling us to smarten ourselves up.'

We found him about twenty feet from where we were. He had been mown down by what looked like a machine gun and was dead, next to him was our Rupert. It suddenly hit us, two of our lucky group gone. No more would we hear Spelk pulling rank on us and him being wound up. As for Rupert, well, that would be another country estate that would be without someone to inherit and take over the mantel. We really were shaking up and a couple were even seen to be shedding a few tears."

"Granda, Granda," said James, shaking him, "are you all right? You're crying."

"Aye, lads, don't fret. I'm fine. Just forgot myself for a while. Now, if you don't mind, I think we'll call it a day, eh?"

*

On their way home, the boys were unusually quiet until George, turning to his mother, said, "Mum, do you think there'll be another war like Granda's? I mean when I join the army will I have to fight?"

She looked at him and then at James and Claire and said, "Well, when Granda came back from the war, there was another many, many years later and both your dad and granda were in that one. But I really think that the world has had enough fighting and killing, so I honestly hope that there is never another. If women had anything to do with it, there certainly wouldn't be. I hope that when and if you join the army, things will be different. Now get yourselves on and play. We'll be home shortly." *I certainly hope there will be no more,* she thought.

*

"Hello, love," Ralph said as they all walked in, "and how were the two of them today then?"

"Are you in about Mary-Ellen and your dad or the boys?" She knew what he was on about, but for some reason or other, the question just miffed her.

"Da and Mary-Ellen, of course. How were they?"

"Well, they had had a row over something or other and they had gone for a walk up the fells to pick some bilberries and she'd made a couple of small pies but your da was in a funny old mood, so rather than linger down there I brought the pies home. Apparently, he has been really enjoying talking to the lads and

119

reminiscing but today there were wet eyes. I think he had been remembering his pal Spelk and the Somme, he kept saying 'bloody victory, bloody victory'. Aye, that might be so and at what cost? I thought that the lads would be better off out the way. I can never understand the horrors that him and his mates and all those other poor souls would have gone through. Who will listen to the likes of him and who will understand? Not the politicians who weren't there. Your generation will, but who is going to listen to your generation as you won't talk either. Damn men and your stupid pride," she said, looking at him. "If you'd only open up and talk, we all may learn something that may stop all of the waste of life."

Going in the kitchen, she put the pies in the oven to heat up and, putting her pinney on, came back into the sitting room and said, "Ralph, why don't we take the kids down to the paddling pool at Chester-Le-Street tomorrow? I can do a picnic up; they can take their pails and a towel and have a good day out. They don't have to go to Sunday school. Anyway, I think God's got enough to worry about apart from the three of them. What do you think?"

"Sounds a good idea and I agree with you about God, he's got enough on his plate. The forecasts, according to the wireless anyway, supposed to be decent tomorrow. I'll take a couple of bottles of export for us and some lemonade and we can really lash out and a have a shandy. The sheer devilment and excitement of it is setting my pulses racing, so you had better watch out, and on a Sunday as well. What would the neighbours say, eh?"

"You can behave yourself and knock any of those ideas out of your head, Ralph Hardy, before you start."

"Story of my life that is," he said playfully, smiling at her.

*

Ralph was up bright and early getting the Sunday papers, he always got *The People*, *The Sunday Post* and the *Sunday Sun*, he also bought some Tudor crisps, they didn't have the blue bags of salt in now though and were already salted. There was something exciting about looking for that little blue bag she thought. Sad that she missed that little pleasure she thought to herself.

Opening the door at the bottom of the stairs, she shouted, "Right, you three, up, get washed and dressed and down here for your breakfast, and I don't want to be keep shouting up there. And before you start, I want no fighting. Do you understand?"

"Yes, Ma," came the reply followed by George saying, "But he always starts it."

Claire had to have her pennyworth also, "Tell them not to pick on me and not to throw the water at me."

"The three of you get up and sorted right now and without any more noise. Remember the dog needs a walk before we go out."

"Where we going? When are we going out and do, we have to take Claire?"

"If you don't get cracking, we'll not be going anywhere, and as for not taking Claire, believe me if I could leave anyone it would be you two, so get a move on. And don't forget behind the ears."

She went back in the kitchen and Ralph was back from the shops and he'd even bought her a bunch of flowers. "My goodness. What's up? You've either been up to no good and you're feeling guilty or you've had a treble up. Which is it?" she said teasingly.

"My sweet," he said, pulling her to him, "you know I've only eyes for you," and kissed her.

At that moment, George and James came in all excited and stopped in their tracks when they saw their parents kissing. "Yugh," said George. Ralph was silent but looked at them in an embarrassed way.

"Peace is now shattered, and a moment of intimacy gone. Oh well. That's married life, pet," she said.

Ralph laughed at young George and said, "I hope that one day he'll look back on seeing us and think that it's great and natural. He needs toughening up though. After piano practice, he should be out with the lads kicking about and getting a few knocks, especially if he really is keen on joining up. Won't hurt him one little bit."

"Leave him be, Ralph, he enjoys the piano and the music, but I must admit that if I hear 'London's Burning' one more time, I'll set it on fire myself. Seriously though Mrs Thompson is pleased with him and is putting him in for his first exam which will be in Newcastle and costs ten shilling. I also thought that as James is in the scouts, then George could join the cubs, same place and same time. He'll probably love the idea of dressing up in a uniform."

"Never mind him, have I told you? No, I haven't. I think it must have been Mary-Ellen I was telling, or she was telling me."

"What on earth are you rattling on about? Who told who? Who told who what?"

"Apparently, Claire has been talking about joining the gazoo band at the Plain."

"Piano, recorder and now a gazoo. I don't know if my nerves would stand it. Anyway, some of those mothers that are in charge of the kids on those bands look like little Hitler, all dressed up. Bit over the top some of them, but I suppose it would also do her the world of good, but you realise that we'd be having to go to competitions on a weekend in the summer with them for support. I can just imagine it George in one room on the piano, her marching up and down blowing a gazoo in another and the other one kicking the ball against the wall."

"Well, if all that happens, you'll know where to find me," Ralph said, "in the shed at the allotments or down at Dad's."

About 30 minutes later, everything was packed up and the five of them made their way to the bus stop at the top of the street. The bus pulled up and Ralph said, "Two and three half's return to Chester Jack please."

George said, "How do you know that the conductor is called Jack?"

"Ah. That's another secret you'll learn when you get older, nearly all conductors are called Jack."

"Ralph, stop teasing them. Ignore your dad, he's having one of his funny moments."

George and James looked at each other, shrugged their shoulders and turning around kneeled on the seat and starting to wave to people in cars behind. When they arrived, they ran on ahead until they came to main road that they had to cross and there was the paddling pool. It was alongside a river and in view of a castle, there were some swings, a shuggy boat and banana slide. They knew George wouldn't go on the shuggy boats as he didn't like the height it went. Off the three of them went straight into the pool. It was a beautiful day, not a cloud in sight, and even at this time of day, the ice cream man was doing a roaring trade. The lads wanted to take their small boats down to the side of the river, so Ralph went along to supervise. Everything was going well until George let go of the string attached to his boat and it started to drift slightly.

"Da," he shouted, "my boat's gone. Can you get it?"

Ralph decided to play along with them and shouted, "Here I am. Superman to the rescue." He took off his shoes and socks and rolled up his trouser legs and started to walk out to the stricken boat. He looked at the kids and Penny and said, "Superman is on his way."

Penny shouted, "More like Captain Pugwash," and everyone laughed.

Then splash. Ralph had slipped and fallen into the river. He stood up and in his hand was not a fish but the boat. "Look, I told you Superman would get it."

By this time the kids were in stitches and everyone was now looking at Ralph who had suddenly become the centre of attention looking like a drowned rat and worse than that his trousers were clinging to his body and were virtually see through. Embarrassing but funny.

Climbing out, he said, "Right, lads. Get your nets and jars and see if you can catch a couple of minnows or go back to the paddling pool while I try and dry off."

Penny looked at him and said, "We have nothing for you to change into so you'll just have to strip down and pretend you are wearing shorts and dry everything off in the sun, won't take long."

"Your mother never told me that you were secretly a shameless wanton hussy. Any excuse to get my clothes off me, and in public. We'll be arrested for indecency."

"If anyone is arrested for indecency, it'll be you Ralph Hardy, just look at yourself. You'll have all the fair maidens of Chester-Le-Street swooning. I'll go and get a wind breaker from the parkie and that should give a bit of privacy."

The lads kept running back to show some tiddlers they had caught and then wanted an ice cream. Penny looked at them and said to Ralph, "I think we should think about heading back, they've caught the sun and they should sleep tonight then we can have five minutes to ourselves."

"There you go again. After my body. Shameless."

She picked up one of the buckets, minnows and all and threw it over him. "That'll cool you off," she said, laughing.

"You so and so. I've just got dry, now I'll have to get on the bus wet again and it looks as though I've wet myself."

"Talking of wetting themselves, I'd better see to Claire, she is dancing around as though she wants to go." She went up to Claire who was beside the paddling pool and said, "Do you need the toilet, pet?"

"I need a wee but I need it now."

"Come here and sit on the side and you can just wee into the pool."

George heard the conversation and shouted, "Mum is letting our Claire tinkle in the pool."

"George, will you be quiet and keep your voice down please, after all it is Sunday and go and get your da to dry you off. Now. And you can go also, Ralph."

Everyone was dried, packed up and ready. The lads wanted to take their tiddlers on the bus but their da told them as they didn't have tickets for them the conductor would not let them on, so it would be better if they were released back into the river and they could re-join their own families as they would have been wondering where they were. George accepted the story but James was now starting to doubt everything. "Can I call the conductor Jack?" said James.

"No, Son, you're too young to be using first name terms with adults. Grown-ups don't like it."

On the way back to the bus, they were approached by a couple of strangers who were lost and were seeking directions. Penny could see her husband freeze and his back stiffen. They were Japanese, probably from the university, but to Ralph memories came flooding back of prisoner of war camps, their treatment received. Penny jumped in and said, "If it is the university you're after, then you need to catch a bus at the next stop, and it'll be signed Durham City. If you want the one that goes passed the Oriental University, then get the Darlington bus."

She grabbed her husband and said, "You all right, pet? Don't let that spoil a good day and the lads are looking a little frightened."

James said, "When we get home, can we go to Pyles and get some chips and cherryade pop?"

"We'll see," said Penny, thinking that when she was younger, she had said to herself that she'd never say 'we'll see' because she'd heard her parents saying it all the time and now here, she is doing and saying the same things that they said and did.

Getting on the bus, George noticed his da say, "How do marra…" and then again, he called this conductor Jack. *Will I ever learn to be grown up and what you have to say to different people?* he thought.

More Questions

"You can have another half an hour kick about while I sort stuff out and then we'll be off to Granda Fred's. Claire, don't forget to pack that box of cakes that you made for Aunt Mary-Ellen, she'll be over the moon when you tell her that you made them."

Claire came into the kitchen and, looking very deep in thoughts, said, "I've been thinking."

"What have you been thinking about, pet?"

"Well, I've decided that when I grow up that I am going to be a teacher, meet a tall dark handsome man who will go to Durham and we'll have three children."

"Well, you've got it all worked out, haven't you? Tall, dark and handsome, educated and three children."

"Yes, definitely three. One of each."

"What do you mean, pet? One of each?"

"Well," she said all very serious, "there will be a boy called Robin, a girl called Sarah Louise and a little black girl called Wilma Jane Penny. Penny after you and Jane after Grandma Jane that we never saw. I think Granda Fred would like that, don't you?"

"I do, pet. I'm not really sure about the black one though."

"Mum," Claire said.

Now what, Penny thought. "Yes, pet, what's up?" I heard James and one of friends whispering and giggling yesterday and James's friend said that girls had 'Marys' and boys had 'peters' and they were doing something, but I don't know what as I couldn't see. I shouted at them that I didn't have a Mary and they laughed at me and I ran away."

"Were they now," said Penny, thinking on her feet. "I shall have a word with him later, in fact his da can have a talk with him. Boys and girls are different in lots of ways. They are stronger and tougher and dirtier," she said, pulling a face and making Claire laugh. "Horrible creatures, you are better off being a girl. They are dirty things that think water is for playing with and not for washing and they are always trying to be tough in front of their pals. Have you noticed they never come home from football with clean kit? They dirtied it on purpose, so we think they've had a good game. They pretend not to be soft and kind and say they don't like all the hugging and kissing that we do. But, as you grow up, you will watch them at a football match or with a dog and there will be hugs and kisses galore. But suggest giving their sons a hug and you'd think that you were talking in a foreign language. No, you are better off being a girl. You can get nice scent

124

and nice jewellery which you get them to buy. But times are changing, the war saw to that. Women had to do jobs that men used to do. Women worked on farms, drove buses, built tanks and made ammunition. Women found out that they could do the majority of things that a man can do, but you ask a man to cook a meal then disaster and a mess are the results. No, it is useful to learn some of the things that men do but the secret is to never tell them. We have to make them think that we can't manage without them and that we are helpless."

She skipped away, shouting, "James, George, are you going to be all day? We've been waiting ages and are starting to get cross."

Coming into the kitchen at that moment, Ralph laughed and said, "Listen to that little madam. Pity help her poor husband and the children."

"Wait until I get back and tell you what she has been telling me and you'll be needing to talk to James also," she said, raising her eyebrows, "anyway, must go," and giving him a kiss they headed off.

On the way to Fred's, they passed the allotment as usual but there was no sign of Dolf at all. *I must mention it to Fred when we get there, in case there is something wrong with him*, she thought. When they arrived, the kids did their normal and rushed straight into see their granda, but Mary-Ellen said, "He's been in a funny old mood this week, I think remembering the battle last week took it out of him a little. I suppose one day the lads will read about it all in history books. To think all those poor young lads lost and for what? I think that those that survived often ask themselves why they did and why others didn't, the luck of the draw I suppose. He always says that if there is a bullet with your name on it, then that's it. Stupid thing to say really when you think about it, isn't it?"

"Wow, I have never heard you wax so lyrical," said Penny.

"Aye, well, I am a silent, deep thinker," she said and laughed. "Anyway, how are you? I hear that you had a good day out last Sunday."

"Hello, my young soldiers," said Fred to James and George. "I know you have got a lot to tell me about the paddling pool and what you got up to."

"Wait until we tell you what happened to da," said George. So they then proceeded to tell him about their da falling in the river and how he had to lie there in his underwear trying to dry himself off.

"Well, I wish I'd seen that. Must have been funny, anyway, he's too old to be playing with boats and paddling. It must have made your day a lot more fun and I hope that you didn't laugh too much at him?" he said with a twinkle in his eye, imagining the scene.

"Anyway, we were talking about that big battle last week, weren't we? The destruction in such a small area was awful, both sides were busy clearing up, bodies had to be collected, weapons, equipment, identity tags. There was such a lot of nastiness. Friends injured and killed. Some of the locals were even out getting their share of the loot and they would sell it on the black market. It was strange in that the locals had more of our kit than the quartermasters did. You know among all that carnage and waste, there was always something to break the reality and make you laugh.

"I remember part way through that day a group of Jocks were coming back from further up front and said, 'Good luck, lads, we're off home.'

"Woody piped up and said, 'Home, bloody home. Damn Jocks, all talk and full of wind like those damn things they blow.'

"'I must admit to being a little envious of them and I wish I could fit in their kit bags.'

"'You, fit into their kit bags? You have to be joking. You're the only one of us that has put any weight on. Did someone get to you and make you pregnant? I wonder what you'll have.'

"'Well, whatever I have it will still have more sense than you.'

"'It was probably one of those conception things that Mary was supposed to have with yon man.'

"'Aye, Joseph must have been a bit of a wimp to believe all that nonsense and fall for that excuse.'

"'Will you lot have some respect and stop all that blaspheming, or you'll go straight to hell,' said Woody.

"'Since when have you gone all religious like? I suppose that you thought that the shells exploding in the sky was the Archangel Gabriel. Suppose you'll be running for the next Bishop of Durham or even the Pope when you get back. And as for hell, look around you. We're there already.'

"As we were gathering kit and piling it up to be sorted and repaired, some of the officers were sitting down and writing letters to families saying that their sons, fathers, brothers had been heroically killed in action and what a good chap they were and what a miss they would be. It was one job that I didn't envy them. It was also strange to think that at the same time we were doing all of this that the enemy were doing the same thing. It really does go to show that underneath everything we are all the same. Of course someone had to comment, 'Aye and we all shit the same.'"

Turning to look direct at the lads, he said, "See that old brass cane stand that we use for to put an umbrella in? Well, that was once a shell from a gun. Aye, some of the lads to ease boredom would make things out of old shells and then they would end up back at home, or they'd sell them to get a few more fags. That one was made by my old pal Spelk. I caught Mary-Ellen about to give it away to old Mrs Clegg for a chapel white elephant sale last week. And before either of you ask, I don't know why they call it a white elephant sale, it is just another of those things that we adults say."

George muttered, "I'll never be an adult if I can't remember all of these things."

Fred was mimicking Mary-Ellen by crossing his arms and saying, "'And why do you want to keep something that has probably killed someone else, I don't understand you lot, I really don't.'

"So, I said to her, 'And why do you want to eat something that has never harmed anyone?'

"'That's different and you know it is.'

"'You're crackers, woman. All of this is really because your boyfriend still hasn't come home.' At that she went out of the room in tears."

The lads were enjoying watching their granda playing the two parts and pulling faces.

George said, "Is Aunt Mary-Ellen really crackers, Granda?"

"No, it doesn't, and I shouldn't be saying things like that to you both. It was just hard for her when we were all coming back, and the war was finished. All she had been told was the he was missing and believed to be dead. She waited and waited, she still loved him, and in fact I think that she still does and always will. He was like many a young man who marched off to war full of pride and hope that what he was doing would see eternal peace and his loved ones and country safe. She gave the best years of her life living in hope."

"Does that mean that he'll never come back then?"

"Probably. If he had been taken prisoner he would have been released when the war ended, but if the truth be known there were thousands of men whose bodies were never found. It was the conditions that we fought in. They'll probably turn up one day when farmers are tending their land in France, Belgium or Holland. Sometimes I think and hope for her sake, that one day a miracle may happen, and he turns up having been injured and lost his memory or something."

James said, "Da says that she'll turn into a wizened old prune."

"Now, James, don't ever let me hear you say anything like that ever again, and your da shouldn't be saying it to you either. It's not a joke nor a funny matter. How'd you like it if someone you loved, your da, your mum or Claire walked out that door and never came back, and you grew up never ever knowing what had happened to them? Think about it. I'm really disappointed at you and at your da for saying such hurtful things. Can you imagine how your aunt would feel if she was to hear it? She's a good woman. A proud woman. She would still make a grand catch for someone and I would miss her like mad, but would never dream of telling her as such, she'd think that I'd gone soft in the head. She, like many other women of that age, were the real unsung heroes of the war, in fact of any war. It was and is them that keep family life alive. They keep the country alive. Aye, each of them should have been given a special medal, as their type of bravery is different and far more heroic than what we had to face. For us, it was a case of kill or be killed but for them, no matter what happened, they have to ensure that the country and family carry on and prosper despite anything the government and the enemy throw at them. Next time, you look at your aunt and women like her, don't see a grumpy old person but see a hero. Right, lads. Enough for today and I may have a surprise for you next week, we may do something different. Now there's a tanner each and one for Claire. There's also two shillings, James, get your ma a bunch of flowers at the corner shop from me when you get home, but don't tell her until you get there. Okay? And don't lose it."

"Thanks, Granda Fred," they both said in unison and ran out to the kitchen where their mum was tidying up after Claire had had a baking session with Mary-Ellen.

"Mum, we can't tell you what it is yet cos it's a secret but we have to get something for you on the way home off Granda."

"Big gob," said James, giving George a dig in the side, "you can't keep a secret, can you, idiot?"

"Oh, Mary-Ellen, will it ever end, the bickering and name calling?"

"Doubt it, pet, just look at that old so and so in there and he's supposed to be a responsible adult. Men will always be boys. It just a good job that we grow up and keep them in order," she said, and they both laughed.

"True. Definitely true. Ralph's no better either. A big bairn at heart and behaves like one sometimes."

A Grave Visit

It was Friday and Fred was sitting having a cup of tea and reading the local paper when he had a brainwave. "Mary-Ellen," he shouted, "was it today that you were thinking about popping up and seeing Penny?"

The answer came back from the kitchen, "Yes, why?"

"I was just thinking that instead of her bringing the kids down here on Saturday that I'll pop up and take the lads out with me for a walk."

"Bloody hell, Fred Hardy, what's got into you? Firstly, lashing out money on flowers for Penny, and now setting foot outside of this house. Is the world ready for all this activity?"

"Sarcasm, my dear sister, is supposed to be the lowest form of wit, don't you know?"

"Yes, I do, and I also know what the next line to that saying is, so don't even think about saying it. Anyway, if you are intending to go up there, then I'd better notify the hospital, the fire brigade and the police as something is bound to happen to someone. You do know that your Ralph won't be in, don't you? He's off with the club committee somewhere or other."

"It's not Ralph I am going to see. I just thought that as the lads are learning about their Grandma, I'd take them up the grave, as I don't think they've ever been up there and it's a nice walk and a bit of fresh air will do them good. In fact, why don't you come up and then you and Penny can pop out for a cup of tea somewhere and chat till your heart's content?"

"I suppose I could, the change of scenery will do me good as well. Just don't go getting yourself all worked up though."

"Diffent fret yourself, bonny lass, it'll be fine."

*

Saturday morning came around and the weather was even better than the forecast had said, so once they'd had breakfast, they went and caught the local bus, it was only about four miles but they had to change buses. The local town had changed a lot over the years, there were far more Paki shops now he thought. The indoor market was not doing so well and he had put that down to more people owning cars and were able to get out and about to bigger towns and that meant the smaller ones were suffering. At least, they still had two picture houses where the young lads and lasses used to go and pay nine pence to sit on the back row and have a kiss and cuddle and, if you were lucky, have a grope and think

129

that you had climbed Mount Everest and then tell all your pals that you 'had done it' and even said to some of them, offering your finger 'here smell it'. There was also a local dance hall called the Palais. Wonder if the lads and lasses still sit separate and look at each other daring to ask someone for a dance? He was miles away, lost in his own dream world when he felt a poke in the ribs and Mary-Ellen's voice saying, "You haven't listened to a word I've said, have you?"

"Of course, I have. Every word."

"Come on then. What did I say?"

"You were going on about the bairns, weren't you?"

"As I thought. Not listening."

Quickly changing the subject, he said, "I thought that I'd take them up the park, show them where Ma lived and then up to the graveyard."

"What about some flowers?"

"I'll get the lads to pick some wild ones and they can feel that they have done something themselves."

"As long as you keep an eye on them and make sure they don't touch any in the park."

Penny had been shocked when Mary-Ellen told her yesterday that Fred was coming up, but she hadn't told the kids in case things didn't go as planned. They were out on the field having a kickabout. George had gone up under duress. They had asked why they weren't going to see Granda Fred today and Penny said, "The mountain might be coming to see Mohammed."

Of course, no sooner had the words come out of her mouth when George asked who Mohammed was and why, and how could a mountain come to see them.

While they were out playing, she thought that she'd ask Fred and Mary-Ellen to stop for a bite to eat. *Fred likes liver and onions with some veg and mashed potato. He always says that 'she', Mary-Ellen couldn't do mash as well as her, but I am sure that he tells Mary-Ellen that I can't make mash as good as her, that's what men do, play us off against each other. Probably does, the fly old so and so. The kids won't be too happy with that though so they could nip up the chip shop and get some chips and batter.* Fred also liked tripe but the thought of it didn't appeal and Ralph always told her that getting it once a week as a boy was terrible.

Startling her, the front doorbell rang, Fred and May-Ellen were probably the only two people to use the front door, so she knew it would be them. Sure enough when she opened, there they were, standing there.

"Hello, love, and how are you?" said Mary-Ellen, giving her a kiss and box of chocolates.

"I'm fine, but when are you going to just come in instead of standing on formality?"

"Don't like to do that, pet, might catch the pair of you in a compromising position."

"Ignore him, love, he's probably been reading one of those magazines from the top shelf."

"We saw the kids as we got off the bus, but they were too busy tying Claire to take any notice of us two old things."

"Feeling sorry for himself, is he?" she said to Mary-Ellen, "They'll be the death of me, the pair of them. I'll give them a shout."

"It can wait a minute or two, pet, get yourself a sit down, and I'll put the kettle on. Make most of the quiet. He," said Mary-Ellen, nudging Fred, "can go out and speak to them and rescue the bairn from the clutches of the Red Indians. Go on, get yourself out there and make sure they don't do what you once did to that lass, what was her name again? Margaret, yes Margaret that's what it was."

Penny looked startled and said, "What did he do to Margaret?"

"Do I tell her or do you?" she said, looking at Fred.

"You might as well tell her; you're breaking your neck to do so. I'm off out to play the hero or villain depending on whose view you take."

"Well, he was probably about eight years old and they were all out playing cowboys and Indians, obviously he was an Indian chief and they had attacked a wagon train and taken this Margaret girl prisoner. All well and good and totally innocent, until that is, he decided to scalp her."

"He what?" said Penny. "Did he really scalp her?"

"Yes, with a pair of old scissors and what a mess her hair was!"

"I bet her mother went crackers,"

"Crackers wasn't the word. She used words that wouldn't have been out of place in an army barracks or something heard on the quayside. The parents fell out as a result and didn't speak for nearly two months, and of course, Margaret wasn't allowed to associate with common ruffians for a while."

Meanwhile Fred shouted at the lads, "Hey, you two leave her alone and pick on someone your own size."

Their faces were a treat when they saw him and ran straight over and were saying, "We didn't know you were coming."

"Emmm, I think that you've forgotten something or someone, haven't you?" he said, pointing at Claire who was still tied up. "Go and get her undone, then in the house and get yourselves tidied up as you're coming with me for a walk."

They went and released Claire who was looking very smug that she had been rescued by her granda but she was still old enough to realise that they would get her again sometime when he wasn't around. *I wish that I'd been born a boy,* she thought to herself.

"Where are we going, Granda?" asked James.

"That's for me to know and you to find out. I have decided that we are going for a long walk off a short pier."

Here we go again, thought George. *Something else that grown-ups say that we don't know what it means. I wonder why they do it. Should I ask?* Then thought better of it as no one ever told you what they were on about.

"No, we're going there and back, and, if I decide it's too far, then we're not going, okay?"

Just as George was about to say something, James couldn't contain himself and said, "Da says that, Granda, but it doesn't make sense. If they've gone and come back and decided that it was too far for them to go, how can they not go if they've already been? Last week, Mum had told George off for climbing and said, 'If you fall down and break your legs, don't come running to me crying,' how could be run if he had broken his legs?"

"The pair of you stop asking so many questions and," said Fred, turning to George, "and catch up, George."

"I was thinking, Granda."

"Thinking, eh? So that was what the strange smell was, you thinking. Come on."

George caught up with them and looking at James, he said, "I think that when you become grown-up you go crackers," and made a sign and pointed to his head.

"We're going up the park first to show you where your Granda lived and then up to see her grave. So, I want you to pick some wildflowers, not any proper flowers from the park or from anyone's front garden, mind you, Granda would like that."

For the next five minutes or so they scavenged around, making Claire pick the flowers as they thought it too sissyish to do.

"Right, well done. They look nice and colourful. Now, put your bums in that old log over there and we'll have a five-minute breather." Claire put her coat on the log and sat on that because she thought that was what ladies should do, but wouldn't let the lads anywhere near it.

"See that row of cottages over there," he said, pointing to about twelve little bungalows all in a row about 100 yards away. "That's where you're Grandma Jane and Mary-Ellen used to live just after I went off to war. Nice spot, isn't it? Third one from the left. No busy roads, the pit in the distance, kids playing footie in the winter and then cricket in the summer months. The vicar and his family lived in a big house down to the right. Great garden parties and jumble sales if I remember rightly. Just over there, we'd enter the woods and it was a fantastic spot for bilberry picking and walking dogs. Aye, at the bottom of her garden, just as you enter through the gate, your gran had a nice little allotment as everyone was encouraged to grow their own veg. There were tatties, carrots, cabbage, and the like. There was also plenty of rhubarb and a goosegog bush. I remember she used to grow red cabbage and then pickle it. She also managed to have some marigolds and other small flowers to brighten the place up. If there were plenty of them, she'd often give passing children a bunch to take home for their mams." He paused for a moment lost in his own thoughts and then said, "It was strange, and the Germans even dropped two bombs at the corner of the row, knocking a couple of walls down."

"Why would they want to bomb Grandma Jane though?" said Ralph.

"Well, though Grandma Jane was a hero, it wasn't her they were trying to bomb. I think that it was either the steel works or the ball bearing factory. Must've misread their maps or something, but she said that the weather that night was bad so that could've been to blame. You know when your mum brings you down on a Saturday?"

They all looked at him and answered, "Yes," virtually at the same time.

"Well, you pass a brickwork where two footpaths cross, and at that spot, there are wild blackberry bushes growing, and I am sure that you have either hidden in them or picked blackberries when the fruit was out. An aeroplane crashed there during the war; 1942 I think it was. It went quite deep but they managed to recover the pilot's body and some of the aircraft, but if you ask your da, he might still have a piece of the metal from it as he found a bit."

"Wow," said George.

James said, "If we'd known that a pilot had been killed there, then we wouldn't have played there."

"No, lad, life goes on. It has to. I know that there is no plaque there but there should be, maybe one day when you're older you'll remember the story and do something about it. Now we'll head on up to the grave, but I think we've earned ourselves an ice cream at the King's café, and we'll be adventurous and have a big cornet each, eh?"

"Can we have blood on it?" said Claire excitedly.

"Aye, you can have blood on it, pet," he said, grabbing her hand and thought, *The innocence of childhood.*

"I'll be able to show you where my piano teacher lives, Granda," said George.

"Why does he want to know where your piano teacher lives?" said James, "Granda isn't interested in that, are you, Granda?"

"Actually, young Ralph," he said and thought, *That'll annoy him, he doesn't like being called Ralph.* "I'm very interested. When you become a granda, you have to learn to be interested in everything that everyone does. Everyone says that older people become nosey, but what would you think if I never asked you about school or your football and only talked to young George here? You wouldn't be too happy. The same would happen if I was only interested in what you did and didn't bother with George or Claire. Think about it, the pair of you have a lot in common, in many ways you both want to be entertainers. You want to entertain people with your football skills and George with his music. This month Claire wants to be able to heal people. So, I consider myself to be a very lucky granda indeed. All that talent, and in one family and more importantly, it stems from me."

About ten minutes later and having finished their ice creams with blood on, they arrived at the gates of the little church and Fred said, "Whilst we're here we'll look at Grandma Jane's grave, then her parents and then at your mum's mothers grave. I think that you'll have to try and work miracles with the flowers, but a few on each will be nice." They stopped in front of a head stone that read:

Here Lies
Jane Hardy (nee Wilson-Roberts) 1900 – 1924
And twin daughters Grace and Iris 1924 – 1924
May God Bless and Protect Them

Fred stood and looked and looked, and wondered to himself what Jane would have made of the bairns and also thought about Grace and Iris, *She would've made a great mother. They would have been the bairns' aunts. Strange to think of that. Aye, it's strange what life throws at you.*

He knew it was coming but this time it was George and not James.

"Granda Fred? It said on there that you had two children but that they died the same time as Grandma Jane. How's that?"

"You're right, lad. Your Grandma Jane died giving birth. The war had finished, and we were living where me ma and Aunt Mary-Ellen were living. When we got back from the war, nothing was the same as when we had left, the place had changed, we had changed. There wasn't the work that had been there before. There was still the pits and the steel works, but everyone was after work. The country had won the war but for the people, there was unemployment, lots of it. We couldn't stay permanently with me Ma and Mary-Ellen, there just wasn't the room, so we went and lived with your grandma's parents, George, who you're named after, and Rosalind, the she devil. Life was comfortable I managed to get down the pit and some nights and then on a weekend if I was off, I helped out in the back of your granda's butcher's shop. It got me a few extra bobs to be able to get Grandma Jane a treat every now and then, and me a pint at the local with the lads. Your da was a real twisty bairn, couldn't put him down for five minutes peace, don't you tell him that mind."

They all laughed and James said, "I'll tell him when we're getting telt off."

"It's told off, and not telt off, if your ma hears you saying that you'll get into trouble. Then one day, your Grandma Jane said, 'Fred, I think I could be pregnant.' We were delighted. We even decided there and then that your Aunt Mary-Ellen and a couple of the lads would be godparents. We couldn't tell anyone for definite as in those times it wasn't always easy for women giving birth. Then one day, near the baby's birth, your Grandma Jane's mother died. It hit her really hard and was a big shock and I don't think she ever really got over it. Several days after the funeral, your Grandma Jane fainted at the top of the stairs. I was at work and the next-door neighbour came to the pit yard and asked for me and we ran all the way home. When we arrived at the house, we found the doctor there and he told me that he was sorry and there had been nothing he could have done, she had fainted and fallen down the stairs. Your Grandma had died. I asked about the bairn and he told me that there actually, had been two, twin girls and they had also died. Grace and Iris." Fred started to cry a little.

George said, "Granda, are you all right?"

"Aye, lad, just me being soft for a minute or two that's all. The two lasses had been still born which meant that they had both come into this world dead. It was a terrible time, everybody kept coming around and trying to help me and your da. Then we found out that the girls had to be baptised, otherwise they wouldn't be able to be buried in consecrated ground, blessed by the church and they would go to hell. Your Aunt Mary-Ellen and Grandma Jane's da were fantastic and kept me together. Granma Jane's da even changed the name of his shop to 'Roberts and Hardy, Family Butchers', he wanted to pass on something to your da. It was a nice gesture and meant a lot to me."

"So, Da owned a butcher's shop?"

"Not quite. I think that his granda wanted to make him feel that he hadn't forgotten his name, so put his surname on the board. Anyway, having a young son at home presented a few problems, but both my mum and your Aunt Mary-Ellen used to come along and help out which worked well until your Grandma Maud died. The house at the Plain had to be emptied as there was now no one working or had any connection with the pit, so thanks to your great-granda we all moved in there with them. There was plenty of room and it also ended up that Mary-Ellen became a shopkeeper. Your poor da had had a bit if a rough time growing up and was always looked after by someone or other. He never went hungry though, and, despite everything, was doing well at school. He even went up to the grammar. The first one in the family and, believe it not, it was there that he even met your ma. So, little Ralphy, you obviously get your brains from two good people. Now what was strange, was that it turned out that your mum was also the daughter of a shopkeeper, a grocer. When they were old enough to start courting, your da even found out that your mum's mum had also died in childbirth, quite odd that."

"Granda Fred," said George, "it must be a dangerous job having a baby. Do you think that it's as dangerous as working down the pit?"

"It is dangerous, Son, but having a baby isn't a job, but women will always tell you that if a man had to have babies, then there would only ever be one child in any family as they couldn't stand the pain."

"I'm still confused though. Mum always told me that babies are delivered by nurses who carry big black bags to put them in. Then sometimes they are delivered down chimneys by storks."

"You're gormless," said James. "Babies don't come out of bags or delivered by storks. You know nothing."

"Hey, Mr Know-all. You think you know everything, but you know nothing. Each of you will learn things at different times of your lives. You, George, will sometimes learn things from your brother but they may only be a little bit right. Now drink your pop up, and we'll head off back home, and on the way, I'll show you the school that I went to."

"It must be really old, Granda," said George. "Will it still be there?"

Laughing, Fred said, "You cheeky little so and so. I'm not that old you know. Of course, it'll still be there. When I left that school to go to the senior, there was still a picture on the wall of the first class, in a frame that I had done in my few weeks there. Opposite is the infant school which is made of white tin and next to that is the Sunday school that is also tin but painted black. I don't suppose they'll be around that much longer; everything's being pulled down and replaced by brick."

*

135

"We're back," shouted Fred as they walked into Penny's. "They have had a good walk, so I'm sure that they'll sleep like logs tonight."

George looked at James and was about to ask how logs slept but, the smell of tea made him forget the question.

"Instead of you rushing back, why don't the pair of you stop for a bite to eat? There is Ham Shank, some fresh made Pease Pudding, homemade Stottie and salad."

"You've twisted my arm, hinney. She," he said, nodding to Mary-Ellen, "she says that making stottie is too much hassle for just the two of us,"

"Nothing's too much hassle for you," said Penny with a smile and a glint, "you can even take some home with you and the shank is stripped, so you can take that and make some broth, I'm sure Mary-Ellen loves you enough to do that."

"Humph," said Mary-Ellen, "he's worse than the bairns sometimes. In fact, forget that. He is worse than the bairns, most of the time. No other woman would put up with a moaning old brother."

"Isn't it nice? You can tell just by her tone that she really loves me."

"The pair of you are as bad as each other if the truth be known," said Penny.

"While we're waiting for the kettle, I must tell you something that Claire said last week on her way down to yours," she said and dropped her voice down to a loudish whisper. "She said that when she grows up that she is going to have three children," she said, looking around to ensure that the kids weren't within earshot and continued. "Apparently she is going to have one of each." She paused again for effect.

"One of each, be buggared, that'll hit the front pages," said Fred.

"Yes, that's right, one of each. There'll be a boy, a girl and, wait for it, a black one."

They all laughed, and Fred said, "Now I would love to see the expressions on people's faces when that one was explained. I don't know if I'd want to be around for that one. It's a good one though. It would certainly make the front pages of both the *Stanley News* and the *Journal*, may even make headlines in *The Daily Herald*."

*

Mary-Ellen had had a bad cough all week and was certainly not getting any form of sympathy from her brother. All he could keep on saying was, "Needs a good rubbing that does. Surprised that you haven't asked all Laverick to rub some horse liniment on. He'd enjoy that, mind you, so would you? Unless of course he's already done it?"

"What did you say, Fred Hardy?"

"I just said that you should get old Laverick to rub that chest for you."

"After that."

"Nowt. Didn't say a word. Your hearings getting as bad as your eyesight, lass."

"Eyesight. What are you on about? There's nothing wrong with my eyesight, and as for my hearing, you're always muttering instead of speaking clearly."

"There has got to be something the matter with your eyes. Fancying Old Laverick, come to think on it, it may be your brain that needs attention."

Changing the subject before she threw something at him, she said, "Do you think they'll come down today, it's a bit miserable out there?"

"Penny was in a strange mood last week. I wonder if she's carrying?" said Fred.

"No. I don't think so. I think she's happy with the three they've got, unless of course that little black one comes along."

"You know we've still got quite a nice little sum from Jane's dad's place?"

"Aye, what about it?"

"Well, I was thinking that as we're comfortable and have everything that we need. Why don't we put some of that money in some kind of savings for each of the kids for when they get married? Nothings getting cheaper, and they seem to want more than we ever wanted. It would help set each of them up. What do you think?"

"We could go to a solicitor and speak to them, but you know they'll charge an arm and a leg for the privilege of giving us advice."

"What about Penny and Ralph? Do you think that they need a helping hand as they'll not want to stop in that pit house all their lives?"

"Strange, isn't it, you bringing the subject up? I was just talking indirectly to Penny about that same thing a few weeks ago and she told me that they had money put away from the sale of her father's place as Ralph had not wanted to go into the business and they were going to start looking around for somewhere nearby soon. She worries about all the nightmares Ralph has which are the result of being a prisoner, but she can't get him to go the doctors or talk to anybody about it, as he's frightened they'll send him off to St Nicks."

"Of course, he won't talk about it, but people are now starting to write about their experiences and making a few bobs out of it, but that's not our Ralph's style, is it? According to him, there is nothing that a few dead Japs wouldn't cure. He should be able to talk to me, ahm, his da."

"Listen to yourself, Fred Hardy. It has taken all these years for you to start talking, and the bairns know more about your war years than I do. But at least you are talking, and you know yourself how it sometimes affects you. Remember how you were when you told me about that poor kid being shot for being a coward? Your Ralph has the same sort of demons to contend with. We can't change the world, we're just little cogs in a, sometimes, well-run or not machine, depending on your view. One day, they are going to ask your Ralph about his time in the war as I know they have already broached the subject with you. And one day, he is going to have to answer them. Why don't you get your old buttons, badges and medals out and I'll give them a polish?"

"Isn't it strange though, that to think our grandparents were alive when cowboys and Indians were fighting and it was about Geronimo, Sitting Bull, General Custer and Billy the Kid. Then there was Davy Crocket, Wild Bill

Hickok, Crazy Horse. Strange, isn't it. And the kids have this fascination for wanting to scalp Claire."

They both laughed and Mary-Ellen said, "Why don't I make a new pot of tea and have it with a piece of rice cake?"

"Aye, sounds like a good idea," as he watched Minnie in the field, "Aye, life's funny how it keeps on going around."

"I've just been out to the bin and looked down the street and they've just got off the bus, they look drenched already," said Mary-Ellen.

*

"Well, you three, before we start, what have the three of you been up to this week?"

"I've just got my new uniform for the grammar and the school has a swimming pool and a good football team," said James.

"I've been practising some new pieces and Dad says that I am driving him mad with scales. He says that he likes listening to me but I'm not really sure, because when I start, he either picks up the paper or goes into the garden."

"That's where you are wrong, George. When you're grown up, you learn to do several things at once, so you can be certain he'll be listening," said Fred with a smirk.

"What about you Claire? How are Wilma and Holly behaving?"

"Granda, don't be silly. I'm not a child anymore. Wilma and Holly are only dolls, they're not real," said Clair, and off she tottered into the kitchen.

"Sorry, I'm sure," said Fred. Looking at the lads, he said, "Now, as I was telling you last week, the end of the First War and the years that followed brought a lot of changes. There was a miners' strike and men marched from Jarrow to London to beg for work. The government called in the army to stem the unrest as nearly everyone was on strike. Things did change, slowly. Working conditions improved and people felt better in their own little worlds. When you looked at a map at school, nearly one third of the world was pink. Pink meant that it belonged to Britain and the King was king of all those places. There were other colours which represented places that belonged to other nations such as the Dutch, the Belgians, the French, the Italians, the Spanish and the Portuguese, but the main one was pink. Places like Canada, Australia, India, New Zealand, and South Africa. The King was king of all them and the people were all different colours, red, white, brown, black, yellow. The big cities that had shipyards were busy building ships and they were Newcastle, Sunderland, Liverpool, Glasgow, Belfast and the steel works at Consett was producing lots of iron. It was a dirty industry and the town was dirty, it wasn't black but red dust that got everywhere. God only knows how the poor women did their washing and kept a clean house. It was a place you went for the market, which was always busy."

"What about Mum and Dad?" said George.

"Well, your da met your mum at a dance at the local welfare hall, it was the normal thing, and virtually the same as in my days. It was your mum that went and asked your da to dance and he ended up getting a lot of ribbing from his pals. From that moment on, they got on like a house on fire." He knew George would ask so he rushed on with the story. "Many weeks later, she asked him to go and meet her father. That was something a lad feared. It meant that they were getting serious and a girl's dad could frighten the death out of a young lad. I remember the day well. He spent ages having a good bath in the tub, then a shave, although he didn't need to and then covering his hair with brylcreem and then throwing a cheap aftershave on. The smell was terrible, and he'd even borrowed a tie from me."

"So, what happened when he met mum's dad?" said James.

"I think that I'll leave that story for your da to tell you. When you get home, and if he's not busy, just ask him if he'll tell you the story about the brylcreem. He'll know what you mean. But, whatever you do, don't pester him, especially if he's busy."

Then Fred had a brainwave and turning to George, said, "George lad, pop into the kitchen and ask your aunt if she could dig out the old atlas that we have somewhere, she'll know where it is. Knows everything, that woman. And smile when you ask, as that'll melt her heart, if she has one. And don't you go telling her I said that or there'll be trouble for me when you go home."

Five minutes later, in walked Mary-Ellen with the map, a big one, like you have in schools and with a look of annoyance, said, "Do you think that I've nothing else better to do than look out a dusty old map for you?"

"Haddaway with you, man. You were probably only standing gossiping while we have the world on our minds. Important stuff this."

"Hmph, I don't know who's the daftest you or me for jumping to your every command. Second thoughts I know the answer to that. Is there anything else that your highness would like? A pot of tea perhaps? Or perhaps even a piece of cake to go with it?"

"Now you mention it, pet..." he said as she smiled, shutting the door, not slamming it, but shutting it very loudly.

"Granda," said George, "can you show us on the map where you went to in the war and the pink places?"

"I am going to test your geography now, and especially for you, young Ralph, now you're going up to the grammar. Ralph, can you point out England?" James leaned across the map and got the answer right.

"Well done, now what about Germany? Can you manage that?"

James said, "That's easy."

"You got it right because the letters are big enough for you to see. I hope you are watching and learning, Georgie? Now, if you look at the top right corner of the map it shows different colours, and next to them, it tells you which empires they represent. It is a good thing to learn them and the colours also help to give you some idea of the size of countries. When you look at England and then all of the pink you wonder how a small country like ours managed to conquer and rule all of the other countries. Fascinating stuff is history. Now, getting back to where I went in the war. In the first war it was mainly in France," he said, pointing it out on the map. "But in the second one, I went to Belgium, Holland, France and Germany. I even passed through Luxembourg but can't remember a thing about it," he pointed them all out. "Now your da, when he went to war, he sailed," he said and pointed the route out, "right across the world and was in Burma, Singapore and was a prisoner in Japan." He pointed them all out to the boys.

"Did those people in the pink places not do anything to help?" said George.

"Aye, they did, lad, and we would have struggled without their help. You have to remember that some of those countries were taken by the Japanese, so they had to fight. The Japanese had their eyes set on those big ones there," he pointed to India, Australia and New Zealand. "Nearly all the world was involved, except," he pointed to South America, "most of the countries there were neutral, which meant that they didn't take sides, a bit like Aunt Mary-Ellen when you two fight."

"But I always think that she takes his side," said James.

"Maybe so, lad, but that really is what being neutral is about, pretending you're not taking sides but at the same time helping one side. In fact, some countries helped both sides which meant that no matter who won they would appear as though they had helped the winners and ensured that they weren't next on the list."

"Right, you two. It's about time we headed home. Your dad will be wanting his tea, unless he has won the pools, which I very much doubt," she said, winking at Fred.

"Aye, off you go and remember, don't pester your da about the brylcreem." Of course, soon as he had said it, he knew that it would be one of the first things that they'd do when they got home.

"I dread to think what that's about, so I won't even ask. Bye and look after yourself and get yourself out and see Dolf. Put the world to rights," she said and gave him a kiss.

*

No sooner were they back in the house than it sounded as though World War Three had started. The peace was shattered. "Da," they both shouted, "Da, are you there? Can we come and ask you a question?"

Ralph looked at Penny and said, "Now what has the old so and so been telling them?"

"I don't know but they are certainly interested in what you have to tell them. Seriously, I haven't a clue what they have been talking about today. Your dad didn't give much away."

"Da," they said as they ran into the main room.

"Whoa, slow down. Now what are you so excited about?"

"Granda Fred said that we had to ask you a question, but not to pester you or disturb you if you were busy."

"Well, I'm pleased to see that you have taken notice of his advice… What's the question?"

"He said that we had to mention Mum's da and brylcreem."

"He did, did he? Telling tales out of school, is he? Don't know what he's talking about."

"Ah, Da," said James, "he said that you would certainly remember."

"Sit yourselves down then and I'll tell you. When a young man is courting a young girl, they dread meeting up with the girl's father. To a dad his daughter is always his little girl. They become very protective of them. They want to know who the lad is, what he does for a living, where he lives, what his parents do. The lad has to pass the inspection, so you get all dolled up for that first meeting. After that first dance your mum and I saw each other quite a lot, then one day she asked me, or rather told me that I should come around and pick her up and meet her dad. Your Granda Fred kept telling me that it was inspection time to see if I would make a good son-in-law. So, yes, I had a shave although you couldn't really tell that I needed to shave, put some of my da's brylcreem on to keep the hair in place and threw some after shave on. When I got to your mum's, she opened the door and said, 'My goodness, Ralph Hardy, you're looking quite dapper today. Come in and don't worry he won't bite.' Well I went in and there he was sitting in the chair having just out the paper down. And your mum said, 'Dad, I'd like to introduce Ralph Hardy who I am going out with.' He looked at me and replied, 'We'll see about that,' and got up to shake my hand. I said, 'Good evening, Mr Robson. It's nice to meet you and I hope that you are well?' He looked at me and said, 'So, your Fred Hardy's lad then. A chip off the block, you are just unfortunate that you got your looks off him and not your mother, a fine-looking woman she was.'"

"He doesn't sound that he was very nice or friendly to you though," said James.

"No, he didn't sound it, but in actual fact, he really was, and it had all been to make me worried, but he really was very welcoming. He then said, 'Well, it is good to meet you finally and the name is George, by the way. And how is your dad?'

"'He's well. Even now he still feels some resentment towards the government with their treatment of the miners and also with the mine owners after the pit disaster, even though it was year's ago.'

"'That's as may be lad, but your dad's right. The miners and their families were treated disgracefully by the mine owners, and now things are starting to bite again. Work is getting scarcer, and basic things are costing more and more all over the world. We're in for difficult times ahead.'

"'Dad, Ralph hasn't come here to listen to a political discussion.'

"'No, lass, you're right, he hasn't, but it gives me the chance to see what he's made of. The future's not looking bright for any of us, but more so for you young ones. There is too much happening over the water there.'

"Your mum raised her eyebrows and looked at me then her dad. He turned to her and said, 'And don't think that I didn't notice you pulling faces, young lady. Now why don't you put the kettle on, or if Ralph would like something stronger? Myself I don't drink. Homemade Ginger Wine or Ginger Beer is my level of excitement these days but there's always some Sherry in the cupboard.'

"'No, thank you. A cup of tea will do nicely for me, thank you, Mr Rob... sorry, George.'

"'I admire men like your dad, Ralph, working down the pits, the dark, the wet and the danger. No, I couldn't do it. The shop does me and before that the horse and cart as I went around the streets.'

"'I remember you going around the streets as me da used to make me follow you and get the manure for the garden.'

"'I saw that, and I then saw another way to make a few bobs. I started taking little sacks and picking it up myself and then selling it. Your da probably wondered why the horse had stopped shi... making a mess.'

"We all laughed at that and then he shocked me and your mum and said, 'I expect you to treat my daughter right and I have no problem you staying over some night, there's a spare room and the bed is always made up, save you rushing off, especially if you're not working or on the early shift the next day.'

"'Dad, that's very sweet of you,' your mother said and rolled her eyes and flickered her eyelashes like a little angel. Her da was like putty in her hands and she knew it. So that, me laddos, is the story of your mum's dad, me and the brylcreem. Nothing exciting but I can still picture it in my mind even now. I wonder if you two will have to go through all that palaver when you're older. Right, now go and get yourselves washed and ready for bed." He had a little smile to himself just thinking about the whole prospect of them having to do it and the thought of a future boyfriend of Claire's going through it.

*

"Granda, Granda," Fred could hear them shout as they ran through the back door and even bypassed Mary-Ellen.

"Whist, lads, you're making that much noise that I can't hear myself think. That's better. Now, what is all the fuss about?"

"When we got home, we waited until Da wasn't busy ad then asked him about the brylcreem and mum's dad," said James, "and it was quite funny."

George had to have his tuppence worth and said, "He told us that we'd probably have to do it when we grew up and got a girlfriend. That can't be true, can it? You and Grandma Jane just ran away."

"We did, but I still had to meet him, before and after the event. Besides, when I met him after we had run away, I think that I was more frightened as we had already married by then and he couldn't protect his daughter even if he'd wanted to. Now then, before we have another look at that big map, which I have ready, so we don't have to ask old grumpy boots again. The 30s were strange times. Everyone was that busy trying to keep a job and keep their families fed that they were too busy to watch what was going on over the water. They were even in more debt than we were and in Germany their money was that worthless that they had to take a barrow of paper money to even by such essential things as bread. Can you imagine that? Then along came a little ex First World War corporal and suddenly Germany had picked itself up off its feet. There was work for all. They were secretly building an air force and their army was getting bigger. After the first war, they weren't allowed to but they did and no one did anything about it. Even when they took back some of the land they had lost, still no one did anything and then some emperor or prince was shot and turmoil broke out with different countries blaming the other for the murder. Hitler, that was the little corporal, suddenly marched into Austria and then Czechoslovakia under the pretext of returning, or re-uniting and protecting the German speaking populations of these countries. Again no one stopped him. At that stage, he was feeling that the big countries like France and Britain would not stand in his way. He was even visited by our prime minister who came back and told everyone that Hitler had no further ambitions to invade anywhere else. We, the British were over the moon, but we soon found out that what he said and what he did were two different things. He made threats towards Poland. France and Britain had treaties with Poland which meant that if he was to attack them, then we would come to its defence and declare war on Germany. I remember it well. Britain had given him twenty-four hours to withdraw its troops and if nothing was heard, then war would be declared between Britain and Germany."

He paused as his mind went back to that day. "There, in the front room were me, Penny's da, Mary-Ellen, Ralph and Penny. All waiting for the news.

"It was getting near time for the news and the announcement from the prime minister and the King. 'Let's hope that it is good news, eh?'

"The BBC world Service came on and an announcement was made stating that as Britain had had no reply from the German Government about our ultimatum that Britain was now at war with Germany. It was followed by the National Anthem. Switching the wireless off Mary-Ellen came over and held my hand and said, 'Fred. I never thought that we would see this again. What are we going to do, Fred? Why? Again?'

"'I'll tell you what. Why don't you go into the tall-boy in the back room, get that bottle of medicinal whiskey and sherry out. We'll then have a toast to the King and the country.'

"Once the drinks were poured, Fred stood and said, 'Raise your glasses everyone and salute the country and the King.'

"'Britain and the King,' everyone said. There was no cheering, just a silent solidarity with each other, whilst at the same time we were all lost in our own little worlds.

"Art that moment, there was a cough followed by Ralph speaking. He said, 'Well, I think that this may be as good a time as any.' He looked at Penny's da and said, 'Sir, may I have your blessing in asking for your daughter's hand in marriage?' He looked at Penny and she was just standing there speechless and then her dad said, 'Son, it has been a long time coming and I thought at one stage that you'd never get around to asking her. But, yes, you have my blessing and I hope that you'll both be very happy.' Poor Penny, she was still standing speechless and said, 'Ralph Hardy, you never…'

"Getting down one knee in front of everyone her da, said, 'Penny Robson, will you do me the honour of agreeing to be my wife?' Funny though, your mum still stood speechless while we all waited with baited breath for the answer, then it came.

"'Ralph Hardy. Of course, I will but I wish you'd warned me and I hope that we're not going to have too many surprises as that.'

"'I haven't had time to get you a ring yet though, I just thought, with the news we've just heard that now was as good a time as any.'

"Meanwhile I noticed that your Aunt Mary-Ellen had nipped out of the room and shortly after came back in with a small velvet box and handing it to your da said, 'I know that you haven't thought about a ring yet but, I would like it, in fact I would consider it an honour, if you both would accept this,' and opened the box to produce a beautiful engagement ring. "It was given to me and we were to get wed after the war, but as you all know, he never came back. We would both feel it an honour if you would accept this as your engagement ring. It would also make me feel closer to him if I knew that someone whom I loved was wearing a ring that was meant for me and our love.' Your mum ran to Mary-Ellen and there were tears in her eyes as she said that they would be delighted and honoured to accept such a beautiful ring.

"I can tell you, there wasn't a dry eye in the room at that moment. It seemed to me that your aunt had finally come to terms with fact that her lover would never be coming back and that this was her way of closing a chapter of a story in her life. Well, she wasn't closing the book exactly, but more like keeping it slightly open. Once everyone had something, even if was only Ginger Wine for George, I proposed a toast to the health, wealth and happiness of the future Mr and Mrs Ralph Hardy.

"'To the future Mr and Mrs Ralph Hardy,' everyone said.

"Mary-Ellen whispered in my ear, 'Such short notice. I only hope that the lass isn't pregnant and they've been living over the brush.'

"'Hush woman. Penny looked as surprised by the proposal as the rest of us, and anyway, that's how the gossip starts and when you think about it, they are going to have enough worry on their plates, especially now the war is here.'

"'Fred,' she said, sounding very serious, 'you don't think, do you…?'

"'Well, knowing our Fred he'll probably volunteer, the same as I did all those years ago. The thing is that it was over twenty years but it now seems just like yesterday. We and her da are going to have to be there to support them, love, no matter what.'

"'Well, blow me, Frederick Hardy. I never knew that you had such a soft side to you. You've certainly kept that hidden all these years, I know that I've never seen it. The next thing you know is that you'll be saying that you love him.'

"'Haddaway with yourself, woman. You should hear yourself, love. He's my son and a man is allowed to be proud of his son. But no, if I'm honest, I don't want him to go but if that's what they decide then that is between the pair of them. We're not sticking our noses into it, understand?'

"'I suppose that I'll have to start and make a spice cake for the wedding, so you'll need to get a couple of drops of brandy.'

"'Don't go rushing things, let them decide.'

"'Fred. Will you listen to yourself? If war is coming, and according to the wireless, it is then he'll be thinking of enlisting soon. It makes sense all around if they get married before he goes off to war. If they don't, then just look at me. In fact why don't you speak to George and discuss giving them a treat. A weekend away somewhere nice like Tynemouth, Cullercoats or even Blackpool. They don't want to spend a one-night secret honeymoon like you and your Jane.'

"'Do you know something, pet? For an old biddy, you aren't often right, but on this occasion, I think you are. Cullercoats or Tynemouth would be nice. Blackpool is probably as bit too far but I'll go and speak to George later on. I wonder if I could get him to go up the pub and have s chat there over a pint.'

"'You've got more chance of winning a game of bingo.'"

Fred paused from the story and then said, "Your da and his fiancé then started to make plans for a wedding. There was no sign of an actual war. We hadn't been bombed or anything like that and people still hoped that common sense would win in the end and there would be peace. But things were moving fast. We even had a new King and he wanted to marry his lady friend who was a divorced American. The government wouldn't allow it and he abdicated meaning his younger brother and his wife became king and queen."

"So da joined the army then?"

"No. At least not at that particular time. I think that his first plan was to get married. When the big day finally came, it was at the Registry Office in Stanley. I remember some of them that were there. There was me, Your Aunt Mary-Ellen, your mum's da, a couple of friends of your da. If I remember right, and I can still see them, a couple were worse for wear. Ian Metcalfe, Gordon Embleton, a couple of the Kelly lads, some of the Clarks. A couple of them were canny footballers and one was good on the old arrows."

"Arrows," said George very quizzically, "like Red Indians or William Tell?"

"No. Arrows like as in darts. If I remember correctly it was Ian, he was useless at sums at school, but give him a dartboard and he could work out exactly what darts you needed to throw. Never knew how he did that, unless of course his schoolwork didn't interest him. A couple of your man's friends were also there and the lads fancied their chances, Jennifer Beer she was to lose her husband at Dunkirk. I also remember a lass called Eileen, she married quite well, some toff up in one of the villages in Northumberland. He had a few bobs and I think he ended up in the Durham's and got Military Cross for his troubles in North Africa. There was a lass called Margaret who was a bit of a tomboy, she married a lad in the Fusiliers who was reported missing. So she joined up and ended up as a nurse in Belgium, Holland, and was always in the thick of it. She even got a medal from the French President, don't know what for though."

"Wow, so she was famous then? I didn't know that girls could fight. I bet our Claire would be useless."

"Don't underestimate women, lads, they can be as tough as nails and as sly, which makes them someone to be weary of. We all got tiddly that night except for you mum and da, they went off by bus and then train to Tynemouth for their honeymoon. It was strange, George even got tiddly, I think he had smelt the beer rather than drink it. But as he wasn't used to it, he ended up being sick in the toilet. The way everyone kept congratulating us you'd have thought that it had been me and him who'd got married and not Ralph and Penny. Anyway George and I got chatting, purring the world to rights is how you're Aunt Mary-Ellen would describe it. I also noticed that when George did decide to have a drink that the real reason he didn't drink wasn't because that he didn't like it but, was in fact, the opposite. I know you'll not understand that now but one day you will."

He could tell they didn't understand but continued. "'George,' I said, 'I never ever thought for one minute that we'd be back at this time, but I don't think that the Germans'll stop so easily this time. I often wonder about the neutral countries like Sweden, Switzerland, Norway, Holland, well, the Germans take any notice of their neutrality?'

"'I doubt it,' said George, 'anyway Switzerland has enough of their own crooks and German speaking people so are probably safe. As for the others, I suppose that's up to the Germans.'

"'It's the young'uns I'm worried about, like Ralph and his mates. We both know that he intends to join up and his pals will do the same. Their pride will make them think that they're going to fight for King and Country and that'll it'll be over in a year. Poor buggars. Those in Downing Street and Buckingham Palace'll be all right, they don't have to go and do the dirty work, they just send someone else. Then if things get too tough here, they'll all bugger off to Canada or somewhere safe. Plus their country estates are far enough out of London that'll it'll be the same sods again who get it. Those in London, Birmingham, Liverpool, Newcastle, Belfast, they have struggled to get their lives back on keel after the last one and here we go again. I just hope that they don't cross that channel.'

"If they get to that stage, Fred, then we'll be alone. A group of local businessmen have been up to the ranges practising shooting. More are likely to join. So, this time if it is needed, I'll be there. Last one, as you know, they wouldn't let me in because of my disability, but this time, I am determined that even if they won't have me then at least I can be of some use.'

"'Aye, well at least they haven't got to that stage yet. But I dare put a couple of bobs on it that by the time they get back from their honeymoon that the bands and posters will be out and recruiting and telling us that God is on our side. I know that he's in a protected trade but he's like me and he'll be thinking buggar that, my country and family need me. He's a stubborn sod, so I'm not even going to waste my breath trying to stop him. All I can do is to be brave for him and wish him all the best.'

"'When the time comes around, several of the local business people have already started a fund for them and their families. We've also agreed that the local hall will be used for a send-off for them.'

"'Well, I'll be beggared, George, I never thought that the shopkeepers would rally around like that.' George didn't like being called a shopkeeper, a businessman had better standing, especially with the bank. 'I think I'll encourage all the allotment owners to do their bit and try and help the wives and basins of those who'll go off to fight,' I said.

"'I think that it'll be similar to the last one in that us lot up here, I'll have to look after themselves as those down south never think of the north.'

"'All we need is for the bloody paddies to start up again and then there's that Mosely fellow, should be in the Tower for treason.'

"'Anyway, Fred, here's to our families. That they have a safe future.'

"'Mmmmmm,' I said, raising my glass and silently saying to myself. 'Here's to the poor buggars, good luck and watch your back.'"

Ralph and the Call to Arms

Penny and Ralph walked through her dad's door and shouted, "We're home, Dad."

"Come and give us a kiss, pet. No need asking how you both are, you certainly look in the pink, the pair of you. Obviously, bed-rest did you the world of good."

"Dad, behave yourself, you'll embarrass Ralph," she replied with a little cheeky grin.

"Better tell you before you go upstairs, some of your friends. Both yours and Ralphs visited the other day and delivered some flowers for you which are up in your room. They were up there ages, so all I'll say to you is be careful as God only knows what they've done."

"Oh Ralph, they wouldn't. Would they?"

"Alan and Eileen were there also and they seemed to be very interested in each other, if you know what I mean."

"Dad, you're supposed to be my dad and not talk about things like that to me. In fact at your age, you aren't even supposed to be thinking about it," she said, laughing.

"I'll have you know, young lady, married or not, you are not beyond getting a smack from your dad. Anyway, there's been a certain lady, of, let's say, mature years passing the garden every time I'm out in it. I think she must be spying on me. We've been chatting and as she is by herself, she feels restricted as to where she can go so, I'm thinking of asking her out for a walk one day."

"Did you hear that, Mr Ralph Hardy? We're going to have to act as chaperones to ensure they don't misbehave. You haven't said who it is yet and she must be local if she conveniently knows when you're in the garden. She's only after one thing though, so beware."

"And what, if I may ask is that?"

"Your chrysanthemums, of course, what did you think I meant?"

Ralph coughed and said to George, "I, or rather we, must thank you and the family and friends for giving us the great wedding day and the hotel. It was excellent. The owners were very kind, there was a turn on some nights. When we went out during the day, there were flags everywhere plus people going into the both the town and the church hall to get information about signing up. No matter where you went, the war was the topic of conversation. The old 'uns voicing their concerns, and my group showing their enthusiasm. As you no doubt have worked out, we have both talked long and hard and Penny has said that I

148

must do what I feel is my duty. There were posters being put up showing the King and Queen, others were showing a finger across your mouth warning you to be aware of who was listening and what you were saying. We also came across a very nasty incident. Next to the church hall, there was an ice cream man, Italian and his son had just gone in to join up. Apparently, when he got to the front of the queue, he had been told that they did not want friends of Hitler joining the army. No, Italians weren't welcome. We could hear the row. The young lad said that he couldn't speak Italian, and I must admit he sounded broader Geordie than me, he'd never been to Italy or even wanted to go. Because you could hear all of this, when he came out, this woman came up to him and told him that he should go back to his own country, and we didn't want wops here and then spat at him."

"Dad," said Penny. "You would have been so ashamed and angry. We spoke in his defence but were told that if we were lovers of them, then we should buggar off. Then guess what she did? She went and bought an ice cream from his father."

"There'll be a lot more of that, pet, before we're done. You mark my words."

"Anyway, Dad, it's nice of you to ask if we'd like a cup of tea. No, don't bother, I'll go and put the kettle on. You take it easy."

"She gets the sarcasm from her mother's side you know." Dropping his voice to a loud whisper he said, "You do realise that as the pits are vital to the country working, it is a protected industry and enlisting may not be as easy as you think."

"I know and realise the importance to the country but I couldn't live with myself if all me mates went off to fight and I was still here. They'd be risking their lives for me. Plus there are all those making a few bobs from the war and I don't want to be considered a shirker or a flyboy."

"That's a loyal thought, Son, but you risk your life everyday down the pit. That in itself is brave, it'll never get you a medal or a decent wage, but it's brave, even if you don't realise it. I couldn't do it. Just think. If there were no pitmen, then the countries industries would come to a standstill and along with it the war. There'd be no factories working, no steel works, no ships being made, we'd be overrun in no time. As for being a shirker, don't even think that. A flyboy, well, there always going to be those that'll make a few bobs out of others misery and bad luck. They see that as an opportunity, someone needs something someone else has and that someone is exploitable whether we like it or not."

Penny came in with a tray with tea and some left-over wedding cake and looking at her dad said, "I didn't know you thought like that, Dad. You'll be standing for parliament next. A caring socialist. That sounds a good title, doesn't it? But then again, isn't that what a socialist is supposed to be, caring? Or have I got it wrong?"

"I don't know whether you're being sarcastic or not, young lady," looking at Ralph, he continued, "You've got all this coming, my lad. Poor soul."

Leaving them to this friendly banter, Ralph said, "Think I'll go and get sorted then pop up to see Da, see if he fancies going up to the pub and see who's there. That's all right, love?"

"Hen pecked already. Asking the wife's permission so soon. That's just the start of it," said George.

"Before I go, I think we should nip upstairs and see what they've been up to."

As they ran upstairs chasing each other and giggling, George remembered when he and Penny's mum had done the exact same thing. *The innocence of that night. Neither of us had ever slept with anyone before that night. It was a strange night, one of fear, tears, enjoyment, amusement, fun, exploration and fumbles. Plenty of them,* he thought and smiled to himself. Penny's parents had let them have the house all to themselves and they went to stay with relatives. As they lay there, they could hear men going out on first the late shift and then the early shift. The pit buzzer going, women gossiping over the back gate, children shouting on their way to school but, in reality, hearing nothing as they explored each other and enjoyed the new experiences. Their sex was hard, rough, gentle, quick and slow, all at the same time. He remembered Maude leaning on her elbow and looking down at him saying, 'I never ever for one minute that it could be like this,' as she stroked his nipple through his chest hair. 'Will it always be like this, George?'

They had kissed and then fallen asleep in each other's arms and George suddenly came back to the present time when he heard, "You all right, Dad? Do you fancy another cup of tea and a sandwich or something?"

He looked at her and for a moment, a very brief moment, he saw Maude standing there asking the same question.

"Sorry. What was that? I was miles away. A cup of tea. Yes, that would be nice, pet."

*

Opening the back door, Ralph shouted, "It's only me. You in, Da?"

"Aye, in the other room, howay in and tell me everything."

"Firstly I want to say thanks to you and Mary-Ellen for everything you did for us, the wedding, and the honeymoon. But more importantly, what is that I hear about you and your new bosom mate George and getting him legless from all accounts?"

"For a teetotaller, he can certainly knock it back when he sets his mind to it, aye, I'll give him that."

"On the way to the pub, so I thought I'd pop in see if the old man wanted to treat me to a pint. Only joking. Have a chat with the lads and catch up on everything."

"Good idea, could do with getting away from her that must be obeyed," he nodded towards the kitchen, "Just off to the pub for a couple with young Ralph, I'll bring you a bag of chips in."

"Better not come in drunk. I'm not putting you to be again. You'll just lie wherever you fall."

"Anybody would think she was my wife the way she goes on."

When they walked in the pub, the comments started. "He's looking tired, obviously being kept awake."

"Too much of the other."

"Did you get permission to come out then?"

"You lot can shut up for a start. You're only jealous that you've only got your hand for company. Anyway, I owe you lot a hiding for what you did to the bed."

The ribbing started again and his da said, "You're on a losing streak, Son, just get the round in, that'll keep them quiet."

"Bloody hell, not back five minutes and tried the bed already. Penny's going to need a week's holiday after all this to recuperate. Nudge, nudge, say no more. I suppose you take after your old man. Is that right, Mr Hardy?"

"Less of the old and mind your own business. You lot still think it's for peeing over high walls."

They all cheered and clapped each other's backs.

Pints finished and another round on the way and Alan said, "I suppose that I should bring the subject up, Ralphy. We've all been talking and have decided that we should all join up and go and get them. Our loved ones have given their blessing, they don't necessarily agree with our decisions but know that we have to, after all, our own das did it. Isn't that right, Mr Hardy?

"We did, lad. We saw enough blood and tears to last a lifetime or so we thought. That's life nowadays, we sign treaties with people and hope that they never come to anything, but when they do, then we have to do what is right. You all have to remember that some of you are in protective industries and they may not let you go."

"They'll have to if we were to get the sack."

"All I'll add is for the four of you to think long and hard before you do anything, and remember that this time I think that there will be a lot more countries involved and a lot more destruction."

"That's all the more reason for is to join then, isn't it?"

"Fancy a corporal running the country and telling generals what to do."

"He may have only been a corporal in the last one but the man is a good talker and sees the need to blame someone for the state of their country and economy. The people to blame are firstly the allies who made the peace agreement at the end of the first one, us, the French and the Americans. Then he has the Jews, it looks like everything will be their fault and he'll try to get them all to leave Germany."

Two of Ralph's pals got up and started strutting around the place mimicking Hitler, arms outstretched and pretending to have a moustache. Everyone in the pub was laughing and some shouted, "*Sieg Heils.*"

Everyone laughed except the landlord. "Now, now you lot. I'm not having any of that stuff in here and if it continues you will find yourselves out on your arses and banned permanently. There's enough of it over there without you lot joining in."

"Sorry, Sid, we were only joking and didn't mean to cause any offence to anyone. We just want to get over there and stop it all."

"What do you really think then, Mr Hardy?" said Alan.

"What do I really think, lad? If I thought that stopping you would make any difference to the future then I would. If I could take you all over to Berlin and kill the little sod, even though it may mean losing some lives, then I would. I can't do any of those things but what I can do," looking at Sid, he said, "Get shorts in for them and one for yourself. What I can do is to raise a glass to you all, wish you godspeed and tell you to keep your heads down. Remember you will see sights that you never ever thought for one moment that you would see. You will have to see your friends hit, maybe killed, and leave them. You will see destruction of homes, property, families, and people on the move, just wandering anywhere they can, people begging and children and mothers crying. But whatever you see and whatever you experience, you must remember that you are there because you made a decision to do right by the world. Some of the people you see have never had that right given to them. That right to make your own decisions is one of the principles that you are fighting for. Remember that."

They all stared at Fred but Ralph said, "I've never heard you talk like that before."

"War, Son, is a strange thing. It isn't something that people find easy to talk about, no matter how long after the event. They find it hard to talk about it because if you've never been there, then how can you understand. People nod sympathetically but we don't want sympathy. Empathy, yes. Justice, yes. But anything but bloody sympathy," he said and went to the gents.

"Quite a canny da you have there. Proud as well. You can see it in his eyes and hear it in his voice, the horrors he has seen. We owe it to the people like your da to go there and finish the bloody thing good and proper."

"That's all right saying but will we have the Yanks this time to help? When you read the papers, they seem that they don't want to be involved in another European war."

"Right. What day are we going into the town and sign up?"

After a bit of discussion regarding shifts etc., it was decided that they would go in on Saturday.

When he came back from the toilet, Fred said, "Whatever you decide, lads, don't become spies. It is written all over your faces that you are going ahead, so, again, gentlemen, I wish you all good luck."

"Gentlemen. Gentlemen, Da? I have never heard you call anyone a gentlemen. Wait until I tell Penny. I wonder if she'll be asleep when I get back in."

"There he goes again, he's just back from is honeymoon, left her a few hours ago and now he's wondering if she'll be in bed waiting for him. Lucky buggar. Just think when we get to war how long you'll be without female company."

"I'm not worried because I've worked out who is going to be the pretend miss and all I'll say is watch your back and I'm going first."

"You dirty twisted pervert." And they all laughed.

"Now it's getting to that stage I think I'll be off home and don't you forget you have a new missus to go home to, bonny lad," he said to Ralph.

Everyone was shouting different farewells, "Cheers, mate." Night, Mr Hardy. Tarra." Fed turned and looked at Ralph and winked. They understood each other. He thought, *I'll miss him as well but I cannot tell him that. Dads don't do that.*

*

The week passed by quickly, and whilst Ralph had been out at work, Penny had been making some changes, minor adjustments she said, to her dad's house. He hadn't really minded as it had been something that he been promising himself to do for a long while now, but, like many things, had never got around to it. She also helped him to sort through her mother's clothes and they decided with a laugh that some things would never come back into fashion and they were cut up rolled into balls for the next clippy mat to be made. Making a new mat would give her something to do when Ralph decided to go off and fight. There was also the exciting prospect of the ragman coming on Friday and the possibility of getting a goldfish off him. The bits of jewellery that they were she put to one side and they could look at another time. She picked up a long necklace that she remembered playing with when she was small and she remembered that she had broken it and then hidden it, but there it was staring at her in the face. *Poor, Mum, I wish that we had met,* she wondered if her mum had even seen her before she died. It was nice to see dad and Ralph getting on so well, even if they appeared to be keeping secrets from her. The other night when she had gone into the sitting room, they stopped talking and looking at a paper said, "I was just saying to Ralph that I wouldn't mind this cardigan that's on the front of this pattern."

"Cardigan? On a knitting pattern. Do you think I'm daft altogether? Don't answer that and when have you ever looked at, let alone be interested in a knitting pattern?"

"I was just saying to Ralph that when this war is over, I would like him to come into business with me. He's good with people and the old dears would love him. What do you think, love?"

"I think that it's a brilliant idea. Don't you, pet," she said, looking at Ralph who was standing looking a little embarrassed by George's generosity.

*

It was that time. Saturday morning had arrived, and as agreed there were the four of them on the bus to Newcastle. It was always busy but today more than normal for two reasons, firstly the war and secondly there was a local derby being played at St James's Park. The recruiting people had taken the match into account and had set up tents and tables at the top end of Northumberland Street, The Haymarket, The Rail Station, Fenham Barracks and outside St James's Park.

Ralph laughed and said, "Well, they really are clever sods, aren't they? Outside of the ground. Whoever wins the lads'll be feeling on top of the world

153

and will sign up to win the war and whoever loses they know they'll be feeling suicidal. So, for the recruiters it is a no-lose situation."

Ian added, "And, look, what the uniform does for them. The place is buzzing with lasses. They're like flies around the old proverbial. I'm going to have some of that."

"Behave yourself, man," said Fred, "you're like a kid in a sweet shop."

"Listen to him. Mr High and Mighty. Mr, I'm getting it on a plate every night and wouldn't dream of coming out with a comment like that."

Fred knew that they were joking but sometimes he felt like punching someone. Then again, he secretly knew that he would be doing the same thing in their place.

"Aye, whatever you say and you're just jealous, the lot of you. Anyway, where are we heading to do it?"

"Stations nearer, then we can always swagger up to Fenwick's," and putting on what he thought was his posh voice, he said, "and have a scone and jam."

"Posh people don't say jam, the say preserve. You're a gormless buggar, and remember I know who the secret miss is going to be when we get frustrated at the front and I wouldn't be so cocksure of yourself." It was his turn to tease but he needed to remember that he was joking or they might take him serious.

When they got to the station there was already a queue. There were several army vehicles and about a dozen men in uniform, some were wearing a red and white feather in their cap and others had what looked like a bugle in theirs. Plus there was also a bloke dressed to the nines with a little stick, he looked and sounded like a real pansy. *Wouldn't last five minutes in the club on a Saturday night,* he thought.

"Oh look, chaps, daddy's little boy has joined up. I wonder what he's thinking about the riff-raff in the queue."

"Keep your bloody voice down, Ian, we don't want to be upsetting someone who may be in charge of us, do we?"

"Him? In charge of us? I don't think somehow that the country is that desperate."

The men went in one at a time and some stayed longer than others. Some came straight out and said, "I'm too old," or, "I'm short sighted," or, "Flat footed," and others came out shouting, "I'm in," and then went straight into another tent. One came out and said, "Don't be shy, lads. You have to drop your drawers and stand naked while they look at and touch your tackle. I'm sure," looking at the lasses, he continued, "that yon lasses have a hole poked in the tent and have already picked out the biggons. But looking at you shower, I wouldn't worry on that score, but I would worry about the bloke who feels your tackled, spends a little too long doing it for my liking, but beggars can't be choosers," then walked into the next tent.

"Do you think he was serious about you know what?" said Ian.

"Aye, I am," said David. "I can see why you'd be worried, nothing there to hold and remember Ralph has already got you ear-marked for when we are at the front." Again they all laughed except Ian, he was really taking it all to heart.

"Anyway, I'm pleased I put clean ones on this morning."

"God, I didn't. Me ma would have gone mad if she'd been alive," said Ralph.

"You mean to say your lass didn't have time to check before you came out? It'll be all smelly. Poor sod that has to touch it, he'll not know where it's been."

"Well, it has a t least been somewhere not like Mr Cherry boy."

About thirty minutes later, they all finally met up with each other outside the other tent and Ian said, "We mustn't have measure up, there's no lasses waiting."

David said, "Well, we're all nearly soldiers of the King."

"Aye," this bellowing shout shook the ground, "and if you don't get yourselves smartened up and start behaving like soldiers, then I can guarantee that when I get my hands on you in ten days' time, you'll not last five minutes."

"God, if he is anything to do with joining up then I think that I've changed my mind."

"I heard that. My hearing is sensitive to high-pitched whining. Look at my face and remember it. In ten days' time, if you finally get accepted, I shall be your mother, your father, your girlfriend, your wife and, for those of you that way inclined, your boyfriend and I can see that there might be a few among you who may be of that persuasion. Remember this face. You will only remember me as bastard. You'll never say it to my face. You shall be in my tender loving care for three months. No one to love but me." Then all of a sudden, he changed his tone and said quietly, "Right, lads. Once you have finished in the next tent and you have sworn your allegiance, you will be in the army. Be proud. Be courageous and I'm sure that," looking at Ian, he continued, "we can even make a man of you. Once finished in there, you can pick up some money and travel warrants, and we shall see you in ten days' time right here as per your instructions. Good luck and welcome to the army."

They stood there with their mouths wide open. "Did he mean everything he had said? Was he really going to be in charge of us for the next three months?" They all looked at each and then Ralph said, "To hell with him, for now anyway. Let's go and have a pint to celebrate."

"Did you notice that bloke who said that they had told him he was too old? He only looked about forty. So that's got to be a good sign."

"Why has it got to be a good sign?"

"Well man, it's obvious. It means that they think that it is going to be a quick one and it's a waste of time picking oldie."

"On that theory then bright spark. Once we see them taking on people over forty, we then know it's going to be a long one and they are desperate. Is that right?"

"Aye, summit like that."

"Did you notice that Jew lad? Poor sod, not only is he English but a Jew, Hitler isn't going to like him at all. Having never met one, I didn't realise they sounded Geordie like us."

"What did you expect someone who has probably lived all his life here to sound like then? Anyway, did anyone notice who dodged the round again?" They all looked in the same direction.

"Not me," said Ian. "I got the last one last night. Tight as duck's arses you lot are."

"And, pray may I ask just how tight is a duck's arse? Hope it's as tight as yours will be when we get it at the front."

Ignoring them, or at least trying to, Ian said, "That pansy officer bloke says that we'll all probably be going to the same regiment, probably the Fusiliers and then when they see potential in any of us, me probably, but you lot… Anyway there's the chance for specialist training elsewhere,"

"My God. It didn't take you long to do some brown-nosing. Are you planning on keeping him warm at nights then and two timing your pals?"

*

Penny and Ralph decided that they would try and spend as much time to themselves as they could, but at the same time, knew they couldn't ignore everyone else. The days flew by, suitcases were packed and packed again and then unpacked and repacked for a final time. Mary-Ellen's young man's name from the first war had been added to the local war memorial and Mary visited often. "Just going for a walk," she would say. Since his name had been put up, she had become like Queen Victoria and was always dressed in black.

Fred had said, "Eeh, lass, at least you'll never be caught out by someone's funeral. You're dressed already. As for the beret, it makes you look like a French Onion seller, a big one at that."

"It's a good job I know that you are joking, an Onion Seller indeed."

The letter had come in the week and Penny's da had taken it from the postman, saying, "Your letter from the King has arrived, Ralph, even stamped O.H.M.S. All very official."

He opened it and pretended to read what was not in the letter to his awaited audience,

"Dear Ralph. I am writing to you to ask a favour. As you know there is a war on and I'd be grateful if you and your pals could come down to London and see me at the Palace. Yours George Rex. P.s. I've already squared up with the pit for some time off for you all."

"All right. I know you're having a laugh at my expense but what does it say?"

"It says that I am to report to Newcastle on the fourth which is two days' time and enclosed there is a way ticket for the bus. So they don't intend letting me go soon then. We all get picked up at the station, my truck number is two out of ten. Personal possessions other than a picture, underwear, washing and shaving kit, writing paper are to be kept to a minimum and you are allowed only one small suitcase. There will be a tea and toilet stop somewhere on the way."

"It sounds," said George, "as though you'll be up at one of those big training areas in the backs of beyond in Northumberland. Some blokes say that you go crazy and end up fancying sheep up there."

"Baa, Baa," said Ralph.

"What are you two idiots on about? said Penny, "Sheep? Baa?"

"Come here, my pet lamb, and give your shepherd a kiss."

"There you are again, calling me pet lamb and don't start any nursery rhymes or I'll be serving you up with mint. And don't you laugh, Dad, as the same goes for you. You're both supposed to be grown men. The Germans don't know how easy it's going to be if their all like you."

"I'm pleased you made light of all that, Son, it'll make it easier for her when the time comes. Now give me a proper read of that letter, will you?"

As he came back from the kitchen with a pot of tea each, George said, "Don't forget it says here that there is a number you must learn and be able to recite when you get to where you're going?"

*

As the day went on, Penny became very strange and everything he did seemed to be wrong even if it was right, so he just kept his head down and then a few hours later the world was rosy again. "What was all that about?" he said to George.

"Don't worry, lad, you'll get used to it. Probably women's troubles but don't ever say that to her because even if it is there'll be hell to pay. You'll soon learn the signs."

She came in the sitting room and said, "I wonder which one of your crowd will get the first medal then? If there is any justice, it should be you because you're my hero."

"God the mood changes quick, doesn't it?" he said to George.

"You opted for marriage, lad, so you've only yourself to blame. Anyway, you've only got another fifty years or so, and even by that time, you won't have fathomed them out. Get yourself out and see the others and see what their letters say, while you have the chance and she's in a good mood."

Ian was the last one in and, looking at all their glasses being full, said, "I see you're all okay with beer, so I'll get my own. Cheap round that."

They all looked at each other speechless.

It appeared that they were all on the same truck so they all hoped that they might be in the same block or whatever they called them.

"Has anyone learnt that bloody number yet?" said Dave.

"Plenty of time for that, I want to enjoy the rest of my free time, that can wait."

They others all decided to show off their skills, and with some hesitation and minor cock-ups, they could all nearly quote it.

"Just listen to you three. There are more important things than numbers. There's beer and women. What are we going to do without them?"

"Just do what you always do, use your hand." They all laughed.

"If the weather stays like this, it is going to be very cold, wet and windy up there, but I suppose they have to toughen us up, but for us pit-boys, it won't be as much as a problem as for you Ian, well…"

"We'll have to be tough for that Hitler bloke. There are all kinds of rumours, he has taken France and Belgium and Holland and wants Russia."

"Where'd you hear all of this? From the prime minister himself no doubt. We'll only get to know what they want us to know."

"Well, it's supposed to be true that the King and Queen of Holland and Belgium are staying at the Palace, it must be getting a bit cramped there if all their relatives turn up and what about the German ones, and the Greek ones. I suppose they'll have no problems getting a council house overcrowding they'll say."

"Will you listen to yourself? Council house. Overcrowding. The King and Queen."

They all laughed and headed home before the off tomorrow. It was funny to think about the King and Queen living in a council house though.

The Day

The day finally arrived and it was like starting school all over again. There was Penny, her da and my da all at the bus stand to see me off. I thought for one moment that I was moving to America instead of going to Newcastle. Penny had checked me over from head to toe and passed me as spick and span, shoes were shining, I'd had a haircut and was even wearing a tie. I thought the fact that my family being at the bus stop was embarrassing but when David turned up his family were carrying a large Union Jack with a banner saying 'Go get 'um,' or something like that. When the bus did arrive, we found that the driver and conductress were very patient, because looking up the aisle there were already a few blokes on and they had obviously been seen off by families. It was a case of handshakes and kisses and then one last wave. The patience of the conductress had obviously worn off as she said, "Come on, you lot or the war'll be over before you get there."

When the others got on a couple of stops further on, the whole process was repeated all over again. Then, full of bravado the bus crew were wishing us good luck as we walked the last few yards to the station and the awaiting trucks. The conductress said, "My lad went off somewhere last week, down south I think so at least you are up here somewhere for a while."

We saw the trucks and there waiting with them were what we were later to become familiar with Military Police and bug ones at that.

They took one long look at us and shouted, "Before you get on the trucks, get your arses over here and give your regimental number and name then when you have done that you get on the truck assigned to you. A warning though, we don't leave until you get your number right and the longer that takes, then the less time you'll have for your food, if the cookhouse is still open when we get there that is. Plus, you'll be sleeping on the floor if the quartermaster and his staff have gibe home for the day. So, you useless pieces of shit, it's up to you and how you learnt your number when you were being pampered by your mammies and daddies."

Training

We arrived at this camp slap bang in the middle of nowhere. It was damp, foggy and the air seemed heavy. On what I assumed was the parade ground, a concreted covered area with three flagpoles and little else, stood about fifty soldiers and that horrible man we had met when we signed up. *So, he hadn't been telling lies then*, I thought. It was obvious several of us thought the same thing when I looked at Dave and Ian. In a pile at one corner were all of our belongings, suitcases and bags of various sizes and descriptions. Then all of a sudden, just to stop us daydreaming.

"Right, you shower of piss. When I call your name out, I want you to come to attention like this," he said, indicating a soldier, "watch what he does when I shout out his name and his response. It will be shown to you three times, and three times only, so watch and learn."

"Clark," shouted the soldier in charge.

"Sir," replied the other soldier who then brought his feet together by lifting one, and bringing it down next to his other with a loud bang and the calling out his number and name followed by 'sir' again.

This was done three times in total and then the other soldier said, "Right, you will have noticed that all he said was 'sir' followed by his number, his surname and sir again. He did not, and I repeat, he did not use a Christian or any other name. The reason being is that we, who are going to be looking after you are not interested in your first name. As far as we're concerned, you don't have one, you are whatever we want to call you. That's who you are. The orderly room will be interested in your other names because they'll need to know who you are in case we kill you and they have to notify your next of kin, that is, of course, assuming that you have one. To me, where I am standing right now, all I can see in front of me are a load of useless bastards, the dregs of society who have volunteered before you were volunteered by others. Good that's sorted then, we all know where we stand. Now let's get started."

For the next two hours at least, people were stamping their feet and shouting out their names and numbers. Of course, there were those that even after three attempts still couldn't do something right. It was either they couldn't remember their number, or they didn't say 'sir' or didn't bang their feet loud enough and they were pulled out to one side.

The soldier who appeared to be in charge then said, "I told you that you were useless bastards, well, it appears that I was right about some of you and these," indicating those standing to one side, "are a prime example, but we'll alter that.

It also appears to me that because of these creatures you've all missed your hot meal. No noise or comments I didn't ask for them. From here your names will be read out again and you then go and stand in front of one of those corporals. So listen for your name, come to attention and do what you have been just doing and a block number will be given. You then go over to the NCO who is carrying your block number. Once assigned to your blocks, you will be taking there by your corporal, who will then brief you himself. If he feels happy, he'll then escort you to the cookhouse where there may be something cold waiting for you but there just to show you that we do care for you there will be tea. Are there any questions and, remember, if you have a question, then follow the procedure. Now any questions?"

I came to attention and bellowed out my number and name followed by sir and waited.

"Well, Hardy, what is your question?"

"Sir, what happens to our suitcases? Will they go to our blocks, sir?"

It all went deathly quiet and then all hell broke loose.

"Will it be in our blocks, sir," mimicked the soldier, "will it be in our blocks, sir? Of course, it won't be in your blocks. Who the hell do you think is going to take it there? You are not at the Ritz now, your mother isn't here to run around after you. It is you soldier, that will be taken it to your blocks. When your block corporal tells you that you can. Does that answer your question, Hardy? Good and there being no more questions listen out for your names."

"What a welcome that was," I said, looking at the others.

"I've decided that I either want to go back home already or at least drop him."

"It's now starting rain, so I suppose it stays there until we're told to get it."

"You four. I hope that you're not going to be a problem to me. Because, if you think you can beat me, then I'd better tell you now, you won't. When you meet your corporal, tell him from me that you three are the on extra duties and restrictions for a week. Understood?"

"Sir, yes, sir," we all shouted as much in unison as any pit choir could be.

We were all gathered under the watchful eyes of our block corporal, whose name as yet we didn't know. He brought us to attention and tried to march us, in step, but some of the blokes could only march in step to a pit band at Durham Big meeting, and then only if they were pissed. We were all laughing, again the wrong thing to do and we soon found out that laughter often meant some form of army punishment. When we got to our block and went inside, there were metal bunk beds and lockers and a stove in the middle. At the far end was a pile of blankets, mattresses, pillows and sheets. The stove, we noticed was unlit and the block was freezing. There was also at one end a large wall furnished room for the... our NCO. As we stood gaping and wondering what was next, we were told to get outside and fall in in threes. The next half an hour was a marching tour of the camp, Officers' Mess, out of bounds, Sgts mess. Out of bounds, cookhouse, orderly room, quartermasters, guard room and jail, chapel, training huts, ranges, assault coarse and then back to our accommodation.

161

"Right, lads, pick a bed and sit on it. That was a mini-grand tour of your home from home holiday camp. You will learn either to enjoy it or hate it. What we do aim for is for you to love and hate it. My name is Corporal Williams and to you it is nothing else but corporal. I shall be living in that room there. One of you will have the task of cleaning it and that will change on a weekly basis, Hardy, you are on that for a month because you and your three pals have already started to make enemies."

I jumped to attention and shouted, "Corporal."

"You other three needn't think that you've escaped because I can guarantee you haven't. The four of you will still be required to carry out other duties as well as those. How you achieve that I am not interested in but achieve it you will. Now all of you have five minutes to get to the cookhouse and get whatever's been left for you then back here and in threes in thirty minutes and not a minute later, woe betide anyone late. Now get lost."

"Corporal," we all shouted, *Better get used to it*, I thought.

Two curled cheese and tomato sandwiches and a mug of tea we were already outside the hut waiting for Cpl Williams.

"A couple of you just made it, Hardy, your one of them. We're now going to try and march you onto the parade ground and for the thick amongst you, which looking at you, is the majority. We start off one the left foot and then follow it with the right and then the left and so on. Now that isn't too difficult, is it?" There was no answer.

"I said that wasn't too f... difficult was it?"

"No, Corporal," we all shouted.

"Good. We're starting to get somewhere. The Regimental Sgt Major who you all saw at the recruitment station and then when you went to get your trucks will be introducing himself and the rules. Tomorrow, you will meet the Commanding Officer and some of the other officers. When the RSM speaks and wants an answer it is sir, not corporal or Sgt but sir."

The whole regiment was standing at attention when the Regimental Sgt Major strode on and Sgt marched up to him, halted and said, "Two Hundred and Eighty new recruits on parade, sir."

"Thank you, Sgt Embleton, stand them at ease, easy."

"Sir, new recruits, stand at ease, stand easy," he said and marched off to take his place alongside the other senior ranks.

"Right, you lot. Stand easy means to relax, it doesn't mean to start smoking, talking, scratching your bollocks, arse or even scratching someone else's bollocks," he paused and we all laughed. "Nor does it mean talking either. Listen in because I am only telling you once and heaven help any of you who don't listen. My name is Regimental Sgt Major Corclough. Behind my back you can call me what you want as long as one of them is God." Again there was laughter. "But to you, I am sir. I am the man that you will learn to love, or if you have already not done so, to hate. Each of your blocks is a squad and four blocks form a company. Your block corporal will explain what you are in. Some of you will have noticed that you have been separated from your bed partners, Hardy, where are you?"

"Sir. Pte Hardy, sir."

"I am keeping my eye on you and your mates, don't know how you weren't separated but that may change tomorrow."

"Sir," I shouted and stood at ease. I thought, *It isn't a good thing being remembered for all the wrong reasons on day one.*

"Firstly, the block is your responsibility. No one else's. The cleaning, the heating of it falls down to you. There will be block inspections, at least every day. There will be no smoking in the block. Irrespective of the weather all windows will be open and two at night. The parade ground unless you are training on it is out of bounds. There will be no short cuts across it to the cookhouse. If you hear the bugle at night and you are outside, you will stop what you are doing and stand to attention facing the Regimental Flag. Tomorrow your block corporal will show you how to make your beds. You will also collect your uniform from the quartermasters and remember you are not going to either Burtons or the co-op for clothes. You will be shown how to wash and iron them. Your boots will also be bulled so you can shave in them. For those of you that can shave. For those that, then stick your heads out of the window or let the cats lick you, but shave you will. You'll also be getting a proper haircut gentlemen, what you have now is not army proper. When you fall out from here get your cases and get what you need out of them, because after tomorrow it will be too late and you will not need what you are wearing, so they'll go in the case. Ensure that your number and name is on the suitcase." He paused for effect and he was certainly getting it, plenty of heads were turning looking at pals but no one spoke. "I nearly forgot. Welcome to the British Army, the finest fighting army in the world and welcome to your new homes and remember, I am there if you need me – but you had better not." He paused again and I think he knew what we were thinking and he also at the same time knew that no one would say anything.

"Sgt," he yelled, "take over."

"Right, you heard what the Regimental Sgt Major said. Hope you've taken it all in for your own sakes. It'll make life easier for you. Fall out and get your cases and back to your huts. It'll soon be lights out and you need showers, that is not voluntary, it's compulsory, and for those of you who don't know what soap is then ask your mates then ask me." What a series of shocks, first the RSM, then the grub, we all agreed that we had better in our bait boxes, then the showers, there was no hot water. Ian shouted out that his willie was not normally that small and everybody laughed. When we got back to the hut there waiting for us was our corporal Williams.

"Right, you lot, gather around and cover yourselves, I've seen bigger ones on animals. As you will notice it is cold in here, reason? Not one of you have thought about the stove. It is too late to go foraging for stuff to light it with. You have thirty minutes to get yourselves the following, a mattress, one pillow, two sheets, one pillowcase and three blankets, make your bed whichever way you want because tomorrow you'll be taught how to make it properly, then it will be lights out. Seeing as it is your first night, you can talk for thirty minutes. Reveille, for those that don't understand, you will be woken by a bugle call at 0500hrs, followed by me who will be tipping you out of bed. Right, get your stuff and have a good night. By the way, Hardy, one of your tasks when you're cleaning my room out is to clean my stove and ensure that it's relit."

"Corporal. Yes, Corporal," I shouted.

"Yes, Corporal. Thank you, Corporal, and Goodnight, Corporal," we all said.

Beds were made and light were switched off and then we all started talking. Ian said, "They've got it in for you, Ralphy lad, haven't they?"

"At the minute, yes, but they haven't said what the punishment for you three is going to be yet."

"What about the food and the bloody hot water, or lack of it. Is it going to be like that every day?"

"And up out of bed at five every morning. We're going to be too knackered to fight the Germans. And what about the man with the voice, God I think he calls himself?"

"All I can say is that if he is God, I am not looking forward to meeting the Devil, and I think I'll stop going to church. Stuff that for a game of soldiers."

"That's a good 'un, mate. Stuff that for a game of soldiers. I like that."

"Right, you lot, that's enough now. Get you heads down and sleep, you'll need all your energy for tomorrow, plus you also need plenty of beauty sleep because looking at you all God was not generous in that department with you," he said and went back into his room.

*

"Right, you lot, hands off cocks and on with socks. Get yourselves over to the ablutions, back in here in ten minutes, put some clothes on and then to the cookhouse. I will expect you back here at 0600 hrs. Go."

"We looked around and there on the floor on its side was the bunk bed that Ian and Dave with the two of them in a heap on the floor. This is like being on first shift at the pit without the niceties. I bet that water isn't hot either and if not, how do they expect us to shave?"

"Hardy, I heard that. You will shave irrespective of the temperature of the water, it won't be warm when you are in France or Germany fighting. Anyway you have enough jobs to do to keep you warm and there's always my bed if you are that cold," he said jokingly. "Now bugger off, the more time you spend here moaning, the less time you have to eat."

Thirty minutes later, we were back and dressed in the block waiting for Corporal Williams.

He walked out of his room and said, "Get yourselves a pew or something to sit on. There are a lot of things that weren't said by the RSM yesterday, so I shall go through them for you. He told you that the blocks were responsibility but let me tell so is everything else. The cookhouse, it will be the job of every recruit to clean it, peel spuds, scrub floors, clean pans in fact anything that the cook Sgt says. The ablutions... Again every person will take their turns, on a block-by-block basis and will be responsible for cleaning, polishing the whole place. As you've noticed, hot water can be a scarce commodity, get used to it. Remember if you make the mess try and clean it. Letters... Incoming letters will be given to you at the end of the day and you will write home once a week. Letters are censored so think about what you say.

"Reveille... Reveille is the same time every morning and is immediately followed by either a cross country run or circuit training in the gym, or if you are really lucky or it's your birthday, then sometimes both. Meal times... These are breakfast 0700hours, lunch 1230 hours and evening meal 1800 hours. Your day finishes when either I or the Regimental Sgt Major says. The Commanding Officer is Lt. Colonel Robinson, he has a pip and a crown on his shoulders, the Adjutant is Captain Smith, not Smith so beware. You are in A Squad, X Company and your company officer is Major Jones and he has a crown on his shoulder he is support by two Lts. The Company Sgt Major is Warrant Officer Class Two Roberts. Notices... As you come in through that door, on the left is a notice board. On there will be names and pictures of all the major personnel in the camp including your own company. There will be other information regarding who is on what duty and when. Now for the next hour, we are going to learn how to make a bed. Once we have gone through it and you each have followed my instructions you will make it again under your own stream. Right, gather round."

Nearly an hour passed and everyone was finally successful. The best one at it was a lad from Gateshead, he looked kind of coloured or half cast as me da used to say or as the gossips would say, looks like some young lass has fancied a bit of coloured, shame on her. To me, he was a bit like the pictures you see of Indians in the Wild West. We found out later that he was a descendent of a real live Red Indian and one of his ancestors had married a white man and then moved over here. His name was William Bill Smith but he had been born with an Indian name, so we decided to call him Sitting Bull but he didn't like that and fearing being scalped, we settled for Bull.

Corporal Williams had gone out of the room for five minutes and was now back. "Now that you have learnt to make a bed box that is how it will be everyday as soon as you've washed. You don't sleep or sit on the bed after that either. Each block has to appoint someone from among you to be block leader and no, it won't be you, Hardy. Anything that goes wrong, any inspection that fails, that person carries a lot of the blame. So you have to decide whether you're going to drop him in the proverbial or you're going to learn to work as a team. The person that's going to be your block leader is Private Smith."

Ian said, "Bugger me. A bloody red Indian in charge, we'd better behave now."

Bull replied, "White man had better beware. Sitting Bull will scalp him otherwise." And we all laughed, including Cpl Williams.

"Well, I'll be buggered. I've heard everything now and this should make for an interesting hut," said Corporal Williams, but not loud enough for anyone to hear, "wait until I tell the Sarg."

"Smith will be responsible for ensuring that everything from the windows to the stove are correct, clean and workable. He is not excused the work but has to ensure that it is completed and then reports to me. He is also the contact between you and me. Each of you, if you have a problem, I am there to listen and to assist where and when I can. But if you don't want to come and see me, then speak to Smith and he will come on your behalf. I want you to remember that if you let me down, then you let your roommate down. It may be your turn after Smith or it may not, depends on how I feel."

When he went back to his room, we all gathered around Bull, as he was now known and we all talked at once, "We'll not let you down, mate. We'll make sure everything's okay. Wouldn't fancy your job? What do you think about it?"

"What do I think? I can't think anything about it. I don't have any choice, do I? But I'll tell you all one thing, any cock-ups, messing about that gets either me or this hut into trouble, you'll be answerable to me and there is a lot of Indian in me."

We all looked at him and none of us was sure how much was true and how much was bullshit, that's funny, isn't it? Bullshit – get it?

"Smith," came a shout from the corporal's room.

"Yes, Corporal, coming Corporal."

"Right, Smith, get them all outside in threes, we're off to the quartermasters stores."

"Outside everyone in threes."

Corporal Williams marched us all in a fashion, Ian still couldn't get the hang of his left leg following his right and then the problem of swing his left arm at the same time as his right leg went forward. He was already on extra duties which had not been decided yet and was heading for more.

On arrival at the QM's, there was a Sgt, another corporal and two privates behind long counters. You shouted out your name and number and then they handed you your kit. There was no measuring or anything like that. They took one look at you and guessed your size. The kit never seemed to stop, socks, towels, shirts, berets, badges, button sticks, buttons, belts, it just seemed to go on and at the end was a big kit bag in which you could put the majority of it in. The remainder you just had to carry as best as you were able. If you thought the marching there was funny, then the marching back to the block afterwards was even funnier and woe betide anyone who managed to drop something. In fact, I think you deserved a special award if you didn't.

When we got back Cpl Williams said, "Right, you made a right arse of yourselves there, didn't you? Remember when you march into battle, you'll have a lot of this kit with you. Put your kit down on your beds, wait for the bugle and then get yourselves to the cookhouse. At 1400hours, we shall go through your kit and explain everything to you. Now start sorting it out."

When we got back from the cookhouse, some of us noticed that our piles weren't as big as the others and Ian said, "Some sod's been in and nicked my sandshoes and vests."

Someone else said, "Yeah and my beret and badge and long johns have vanished. If I catch the buggers that nicked it, they'll swing for it."

"Hey, Bull, what are you going to do about it. You're the block leader?"

"Yeah, that's right," someone else said, "Come on."

"I'll go and see Corporal Williams."

Smith knocked at the door and a voice within replied, "Come in."

We watched as Smith opened the door marched in, halted and gave his number and name."

"Yes, Smith. What is it?"

"It's the men, Corporal. They have requested that I come and see you and tell that when they came back from the cookhouse some of them had found that someone had been in and stolen some of their kit, Corporal."

"Did they now?" he said and stood up and walked around his desk with Smith following.

"So someone has stolen your kit, eh? You do realise that to lose your kit is punishable and costly. You have to buy new ones and also pay for the item that you lost. How's your money going to hold up against that? You have signed for every single item that His Majesty has been gracious enough to provide and this is how you repay him. Losing your kit?" He paused and then continued, "No-one stole your kit. I took it. Why? Because I could. Because you dim-wits had been stupid to leave it lying there. I am not a babysitter for you. You have lockers in which you have to use and lock away your kit. Not you shower, you thought that the Corporal would keep an eye on it while we go for something to eat, didn't you? Well, didn't you?"

No one wanted to say yes to that question but at the same time if we said no then we would also be in trouble.

"As you are all incapable to answer a simple question, there will be an extra hour of PT before your evening meal, and if we get back in time, then you can go to the cookhouse, if not, then it looks as though you will do without. In ten minutes' time, we shall do a kit check and woe betide those that have kit missing, so get yourselves sorted out. As we go through each item on the list, I shall explain its purpose and you will listen because tomorrow you will be telling me the purpose of each item. Be prepared also to say goodbye to those poncy outfits that you are wearing now. From this afternoon, we are going to try and teach you to dress like a man. A man, Hardy, you understand?"

Here we go again, I thought and answered, "Yes, Corporal, I understand."

"Good, get yourselves sorted out."

For the next four hours, we went through every item of equipment, I never realise that a belt had a cock and fanny. The swimming trunks were a dark blue and seemed to be very like the big blue hairy knickers that girls wore. I think that when you come out of the water the crotch will be down near your knees. The shirts were hairy and itchy and we were then shown how to iron things, how and where to put creases in trousers and shirts and then how to get the shine on the boots. Spit and polish they called it, but I think the worst thing was the cleaning of the belts and gaiters, they had to be scrubbed with something called Blanco that was then left to dry and then you had to clean the cock and fanny and the brass clips on the back with brasso and without then marking the belt. To make matters worse, we even had to pay for the brasso, Blanco and polish ourselves, there wasn't going to be a lot left of our money when we got it.

"They have names for everything, don't they? I mean I can see why they call the belt parts cock and fanny."

"How do you know what a fanny looks like you're still a cherry boy, aren't you?" someone shouted in response.

"Bog off. I've had more than you've had hot dinners."

"Dream on."

"I'm pleased they issued vests because those shirts are going to be terrible next to your skin, and as for the uniform, they call battle dress, that's going to be hellish to iron. Incidentally has anyone seen an iron?"

"No, and I suppose that we have to all chip in to buy that as well?"

"Smith. Here."

"Corporal, coming Corporal."

When he went in the room Cpl Williams said, "Everyone outside in PT kit in ten minutes."

"Right, lads, the Corps wants everyone outside in PT kit in ten minutes and remember to put your other kit in your lockers, otherwise you know what will happen."

"Well done, Bull, for remembering that. Do you think it matters what colour top we wear?"

"We only have a choice of two, red or white, so let's all put the red one on, then he can't say anything."

An hour later and knackered, we were back. Cpl Williams said, "Right, the cookhouse will finish in thirty minutes, so you'd better get showered and over there sharpish if you want something to eat, and no bringing anything back. Food isn't allowed in the hut. It also looks as though you're going to be cold again tonight as no one has sorted out a rota of any kind for the stove, Oh, well. That, by the way, is your fault, Smith."

"Corporal," Smith shouted. "I'm fed up with being block leader all ready. Smith this. Smith that. Smith do this. Smith do that."

"Smith. You're not complaining at all, are you?" came a shout from the end room.

"No, corporal. I was just telling them to get a move on or we'll miss the cookhouse."

"Thought so. Good."

The next morning all what a cultural shock all hell broke loose. The light went on and all the windows opened letting a howling wind in and standing there all shining and immaculate was Cpl Williams who was banging a dustbin lid with a stick, "Out of you pits, you shower of shit, and in your PT kit, you're going for an early, early morning run." He looked over and Bull was still in bed, so he went over and tipped the bed over sending both Bull and Robbo who was on the top bunk flying. "You," he said, pointing at Bull, "might be some Indian chief, but you get up at the same time as everyone else. Extras."

Penny would have a fit at all this language and she'd say, "He can't talk to you like that. I'd report him." Can you imagine?

When we got back from the run, we showered, made our beds up in bed box fashion as we had been taught, then ran to the cookhouse for what was left from breakfast. We were getting used to being the last block at meals. Cpl Williams obviously thought that we all needed to slim. On getting back to the block, chaos had happened whilst we'd been at breakfast. It was either a tornado or Cpl Williams. Our beds were all tipped up with bedding and kit on the floor all mixed up and there standing in the middle of it was our version of Hitler, Cpl Williams.

Your bed boxes were an utter disgrace. Kit had been left out of lockers. Do you shower of shit never learn? Sit down where you can. Every month there is an assault course competition between the companies and the blocks. The winning company gets a crate of beer and a week off all outside cleaning duties. The winning block also gets a crate of beer and if the block corporal feels they have earned it, they also get Saturday and Sunday, apart from church parade free to what you want. You are not allowed out of barracks though, the local sheep have just recovered from the last shower we had here. The other companies have to do the whole assault course again with an hour break. The company that comes last loses all privileges for one month and they take over all fatigues for a month. So, you don't want to be in that loosing company. If you think that there is someone in your block who needs the extra kick up the arse, then that's what you do. Get this lot cleaned up and everything put away as per regulations, this afternoon you are going to learn how to sew and darn."

"Sew and Darn. It's supposed to be the army, not the mothers' union. That's what mothers are for sewing and darning."

"That's as maybe but she's not here and so who is going to do it for you? Are you man enough not to sew a button back on your uniform because you think it's not a man's job? I don't think so," said Robbo to Dave.

"Yeah, but what the hell are they trying to turn us into?"

A voice shouted out, "What are you worrying about, man, you're halfway there already."

"Listen you," Robbo was starting to get annoyed, "I've seen you in the shower and I've caught and thrown back bigger tiddlers."

"So you've been watching then, have you?"

At that stage both Smithy and Bull jumped in and said, "Stop winding each other up for Christ's sake, we've got enough to worry about what with kit, Cpl Williams and now this bloody assault course. I know I'm hopeless for climbing over walls. Always got caught when we went bird nesting up the park by the keeper. Why they couldn't have made them smaller I'll never know?"

"All I'd say if he keeps this up, he'd better watch his back."

"Diffant worry, when you're in the shower I will."

"Right, pack it in now, the pair of you, or I'll be the one you've both got to watch out for. I'm not getting extras because of two wankers like you. Grow up, and if you can't take the teasing, then don't bloody give it out. Right."

Smithy had stood watching and listening and knew that this was all out of his control he couldn't handle blokes like Ian, Robbo, Dave and especially not Bull. He just wished that Cpl Williams had given the job to Bull. But I decided that we'd all though Robbo was a bit of a girl's blouse but I think if there's trouble I'd sooner have him on my side as long as he could control that temper of his.

This all went on for at least four weeks, cleaning and cleaning again, peeling spuds, sweeping the parade ground, kit checks, assault course, drill, weapon training, and then one afternoon while we were doing map reading, Cpl Williams came in and said, "Right, everyone, listen in and pay attention. Because of good marks we've been getting I can tell you there will be no assault course this weekend and that you are free all weekend including church parade. You are free to go down to the local pub in uniform. You will not get drunk and woe betide anyone who does, so if you can't take it then don't. Know your limit. No hanky-panky with the local lasses, their dads are nearly all farmers and have shotguns."

I thought I'd sit down and write a letter to Penny and Da.

'I wish he'd told me all about the army, the bull, the cleaning. All you seem to do is clean, clean and clean again. If it is not your kit, it is the room or your rifle. Inspection after inspection and assault courses. We have a lad here whom we've nicknamed 'Wordsworth'. He's as thick as you know what and speaks broad Geordie but writes poetry and it's really beautiful, he's making a few bob on the side for fags with writing poems for the lads to send to their lasses. Hope that they never catch on that it is someone else doing the writing. The area around here is nice, in a wild sort of way. There are flowers that I've never seen before, lots of sheep and the sunsets and sunrises are really spectacular, it is something you don't really see or notice at home. Everyone seems to be losing weight but filling out more with muscles. I am starting to look like Popeye. Some of the lads are talking about putting on a show, a sort of 'Gang Show' before we leave here and have even been seeing rehearsing. Widow Twanky doesn't have a look in. They've been pestering me to do something, me without an ounce of musical talent. There are some things that you and I know I am good at but I don't think that anyone would volunteer to partner me (only kidding, my pet). I hope that you're well and no doubt looking as gorgeous as ever. Give my best wishes to your da. We've all been reading and listening to the news about the men at Dunkirk and isn't it amazing that those small boats could save so many? I'm sure that if we'd been there, then it wouldn't have happened, we'd never have let that little corporal get that far. In fact I think that we should swap corporals. They can have our Cpl Williams and we'll take their Cpl Hitler. That'll probably get censored. It's like getting a jigsaw by the time they take stuff out. Anyway, I love you and hope to be home soon. Xxxxxxx.'

'Hello, pet. Thought as it's quiet I'd write another few lines. We went to the local, I say local, it was about four miles away and we were looking quite smart in our uniform. Of course, it all went quiet when we went in even the blokes playing dominos and darts stopped. I think they'd had trouble with some other outfit recently and had just been put back in bounds by the military police who popped their heads in every now and then. There were a few lasses in but I think they were the ones that didn't stand a chance in town, they really were gruesome. Once the older blokes got talking, they were pleasant and full of old soldier stories and kept saying, "In my day things, were a lot harder, you lot don't know you're born, uniforms that pull the lasses and all that money" and went on but some of us played them at darts. Two of the lads were arrested by the local bobby for fighting and it was over football, one supported Newcastle and the other Sunderland. They spent the night in the guard house. Heaven help them when they have to go and see the RSM. Any, just a quick one. Take care and all my love pet lamb, xxxxx.'

*

"Right, run on the spot. Knees up and backs straight. Come on, you aren't on a Sunday stroll with the missus. You're not going to get any oats at the end of this, well, at least not the type you think. That may be all that's left in the cookhouse the way you lot are dawdling. Smith, Hardy, report to me when this is finished. No talking, no one gave anyone permission to talk. When I say go, you run to the end of the parade ground, ten press-ups and then back. The last one back will be on extra duties tonight. Go."

Off we went like whippets at the track on a Saturday. The thing was Bull was always good at this at, it would probably be Robbo last, apart from me, his was the name that was nearly always singled out. I often think that our Cpl Williams had been born with my name on his lips it was Hardy this, Hardy that and Hardy the bloody other. Sure enough it looked odds on that it was going to be Robbo last but Bull seemed to be hobbling and then he fell, so in theory he was last.

"Hardy, go and see what's up with him and take him to the medical centre. The rest of you showered and changed before your meal. Hardy, don't forget the pair of you see me as soon as you get back."

"Yes, Corporal."

Going up to Bull, I said, "What the hell happened to you, there was nowt the matter earlier?"

"I know. I knew that Robbo was going to be last so I pretended to fall, that way Robbo beat me in. He couldn't take anymore extra duties now, could he?"

I helped him up and said, "There's a heart under that cool exterior," and laughed, "Better limp a little to convince Hitler."

When we got back, we went straight to see Cpl Williams.

"Come in, the pair of you. What happened, Smith? And you realise that you were last, don't you?"

171

"Corporal, I think I just twisted my ankle and the medical corporal put a cold compress on it and said to take it easy."

"God, the way they mollycoddle, you lot we'll never win this bloody war. They'll have you as soft as shite. Right the pair of you get yourselves dressed, full uniform, pressed and polished. You are both going to see the RSM in 30 minutes."

"But, Corporal, we haven't…"

"Smith, for once just do as you are told. Now get out of my sight. I'll be taking you over there in," he said, looking at his watch, "in twenty-five minutes from now. Go."

We were standing outside of the RSM's door, both a little nervous, no that's not correct we were both bloody terrified.

"Bring them in, Cpl Williams."

Cpl Williams marched us in and then stood us at ease. The RSM said, "Stand easy." He looked even more intimidating sitting behind a desk. There was picture of the King and Queen on the wall and a calendar.

"Right, you two, Hardy and Smith. I have in front of me reports made by your block leader and squad Sgt as to how you have been behaving and how your training is going. You both appear to be excellent marksman, both smart and presentable and both are seen as a good example to the men. It has been decided firstly that you both will be enrolled on a sniper's course, which will be in a few days' time. It has been recommended, although I don't know why, looking at the pair of you, that you should be promoted. You will both be made a local lance corporal. That basically means your will wear a stripe on your arms, but for the moment, you will not be paid. This will be a trial period and once that has been reached and passed, you shall become an acting lance corporal, which in effect means that you'll be paid for the rank. Well done, now your next stop is the quartermasters where you will get your stripes and then you must have them on tomorrow morning. Your names will be mentioned on the Regimental Orders tonight. Congratulations and well done. March them out, Cpl Williams."

*

'Hello, pet. There is so much to tell you that I don't know where to start. Bull and I have been selected for a sniper's course because of our shooting skills. But the most exciting thing is that we have both been promoted to Lance Corporal which means I am only one stripe below Hitler and Napoleon. We don't get paid for it yet as we have to have a trial period but isn't that great news? Remember to tell Da, won't you? He never made the dizzy heights, or if he did, he never mentioned it to me.

We are in a final, two weeks here and, nearly forgot to tell you I also have my driving licence, brilliant, eh, pet? You, Da, Mary-Ellen and your dad will be getting visitors passes soon. We are having a passing out parade and some big wig General is coming up from Catterick I think. (That'll probably be censored). There will be buses laid on from the town to bring families here. Isn't that good?

There will be a Regimental Band and drummers, then families can look around the camp and see our blocks and then there are refreshments in the cookhouse for everyone. There will also be awards given out for various activities. I'm afraid that if there was one for sewing and darning, I wouldn't even be in the running. My socks, you should see them. Then we are all to get seven whole days leave before we report for the next stage, whatever that will be. The gang show is going ahead tonight and I have been coaxed to dress up as a worm while somebody sings the Lambton Worm, please, don't even try to imagine it and whatever you do, don't let on to Da. Until I see you in a couple of weeks' time, take care and all my love to everyone.

Ps...We have some lost time to make up for!!! Wink wink, xx I think it might be making babies time!!! Xx'

*

The day of the passing out parade arrived and there were about twenty buses all full of excited and proud parents, gushing wives and girlfriends and very proud grandparents all dressed in their Sunday best. There was plenty of brass on display with visiting officers and we were surprised at how smart the band were in their scarlet tunics.

People were waving at us but we couldn't wave back we were forming up for the parade and I'm pleased to day that the weather was good, probably one of the best we've had up here since we arrived. Cpl Williams checked us over, then the Company Sgt and then the Company Commander. They all managed to find something wrong, if one missed it, then the other seemed to find it and this was despite having our mates go over us with a fine toothcomb. The bull on the boots was starting to look a bit worse for wear with the sun and the dust, but before we marched on, someone came along and rubbed a cloth over the toecaps. Then the order, "Battalion, Battalion shun," came from the Regimental Sgt Major. "By the left, quick march," and the band stuck up, boom. Boom went the bass drum and then it felt we were on guard at Buckingham Palace or somewhere nice. You could see people holding little cameras out the corner of your eye. I saw Penny and the rest of the family, in fact, I had to virtually counter-march in front of them. I was that close I could have kissed her. She threw me a kiss and I thought, *Mustn't even acknowledge*, although I did raise my eyebrows.

Then the Adjutant took over, handed to the second in Command and then we waited for what seemed an eternity for the Commanding who would be escorting the General. The band struck up a salute and we presented arms and then everything we had been working for started.

Apart from me and Smith, there were another eight people selected for promotion and we nearly died laughing when they called out Robbo's name. Totally unexpected, he was a nightmare for the physical training staff but he was good at admin and paper related things, so I think he was destined for the orderly room. Then Bull and I were presented with our crossed rifles to go on our sleeves. Then the announcement was due for 'Best all-round recruit'. We all waited with baited breath, I mean we all felt that after Robbo was promoted anything was possible. The Colonel announced, "Best All-Round Recruit and winner of the Shield is… Lance Corporal Smith." He handed his weapon to me and marched up as proud as punch. He deserved it. Alan had received the award for best sportsmen, and if there had been an award for best whinger, then Ian would have received it but he got nothing and then started to moan that he was better than some of the others. Overall our block had done quite well. Someone was heard to remark, "Load of arse creepers that lot." Of course Ian bit and Bull had to step in yet again before anyone saw. I think Ian was still working off all the extras that he had accumulated. The day went off well and our families departed all smile and full of anticipation about our forthcoming leave.

The normal duties had to be carried out, kit stored, beds made up, forms to be filled in, leave passes and pay to get, bus and/or train warrants to be issued and of course the proverbial talk about behaviour when out in uniform and in public and you are now in representing the King, blah, blah, it went on and on, and there were trucks lined up on the parade ground that would take everyone to Newcastle and then they made their own way home, when and if we ever got this talk finished.

A Week's Leave

The four of us were still together and got the same bus home, although getting off at different stops and there at stop was flag waving families. The bus conductress said, "There's going to be fun tonight I can see," and we all laughed.

When I got off, there was no one there. I thought had they forgotten but how could they when the others all knew? Then I turned the street and there was a sheet hanging across the road saying, 'Welcome Home, Soldier Boy', there were more in the backyard and on the door, but then when I opened the door, you would have thought that the King and Queen were visiting, there were streamers hung form corner to corner and enough food laid out to feed an army. They were all there, Da, with his little box camera, Penny's dad, Aunt Mary-Ellen, some of the neighbours and even a couple of George's customers, being nosey no doubt.

While everyone was shouting 'welcome home', Penny ran to me and putting her arms around me tightly and kissed me passionately then said, "Well done on everything and congratulations," and gave me another kiss.

Da said, "Will you leave him alone, lass, you've plenty of time for all that messing about later. Let the lad get in the door before you rip his clothes off."

"Mr Hardy," Penny said, mockingly, "Please, I'm not that kind of girl."

"Bloody hell, Son, looks like you're going to be disappointed tonight," he said, and everyone then joined in the joke.

George said, "We've already made a space in the cabinet for your trophy and certificate, and then we get the picture back from the chemist we'll have one framed, show you off Lance Corporal Hardy."

"Come on, you must be starving," Penny said.

Grabbing her, I whispered in her ear, "Yes, but not for food."

"Behave and I can feel," she said, pushing closely together.

"God, they're like dogs on heat, the pair of them. Remember you have company."

"You're only jealous 'cos you've forgotten what it's all about."

"You cheeky wee monkey, you're not too old or big to still get a clout, you know. Lance corporal or not. Lance Corporal, you'll be an officer next time we meet, you mark my words, they know a good one when they see one. A bit like that general with all is medals and sword, bet he's never cleaned any of his own kit for years. It was a good parade though."

"Can I ask a question?" said Mary-Ellen. "Having seen your room and bed space, why couldn't you keep your bed like that at home?"

"What, and give you nothing to moan about?"

Da looked at me and hugged me, which felt strange as he wasn't into displays of affection and said, "Well done, lad, you survived and prospered. Your mum would have been proud of you. Well done." I'm sure that there was a tear in his eye.

"May I have your attention please? Thank you. I would just like to say a few words, and they will be few. The whole three month up there was an experience that I'll never forget and it has done me well. I realise that the hard stuff is just beginning. So it looks like I'm in for the duration or for the end of war, whichever comes first. There are rumours, even in the army that they are planning on starting conscription. I would like to thank you all for coming to the passing out parade, it made me proud seeing you all there. I also even saw a human side to Cpl Williams and the RSM when I saw him talking to you. I even saw him smile."

"No, lad. That wasn't a smile or even a grimace. That was wind."

Everyone laughed because Penny's da was not known for making funnies.

"I also want to thank you for all your support and letters and for the welcome today. As for the food, I'm not sure what I'm looking forward to most, the corned-beef pies of a bit of something else," he said and smiled at Penny.

Fred said, "Will someone get a bucket of cold water and throw it over him for Christ sake, and remember your manners, lad, there are women present."

I replied, "Where?" Then got a slap on the back of my head from Aunt Mary-Ellen, who said, "I'll where, you so and so."

Penny's dad wanted his say, "Well, I'd like to welcome Ralph back home and that we all hope he has an enjoyable leave."

"Here, Here," they all echoed.

"Now everyone else has had their say," said Penny. "I'd like my tuppence worth. There is something that I want to tell you all that not even Ralph knows." She waited a moment until the eyebrows that had been raised were lowered and continued, and looking over and grabbing Ralph's hand said, "I'm pregnant."

The place just erupted, hugs, kisses, handshakes, tears and glasses refilled.

We just looked at each other and I kept saying, "Us a baby. Us a Baby. I'm going to be a da. Me, a da? I can't believe it, us, a baby."

Penny was suddenly lifted in the air by Ralph and Aunt Mary-Ellen said, "You stop that, Ralph, you can't do things like that now she's with child. Put her down."

"Well, if I can't swing her, I think I must swing you," and she ran and he ran after her.

Fred said, "She's pulled at last. She's finally got someone chasing her. Must be a name for that, George, eh?"

"Aye, there is. It's incest," he said and they all laughed again.

The day continued one round of celebrations as the tom toms must have been out and the neighbours got to know, so they had to pop in to add their congratulations and get a free drink of course.

Penny was in the kitchen and Ralph went up behind her and put his arms around her and said, "How can we get rid of them all and give us some peace?" as he tapped her belly, "Do you think it'll be a boy?"

"My dad said that he was going to stay over at your das for a couple of night to give us some privacy, which I thought was a nice gesture."

"Even with this was on life is still good, isn't it?"

When they went back into the sitting room, they were amazed to find it empty, everything had been washed and tidied away. There were three envelopes on the table. There was one from Fred's da, he recognised the writing also one from Mary-Ellen and a third from Penny's dad.

Each envelope had written on it 'Congratulations on your special day'. "Your aunt Mary-Ellen must have guessed, do you think?"

They opened the envelopes and could not believe what they saw, Fred said holding a pile of money, "And it just got better."

They ran upstairs, with Ralph chasing Penny and trying to bite her bum as they went until they reached the bedroom. The chase had culminated, it was now more like two hungry loving animals coupling and who had now satisfied their initial lust and then settled down to making long, slow passionate love...

*

The week passed far too quickly, they made a lot of arrangements about the baby, about the money they had been given, the total was far more than either of them had ever seen and would make a nice figure in the bank for the future. They went for walks, made love, went to the pictures and penny even managed to get me to go to a dance at the local church hall and both Ian and Dave were there. Ian was doing his normal, looking to make trouble and Dave was sniffing around the barmaid. He had no chance because her boyfriend, built like the proverbial, was standing at the end of the bar in an RAF Officers' uniform. I only hoped that he had noticed, if not then I'll have to pint out.

Penny said, "Keep out of it, Ralph, he's old enough and big enough to look after himself."

"Can't do that, Pet. I'll have to warn him, the last thing we want is trouble and it getting back to camp and Ian is just looking for some excitement. Why he can never just settle for a game of bingo like the rest of us I'll never know. Back in a minute."

Everyone was all right and Ian had settled and Dave had put his brains back in his head where they belonged. At the end of the dance, they played a selection of songs form the first war and its strange how you know them. Then they played the National Anthem and wished every one of us good luck and to hurry home.

We both knew that this would be the last night home for I don't know how long. We were due to return to camp tomorrow. There was not munch said between us but what we did say was important, and we had little Ralphy to look out for now, *Wonder what I'll do if it's not a boy?*

The weeks leave was over and there were lots of tears at every stop with people saying goodbye and waving flags, I think that Woolworth's must have done a good trade on them.

When we got back, there was a lot of gossip to catch up on and I couldn't wait to tell them all my news, I was going to be a dad.

"Haddaway with you, man. Must be somebody else's, you haven't got a good one in you."

"Eh, if you're going to take the piss, remember it's Lance Corporal now."

Everyone laughed, then someone said, "Oooo, listen to her. Lance Corporal, if you don't mind."

I learnt a lot more about Smithy alias Bull. His grandparents had been on an Indian Reservation which he said was terrible, a lot of hunger and no employment, so the family decided to come to England. His Indian name was 'He Who Gives' which stems from the fact that they were traders rather than warriors.

I said to him, "I never thought in my life that I'd ever meet a real-life Red Indian, the only ones we knew, and that was because of comics and the pictures were Sitting Bull, Crazy Horse, Geronimo and Hiawatha. Now I can add 'He Who Gives' to that list.

Paperwork completed we were all gathered together on the parade ground and a roll call taken, which took ages. It was explained that we would be staying together as a new battalion of the Regiment and the majority of us would stay in the same companies. It was announced the whole battalion would muster on the parade ground tomorrow morning at 1000hrs in full battle dress as though going to war. Anything not on the list would be packed up and given to the quartermaster for safekeeping. Nothing else was said. We went back to our blocks and started work on all of our kit ensuring all buckles were done up and everything that we were supposed to have we had. We checked each other's kit just in case. The talk was all about war. Were we finally going? If our training corporal knew he never said anything.

The next day, we paraded as normal with all the handovers that took place until finally the Commanding officer was standing there. He announced that every single person and their kit would be inspected and checked by their Company Commanders but the CO chose our company for inspection. It took several hours, everything was unpacked and laid out in front of each soldier. There items were checked against lists again, weapons checked and then about two hours later, we handed the weapons into the armoury and everyone went off to the cookhouse where we tried to find out what other people had been picked for. Robbo, not to our surprise was destined for the Intelligence section of the regiment. Then we got a surprise and that at 1200hrs, Friday the following day, we would be leaving for an undisclosed destination. We were both excited and frightened, it had finally come.

The following morning the trucks were all lined up and we climbed on with all of our equipment and the next stop was the railway station in Newcastle. The signs read, 'Troop Train – South', 'Troop train – East', plus all the normal trains going to London, York, Scotland and plenty of freight trains passing through. The station was bunged with uniforms of every description, Army, Navy, Air force, Red Cross, Salvation Army, French and Dutch service personnel. The excitement reminded me being a bairn and going on a trip to the seaside, except this time the excitement was coming from grown men. There were separate carriages for the officers and then a group of military female nurses matched up led by a female officer, with huge bosoms and built like a gorilla and I thought, *I hope I never get taken into her care.*

The noise in the station was horrific, trains hissing, the tannoy system, people shouting orders and the smoke. We climber on board the train marked 'South' and people were leaning out of windows waving, not to anyone in particular, just waving to anyone who would wave back.

We passed Durham with its beautiful Cathedral situated on the wear, then York. The lads were playing cards, smoking, farting. That had become a contest in itself to see who could do it to order and Bull always won, and the smell, even with the windows open. Some of us had just fallen asleep when we pulled into Sheffield where there were hot drinks and meal waiting for us on the platforms, which we were not allowed to leave. The Military Police were there to ensure you didn't. Everywhere we looked there were flags and patriotic posters encouraging everyone to do their bit, whether to enlist, grow more veg, knit things for the troops, telling us to be careful what and where we say things and to whom, to report anything suspicious. We still had no idea where we were heading for but assumed that it was the south coast and certainly further than the majority of us had been in our lives. Before we left, the station there was a roll call and a general tidy up of the carriages and more hot tea handed out by the Salvation Army and Red Cross wagons, they really were a godsend and worth their weight in gold those ladies, and they were of all ages, even me da could have scored, picked a woman up in uniform, now that would have got them talking in the pub and kept the gossips busy for hours. Just then Bull dropped another one and I said, "I wonder if it smells like this in the Officers' Carriage?"

"Why wouldn't it? It's something we all do, even The King and an old Indian pal of mine. Running Water used to say, 'Him who smells shit must be dog, 'cos dog smells own shit first.'" We all laughed and he continued, "So because you smelt it first, he would call you, 'Him who shits first'."

"Get away, you daft bugger, you're taking the piss out of a simple north country lad but I liked your accent, you sound just like the Indians at the when you had captured a fort and you were about to scalp people. Anyway, there's a question, why did you scalp people?"

"Well, here is some truth for you. The Indian did not start the scalping, the white man was doing it for souvenirs and many an Indian village was wiped out with woman and children killed, women were often mutilated and had their breasts sliced off. All at the orders of the great General George Custer. The white man had to make out the Red Indians were savage, how else could they justify taking his land and wealth. The Indian was only doing what we are doing now, defending theirs and their families. We were supposed to be heathens and savages because we worshiped totem poles and gods in the earth, the sun, the moon but what was any different from a totem pole to a wooden cross? We killed for food and survival, the white man killed for profit, gain and a religious belief in a man who valued lives, as long as that life was white. We now have men of god telling us that what we are doing is right. The Germans have the same man telling them that what they are doing is right. Who is right? Answer me if you can. He's a strange man, this God of the white people who can convince us that those that don't believe in his God are heathens and savages."

We all went silent and you could tell that there was a lot of truth in what he'd just said. Whose side was God on?

"Yes, the Red Indian was brought to the white man's god, through rape, murder, some kind of Christianity that was and is."

"Yes, I suppose that you could be right but look at what the settlers brought. Civilisation, advancement, medicine, peace."

"And they also brought disease, greed, poverty, weapons of mass destruction, drink. I often think that we would have been better without the white man's advancement and we would have evolved in our own way. Now we are left with no land, despite all the treaties and promises that were made. We were herded away from out hunting grounds to reservations that were hundreds of miles from our natural homelands, that were ran by the white man, not the Indian, for the white man. Our food was lost, our wealth in the gold. Our feeding pastures and wild horses all lost for what? White man's advancement. Could you imagine if one day someone came along and moved you and your family lock, stock and barrel away from the North East and resettled you somewhere in the middle of nowhere? You would have fought. Of course you would. Your upper classes came to our land and encouraged migration to our lands the same as they have down trodden people in the North east and North West, Wales and Ireland into the pits, to make them prosperous whilst the poor remain poor but feel grateful to the top for giving them work and it starts from the top down. Did the Royal Navy turn up at Russian ports to take the poor downtrodden to safety from the revolution, of course not, they turned up to pick members of the Royal family, the aristocrats to safety. Did they turn up in Greece for the people, no, they went to take the Royal Family to safety."

"God, Bull, you sound as though you would like to be a commie."

"Anything but, pal, I feel that the people need justice but also know that no matter what system we have we shall never all be equal. Someone has always got to be in charge and if they are in charge then their lives will be better than those at the bottom. People dream of their son not going down the pit, they dream of them getting to grammar, to better themselves and better their prospects and dream of them becoming a white-collar worker and having more opportunities than they themselves did. There is no harm in dreamer but the man at the bottom needs to know that that dream is not impossible and that there is a chance for them to their kids to win. A white-collar job means a better lifestyle, a pension, no more coming home filthy, having to scrimp and save every penny and all for a pint at the pub on the weekend and his kids getting a chance to go on either, or if their lucky, both the pit and Sunday trip."

*

"Granda, last time you were telling us that Da joining up to fight the Germans, so what happened?" said George.

"Well, me laddos, your da did go off to fight but not the German's, he went off to fight a war many, many miles away in Singapore. Remember that atlas I was showing you with all the pink on it well one of those countries was Singapore and it is near Australia. The Japanese had been at war with China for many years but they decided to attack the American naval fleet at Hawaii and then came into the war on the side of the Germans and Italians. They swept through the Far East, taking Malaya, Burma, parts of China and Singapore was considered by the British to be untakeable but they took Singapore without much trouble and they took thousands and thousands of prisoners, your da being one of them."

"But why does Da not talk about to us like you do?"

"Well, there's a strange thing. I never used to talk about it and a lot of men who've been in wars don't, sometimes the memories of what they've seen and what they themselves had to do is too painful to remember and talk about. If that is the case, then it's easier to bury it away in their minds. One day, he will open up and I hope I'm there for when he does because I would just love to give him a cuddle. The Japanese were unlike the ordinary German soldier, they believed that to surrender was not honourable and that soldiers should fight to the very end. So they treated their prisoners very bad, very badly indeed. Not many prisoners survived Japanese camps and they were made to work and had very little food. I do know that he managed to keep a log though."

"What do you mean by a log, Granda?" said James.

"A log, Son, is like a diary. They would write on anything they could find. They would have to hide it in all the strangest of places because of they were caught it would mean more punishment or even death. You can't do it every day, just when and if you could and only a few lines. I imagine that one day, when he feels the time is right, he may talk about it all to you both, but you must never, ever ask him about it. You may have noticed how he is when he sees a Japanese person in the street. I believe that you met two at the paddling pool the other day. Well, to your da that is like an explosion waiting to go off in his head, when he sees them all he sees if the pain and suffering that he and his mates endured. He also sees in his mind the mates that never came back with him. To your da, it's like it happened yesterday. I am trusting you both on this one so I want a big promise on your mum's life."

They both said, "Cross my heart and hope to die, Granda, we promise."

"I'll make sure that blabber mouth here doesn't say anything," said James, digging George in the ribs.

"Granda, tell him to stop picking on me. I have said that I won't say anything."

"The pair of you grow up, will you? As I had been telling you earlier, the war was not going well for us and it was taking a lot longer than we had ever believed so the government starting calling up people that were older. I was working down the pit, and although I was of a call up age, I enlisted as a part time soldier, the Home Guard we were called. A lot were ex-servicemen. I suddenly found myself promoted to Sergeant and became a drill instructor because of my previous experience. Me, a Sgt, I didn't really know my... from my elbow. No, that's not really correct, I could teach men to drill, to do guard duties, and I was still fairly fit. Your mum's dad also joined up and he became a storeman in the home guard and was responsible for the issue of equipment, I think they felt that his retail experience could be put to good use. We were sometimes known jokingly as Dad's army or Fred Carno's army."

"Granda," said George, "who was Fred Carno?"

"Well, I knew as soon as I said it that you would ask, but I suppose that is the only way that you'll learn things. I believe that Fred Carno was an American showman and all the rage with plenty of slapstick comedy. People started thinking about us like that. A lot of us didn't even have weapons and we were supposed to stop parachutists if they invaded. I often think that of the Germans had realised what was waiting for them here they would have invaded straight away. Some of the big country houses were turned into makeshift hospitals for returning wounded. The home guard was used to look after places on the seaside that had concrete pillboxes with little slits in them where you could put a rifle through. We looked after ammunition factories, and places like the steel works. If we saw planes then we radioed to headquarters and they sounded air alarms to different places. They came and bombed places like Coventry, Birmingham, Glasgow, Belfast, Newcastle, Hartlepool, Liverpool places where there was industry and ship building."

"But it wasn't really fair for you, was it? You'd done it before and now you were doing it again. Did you get used to it?"

"Life isn't always fair, lad. You never ever get used to it. I always hoped that your da would never have to experience it or anyone else for that matter. I also hope and pray that you and your generation never have to go through it. As I told you I was with the home guard and because I was a pitman I didn't have to go and fight, but I decided to enlist. I was still young and fit enough to play a part. Although I was Sgt in the home guard, they made me a corporal in the regular army because of my experience. When I came home and told your Aunt Mary-Ellen she went crackers and the air was blue."

"Blue?" said George.

"Yes, George, blue, and before you ask it is just another one of those things that us old ones say. Now, where was I? Oh, yes, me joining up. They said that I would be used for training new recruits and they sent me off to the South of

England to a place called Aldershot, which was and still is a big army place. They also had their own military hospital there. Because of there being a lot of soldiers there, there was often trouble between the local and soldiers normally involving drink and women. The new recruits looked on me as some kind of antique war hero."

"But you were. Weren't you?" said James.

"Well, I was old but as for being a hero, no, I wouldn't say that at all. I was just one of thousands that went off to war and done a job. I was lucky, I came back, and they were the heroes, the ones that didn't come back. Men never thought that what they'd done was heroic. We were all frightened, anyone who says that they weren't is lying. We all put on a show of bravado in front of others. Fear is something that we all have in us, but how we handle it is different in each of us."

Neither James nor George really understood what their granda was talking about and he was aware of that so he continued saying, "I decided that I would volunteer for extra training and picked parachuting."

"So you volunteered to jump out of planes?" said George and they were suddenly both interested again.

"You mean you really jumped out of an airplane?" said James.

"Aye, I did at that, lad. After months training, I was actually going to jump out of a plane over France."

"So you did go and fight the mad corporal then?"

"Yes, me and many more. I was sick at the sights that I saw because it was just a repeat of what I had seen twenty or more years ago. We entered one French Village and there was not a building left intact and there was not a soul alive. The men had been taken to work in Germany and the women and children had been murdered in the church when it was burnt down with them in it. They had all been killed because someone had killed a couple of German soldiers and the Germans considered that a lesson had to be shown so that other villages would not do the same. To march into that village was like seeing what hell was like and what man could do against his fellow people. I asked myself where had been this man called God. Did he exist and whose side was he on? I questioned my faith. Sometimes when I go to church now, I don't know whether I pray or not. I know I ask a lot of questions that I never get answers to. Because of that I can never resolve the feeling about him that I have within me. A different me took over in that village and I found hate. I just wanted to kill any German I found, about like your da with the Japanese."

"Did that village ever become alive again then, Granda?"

"I suppose that it will have done by now. The people in England lived the fear of German bombers and hid under their kitchen tables, in shelters in the garden and in tube statins in London. There was no sweets or ice cream then wither, you queued for your food which was rationed and were only allowed certain amounts of different items. Did you know that when the Queen was married, she had to use her tokens, although the war had ended, to get her cake made? When we left that village, we passed people carrying their few belongings that they had, soldiers were carrying wounded men. The people look tired and hungry, we tried to give them things but we couldn't give to everyone. We came across some Jock soldiers escorting German prisoners and they looked tired, scruffy and I think that secretly they were pleased that for them the war was over. It also meant that we were advancing further and further into the enemy positions. We thought, well, at least the Jocks will be getting hot showers and decent food, we were a bit jealous of them to be honest. The next day we crossed the border into Germany, you didn't know you had done it because there was nothing there to indicate that you had done it. We came across many vehicles and tanks ready to advance. We came across some little collie type dogs and some of the lads tried to make friends with them but I think the dogs were probably frightened they would end up in a pot. We were advancing towards a German town and on the outskirts there didn't appear to be a lot left, the RAF had been and softened the enemy but there were still a lot of snipers hidden in places where we couldn't see them, which was their job and they were doing it well picking off our guys at their leisure. They had also managed to camouflage tanks and had hidden them behind rubble and they were difficult to see from then air. A Sgt near me looked over at me and nodded indicating that we should make a run at a tower that appeared to be hiding a sniper. Several other guys were trying to keep him occupied, and several times, we had to do what you two do when you're playing war games, we had to pretend to be dead. But for us there was no 'tig', for us, it was real. As we were about to go into the building, there was a direct hit on it and everything went quiet. The town was finally taken and we met up with some Americans and Canadians and we were able to get a hot meal at last, not sure what it was but it was hot and tasty and there was plenty of it. They looked at my ribbons and thought that I was some relic from an old war movie. I told them that nothing had changed from the last one except the tanks were bigger, there was more aircraft, there were the same dead, the same needless dead. I realised that I sounded like an old sweat facing these young lads thousands of miles away from home. We listened to whatever news we could and heard that the Russians, who then were our friends, were advancing from the East towards Germany and nearer Berlin than we were. The Italians had changed sides, yet again and the Japanese were on the run. Our Regiment was advancing towards a place called Bergen-Belsen. This was a place that we knew nothing about really except that it was a concentration camp and we were not prepared for anything that we were to see. It was terrible and I am not going to tell you much about it, one day, you will learn and, like us, be horrified. There were piles of rags lying all over the place but inside those rags were people."

"Well, why they dressed funny then and why were they lying down?"

"They were lying down because many of them couldn't stand, they were just bones. They were many nationalities, German, French. Poles, British, Russian, Dutch, and many, many more. A lot of them were Jews. But they were people like you and I. They had done nothing to deserve what had happened to them besides being invaded and occupied by the Germans. Hitler had wanted to rid Europe of Jews."

"But why was da not helping you?"

"Well, Son, while our war was nearing an end, the war with Japan wasn't, and your da was, as far as we knew, still a prisoner. You have to remember, unlike the Germans, the Japs never told countries who they had as prisoners so as far as we were concerned your da could even have been dead. There was no TV like now to keep up with the news, we had to listen to whatever news we could. Much of it coming by the radio network that the allies had set up and was coming via London."

"Did he go and live in Japan then when he was a prisoner."

"No, he never went to live in Japan but until he decides to talk about it, we shall never know. As I have said, one day when you're older and have children of your own, no matter what their age, you still want to protect them, they are the future and many of us could not do that. It'll hurt you the same way as it did me. You feel that you have let them down. But you have already promised that you'll never mention this to your da. You two have to learn to live with each other and learn to respect each other, you're always going to be brothers, you'll fight and stop talking over nothing as the years go on, but you are always going to be brothers and you have to learn to live with it and become friends."

*

Although the war in Europe was finished, the war in Japan would go on for another six months or so. They never surrounded until the Americans dropped two large atomic bombs on two of their cities and wiped the cities from the face of the earth and many, many thousands were killed. But men were returning to Britain from all corners of Europe, from Germany, France, Holland, Belgium, Italy, Greece, North Africa. Also on the move were people who had lost families and they were mainly Jews who returned to towns that they had lived in to find every member of their families had been killed and their homes occupied by other people who wouldn't give them back. Those people tried to settle in America, Canada, Britain and Palestine, but they still kept searching for survivors of their families. You probably say that we won the war, I used to think that but then I look at us now and I am not sure. In Europe destroyed cities were rebuild exactly as they had been, Prague, Warsaw, Ypres, Dresden but we decided to go the way of American, and rebuild our cities in a modern style, which looked good, but they haven't stood the test of time. Many estates became slum areas. Then our modern buildings had to be pulled down. Men again were returning to high unemployment; after all, women had been doing the jobs that men had done and many wanted to keep that independence."

"Granda, what happened to all of your pals?"

"My goodness, all these weeks and you have been listening. I am quite proud of you both." Fred went quiet as though he were lost deep in thoughts and for once the boys did not push for an answer, they seemed to feel for his thoughts and that they were private.

185

George couldn't contain himself and said, "Granda, Granda, are you alive or have you fallen asleep with your eyes open?"

"What's that, lad? No I haven't fallen asleep with my eyes open, but I am tired, and if the pair of you don't mind, I think that I shall have a little nap and then one day, when I'm feeling more up to it, we'll chat about my pals and your da. Okay?"

He didn't give them their usual sixpence and they went out, not sulking this time, but they went out peacefully.

Fred was tired, but, all of a sudden, he felt relieved, he felt a huge burden had been taken off his shoulders and with what looked like a sigh, his shoulders dropped.

The boys went into the kitchen and Mary-Ellen said, "You two are looking suspicious. Have you got into trouble?"

"No, Granda said that he was tired and started to fall asleep, so we came out."

"Mmmmm, doesn't sound like the old devil. I'll pop in and take a cup of tea."

When she came out, she said to Penny, "Must've taken it out of him today, he's sitting there fast asleep, think I'll leave him be. He needs the rest and I need some peace and sanity. Now lads, be good for your mam and da and stop teasing Claire, after all she's a girl not a tomboy. George, you keep at your music and I want to hear next week that you've learnt something different and good luck with your piano exam next week. And you, young man." She said, turning to James, "Good luck with the new school and I hope that you get on the football team, but don't sulk if you don't, because you have to work your way into these things. I remember how I was with the netball team because I didn't get picked first time. Anyway pet," she said to Penny, "Give Ralph my love and we'll see you next week…

Mary-Ellen sat down with a cup of tea and piece of ginger bread and thought, *This is bliss, he's asleep, and the kids have gone home. It's nice to see them but it's also nice when they've gone. Peace and quiet. Bliss.*

HELLO!

I'm Stuart, aka Ashens. I make videos for YouTube, write scripts and sometimes act in things.

This is my second book about atrocious old video games that are no fun whatsoever, as I've somehow forged a career out of pointing out substandard products and laughing at them. I live in Norwich, in a house full of tat that I pretend to need for my work. I'm planning on moving house soon so I have more space to fill, as I've used this series of books as an excuse to buy a large number of retro computers. My favourite soup is still crabmeat and sweetcorn.

@ashens
youtube.com/ashens
ashens.com

HELP IS HERE

Dear Reader,

The book you are holding came about in a rather different way to most others. It was funded directly by readers through a new website: Unbound. Unbound is the creation of three writers. We started the company because we believed there had to be a better deal for both writers and readers. On the Unbound website, authors share the ideas for the books they want to write directly with readers. If enough of you support the book by pledging for it in advance, we produce a beautifully bound special subscribers' edition and distribute a regular edition and e-book wherever books are sold, in shops and online.

This new way of publishing is actually a very old idea (Samuel Johnson funded his dictionary this way). We're just using the internet to build each writer a network of patrons. At the back of this book, you'll find the names of all the people who made it happen.

Publishing in this way means readers are no longer just passive consumers of the books they buy, and authors are free to write the books they really want. They get a much fairer return too – half the profits their books generate, rather than a tiny percentage of the cover price.

If you're not yet a subscriber, we hope that you'll want to join our publishing revolution and have your name listed in one of our books in the future. To get you started, here is a £5 discount on your first pledge. Just visit unbound.com, make your pledge and type **flicker5** in the promo code box when you check out.

Thank you for your support,

Dan, Justin and John
Founders, Unbound

This edition first published in 2017

Unbound
6th Floor Mutual House, 70 Conduit Street, London W1S 2GF
www.unbound.com

Text Design by Friederike Huber
Art Direction by Friederike Huber

A CIP record for this book is available from the British Library

ISBN 978-1-78352-413-6 (trade hbk)
ISBN 978-1-78352-414-3 (ebook)
ISBN 978-1-78352-415-0 (limited edition)

Printed in Italy by L.E.G.O S.p.A

1 3 5 7 9 8 6 4 2

ATTACK
OF THE
FLICKERING
SKELETONS

STUART ASHEN

Unbound

THIS BOOK IS DEDICATED TO
EVERYONE WHO BOUGHT A
TERRIBLE GAME BECAUSE A
MAGAZINE REVIEW LIED AND
SAID IT WAS AVERAGE.

SUPERFRIENDS

LISTED HERE ARE MY SUPERFRIENDS - PEOPLE WHO
PLEDGED A SUBSTANTIAL AMOUNT OF MONEY TO HELP
ENSURE THAT THIS BOOK BECAME A REALITY.

Alex Blackmon
Michael Bradshaw
Alice Broadribb
Gregor Cameron
Mathew Cooper
Larry Cordner
Philip Corner
Tom Cox
Chloe Cresswell
Michael Cullipher
Fox Cutter
Tom Dongolo
J.J. Dumlao
Neil Dutton
Matthew Faulkner
Steven Feary
Cameron Fray
Bernie Furlong
Thor Gaffney
Frederick Gibson
Mark Green
Damien Marc Greenhalgh
Richard 'dragonridley' Hatton
Matt Honeyball
Rob Hutchinson

Sebastian Hutter
Nigel Johnson
Richard Johnson
Michele Kalva
Euan Kennedy
Kymo Misenica Kobayashi
Steven Lindquist
Joshua Linton
Nick Macey
Jami Martinez
Lizzy Matterson
Connor McKenzie
Scott Miller
Matthew Mitchell
Wayne Muff
John Mylan
Benjamin Newman
Max Nicoll
Will Padgett
Jacob Papenfuss
Tanja 'Tikal' Pattberg
Griffin Percy
Justin Puopolo
Leo Ratner
Shawn Ricci

Michael Sanders
Joseph Saxton
Alexander Schraff
Stephen Shiu
SilentS (JGW)
Dan Silvester
James Simon
Mike Sleeman
Alexander Smith
Natalie May Snook
Brad Sparks
Michael Speare
Benjamin Spence
Ebony Stark
Stuart Stretch
The return of the Rt Hon Sir
    James Rich Esq
Owen Tilling
Mark Tolladay
Tommy Törnqvist :)
God Emperor Donald J. Trump
Bracken Walsh
Andrew Waltman
Snykier Zaerthaun
Janez Zonta

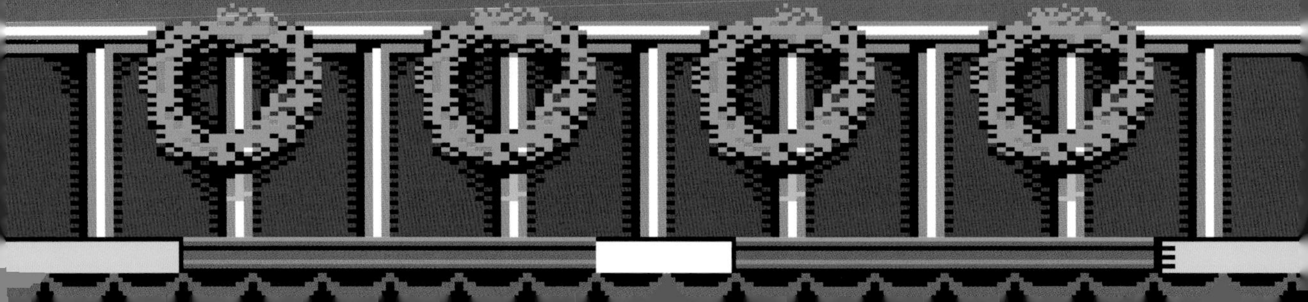

CONTENTS

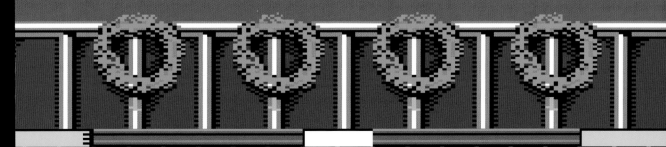

INTRODUCTION

HELLO! AND WELCOME to the second volume of terrible old games you've probably never heard of, a further compendium of some of the worst games to ever be sold for money.

Years ago, when I first started sifting through the video game industry's bins, I thought I'd only find a handful of obscure games so atrocious that they were no fun whatsoever. I was very wrong, and this second book is a testament to the sheer amount of horrifying dross that was shovelled into our faces and called entertainment.

As before, this isn't intended as some kind of definitive guide to the very worst. It's a showcase for games that are not only awful, but that I found interesting in some way. And they're all obscure titles, so you won't find the same tired games that appear in all online lists. There's no *Big Rigs: Over the Road Racing* or *E.T.* in here.

For inclusion as a main entry in this book, a game must have been:

■ released some time between 1980 and 1995 inclusive
■ sold commercially
■ released for a home computer format, not a games console
■ so utterly terrible that it would be almost impossible for a reasonable person to enjoy playing the game.

As well as games so bad they make your eyes itch, I've asked some interesting people what their most disappointing game purchase was. We've all felt the pain of spending cash on an absolute stinker, and these brave people have agreed to share their personal stories of pain with us. The criteria for these games are looser than those for a main entry, mostly as I discovered someone had paid money for *Kris Kross: Make My Video* and I couldn't pass that opportunity up.

I've also sprinkled some articles about other facets of gaming trash throughout the book, because variety is the spice of tat as well as life.

Finally, I'd like to express massive thanks to everyone who pledged for this book via Unbound.

Without you this book wouldn't exist, and the games within would remain mostly forgotten. And we should never let these games slip from history just because they're terrible, they're old, and you probably haven't heard of them.

Stuart Ashen
Norwich, 2017

AUF WIEDERSEHEN PET

FORMAT: BBC MICRO / ACORN ELECTRON
YEAR OF RELEASE: 1985
DEVELOPER: BOB CARR
PUBLISHER: TYNESOFT
ORIGINAL PRICE: 7.95 POUNDS

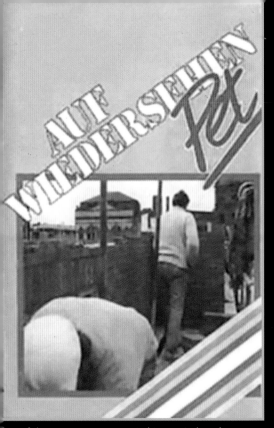

One of the worst game covers in history. It doesn't even show any of the actors from the TV series!

LET'S START WITH a quick history lesson! *Auf Wiedersehen, Pet* was a BBC comedy-drama that initially ran for two series in the mid-eighties. It focused on some construction workers from Newcastle upon Tyne who moved to West Germany in search of work, and it was extremely popular.

Home computers and tie-ins were also popular and the appropriately Newcastle-based Tynesoft acquired the licence, dropped the comma and gave us *Auf Wiedersehen Pet*.

How does one go about converting a TV show based around a building site to a computer game? Tynesoft decided the answer was a set of three mini-games loosely based around what the most popular character Oz might get up to on an average day. Or, at least, what he might get up to on an average day if he lived in some kind of weird nightmare-world.

When the game loads you're offered some very hard to read instructions stretched across the screen, none of which actually help you too much with the gameplay. It does, however, become painfully obvious that the game is written in BASIC, which is never a good sign.

The game itself begins with a painfully off-key attempt at the show's theme tune, 'That's Living Alright', and that's the only sound in the game other than sparse beeps. Amazingly for the time a story cutscene then plays out and we see Oz being overlooked by Eric, the German foreman, as he builds walls. It makes no real sense but it shows us that Oz is portrayed as a tiny little stick man and Eric as a giant head, and it gives us an idea of the weirdness to come.

The first stage involves Oz trying to build as many walls as possible on a yellow screen covered with a blue grid. Presumably as some kind of metaphor, multiple giant Eric heads are impaled on the grid and must be avoided as you build upwards. There is also a rain of deadly trowels each larger than Oz himself – dropping from

The instructions form an eye test from hell.

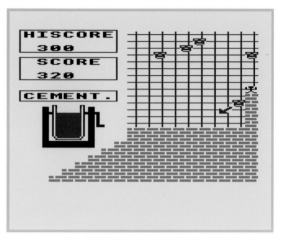

Stage 1: Oz is sadly building a wall directly into one of Eric's many, many heads. He is doomed.

above, which must be avoided. Oz lays bricks as he walks and cannot stop moving at any point. He can build upwards, forming the wall, but any movement to the sides causes him to immediately fall. You basically have to pick a vertical line without an Eric head, then build straight upwards, hoping that no random trowels appear and cave your head in. If Oz does hit anything or fall, then the stage immediately ends and you move on to Level 2. If you succeed in building a wall, then you get some points and have to repeat the task until you do fail.

There are several major problems with this first level. The first is that Oz moves extremely quickly, and the controls, like many BASIC games, are

horrifyingly unresponsive. These two problems compound each other to the point that you will almost certainly fail, not because of poor judgement but because you held down the 'up' key and it took so long for the game to respond that you missed where you wanted to go and instead built directly into one of Eric's lethal heads. The average length of a failed attempt at the level is four seconds – that's how fast things move.

You are then treated to another bizarre cutscene showing a Düsseldorf skyline, as text explains that Oz has finished work and is off to the local Bier Keller for some liquid refreshment.

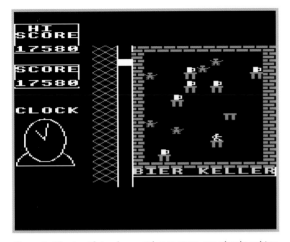

Stage 2: The terrifying barmaid monsters are slowly taking over the screen.

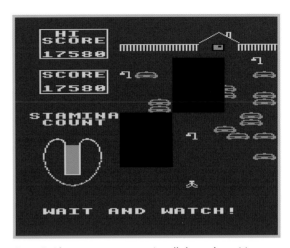

Stage 3: I hope you can memorise all the car's positions as the whole screen will be black soon. And this is one of the easiest random car placements I've seen!

The Bier Keller looks like a dark basement, interspersed with a few tables with pints of lager on them. Oz must run around, again at high speed and unable to stop, and pick up all the lager. Why Oz always controls like he's got a rocket wedged between his bum cheeks is never explained.

Things are made slightly more difficult by the barmaids, who, in keeping with the nightmare-world vibe, appear to be green multi-tentacled alien creatures. They appear out of thin air in random places and must be avoided at all costs. If Oz collects all the lager, then points are given and the level restarts, but touching

the walls, tables or monstrous barmaid creatures means it's straight on to Stage 3. But, as with the first level, the sluggish controls are the real enemy. They're a little better this time round but still give nowhere near an acceptable level of response.

Before Stage 3 is a final weird cutscene of Oz stumbling around drunk in the middle of a road. This apparently raises the ire of the local police, who he must now avoid on his walk back to his place of lodging.

And my goodness, what a walk home it is. This third stage is one of the most horribly designed

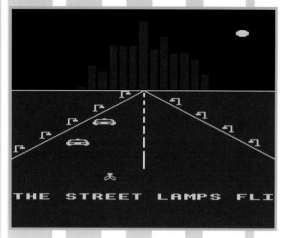

The third cutscene. I'm surprised Oz dodging the traffic wasn't one of the stages – perhaps that seemed too normal?

sub-games I've ever encountered, and I've spent several years playing the worst games I can find.

The Düsseldorf police seem very keen on catching Oz, to the extent that they've sent out dozens of cars which they've parked outside his house in random places. Using his patented method of sliding around at high speed unable to stop, Oz must avoid the cars, street lamps and a security guard to get to his front door.

This would be bad enough given the awful controls, but the street lamps slowly go out before you can move, leaving almost the entire screen totally black. You need to have memorised a route to the front door, which you take with no visual cues whatsoever. If that sounds almost im-

possible to you, then congratulations – you're correct and have worked out something that eluded the game designer! The slightest touch of any object and you are unceremoniously dumped straight back to the title screen without so much as a 'Game Over' message.

Your only chance of making it through is to have failed miserably at the other levels and have a very low score. The fewer points you have, the fewer police cars appear and the fewer lights go out. If you do manage to reach the front door, then some text appears saying 'WELL DONE KIDDA' and it's back to the first stage for another playthrough to get your score up. What joy.

But there's another horrifying fly in the *Auf Wiedersehen Pet* ointment. The lights take a ridiculously long time to go out and fill part of the screen in black, and they go out individually. It can take a full 90 seconds of lamp-watching tedium before you actually get to play. But when they are out, Oz starts moving upwards automatically without warning. As you have no way of knowing how many lamps will go out, chances are you'll be bored and not notice him moving in time to stop him walking into something because that can happen within literally one second.

Auf Wiedersehen Pet is infuriating dross. It's three abysmal mini-games based around you desperately trying to control a tiny, sliding stick man who moves like a greased cheetah. The controls simply don't work properly and there is no fun to be had at any stage. And as an adaptation, it makes little sense – it's less *Auf Wiedersehen Pet* and more *Oz in Purgatory* as he builds walls between giant heads, runs around stealing lager from teleporting mutants then attempts a walk of faith through a black void in a hellish mockery of his daily routine. (That would make an interesting plot idea for a comeback special.)

And now: the twist! I've been describing the Electron version the whole time. Playing on a BBC Micro is slightly faster and thus even more difficult and frustrating! Just when you think it couldn't get any worse, it blasts through the bottom of the barrel and down to the Earth's core.

REVIEW SCORES

Electron User called *Auf Wiedersehen Pet* 'a promising game for all ages, with plenty of variety'. I imagine they also lived in a magical land full of pastel-coloured talking dinosaurs.

OTHER VERSIONS

Both the Spectrum and the Commodore 64 were cursed by *Auf Wiedersehen Pet*. They're essentially the same game with the same character graphics, presumably as the BASIC code was ported across to both. In both versions the instructions are much easier to read, and the game moves slower and is easier as a result. Both have more music, which is a shame. Tragically, the Spectrum version supports the Currah MicroSpeech unit, an evil squawking box that attempts to mimic human speech. Fortunately, said noises were kept to a minimum, with just an occasional 'you lose' or 'well done'. Interestingly, all three versions were written by Bob Carr. *Auf Wiedersehen Pet* was his last game, which is probably a blessing for everyone.

PLAY THESE GAMES INSTEAD

There are no other games similar to *Auf Wiedersehen Pet*, and for good reason. Just play *Exile* or *Citadel* because they're still great.

RECREATE THIS GAME IN REAL LIFE

Become trapped in a hell dimension that exists to mock our own, and then attempt to go about your normal day. Remember to strap banana skins to your feet and run everywhere at full speed.

AND THERE'S MORE

Auf Wiedersehen, Pet was brought back to television in 2002, where it ran for a further two series. Unsurprisingly, they didn't release a tie-in game for the PlayStation 2.

BARRAVENTO

FORMAT: COMMODORE AMIGA
YEAR OF RELEASE: 1993
DEVELOPER: HITEK SOFTWORKS
PUBLISHER: HITEK WORLDWIDE
ORIGINAL PRICE: UNKNOWN

CAPOEIRA IS A MARTIAL ART from Brazil that combines fighting and dance. Practitioners constantly move back and forth in a rhythmic motion known as ginga, and wait for an opening to deliver a decisive blow. It's an acrobatic art that's very impressive to watch, so it's a shame that a game based on it manages to be such an artless mess.

When the game loads you're presented with the game's story while some moody synth music plays. Oddly the text is in Portuguese even if you selected English at the start, but the gist is that every 10 years all the masters of capoeira get together and fight to the death, with the survivor being crowned the Barravento. And – would you believe it! – this time you've qualified and get to murder a load of other people while probably being killed yourself. Great.

Your first fight is against a bald, bearded guy wearing green trousers. It takes place in front of a badly recoloured digitised photo of what appears to be a giant bell. Both fighters start moving in a ginga and the animation is pretty good – I suspect the sprites have been rotoscoped, an animation technique where an artist draws over real-life footage. Unfortunately everything falls apart as soon as you start moving. The fighters just slide across the screen with the same ginga animation as when they stand still. Then you try and fight, and the game falls apart further into constituent atoms of incompetence.

There are only a few offensive moves, and you can only do two of them with any reliability. There's a forward kick which is very effective and usually damages your opponent. There's a leg sweep which nearly always lands and trips the

The militant wing of the Ministry of Silly Walks claims another victim.

enemy up, but does no damage. And that's it fo moves you can actually trigger. There's a differen front kick, a ground-based split kick, a reverse kick and some kind of weird hand thing, and they all just kind of occasionally happen when they fee like it. At one point I seemed to be able to get the reverse kick to work one time out of three b pressing back + fire, but then it stopped working so I had to abandon that theory.

It's also possible to block by holding back which makes you invulnerable to your opponent' front kicks, but you have a tendency to get stuc in that position for a while. By far the best strat egy is to shuffle forward continuously tapping the fire button, which spits out a constant stream o front kicks. In fact the collision detection is so un predictable that it's pretty much the only effective strategy.

If you beat the bald, bearded man in green trousers, then you move on to the next fight which takes place on a bridge. Your opponent is.. a bald, bearded man wearing purple trousers! Yes indeed, there is only one enemy in *Barravento*

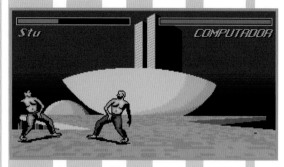

The annual crotch-grabbers convention takes place this year in front of a giant bowl containing two VHS tapes.

Our hero takes a photo of his dead opponent to post on Twitter. Also: what's wrong with the fallen man's arms?

You just have to fight the same man in front of different backgrounds. The only thing that changes is his trousers. Your health does not regenerate between levels so you really need to avoid getting hit, which due to the random collision detection isn't really something you can actively choose.

So you've got a fighting game with totally botched controls and messed-up collision detection, and no variety whatsoever. What could make it worse? How about a constantly looping five-second piece of background music that's just a load of annoying plinky notes? Yep, that'll do it.

Barravento is the very worst commercially released fighting game on the Amiga. It somehow manages to be less fun than *Dangerous Streets*, which is a feat so impressive it would cause the gods of Olympus themselves to despair. Even the simultaneous two-player mode manages to be a tedious experience.

The bald man hits the floor heavily! And loses no energy at all.

Hitek never produced or published another game. I really hope their one attempt was a budget game, because the thought of anyone paying full price for *Barravento* is deeply upsetting.

FIGHTING GAME CHARACTERS THAT USE CAPOEIRA

Richard Meyer (*Fatal Fury*)
Bob Wilson (*Fatal Fury*)
Elena (*Street Fighter*)
Eddie Gordo (*Tekken*)
Christie Monteiro (*Tekken*)

REVIEW SCORES

None. I believe the game was only released in Brazil, which let the magazines dodge a *Barravento*-shaped bullet.

OTHER VERSIONS

None. But there is a free to play online browser game called *Capoeira Fighter 3* which is basically *Barravento*, but good! There's also a PC game called *Martial Arts: Capoeira*, which is less good.

WHAT DOES 'BARRAVENTO' ACTUALLY MEAN?

It translates as 'the turning wind' and is the name of a classic Brazilian film from 1962.

PLAY THESE GAMES INSTEAD

Shadow Fighter is a fun, Amiga-only fighting game with heaps of variety. And there's a great version of the superb *Panza Kick Boxing* (known as *Best of the Best: Championship Karate* in the USA).

RECREATE THIS GAME IN REAL LIFE

Dance around a bit wearing pyjama bottoms. That's it really.

ChinnyHill10 lives on YouTube at https://www.youtube.com/c/chinnyhill10, where he plays and compares many retro games, recording entirely from original hardware rather than emulation. Updates can be found on Twitter via @ChinnyVision.

THE MOST DISAPPOINTING GAME I EVER BOUGHT

BY CHINNYHILL10, INTERNET ENIGMA

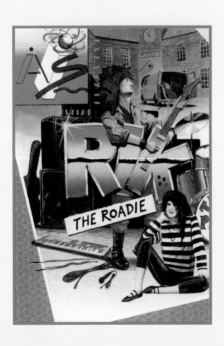

THE ROADIE

RIK THE ROADIE
FORMAT: AMSTRAD CPC
YEAR OF RELEASE: 1988
DEVELOPER: ALTERNATIVE SOFTWARE
PUBLISHER: ALTERNATIVE SOFTWARE
ORIGINAL PRICE: 1.99 POUNDS

IT MUST HAVE BEEN slim pickings on the Friday evening in 1989 when I purchased *Rik the Roadie*. These days you can get hold of any game you like in an instant, but back then the big rack of budget games in our local newsagent was only replenished once a month at best. So the inevitable day would come when your choice of game was somewhat limited. Games you'd previously passed by would become a viable option, as walking out without a game was unthinkable.

So that's how I ended up with *Rik the Roadie* for my Amstrad CPC. The cover certainly didn't appeal. It was the era of pop music producers Stock Aitken and Waterman, not middle-aged men with purple rock mullets.

The instructions explain that you play the eponymous Rik, a roadie for the band Alternative Rock. They promise a three-part game involving a driving section, a section where you move equipment from the van into the venue, and finally a section where you set up the equipment. Everyone loves a driving game, so at least the first section sounded promising.

The game loaded up on first attempt, which was a good start as Alternative Software unusually insisted on doing all their tape duplication in house. Whereas the likes of Mastertronic would proudly boast they used BASF tapes duplicated to the highest standards, Alternative copied their own tapes in the back of their warehouse in Pontefract. It wasn't unusual to find one of their games with the label half glued, the B side missing or, in the case of one Adrian Mole game,

half the game's multi-load sections absent.

The game starts with a simple screen and a jolly tune. The music is on a 10-second loop and you'll be hearing a lot of it. Press fire, and the fun (or lack of it) begins. Big colourful graphics and a top-down view of a road. You must drive your van 200 miles to the venue within a time limit. There are no lives; all you have to do is beat the clock. Crash and you'll lose time.

There are four lanes of traffic and your van has a top speed of 127mph. The road is entirely straight and the only depiction of speed is a flashing red-and-white border. All the other traffic on the road travels at the same relative speed, and as long as you are doing 1mph you can overtake everything else. In fact, between 1mph and 100mph, the comparative speed of your van to the other traffic does not change. Reach 100mph and there is a one-off speed increase.

Steering on your van is responsive; however, braking is not. Your van brakes at the same rate it accelerates. This, combined with the game's strange relationship with relative speed, means that even if you are doing 1mph, you will run into the back of other road users unless you come to a complete stop, which you can't do in time unless you are doing less than 30mph.

So your only option when faced with oncoming traffic is to steer out of the way. This might not be a problem except that the game can often block the road ahead with four cars side by side, all moving at the same speed. First, you won't be able to stop in time to avoid hitting one of the cars, and second, as the cars are all moving at the same speed, there is no way past. They'll happily travel for the full 200 miles all side by side. If you crash into them, the game might reset their positions, it might not or it might spawn another group of four cars in front of you.

All the time, you are running against an in-game clock that starts at six minutes. During the driving section, this clock runs at one game second to three real seconds. However, for Levels 2 and 3, the game clock actually does run in real time. Possibly a coding issue?

Occasionally nothing appears to happen at all. The road is straight and the only thing to crash into is other traffic. I managed to drive for a whole minute in real time without having to touch the steering.

After 200 miles and what feels like several years, Level 1 is complete. After a brief bonus screen, you are on to Level 2. You have to carry the equipment from the van into the venue. You do this by moving one foot after the other before you run out of 'endurance'. Yes – it's a *Decathlon*-style, waggle-the-joystick mini game. Left to move your left foot, right to move your right foot. You must reach the stage door before the endurance meter runs out and beat the time limit. Again, there are no lives but you lose time every occasion you drop the equipment due to your 'endurance' running out.

The critical thing here is that it seems to be impossible to complete the section unless you start waggling the stick before the game is ready. The trick appears to be to just waggle the joystick as fast as you can and not to stop for any reason at all until the level is completed. Not exactly a masterpiece of gameplay design.

Oddly, 'carrying heavy items' is a gameplay mechanic missing from most modern games.

High-speed action as Rik apparently drives through a ZX Spectrum loading screen.

Should your patience stretch to getting to Level 3, you have to set the audio levels for the gig. Too low and the audience won't be able to hear; too high and all the fuses will blow. Keep the levels in the yellow and all will be well. This section is over in seconds, and if you have enough time left on the game clock, you can blow all four fuses and still complete the game.

Achieve this and Alternative Rock will treat you to a performance. And by performance, I mean a static picture of the band that flashes while the background music keeps playing. By then you'll have had seven and a half minutes of gameplay and heard the same loop of music approximately 400 times.

At least by completing the game you will have amassed a high score to be proud of. I achieved 9,270 points, which placed me at the bottom of the high-score table at position 56. Position 55 requires 80,000 points. Top score: 90 million points! You'd probably have to play *Rik the Roadie* for a full month without a break to reach that.

Rik the Roadie was also released on the Spectrum, Commodore 64 and BBC Micro. Every version is unmitigated rubbish. The C64 version has the distinction of having some of the worst music I have ever heard the system's SID chip produce.

Back in 1989 I completed the game within half an hour of purchase and felt so cheated I returned it the next day claiming it did not load. Finally, I was rid of the game... well, until the day in 1993 when *Amstrad Action* magazine put it on their covertape as the only game that month. Bah!

Genius original gameplay concept, or the artist's day off?

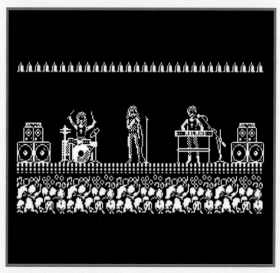

Here's the completion picture, so there's no reason for you to play the game. Ever.

DISTRIBUTED IN AUSTRALIA BY ECP

CODING AND GRAFIX
BY
GLEN COGHLAN
ROBERT RICHARDSON

(C) MCMLXXXIX SECTOR SOFTWARE

BELIAL

FORMAT: COMMODORE AMIGA
YEAR OF RELEASE: 1989
DEVELOPER: SECTOR SOFTWARE
PUBLISHER: ECP
ORIGINAL PRICE: UNKNOWN

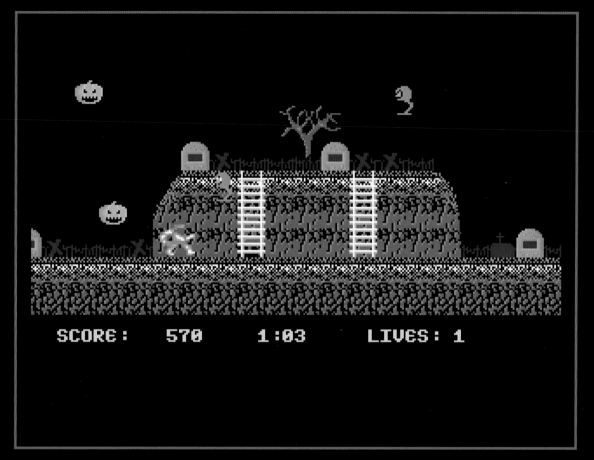

That's our cucumber-wielding hero towards the left. He will be dead within a second.

FIRST THINGS FIRST, for people unfamiliar with the hardware of the Commodore Amiga: there is absolutely no reason why *Belial* should look the way it does. It isn't restricted to four specific colours like early PC graphic modes. The Amiga standard low-res screen mode allows 32 colours to be picked from a palette of 4,096, meaning somebody deliberately picked those hues. Incredibly, the game looks like this on purpose.

A blatant rip-off of Capcom's popular *Ghosts 'n Goblins*, *Belial*'s total lack of quality is legendary. In fact, I didn't include it in the first *Terrible Old*

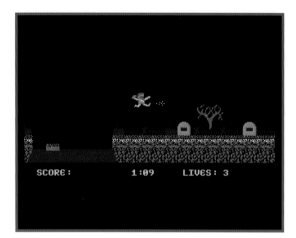

The rarely seen mid-air sneeze.

That fireball is moving extremely fast, and our hero will be dead in a fraction of a second.

Games as it seemed so much like a public domain game, I wasn't sure it had ever been sold for money. But I now have proof that it was sold in Australia as part of a compilation called 1990 Amiga Pak, so there's a tragic possibility that someone spent money on this game.

Did I mention that this game looks the way it does on purpose? I did? Good. Just making sure.

Belial puts us in control of a little guy in armour, whose sacred quest is to run to the far right of the playing area. Various nasty beings attempt to kill him dead with a single touch – zombies, ghastly spitting plants, Halloween pumpkins, tiny wizards and a weird green hopping creature. Our hero's only defence is a cucumber, which seems to allow him to fire a small cloud of dots across the screen. It's never made clear what this represents – it could be a miniature swarm of moths, or he could just be sneezing really violently.

Surprisingly, the controls are actually quite tight and responsive, and the collision detection seems to work as it should. However, the jumping is fiddly, which means it's unnecessarily difficult to leap over the occasional deadly hole in the floor. But the major gameplay problem is the horrifying difficulty. Unlike the two-hit system in *Ghosts 'n Goblins*, one touch from any enemy spells instant death and a restart from the beginning of the level. Factor in the way enemies constantly appear everywhere, and that some of them can spit bullets at the speed of sound, and

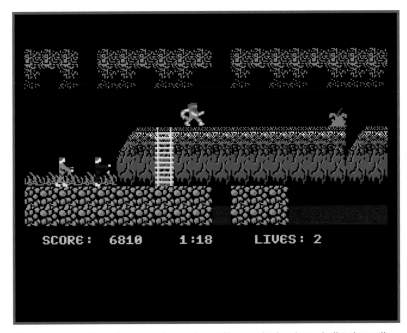

That plant looks like a Xenomorph egg. Soon it'll spit a high-velocity bullet that will kill our hero instantly!

you've got a recipe for a big ol' frustration cake.

The action mostly takes place in a stripe across the centre of the screen, where the hideous colour choices pierce straight through your retinas and into a part of your brain that should never be stimulated. I know I've said this before, but I feel it bears repeating: it was a deliberate decision to make the game look like this. Meditate on that for a moment.

The audio is almost beyond belief. There are no sound effects, but a tune plays constantly and cannot be turned off – and it's an instrumental version of 'The Model' by German electronic band Kraftwerk! Quite how synth-pop from 1978 is supposed to fit a medieval zombie battle, I have no idea. And it doesn't even loop properly, leading to several seconds of silence every minute or so.

There are three levels in *Belial*: the world's ugliest graveyard, a very blue cave, and some woods that lead into another cave. At the end of Level 1, you face a green demon that bounces around the screen while firing blobs at you, an obvious knock-off of the Red Arremer demon from *Ghosts 'n Goblins*. At the end of Level 2, you face two of them, and – yes indeed! – at the end of Level 3, you face three of them. They fill up the screen while zombies walk on from the right, meaning you have a life expectancy of about three seconds in the incredibly unlikely event that you've got the patience to make it that far.

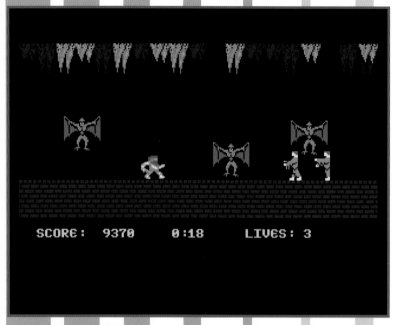

This is the very end of the game, featuring three boss demons! Our hero stands no chance and will be dead in seconds.

And this leads us to another of *Belial*'s major failings. Each level is ridiculously short, to the extent that the entire game can be completed in less than four minutes – in fact there's a time limit of 90 seconds for each level! Not that you're ever going to manage to finish it without using its built-in cheat mode, unless you've got the combined patience of all the saints from human history. Your reward is a screen of text saying, 'Congratulations! You have rid the land of those evil demons called Belial. Now everyone can live without fear.' So we can surmise that the point of the game was to hunt down and kill the six flying demon bosses, which it would have been nice to have known beforehand.

Belial is so slight that it's barely anything at all. For your money, you've got a monstrously annoying, almost impossible game that lasts four minutes if you do manage to get good at it. And worst of all, as I believe I previously mentioned, it was purposely made to look this ugly.

Amazingly, the Australian company ECP that published 1990 Amiga Pak were bought out by major publisher Electronic Arts in 1990. I can only presume that they wanted the legal right to destroy the master copy of *Belial* to make sure it could never be released again.

RECREATE THIS GAME IN REAL LIFE

Wear old-fashioned red/blue 3D glasses and bang your head against a wall while an episode of *Most Haunted* plays in the background.

PLAY THESE GAMES INSTEAD

The Amiga has a fairly decent version of *Ghosts 'n Goblins*, which is probably your best bet. There's also a dodgy version of the sequel, *Ghouls 'n Ghosts*, but if you've got your heart set on playing a knock-off, try Codemasters' *The Sword & the Rose*.

REVIEW SCORES

None. Fortunately, this is a rare game that very few people will have wasted money on.

OTHER VERSIONS

There are no known versions of *Belial* for other systems, so that's good.

OTHER GAMES IN THE 1990 AMIGA PAK

Alpha-1: A dull shoot 'em up.

Caverns of Palle: An appalling, weird *Rygar* rip-off with static enemies and graphics stolen from *Black Tiger*.

Voyager 1: A terrible platformer with graphics stolen from *R-Type*.

Invasion: An almost exact clone of tedious C64 crosshair shooter *Saucer Attack!*.

Select team for Zimbabwe						Wk
R Name	H	Bat	F	Bowl	F	Fd
A Arnott	R	Opener	1	–	2	2
B G.Flowe	L	Opener	1	–	2	3
C Watson	R	Opener	2	–	1	2
D Burmest	R	Opener	2	–	2	2
E Kampbel	R	Stroke	1	–	2	2
F Pycroft	L	Stroke	2	Med	1	3
G Houghto	R	Stroke	1	W/K	2	3
H A.Flowe	R	Stroke	1	W/K	1	1
I Brain	R	Stroke	3	–	2	1
J Dyson	L	Stroke	2	Spin	2	2
K Shah	R	Middle	2	Spin	3	1
L Crocker	R	Middle	2	Med	2	1
M Brandes	R	Middle	2	Med	2	2
N Traicos	L	Tail	3	Fast	1	1
O Pierson	R	Tail	1	Fast	3	1
P Jarvis	R	Tail	1	Fast	1	3
[P]k [D]p [N]m [A]m [V]w [C]n						
1 players 1 bowlers 0 W/K						

This is as exciting as it gets, which is to say not very exciting at all.

LOWEST MAGAZINE SCORE CORNER

AMIGA FORMAT MAGAZINE
Score: 5%
Games: *Test Match Cricket* and
Treble Champions 2
Format: Commodore Amiga

These are two very similar sports management games released by the same company at the same time. And they're both slow, empty, almost non-interactive text-based lumps of tedium. You'd probably have more fun looking through a spreadsheet. The review described *Test Match Cricket* as 'the work of a con artist', which sounds a little extreme until you discover that Challenge Software released five of these identikit boredom fests.

butterfly

© Hugh Davis 1983

BUTTERFLY

SPECTRUM 48k

BUTTERFLY

PULSONIC

This cover is clearly supposed to represent the game being played on a TV, but it contains colours that the ZX Spectrum cannot display. A pox on your house, Pulsonic.

HAVE YOU EVER WANTED to experience the life of a spider stuck on a window, slowly starving to death? If so then seek psychiatric help rather than attempting to play *Butterfly*. It may work to that premise, but the execution is so poor that it will fail to solve your weird arachnid cravings.

The name *Butterfly* is misleading as you actually control a spider attempting to eat multiple butterflies. The spider has been cursed with an insane metabolism which requires it to eat 12 insects every minute to stay alive. Fortunately there are an unending number of butterflies around to munch on. Unfortunately, the spider is trapped on a window in an incredibly unsafe house.

Our spidery protagonist can safely move around the top of the window, but touching the sides or the bottom results in instant death and the end of the game. At the sides are some curtains, which if disturbed instantly send out a purple Pac-Man-style monster, which gobbles the spider up. And the windowsill at the bottom is connected to a live electrical wire which shocks the spider to death. The owner of the window needs to sort these problems out before it affects the price of their house.

Upon loading the game you're subjected to 20 seconds of horrible beeps as the title screen slowly draws itself. And upon starting the game, it becomes painfully apparent that this is a very simple game written in BASIC.

The screen is mostly empty, except for some coloured lines that represent the window. The spider is present, although it looks more like a dreadlock wig with googly eyes stuck to it, and there are two butterflies flittering about which look more like bow ties. The characters flicker about exactly like you would expect from a BASIC game. You can move the spider in four directions and there's a delay between pressing a button and something happening. So far so awful.

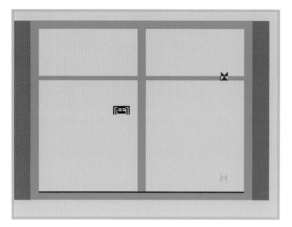

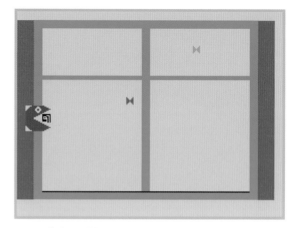

Action-packed is not a good phrase to describe Butterfly.
Also notice the hideous colour clash on the blue butterfly.

*Our eight-legged hero is consumed by the monster that lives
in the curtains. Those curtains seriously need fumigating.*

The entirety of the game involves chasing the butterflies around the screen in an attempt to catch 12 before a minute passes. There are always exactly two butterflies on screen at any one time – when one is eaten another appears in a random position. This sounds like it should be an easy task, but there are major hurdles in the way which make *Butterfly* an utter chore.

The first is, of course, the unresponsive controls. But far worse is the movement of the butterflies, which flicker about entirely at random so it's impossible to predict where they're going next. You just have to move towards them and hope. But the third hurdle is the worst by far – the spider and the butterflies move at exactly the same

speed. This makes catching them entirely down to random chance, and thus makes the game utterly pointless.

If the random numbers fall in your favour and you do manage to catch a dozen butterflies, the time limit extends and you just keep playing until you fail to catch enough. Oddly, when you inevitably fail, the purple Pac-Man appears out of nowhere and eats the spider. Does this mean it's actually the Angel of Death, come to claim the spider as it starves? Or is it some kind of Overlord of the Window, and the spider is actually being forced to eat the butterflies under penalty of death? This poses more questions than a little game about a spider should.

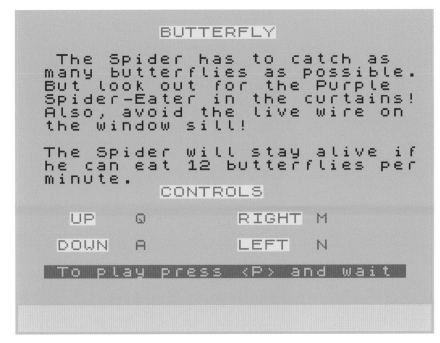

Here are the instructions, since all the screenshots look pretty much identical.

if you get a six – it would certainly save time. It really feels like a weak type-in game you'd find listed in the back of an old copy of *Personal Computer World*.

Pulsonic was one of the first budget software houses and released a slew of games for the Spectrum at the same time. Someone actually wrote in to *Crash* magazine to complain that they'd reviewed too many of their games in the June 1984 issue! It didn't work out for Pulsonic, though, and they disappeared before 1985. And *Butterfly* was Hugh Davis's only game, so we never got a sequel where the spider busts out heavy artillery and fights back against the purple Pac-Man monster.

If you're wondering why I haven't mentioned the sound it's because there isn't really any to speak of. You get a beep if a butterfly is eaten and some more beeps at game over. Perhaps the programmer used up his beep allowance on the title screen.

Butterfly is an astonishingly pointless game. You may as well just roll a dice and say you win

15 OTHER GAMES WHERE YOU PLAY AS A SPIDER

Arachnoid (1982, Commodore VIC-20)
Apple Cider Spider (1983, Apple II / Commodore 64)
Black Widow (1983, Arcade)
Splat! (1983, ZX Spectrum)
Pajaki (1988, Atari 8-bit)
Spider Web (1989, DOS)
Spidertronic (1988, Commodore Amiga / Atari ST)
Pajaki II (1996, Atari 8-bit)
Spider: The Video Game (1997, Sony PlayStation)
Spider's Web (2001, Windows)
Deadly Creatures (2009, Nintendo Wii)
Spider: The Secret of Bryce Manor (2009, Android / iOS)
Along Came a Spider (2009, Xbox 360)
Itsy the Spider (2010, iOS)
Spider: Rite of the Shrouded Moon (2015, various)

REVIEW SCORES

Crash magazine was not impressed, awarding it 17% and a general rating of 'Rubbish'.

Personal Computer Games were also not *Butterfly* fans, saying that Pulsonic should be 'severely reprimanded for offering this particular specimen to the public' and giving it 2/10.

Sinclair User said what we were all thinking: 'What one would expect to find as a magazine listing, not as a commercial program.'

And *Your Computer* plainly stated, '*Butterfly* and *Worm Attack* just aren't that interesting,' *Worm Attack* being a substandard *Snake* clone also from Pulsonic.

OTHER VERSIONS

None. For some reason the 'spider on a window eating insects' genre never took off.

37

RECREATE THIS GAME IN REAL LIFE

Put a spider on a window. If it goes near the curtains, eat it.

PLAY THIS GAME INSTEAD

If you want to eradicate some insects, classic flower-grow-em-up *Pssst* will provide at least a million times more entertainment than *Butterfly*. And if you want to control a spider, the maze game *Splat!* is still good fun to this day.

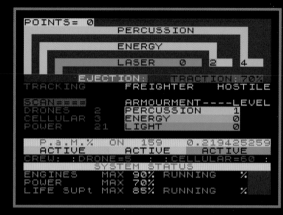

I started the game, pressed the number 3, then no buttons seemed to do anything. Hooray for Kosmik Pirate!

LOWEST MAGAZINE SCORE CORNER

CRASH MAGAZINE
Score: 3%
Game: *Kosmik Pirate*
Format: ZX Spectrum

Crash's least-favoured game is the horribly obtuse *Kosmik Pirate*, a painfully failed attempt at a starship simulator. If you like stunningly dull games full of misspelled text that you can barely read, then... actually still avoid this game, as it's genuinely dreadful. *Crash* nicely summed it up as 'ill-executed rubbish', which I certainly can't disagree with.

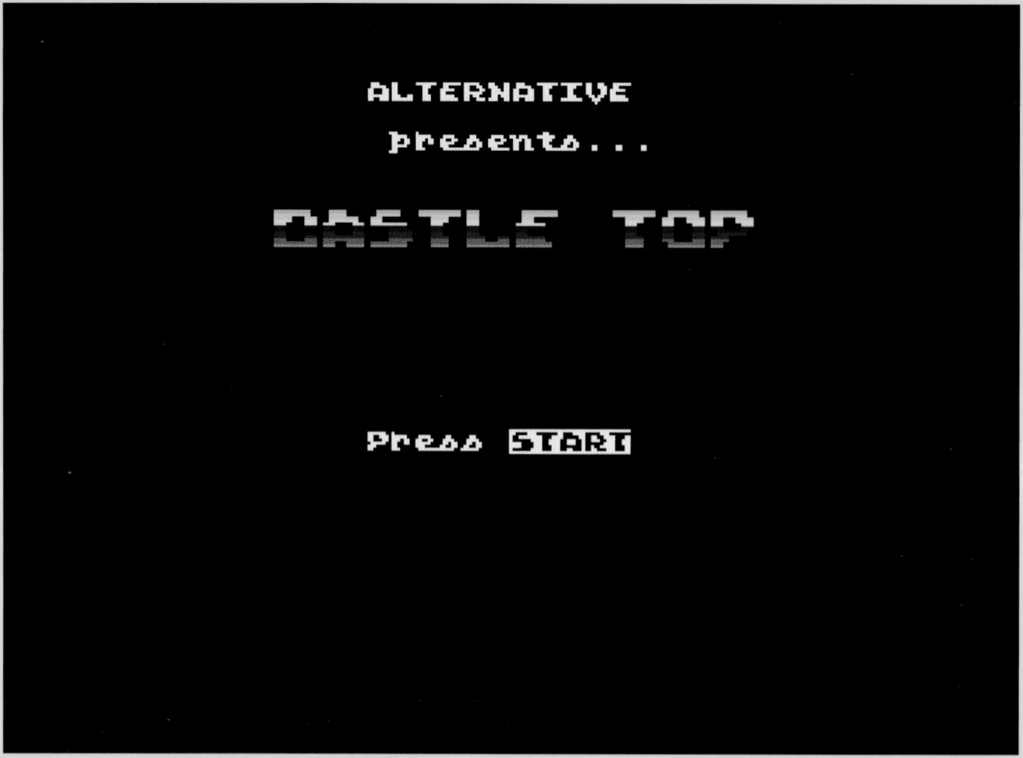
ALTERNATIVE
presents...
CASTLE TOP
Press START

The two covers for Castle Top. *Some mail-order-only cover art was... interesting in the early days of video games.*

T'S ALMOST FORGOTTEN NOW, but the 1983 game *Hunchback* was big news when it first appeared in the arcades. It's a simple platform game in which you have to guide Quasimodo across a castle's battlements to ring bells and rescue his beloved Esmeralda. There was a slew of disappointing unofficial conversions and clones released for the home computers of the time – in fact my ZX Spectrum came bundled with the appalling *Punchy*. But *Castle Top* may well be the very worst.

Originally released via mail order by DBM Software in 1986, *Castle Top* had cover art that could charitably be de scribed as 'charming' But the following year it was picked up for a wide release by budget game publish ers Alternative Software and as was customary i was given a new cover that misrepresents wha you do in the game.

The story stays close to *Hunchback*, excep that Esmeralda is called 'Jessica' and you play as a knight rather than Quasimodo. Well, the instructions claim you play as a knight, bu said knight has a suspi ciously hunched back And due to the poo graphics and odd colour choices, he looks like some kind of zombie.

In fact the first thing that hits you on starting *Castle Top* is how incredibly neon it is. Everything is bright purple or green, as if the screen was stitched together from a pair of those fluorescen socks that were popular in the early eighties. The second thing that hits you is an arrow, because the game is incredibly difficult.

Your character shuffles around on one leg or top of the castle's battlements. Jumping over the deadly gaps is much harder than it appears, a they have a hitbox much larger than the actua

The middle platform is on fire, and there's another arrow coming in at the top right. And everything is horribly coloured, of course.

random, meaning you can't plan ahead and just have to jump about in the hope that the favour of the arrow gods falls upon you.

Between the random arrows and total inability to work out where the edges of the holes are, your first game of *Castle Top* will last less than 15 seconds and be no fun at all. Subsequent games will not last much longer, and will be even less enjoyable.

The sound is also horrible, consisting entirely of odd glitchy noises and irritating swan whistle effects every time you jump or die. It's like an annoying noisy toy you give to the young child of someone you dislike.

holes. Which is a technical way of saying you instantly die if you get too close to one of them and can't tell exactly where they begin and end. And while you're wrestling with that, there's a constant rain of arrows to contend with.

Each arrow is aimed at one of the three safe spaces between holes, and will instantly set light to the entire platform for a second when they hit them. And their targets are picked entirely at

someone you dislike.

Castle Top is maddeningly infuriating – in fact it may be the most annoying game I've ever played. Despite repeated attempts, I always lost all three lives without completing Level 2. In order to see the third screen and beyond, I had to cheat using saved memory states in an emulator!

Here's what the game has in store past the first level...

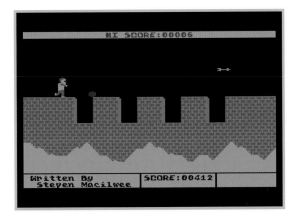

Sticks and stones may break my bones, but an arrow to the back of my head will shatter my skull and pierce my brain.

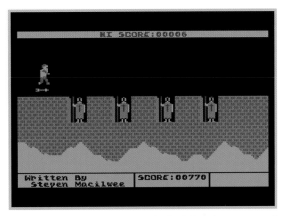

The dreaded Pokey Stick Men, who had their faces removed due to budget cuts.

■ Level 2 – You're attacked by waves of two horizontally flying arrows while you jump more holes. Trying to jump the arrows and holes at the same time is a nightmare.

■ Level 3 – Similar to Level 2 but with more holes, and a constant slew of arrows that are randomly high or low.

■ Level 4 – Stones, which inexplicably float over the holes, are rolling towards you. (They could potentially be very slow-moving cannonballs.) You have to jump them while arrows are fired at the back of your head, and keep an eye out for extra stones that roll in from behind. Despite the number of deadly projectiles, this is the easiest level!

■ Level 5 – Exactly the same as Level 1, except instead of a tower there's a staircase at the right-hand side of the screen.

■ Level 6 – The dreaded Pokey Stick Men appear and hide in the crenulations poking their sticks upwards. Fortunately their movements are rhythmic and not random like everything else in the game, so you can at least plan how to pass them. You do also have to contend with random high and low horizontal arrows being fired at you though.

■ Level 7 – The Pokey Stick Men do their thing while arrows are fired from behind you at your feet. It's insanely difficult and I gave up at this point before I punched my monitor.

I'm not going to mince words – I hate this game. It's an exercise in frustration and futility, and no fun whatsoever. The only thing I like is the amusingly mundane name. It takes place on the top of a castle, so it's called *Castle Top*! Not 'Battlements' or 'Castle Rescue'... just *Castle Top*. It's like calling *Bioshock* 'Underwater Rooms'.

Steven Macilwee wrote a slew of terrible games for the Atari 8-bit machines, including racing game *California Run*, driving simulation *Speed Run*, platform game *Monkey Magic* and action game *Domain of the Undead*, which contains the flickering skeletons that inspired this book's title. He really was the king of awful Atari games.

Ocean Software later decided to develop an official conversion of *Hunchback* for the 8-bit Ataris, and incredibly gave the job to Mr Macilwee! The result was never released, but a prototype version is available on the internet. It's pretty poor but far, far better than *Castle Top*.

PLAY THESE GAMES INSTEAD

If you want a good platform game for your Atari system, you can't go wrong with *Pitfall II: The Lost Caverns* or *Montezuma's Revenge*, both of which are fantastic versions.

REVIEW SCORES

None of the Atari magazines reviewed *Castle Top*, despite it reaching number 11 in the best-selling Atari games chart in March 1988! Perhaps if they had reviewed it fewer people would have wasted their money on it.

OTHER VERSIONS

Castle Top was confined to the Atari 8-bit computers, possibly as some form of quarantine.

RECREATE THIS GAME IN REAL LIFE

Climb up a building site when drunk while friends throw bottles at you. Fall to your death as quickly as possible.

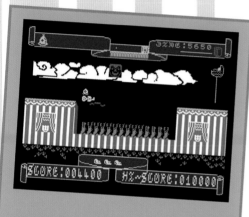

SOMETHING TO BE THANKFUL FOR

At least *Castle Top* lacks the terrifyingly low-quality sampled speech that plagued *Punchy* for the ZX Spectrum. Its screeching cries of 'HA HA! HA HA! ROCK THE BABY!' still haunt me to this day.

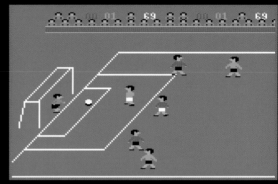

I wish football players really stood around in that pose.

LOWEST MAGAZINE SCORE CORNER

AMSTRAD ACTION MAGAZINE
Score: 0%
Game: *World Cup Carnival*
Format: Amstrad CPC

Yes, that is a zero score for the first-ever officially licensed FIFA World Cup game. The intended game was so heavily delayed that it couldn't be released in time for the 1986 World Cup. In a fit of desperation, the publisher essentially re-released a two-year-old game, *World Cup Football*, at a higher price and pretended it was a new title! *Amstrad Action* was not impressed with this blatant rip-off and withheld all points from it.

Daniel can be found on YouTube at www.youtube.com/user/OfficialNerdCubed and on Twitter @DanNerdCubed

THE MOST DISAPPOINTING GAME I EVER BOUGHT

BY DANIEL HARDCASTLE, JACK OF ALL TRADES

ODDWORLD ADVENTURES
FORMAT: NINTENDO GAME BOY
YEAR OF RELEASE: 1998
DEVELOPER: SAFFIRE CORPORATION
PUBLISHER: GT INTERACTIVE
SOFTWARE CORP.
ORIGINAL PRICE: 19.99 POUNDS

IN 1998, MY INCOME was 50p a fortnight. This wasn't because I was trapped in the worst job of all time... I was simply nine years old. My low (yet mercifully tax-exempt) pocket money meant that any game purchase was literally months of deliberation, research and self-control. One weak moment in the corner shop could put me back weeks.

My pride and joy at the time was my Game Boy. Sure, it was battered, scratched and had a battery cover as stable as one of Peter Molyneux's design documents, but it was mine and I loved it. I still get weepy every time I see the colour greyish-green.

I was, however, behind the times. The PlayStation was out, and with it came graphics and games far beyond the reach of my 160x144 pixel screen. Full 3D worlds? The Game Boy blurred when the 2D ones moved.

My Game Boy and I hit a rough patch. I spent as much time as I could playing on PlayStations, be they in a store or at the house of literally anybody who owned one. (I made a lot of friends that year.) *Crash Bandicoot*, *Tomb Raider* and *Final Fantasy* started to replace *Tetris*, *Zelda* and that Mario & Yoshi game that's disappointingly a puzzler and not a platformer.

But then, on a spontaneous trip to Electronics Boutique, I saw something that would change my entire world. *Oddworld Adventures*. A Game Boy port of one of my favourite PlayStation games, *Abe's Oddysee*. This was it. This was my entry into the world of PlayStation. I marched to the till and paid a full year's salary for the game.

Experts concur that you should probably pull the lever to progress.

Do you know how hard it is to truly disappoint a nine-year-old? Sure, take a toy away and they'll be upset, but they'll start spinning or pretending they're a dog or something and be back up in no time. No, I'm talking real, serious, 'Santa isn't real' disappointment. The kind that aches deep, deep down forever. The kind of disappointment that forces you to grow up to be able to deal with it.

That night I became a man.

I don't even know where to begin with *Oddworld Adventures*. Hell, neither did the developers. It starts by taking a cutscene from the middle of *Abe's Oddysee* and turning it into a slideshow of text, and then it dumps you into the game. Why a cutscene from the middle of the PlayStation game? Because that's where this game takes place. No Rupture Farms. No saving Mudokons from being turned into lunch. Just Abe farting around a much smaller version of the Paramonian Temple until it ends.

Graphically, it's comically poor. Backgrounds are non-existent, the terrain is an absolute mess and enemies look like a collection of haunted tree stumps. Abe himself looks like he was drawn on a Friday afternoon and has less frames of animation than a three-sided zoetrope. There are levers embedded in terrain that are physically impossible to see, bombs still use the 'hit them while they're green' mechanic – which is great on a black-and-white screen – and, most confusingly of all, rocks and meat come from identical sacks, look identical and you only know when you've thrown the wrong one when a tree stump is eating Abe's leg.

The game itself is a faithful recreation of about 50% of the PS1 version. *Oddworld Adventures* is a precision platformer, and as such the developers thought it would be a great idea to get rid of the ability to walk. You can sneak, but to do that you have to hold Up and Left/Right on the D-Pad at the same time. This is remarkable because it's insane. Half of the time it simply won't work and Abe will either stop walking or sprint off the cliff edge you've been creeping towards like a lemming crossed with Usain Bolt.

Jumping involves pressing a direction and the jump button at exactly the same time to a level of precision that even German engineers would think is a bit harsh. Whoever thought that jumping up should be the default while jumping left/right needs an extra button should be locked in a box and flung into the ocean to make sure they never make a video game again. Also, if you pause the game mid-jump, Abe will jump again when

Don't wake the pooch! (As it will slaughter you instantly.)

If only Daniel had seen this tip when he was young. (Although, in his defence, it doesn't mention opening doors.)

you un-pause. This can help skip huge swathes of levels so, in my opinion, it's the best part of the game.

The game maps the 'Chant' ability to the Select button and somehow I never noticed. Seriously, you need to chant to open some doors but I just thought the game was broken. What's worse is that I still managed to progress! If you enter and leave a screen enough times, the game sometimes wigs out and opens doors it isn't supposed to. Combining this with the pause-jump meant that I spent hours and hours slowly crawling my way through the game without realising I was missing a whole mechanic. When somebody at school told me about the chant, I faked a stomach ache, rushed home early and restarted the game properly.

I finished the whole game in just under 30 minutes, then told my mum I felt fine and went back to school.

Oddworld Adventures was a bad idea to begin with. Trying to cram a PC and console game that uses 14 buttons onto a handheld with just 8 is asking for trouble from the get-go. Having to cut major mechanics, story and 95% of the game out should have been the warning signs that this may not come out great. Then again, these are developers that couldn't tell the difference between rocks and meat, so I'm surprised they could program at all.

In the end I swapped the cartridge with my friend for his copy of *Metroid II*. He claimed he liked it. I recently heard that he's in prison. I'm not surprised.

These are doors that lead to different places, not 2001: A Space Odyssey-*style obelisks.*

Two killer dog-things and a mine. The best solution: play something else.

HIDEOUS COMMERCIAL FAILURE CORNER

Let us take a moment to remember the Commodore 64 Game System, a version of the Commodore 64 without a keyboard that could only play games from cartridge. It was released in Europe in 1990 as an attempt to compete in the console market.
Its main features included:

painfully outdated 8-year-old hardware

the same price tag as a full Commodore 64

almost no games – most existing cartridges
couldn't be played as they required a keyboard

a horrible, 2-button Cheetah joystick that broke quickly
and was almost impossible to replace

a UK release date two months after the Sega Mega Drive.

```
PRESS -T- FOR T2
PRESS -M- FOR  MODERN MUSIC
PRESS -I- FOR IMAGE MAKER_
```

Its killer app was to be a graphically impressive game based on the huge movie *Terminator 2*. When it was released, the cartridge required a keyboard to start the game.

Ah, C64GS. You may not have been the worst console ever released, but... actually, you probably were.

CHEF

FORMAT: ORIC 1 / ATMOS
YEAR OF RELEASE: 1984
DEVELOPER: ERIC CAEN
PUBLISHER: SPRITES
ORIGINAL PRICE: UNKNOWN

THE ORIC-1 WAS an interesting computer that is now all but forgotten. Made by Tangerine Computer Systems, it was a little more powerful than the 16K ZX Spectrum models and sold quite well for the time. Its main problems were its horrible calculator-style chiclet keyboard and an excruciating error-checking bug that frequently caused user-written programs to fail when saved to tape. This was a particular problem as type-in programs were extremely popular for the Oric – commercially recorded cassettes were in the minority compared to source code printed in magazines and books. An upgraded version, the Oric Atmos, gave the machine a proper keyboard and a nifty red-and-black colour scheme. It's a lovely little unit and one of the favourite computers I own. Although, amazingly, they failed to fix the error-checking routine, so great work there, lads.

The Oric-1 was big in France, to the extent that it was the bestselling computer there in 1983. Sprites were a French company that released several commercial games for the local market, including the excellent *Space Panic*-inspired *Psychiatric* and *Honey Kong*, the best *Donkey Kong* clone for the system. And they also released *Chef*, which is, as they say in France, 'un jeu terrible'.

You play Luculus the chef, and you have to make an omelette with ostrich eggs sent from the upper floor. This sounds easy but there are several glaring problems. The first is that the people above actually throw the eggs down, forcing Luculus to run about like an idiot, catching them

Luculus is wearing high heels, which probably isn't helping him manoeuvre on the conveyor belt.

being in a kitchen, he's on a conveyor belt. And the third is that there's a rival chef above who throws banana skins to make you fall over. I think we have to consider two possible explanations for these problems: either everyone really hates Luculus, or he's not really a chef at all. You never hear about Gordon Ramsay being locked in a factory while people pelt him with big eggs.

Chef starts off very well – the title screen is well drawn and a jolly, blippy little tune plays to welcome you. Then you get a nice, brightly coloured screen explaining the plot and the controls. Then you start the game and suddenly you're fighting to control a demented cook pratting about on a

SCORE :0000000 CHEF CUISTOT :0000000

Leap, Luculus, leap! Maybe you can escape the screen and end up in a better game.

CHEF

VOUS ETES LUCULUS LE CHEF CUISTOT ET
VOUS DEVEZ FAIRE UNE OMELETTE AVEC LES
OEUFS D'AUTRUCHES ENVOYES DE L'ETAGE
SUPERIEUR.ATTENTION UN CHEF CONCURRENT
ESSAYE DE SABOTER VOTRE OEUVRE EN VOUS
LANCANT DES PEAUX DE BANANES ....

COMMANDES: < .... GAUCHE
                          > .... DROITE
copyright
sprites 84   SHIFT .... SAUT
P.S:VOUS ETES SUR UN TAPIS ROULANT
QUI BOUGE DE FACON DISCONTINUE !!!

Here are the instructions, in French, naturally. They state that the conveyor belt moves discontinuously, and they're not kidding.

The game screen is almost entirely black. Luculus himself at least looks like a chef, and the eggs are fairly egg-shaped. The banana skins could be tarantulas of some kind but we'll ignore that. Our hero chef slides around at high speed in an almost uncontrollable manner – you can force him to slide the other way, and sometimes he'll stop for a second, but there's no predicting it. If you release the controls, he moves to the left, presumably due to the conveyor belt. The belt itself makes no sense – when banana skins hit it they stay still for a couple of seconds, then suddenly slide over to the left. The same thing happens to Luculus if he does stop moving. It's all very odd.

In order to score a point you have to catch an egg exactly in the pan, which is entirely down to luck as it's impossible to line things up precisely due to the unpredictable controls. You can also catch the banana peels as they fall but if you touch one when it's reached the conveyor belt – or nearly reached it, the collision detection is a bit off – then Luculus falls and you lose a life. When that happens, a little seven-note tune plays, which is the only sound in the entire game except for a rare blip noise which seems to play at random. It's also possible to jump over the banana skins as they slide along the conveyor, but a better idea is to hold down the jump button and watch Luculus leap about like an idiot. It makes it impossible to score points, but it's very amusing.

Eggs and peels fall from the ceiling more frequently as time progresses, but you'll have lost any interest before that really becomes an issue. You'll have stopped paying attention to the screen and started wondering when Luculus will pick the smashed egg shells out of his saucepan, because that's going to be a serious task before cooking can start.

I kind of wanted to like *Chef*. It has some charm: the title screen is great, the little tunes are amusing, I like the main sprite... but the actual game is so simple yet fundamentally broken that there's nothing there to enjoy. It may be one of the most pointless pieces of software ever sold. This is not an excellent game.

The game's programmer, Eric Caen, left a message in the code saying he wrote it in three days, which may go a long way to explaining things. He also put in his phone number so people could call him and talk about programming or hacking, which is friendly if a little reckless. He also wrote the bizarre chicken simulator game *Tendre Poulet* and the awful fighting game *Lancelot*, both for the Oric. *Lancelot* is another mostly unplayable mess, but it is possibly the only video game where you have to fight and kill Snoopy.

FIVE ORIC GAMES THAT ARE REALLY GOOD
Rat Splat
Zorgon's Revenge
L'Aigle d'Or
Don't Press the Letter Q
Xenon 1

PLAY THIS GAME INSTEAD
If you want some food-preparation antics for your Oric, *Mr. Wimpy* is the answer. It's a great clone of the arcade game *Burger Time*, but tied in with a British restaurant chain where all the food is like the sort of stuff your friend's mum would cook for you in 1982.

REVIEW SCORES
I checked the French Oric magazines but found no trace of a review for *Chef*. Although, their stock in trade was more to supply software through type-in listings rather than rate existing programs.

OTHER VERSIONS
Chef never cooked for any system other than the Oric.

RECREATE THIS GAME IN REAL LIFE
Break into a kitchen and run around while the staff throw things at you. Then fall over.

THE MOST DISAPPOINTING GAME I EVER BOUGHT

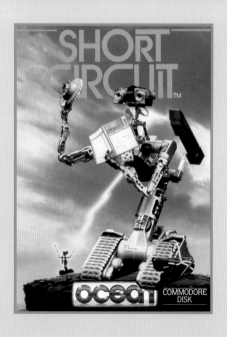

BY JIM STERLING, GAME CRITIC AND #1 KISS BOY

SHORT CIRCUIT
FORMAT: COMMODORE 64
YEAR OF RELEASE: 1986
DEVELOPER: OCEAN
PUBLISHER: OCEAN
ORIGINAL PRICE: 8.95 POUNDS

AS MY ABILITY to earn money has increased, so too has my ability to purchase games. The law of averages suggests that the more recent the era, the more times I've been disappointed by a game I've bought.

Considering I was dirt poor as a child – during the preferable era that Stuart desires – options for stories of childhood disappointment are limited. I was, in fact, delighted by my acquisition of *Primal Rage* despite history's condemnation. If that didn't let me down, what could?

Sod it, let's go with *Short Circuit* for the Commodore 64.

The title screen is fantastic. Just look at it!

Now, to say I 'bought' this particular cassette would be to widen the definition of basic merchantry. It was part of a huge, filthy, plastic sack of similar cassettes and I'm not entirely sure where it came from. At any rate, there were some gems inside. *Wizball* was a wonderful game that united the family for rare, rare moments. Then there was one I'll never remember the name of. All I recall is that it was top-down, had a golem in it, and its manual taught me the word 'hindrance'.

Inside this sack were many great wonders, though it was always a gamble as to whether the game would load. We never did get *Gremlins 2* working, but we scored it big with a text adventure version of James Herbert's horror novel *The Rats*. It was pretty harrowing stuff, all considered. We failed every scenario and it ended with a lot of us being eaten by rats.

Some of these may have been for the Spectrum or the Amstrad, by the way. My memory's incredibly hazy. I remember *Seymour Goes to Hollywood*, though I had to do a bit of googling to recollect the exact name. It was supposed to be part of the *Dizzy the Egg* series, but there were creative

On my first play I decided to go left, which meant an instant game over with no warning. Within ten seconds of starting. THANKS.

someone reading this knows what I'm talking about and is either sharing my pain or sneering at my failure to solve such a simple puzzle; that aforementioned law of averages suggests I'm ad-dressing both.

And that's why *Short Circuit*, for the purposes of this book and the criteria it requires, is going to act as my most disappointing game purchase. Do I get my 50 quid now or after this is published?

differences about it being set in the real world so Seymour was created. He looked weird. Creepy weird.

Anyway, the point is that I don't know what happens in *Short Circuit*. If there's a way to pro-gress past the first minute or so, it's a revelation to me. I remember rolling around as Johnny 5 in the facility where he first becomes self-aware, then the path gets blocked by one of the military robots that mirrors the player's every move.

There was no way to block its movement, no way to trick it or get it to reverse its course. Both my brother and I tried in vain – for no small amount of time – to crack that secret. I'm sure

Jim did not get 50 quid at all. All he got was this picture of a teletext Boglin.

This is the dreaded mirroring robot Jim mentions. I spent about 5 minutes pratting around before looking up the solution, which would have been impossible in pre-internet days.

STUART SAYS

The game with the golem in it that Jim couldn't remember was *Druid 2: Enlightenment* for the Amstrad CPC. I knew which game it was despite never having played it. I need help.

FACT FACT FACT

To get past the mirroring robot, you have to find a 'Jump ROM' by examining a robot chassis in the background. You then have to press the space bar twice, which changes Johnny 5 to jump mode. You can then get past the robot by going to the top of the screen next to it, and quickly jumping down then right. This is the first puzzle in the game and it really is weirdly obtuse.

NTO-THE-SCREEN RACING GAMES on the Commodore 64 were largely an awful affair. For whatever reason, they were a mass of technical messes and gameplay nightmares. The poor C64 had to suffer atrocious versions of *Crazy Cars*, *Chase HQ*, *Hard Drivin'*, *Turbo Esprit* and *WEC Le Mans* (covered elsewhere in this very book). But for my money, the very worst is *Cisco Heat*.

Cisco Heat began life as an arcade game, and it wasn't great from the start. Based around the idea that the entire San Francisco police department was having a massively dangerous race across the city, it worked much like every other sprite scaling racing game with a time limit and Hi / Lo gears. The only interesting addition were 90-degree corners, but they just ended up being an annoyance. It was fast and smooth but suffered from a limited view ahead due to a huge central car sprite and a constantly dipping and rising road.

In order to succeed as a game, the Commodore 64 conversion would need to be fast and smooth with responsive controls. It would be a technical challenge on the ageing hardware, but programmers had nine years to get to grips with the machine – surely they could do a half-decent job? The answer, of course, is very much in the negative.

Cisco Heat is so technically awful that it's almost literally unplayable. PC players these days are disappointed if a game runs at 30 frames a second rather than 60; *Cisco Heat* averages just under 4fps for the movement of the cars and road. Just imagine how unresponsive it feels to play a game running that jerkily. But the lights on top of your police car flash at approximately 3fps, so that's something!

Strap yourselves in, folks – this one's a doozy.

Special mention must be given to the graphics. The cars look fine, if a little boxy, but the city in the distance seems to have been mashed together from giant Stickle Bricks. It's the bizarre technical problems that really top things off though.

There's a bit in beloved TV sitcom *Father Ted* where the titular priest is trying to explain how perspective works to the dim-witted Father Dougal by saying that some toy cows are very small while the real ones outside are far away. Dougal fails to understand, and sadly it seems the makers of *Cisco Heat* were in similar state. The cars in the

The rival police cars take some road with them wherever they go, for efficiency purposes.

Objects viewed through your windshield may appear larger than they actually are.

far distance are frequently larger than ones closer to you, which makes the whole game look farcical. In addition, the rival cars have a big grey square around them, which overwrites the scenery, and roadside objects are drawn on top of each other. It's an absolute mess.

The 90-degree turns of the arcade are replaced with huge stop signs that appear out of nowhere and which you can't possibly stop in time for, causing a huge crash. And that's about all you have to worry about really, as just driving down the centre of the road avoids all oncoming traffic. Which is useful, as the farcically low frame rate means you couldn't possibly react in time to avoid them and the collision detection seems to work at random anyway.

You may be wondering how you turn corners if you just drive straight down the middle of the road the whole time. Well, you don't have to, as there are almost no corners! There are signs advertising that a corner is coming up, but they nearly all lie. This is a racing game where steering makes no real difference – if anything, it actually makes you more likely to crash. It ends up being a mindlessly easy slog through each painfully long level, until of course you smack into one of the sudden stop sign intersections. Level 3 adds obstacles in the road which, much like the stop signs, you frequently can't react to in time.

The audio isn't a joy either. Oddly staccato, thumping music plays at all times and there's a little whoosh sound effect if you closely pass by another car. I won't hold my breath for a collectible vinyl release of the soundtrack.

Here's a fun gameplay idea – huge commands that you can't possibly respond to in time!

Any ideas as to what this obstacle is supposed to be? A jukebox perhaps?

And to top it all off, if you complete the game, you get a thoroughly bizarre end screen. Three clones of the same policeman stand in front of the Golden Gate Bridge and a sign saying 'THE END' while some text congratulates you for winning and breaking every rule in the book. And a thumpy version of 'The Star-Spangled Banner' plays in the background, as if you've done your patriotic duty by illegally racing around like a lunatic.

And there you have it: a mostly incomprehensible racing game with absolutely no sense of speed or the positions of cars on the road, that runs so slowly it's more like an ugly slideshow. It was also insanely expensive, just to rub poisonous salt into the already gaping flesh wound.

Cisco Heat is the very worst commercial racing game on the Commodore 64. Except for maybe

Hard Drivin', depending on your point of view. And *911 Tiger Shark*, but that's not really a racing game. And I'm going to stop thinking about C64 car-related games now, as it's beginning to make my brain melt.

PLAY THIS GAME INSTEAD

Buggy Boy, without question. It's another arcade conversion, but this time the Commodore 64 port is brilliant. Smooth, fast and loads of fun.

You won the race! But are unbelievably bad at your job.

REVIEW SCORES

Commodore Force magazine was less than impressed, commenting that *Cisco Heat* was 'undoubtedly one of the worst games I've had to play' and awarding it a miniscule 7%.

Commodore Format was equally un-amused, flicking a 12% rating in its direction and saying that the only positive point was 'it comes in a nice box'.

The mighty *Zzap!64* was kinder, giving it 30%, although their claim that 'you'd have more fun being fitted up by the West Midlands Serious Crime Squad' implies that they didn't actually like it very much.

OTHER VERSIONS

The ZX Spectrum version is a hideous jerky mess but is still smoother and more playable than the C64 port. Plus it has proper corners! The Amstrad version is basically a far prettier version of the Spectrum attempt, and is the best of the 8-bit conversions.

The Commodore Amiga version is a good deal better. It's still a bit choppy but very nice visually, and it plays much better than any of the 8-bits. Sadly it's spoiled by being overly difficult. As was common at the time, the Atari ST version is similar but with inferior sound, but it is one of the few released games that takes advantage of the hardware in the upgraded STe machines.

FURTHER PLAYING

Cisco Heat's programmer, James MacDonald, wrote five other middling-to-poor games for the Commodore 64. And incredibly, after *Cisco Heat* he was given the job of porting the super-popular *Street Fighter II* to the system! The result is a buggy mess. The most fun game he made was *Postman Pat III*, which is just a bit poor as opposed to a full-on digital war crime.

RECREATE THIS GAME IN REAL LIFE

Get a small child to make a city out of garish knock-off Lego bricks, then put a toy car in front and take a photo. Stare at the photo and shake it four times a second while banging a metal tray on your head.

PRESENTS

D E A T H K I C K

by   D.J.SHAW.

THE YEAR 1984 was very early days for fighting games. It was the year *Karate Champ* – the first modern one-on-one fighter as we understand it Sega's 1976 *Heavyweight Champ* was a bit too simple) – was released in the arcades. And in the same year we had *Kung Fu Master*, a side-scrolling beat 'em up based on the Bruce Lee film *Game of Death*, which proved very influential. It certainly seemed to influence D. J. Shaw, as *Deathkick* is essentially a poor attempt to recreate it entirely in the Amstrad's built-in Locomotive BASIC.

According to the game's instructions, the evil masked warrior rules the Kingdom of Yabbu, but our hero believes himself to be the rightful ruler, so he needs to beat him up. In order to face the masked warrior in combat you need to pass through seventy rooms spread between three stages. I'm not entirely sure this is how a kingdom's ruler is traditionally chosen, but whatever works.

After *Deathkick*'s title screen, you are presented with... another title screen! And this one is absolutely hideous. It's essentially made of two different screens mashed together and stretched vertically, presumably by using the Amstrad's double-width graphic Mode 2 with graphics designed for Mode 1. And the assault isn't just visual – as the protagonist shows off his moves in the left half of the screen, an insane cacophony of whooshing, crunching and bleeping sound effects play. And if you leave it long enough, some weird discordant music starts to play, so it's best to start the game as soon as possible.

The first thing that hits you about the game proper is how ugly it is. The backgrounds are a

The chances of this game being officially endorsed by the estate of Bruce Lee are remote at best.

load of repeated squares and @ symbols, and the characters are terribly drawn – the main character looks like he's pulling an air guitar solo when he's standing still. But let us look beyond its superficial ugliness, and uncover the further ugliness that lies beneath the surface.

As the game starts our hero respectfully bows

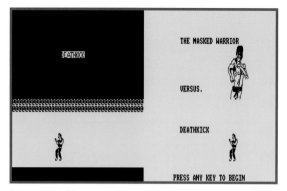

The second title screen. The masked warrior does not look like the leader of a kingdom to me.

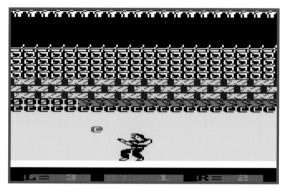

The dreaded purple @ symbol! The bane of all martial artists.

which is strange as there's nobody else there. Then we're given control, and we learn that the controls are odd – they're based around the Amstrad's numerical keypad, and each move has its own button. And as with many BASIC games, they're painfully unresponsive, forcing you to hold them down for half a second before anything happens. The most puzzling thing is that the main character can somehow somersault on the spot without moving forward even an inch.

The titular deathkick is effectively the game's special move. Jam down the 5 button, and our hero eventually leaps into the air with a flying kick while a loud whooshing noise plays, which acts as a kind of smart bomb, destroying certain opponents no matter where they are on screen. However, you only get three deathkicks per stage,

and as the first stage is thirty rooms long, you can't rely on them much.

The first room has nothing in it and can just be walked through. The second room, however, has a vexing puzzle – a floating purple @ symbol! If you hit it with a high split kick, it disappears and you get some points. I can't help but feel that Bruce Lee films were generally more exciting.

Room 3 is where the excrement really collides with the rotary cooling device. Upon entering, you hear a whining noise, and a man with his leg outstretched flies across the screen and straight into your character, killing him instantly and taking one of your three lives. The whole thing takes less than three seconds. The room is immediately re-set and the chap comes flying at you again, and it's at this point you realise that the duck button

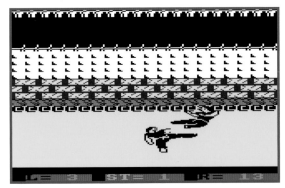

Deathkick beats flying kick. This looks much more exciting than the game actually is.

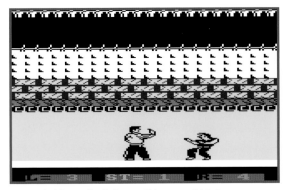

A man holding a leaf. Or possibly a small bird.

has been disabled. In fact, most rooms disable all but a few of your controls. There are two moves that can beat the airborne adversary: the

deathkick, of course, or a well-timed high split kick. Due to the sluggish controls, it's incredibly difficult to time anything, but it turns out that just holding down the kick button causes it to repeat and gives you a higher chance of success.

Most rooms contain a different obstacle, and the trick is in working out which move to perform to survive. Here are all the other rooms I encountered in my multiple plays of *Deathkick*, and how to beat them.

■ Another empty room. Just walk through it.

■ A man holding a leaf Cossack-dances across the screen towards you. Hit him with a low kick. The flying kick guy from the previous room appears again immediately after, and you must kick him as before.

■ An @ symbol falls from the ceiling and turns into a dragon that runs at your legs. If you hit it with a low kick, another one appears, and they seem to keep coming forever. I couldn't work out how to beat this one as all the moves other than the low kick were disabled, and if the dragons kill you once, they disappear and never return.

■ A naked-looking man stands absolutely still, and a shuriken flies towards you at high speed. Simply duck the shuriken and walk up to the man and punch him, as he never moves at all.

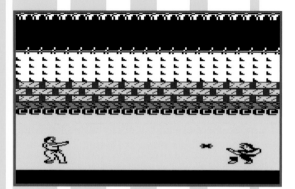

Our hero ducks a shuriken. To duck he removes one of his legs and the status bar.

classic *Karateka* for the Apple II, a technically inferior computer due to it being seven years older!

Blaby Computer Games was mostly known for their games on the Dragon 32, but they did release seven other Amstrad games of varying quality. Their pretty good *Q*Bert* clone called *Jumpman* is their most remembered... for inexplicably having Mario on the cover and thus totally misleading purchasers.

■ A wall of @ symbols blocks the way, sometimes cyan and sometimes red. Just walk up to it and punch it. Be wary though – sometimes a shuriken flies at your back as soon as the wall is hit, and you have to duck quickly.

■ The word 'BOW' is written in small letters. You need to hold down the large enter key and bow, or you drop dead in a few seconds.

And that's all I saw because the game crashed whenever I made it to room 21. I never even saw the second stage, which apparently takes place in the Temple of Yabbu! I'm guessing the background is a different colour.

Deathkick is an utter technical mess as well as a poorly designed lump of digital tedium. It's hard to believe that it came out the same year as the

REVIEW SCORES
There are no known reviews of *Deathkick*, which was a lucky escape for the magazines of the time.

OTHER VERSIONS
Deathkick was ported to the Xbox One in 2016 as part of the Blaby Collection, which could only be purchased digitally... Nope, I'm completely lying, there are no other versions of *Deathkick*.

PLAY THIS GAME INSTEAD
An official conversion of *Kung Fu Master* hit the Amstrad in 1986 and it's very good.

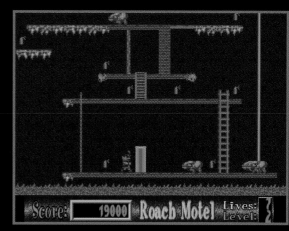

Here's Roach Motel, *one of the games that works. It's not bad!*

RECREATE THIS GAME IN REAL LIFE

Punch a wall while making crazy beeping noises. If the wall breaks, get someone to throw an unshelled conker into your back.

THOSE CONTROLS IN FULL

1 – Low kick
2 – Duck
4 – Punch
5 – Deathkick
6 – Somersault
7 – High split kick
0 – Walk forwards
. – Walk backwards
Small enter key – Block / Stun
8 – Jump
Large enter key – Bow

LOWEST MAGAZINE SCORE CORNER

CU AMIGA MAGAZINE
Score: 6%
Game: *Top 100 Games*
Format: Commodore Amiga CD32

Possibly the most ironically named game product in history, *Top 100 Games* consists of 100 Amiga public domain games that a company called US Dreams stuck on a CD. The vast majority were utterly awful, and the few good ones (the late Edgar Vigdal's superb *Deluxe Galaga* is on there) could be bought cheaply from a public domain library or legally copied from a friend, making the £14.99 price tag look very steep. Also, a large proportion of the games need a mouse to play, which the CD32 does not have as standard, and several games don't work at all. Great job, lads!

Daniel makes historical documentary-style gaming videos on YouTube at youtube.com/ djslopesroom, and can be found on Twitter @SlopesGameRoom.

THE MOST DISAPPOINTING GAME I EVER BOUGHT

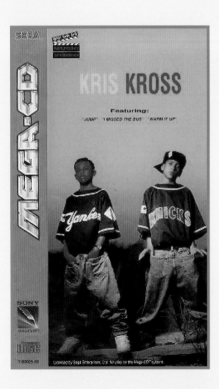

BY DANIEL IBBERSTON, GAMING VIDEO PRODUCER

KRIS KROSS: MAKE MY VIDEO
FORMAT: SEGA MEGA CD
YEAR OF RELEASE: 1992
DEVELOPER: DIGITAL PICTURES, INC.
PUBLISHER: SONY IMAGESOFT
ORIGINAL PRICE: 39.99 POUNDS

It's our painfully hip host, Boyd Packer! And a robot dinosaur toy for some reason.

 WHEN I FIRST got asked to talk about the biggest disappointment in my gaming life, several games came to mind. Perhaps I could talk about *Altered Beast*, *The Flintstones* or even *Superman* for my beloved Amstrad CPC 464. But, if I did, I would not only be lying to you good people... I would be lying to myself!

Back then I was between the ages of five and seven and I didn't know any better – I would actually find enjoyment in games like the ones previously mentioned. Plus they only cost a couple of quid or were completely free thanks to my Amstrad dual tape deck hi-fi (with light-up soundbars, might I add).

For me a game was only a disappointment if it didn't work, which was the case with my copies of *Out Run* and *Ghostbusters 2*. To give a completely honest answer, I would need to leave the home computer era, travel past my beloved Mega Drive generation and stop in 1993 when I finally managed to get my hands on the Mega CD.

The Mega CD is known for having a library of rubbish games, and as I look at the majority of the ones that I once owned, they mostly fall into two categories: ports of classic Mega Drive games or crappy full motion video games. At the time I

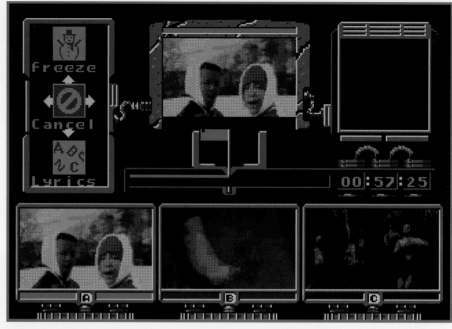

The video editing screen. I think the footage marked B is someone's foot.

was very much into the latter. It was games like *Road Avenger*, *Night Trap* and *Sewer Shark* that blew me away as a kid with their high-quality videos and CD audio. Sure they have dated terribly now, but they were quite groundbreaking at the time and they left me with a hunger for more.

At this point in my life, kid-friendly hip-hop music was also becoming a bit of an obsession, and although I had not read any good reviews for what looked like a totally radical game, *Kris Kross: Make My Video* really did grab my attention. This all happened after I saw Michael Jackson live at Wembley Stadium with support from Chris 'Mac Daddy' Kelly and Chris 'Daddy Mac' Smith (aka Kris Kross), and needless to say, I became a super fan!

I quickly turned all my clothes back to front (which was what the duo was known for – seriously... Google it), I bought the *Totally Krossed Out* album, had the poster and FINALLY decided to ignore the review scores and purchase *Kris Kross: Make My Video*. I started wearing my clothes the right way round soon after.

Kris Kross: Make My Video is not a bad game, because it's not a game! Instead it's a really bad piece of video editing software disguised as a game where you get to chop up three Kris Kross music videos and... that's it!

The 'game' starts off in the Make My Video studios where the host Boyd Packer helps you answer the phone from one of eight callers, who then

73

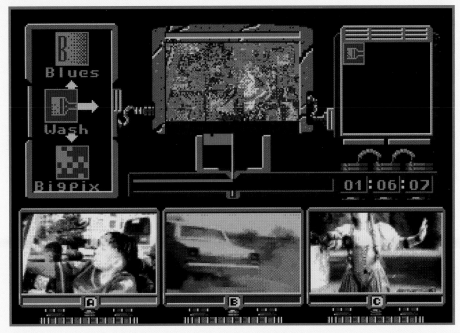

The amazing 'Wash' video effect, which makes your masterpiece look like a corrupted mess.

instruct you on what they want to see in your final edit of the music video. Following said instructions you are then presented with three clips to choose from: the original video, some random stock footage and some other random stock footage. Then, in real time, while listening to 'Jump' (for the second time), you insert the video clips into the final cut with the A, B and C buttons while adding effects like 'Freeze', 'Slow', 'Strobe', 'Flip' and my favourites 'Smear' and 'Bigpix', which just pixelates the video even more than it already was.

Once this is all done you can watch back your creation (listening to 'Jump' for the third time) and if you are like me, sit in complete disappointment, wondering where you put the receipt.

Weirdly enough this *Make My Video* game is actually the second release in a three-game series, and weirder still it's not the worst! Thankfully I wasn't a fan of INXS or Marky Mark and the Funky Bunch anyway so I never had to deal with those disappointments. (Quick side note: Marky Mark was Mark Wahlberg, yes... that Mark Wahlberg! Turns out *Transformers: Age of Extinction* isn't the worst thing he has been a part of.)

So, in the words of the late Chris 'Mac Daddy' Kelly, *Kris Kross: Make My Video* and the entire Make My Video franchise is not only my biggest disappointment, it's 'wiggity, wiggity, wiggity wack!'

DOMAIN OF THE UNDEAD

FORMAT: ATARI 8-BIT
YEAR OF RELEASE: 1986
DEVELOPER: STEVE MACILWEE
PUBLISHER: RED RAT SOFTWARE
ORIGINAL PRICE: 7.95 POUNDS CASSETTE,
9.95 POUNDS DISK

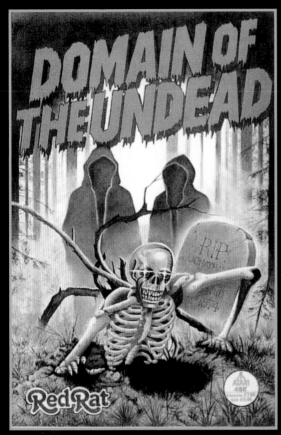

I like this cover – it reminds me of eighties VHS releases of low-budget horror films, and that's always a good thing.

TIME FOR A SECOND *Ghosts 'n Goblins*-inspired game, although this one is more removed from the original than the blatant knock-off *Belial*. *Domain of the Undead* at least tries to do something different, although it fails on every other level.

According to the instructions, the player's character in *Domain of the Undead* must walk through a graveyard to retrieve a master key. Why this key is necessary and what it opens are never mentioned. Unfortunately it's a full moon, which means the undead rise from their graves and attack anyone who enters said cemetery. And rather than come back the following day when the moon is no longer full, our hero stupidly decides to fight through the hordes.

He is armed with 'anti-spectre bolts', which are lines that fire out of his hand, and four crucifixes, which act as lives – if a nasty creature touches him, he loses one, and if he gets hit without any left, it's game over. There's no feedback when a crucifix is lost other than a counter going down, which adds an extra level of confusion and incompetence to the proceedings.

Things do start off well though. The title screen is well drawn, and a good version of Bach's 'Toccata and Fugue in D minor' plays in the background (although this only seems to be present in the disk version – my tape copy had no title music at all). The background music is actually very good throughout the entire game... and that's about all the nice things I have to say about *Domain of the Undead*.

Upon starting the game you see your badly drawn character bob along with a terrible two-frame walking animation, and you know things are going to get bad. But it's the enemies that really set off more alarms than a fire in a klaxon factory. In fact, I named this very book after them!

The enemies consist mostly of skeletons, who rise up out of the floor and walk towards you.

There is another skeleton in this scene, but it's currently in the 'off' phase of its flickering.

The orange thing on the right is a bird or a bat. It flies at you but is really easily shot, posing no threat at all.

They constantly flicker to an insane degree – they flash on and off on alternate frames, as do nearly all the enemies. It's absolutely bizarre to see. They

flash out of sync with each other, which means you can't see half the skeletons in the screenshots on these pages. I don't know if the flickering was a technical problem caused by trying to get more sprites out of the Atari hardware, or if it's a deliberate and hideously flawed attempt at giving them a crude transparency effect. Running the game on my Atari XEGS through an old CRT television, as it would have been when it was released, makes the skeletons flicker less than emulation. But they're still very flickery indeed, and not even close to looking spooky and translucent.

You need to get over the eye-watering effect of the weirdly oscillating skeletons to play *Domain of the Undead*, as they're everywhere. The bony maniacs constantly assault you from both sides but instantly disappear when hit by an anti-spectre bolt. The difficulty comes from certain taller gravestones, which block your bolts and effectively act as choke points. You have to time things very carefully to pass them, as you can only have one bolt on screen at any one time. And as the skeletons just keep on coming, the game becomes insanely difficult, as you will end up being overwhelmed at one of the blocking gravestones. To add to this difficulty, zombie hands reach up from the floor at certain points and require incredibly precise timing to walk over safely, which is hard to work out due to their flickering appearance and your constant need to fend off the skeletons.

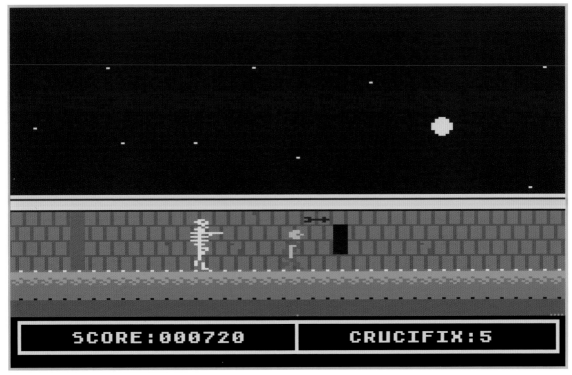

Arrow-ducking action from Level 2. This is as exciting as it gets. Try not to hyperventilate.

There are four stages to traverse before you find the master key, and due to the difficulty I couldn't even make it to Level 2 without cheating – and neither could anyone playing it on YouTube! The second level takes place inside a corridor of some kind, and the last two levels dump you back in the graveyard. The only thing of interest that happens is at one point a giant UFO-shaped cloud follows you and drops bombs, which was different at least. The entire game takes about seven

minutes to play through, which is a bit cheeky for a full-price release – although, of course, nobody ever saw three-quarters of the game anyway.

You may be wondering what happens if you do reach the end of *Domain of the Undead*, and by the power of disabling collision detection in an emulator I shall tell you! You reach a tall column as the instructions mention, then the master key appears behind you. You need to cross several of the annoying zombie hands grasping up from below, then you can pick up your prize. 'THE END' is then printed on the screen... and all your crucifixes drain away and you get sent to the game over screen which says 'THE END' anyway!

Domain of the Undead is a throwback to the days before playtesting and quality control – by 1986 full-price games had moved way, way beyond this type of release. But far worse than that, it's a frustrating, semi-playable wreck that's no fun to play whatsoever. At least the music is nice and it's not as hateful as Steven Macilwee's other entry in this book, the monstrous *Castle Top*.

PLAY THIS GAME INSTEAD
If you feel like battling the undead on your Atari 800, I'd highly recommend *Necromancer*, a uniquely odd multi-stage game that's really good fun.

REVIEW SCORES
Page 6 magazine was bizarrely soft on *Domain of the Undead*, saying it was 'not a bad little game by any means', which makes me wonder if they'd ever played a game before. But they did add, 'I somehow feel *Domain of the Undead* would have been better suited to the budget end of the market.'

Atari User ignored the original release, but when it was released as part of a compilation they tore it apart, criticising the 'appalling graphics, sparse sound and difficult gameplay'.

OTHER VERSIONS
This is an interesting case. Though there are no other versions of *Domain of the Undead*, an upgraded version titled *Night Walk* was released for the Atari ST. Also programmed by Steven Macilwee, it was ported to the Commodore Amiga and is still utterly dreadful. In fact I would say it's even worse than *Domain of the Undead* as it's slower and less smooth, and it takes an age for your character to fire. *Night Walk* was one of the games I covered in my old *Terrible Old Games You've Never Heard Of* video series that inspired these books, and it remains one of my least favourite things ever committed to floppy disk.

WHICH IS WORSE?

It's a tough call between *Belial* and *Domain of the Undead*, but I'll say that *Belial* is worse. It's slightly less aggravating than *Domain*, but even less of a game, even uglier, and looks worse despite being released for a far more powerful computer!

RECREATE THIS GAME IN REAL LIFE

Dig up a load of corpses from a graveyard and turn on a strobe light. Then question your life choices and turn yourself in to the police.

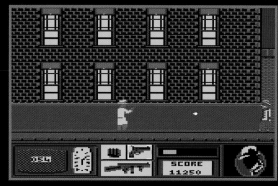

Dick Tracy raids the world's least visually interesting building.

LOWEST MAGAZINE SCORE CORNER

COMMODORE FORMAT MAGAZINE
Score: 11%
Game: *Dick Tracy*
Format: Commodore 64

This hellishly bad scrolling fighter/shooter hybrid based on the 1990 movie *Dick Tracy* is an ugly, tedious excuse for a game where instead of timing punches to take out bad guys, you literally stand there with an out-stretched fist and they walk into it. All the home computer versions of *Dick Tracy* were dreadful, but the C64 really got the absolute pits. *Commodore Format*'s verdict: 'Cobblers.'

TotalBiscuit can be found on YouTube at youtube.com/TotalHalibut, and can be found on Twitter @Totalbiscuit.

THE MOST DISAPPOINTING GAME I EVER BOUGHT

BY JOHN BAIN AKA TOTALBISCUIT, GAME CRITIC AND VIDEO PRODUCER

FACT FACT FACT FACT FACT

Acorn User magazine's review of *The Crystal Maze* said they expected people to be disappointed with it, which is hard to argue with. *PC Format* gave the almost identical DOS version 21%, calling it, 'A hopeless piece of PC software, totally out of touch with what passes as a full-price game. A waste of money.'

THE CRYSTAL MAZE
FORMAT: ACORN 32-BIT
YEAR OF RELEASE: 1993
DEVELOPER: DIGITAL JELLYFISH DESIGN
PUBLISHER: SHERSTON SOFTWARE
ORIGINAL PRICE: 39.95 POUNDS

GAME SHOWS ARE arguably Britain's greatest export. Anything that could feasibly be made into some sort of televised contest has been, and some of the most famous television programming of all time sprouted from this usually cheap, disposable format. However, there was one game show that bucked the trend. A costly, sprawling, majestic affair that pitted challengers against themed puzzle rooms, decked out in props, decorations and sometimes even actors representing the four different 'zones' of the game. It was cooperative yet featured player elimination, tough choices and challenges requiring mental and physical strength to overcome. It was hosted by an eccentric and charismatic bald man with an odd taste in attire, and it ran for half of the nineties. Its name was *The Crystal Maze*.

There was nothing else quite like it back then. For the most part, elaborate affairs like this were reserved strictly for audiences of children. Yet *The Crystal Maze* had wide appeal. Anyone of any age could enjoy its compelling mix of escape-room-like challenges, mixed with the addictive drama of time limits, which, if exceeded, would result in a player being physically locked in the room, leaving their team down a member. Challenges were regularly rotated and themed in zones such as 'Aztec' and 'Futuristic' (my personal favourite). The whole thing was quintessentially British and very entertaining. So imagine my excitement when I discovered that Sherston Software had published a game of *The Crystal Maze* for the Acorn Archimedes system in 1993. Looking back

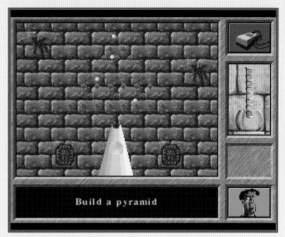

The Aztec zone, and one of the most frustrating mini-games I have ever played. Catch falling crystals in a drain-pipe that you can't quite control precisely enough!

on it, I absolutely cannot imagine why I thought this had the potential to be any good, but I was young and foolish, and I loved *The Crystal Maze* show.

To be an Acorn Archimedes owner in the nineties was to know famine. While consoles were pumping out classic after classic and MS-DOS's twilight was producing some of the greatest PC games of all time, if you owned a variant of the Archimedes, a British-developed computer primarily used in schools, your choices for games were few and far between. We would occasionally receive the PC and Amiga's table-scraps, ports that were for the most part adequate but years late. We also had a small but dedicated native scene of developers who tried their best and on rare occasion produced a genuinely good game like *Star Fighter 3000*. However, most of what we got were inferior clones of already existing titles. To see a big-name franchise of any kind on

82

RISC OS (the Acorn oper-
ating system) was incred-
ibly rare. To see a nation-
ally recognized brand like
The Crystal Maze show
up was like catching a
unicorn.

The box it came in was
impressive, an unusual
octagonal design meant
to invoke the shape of the
Crystal Dome, the show's
giant transparent struc-
ture in which the final
challenge would take
place. Inside the box was
an octagonal manual that
served as the game's copyright protection, requir-
ing you to match colour-
ed segments on the back of it with others printed
on the inside of the box. Lose either of those and
you were done for – thanks to the reliance on colour, photocopying wasn't even an option. It gave
a great first impression, which rapidly sank to the
briny depths of the Ocean zone as soon as you
started playing.

The first thing that strikes you is your choice of
characters. You get to choose 6 from a roster of
12, though as far as I know they all performed
identically. What hits you immediately is the completely bizarre art style. All of the characters look
deformed, I could swear one of them has hair that
looks like a dead cat. It massively clashes with the

game's aesthetic, what there is of it, which is a
patchwork mess of styles with no guiding direction. The gameplay is a set of themed mini-games
broken down into four categories, which range
from mundane to downright broken. The timed
sliding puzzle and hidden object games are serviceable, but they're mixed in with things like a
barely functional 2D platformer or a 'roll the ball
into the Aztec statue's mouth' challenge, which
mostly boiled down to guessing how offset the
camera perspective was. The game switches between 2D and 3D games, with a seemingly random riot of different art styles.

The ultimate objective of each game is simple:

beat the game, get a crystal. Crystals extend your time in the final challenge. Fail the game and your character is locked in, giving you a disadvantage at the end. The final challenge, the Crystal Dome, is the icing on this uninspired slog. A simple wire-frame click-a-thon in which you must collect as many golden tickets as you can while avoiding the silver ones. You might assume your mouse is on the fritz considering how poorly it handles, but no, that's just the game.

I really don't know what I expected. The show itself is just a series of mini-games; the fun is watching the drama of a team desperately trying to complete them or mulling over whether to spend resources to free a trapped contender. Boil all of that away and what you're left with is a set of simplistic, repetitive vignettes, most of which aren't even fun to play the first time around let alone something you'd want to experience time and again.

I was a fool. I paid full price for a big brand. I was suckered in by what looked like a gleaming diamond but turned out to be cheap glass. Common sense should have told me this was never going to be good but I was desperate, I wanted something I recognised, something that wasn't just an obscure clone on a system nobody liked. Barely six months passed before I lost the manual. I'm sure I could find the back of it on the internet somewhere but in the case of *The Crystal Maze*, it'd be wise to leave it locked in the Aztec era forever.

Fans of counting dots will love this medieval zone game. Switch the panels around so every direction totals 18 against a very tight time limit.

Fans of the show will recognise this character as 'Mumsey'. She asks some mathematical questions like the ones in middle-school exams.

COMMODORE 64 COIN-OP CONVERSION BATTLE ROYALE!

In the late eighties arcade conversions were some of the biggest-selling titles for home computers. Everybody wanted to play the latest 10-pence guzzling behemoths in their own home, but they were usually left disappointed by attempts to recreate their favourite game on inferior hardware. For every *R-Type* and *Chase HQ* on my Spectrum, there was a *Jail Break* or *Kung-Fu Master*.

As one of the few home computers of the period to have a substantial user base in the USA, the Commodore 64 had some conversions made specifically for the US market that varied greatly from the European releases. Sometimes this was seemingly because the European version was awful, but sometimes the US versions were produced later and were much worse. Why did it happen? The main suspects are licensing issues, but we may never know for sure. But we can line them all up and make them fight to see which version of each game is better!

Place your bets – who will come out on top overall?
It's the least important intercontinental
grudge match in history!

European publisher: US Gold (1987)

US publisher: Mindscape (1987)

720˚ – Isometric skateboarding game starring some bloke in a hat

Europe got a fiddly, ugly game with astonishingly thumping music. The USA got better graphics but the playfield is too zoomed in, and it feels empty due to a lack of other characters present in the European version. The nail in the coffin for the US version is the multi-load system which means you end up waiting ages between levels.

FIGHT OUTCOME: Never quite able to fight back effectively,
the US version throws in the towel in the sixth round.
EUROPE WINS!

European publisher: Activision (1989)

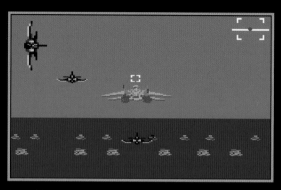

US publisher: Mindscape (1989)

After Burner – Into-the-screen shoot 'em up starring an F-14 Tomcat

The European version has a limited playfield with massive borders. It's jerky, has dull graphics and it feels like whatever you do has little effect on the outcome of the game. The USA got a far better game in all respects – it's full screen, smoother and more responsive, and a clever flicker effect on the main aircraft makes it appear higher resolution (not viewable in the screenshot here!).

FIGHT OUTCOME: The US version punches the European one
to death in five seconds flat.
USA WINS!

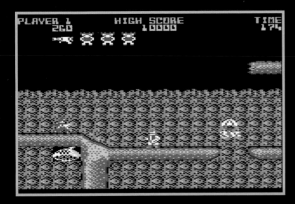

European publisher: Go! (1988)

US publisher: Capcom (1988)

Bionic Commando – Scrolling platformer starring a soldier with a very long arm

The European version is beloved amongst C64 games, and with good reason.
It's fast, fluid, smooth and great fun – and it has some of the very best music for the
system. Now imagine that someone remade it in a weekend from memory. That's the US
version, all the way down to horrible, bleepy versions of the game's tunes that just peter
out as if the musician forgot them. A travesty.

FIGHT OUTCOME: The US version's head falls off before
the European version even lands a punch.
EUROPE WINS!

European publisher: Ocean (1989)

US publisher: Capcom (1990)

Cabal – Third-person shoot 'em up starring very brightly dressed soldiers

Europe got a nice conversion here – it's pretty, fun and plays smoothly.
The US version has fiddlier controls and inferior graphics, the enemies move too fast
and the main character has no death animation. Bah.

FIGHT OUTCOME: The US version is knocked out in the second round.
EUROPE WINS!

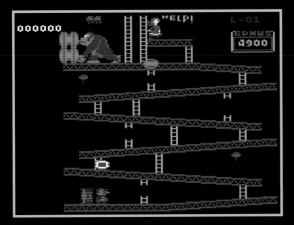

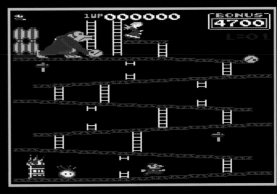

US publisher: Atarisoft (1983)

European publisher: Ocean (1986)

Donkey Kong – Single-screen platformer starring Jumpman, aka Mario

Uniquely in this feature, both of these are pretty good! The US version is impressive considering how early it was made, but it suffers from oddly stretched graphics and slightly slow gameplay. The European version has the different screens in the original Japanese order, and the sound and music are slightly off. This would pretty much be a dead heat but the US game needs annoyingly perfect positioning for Jumpman to climb a ladder, which makes things unnecessarily fiddly and spoils the arcade feel.

FIGHT OUTCOME: After a long match, the European version wins on points.
Fans argue over the outcome for years.
EUROPE WINS!

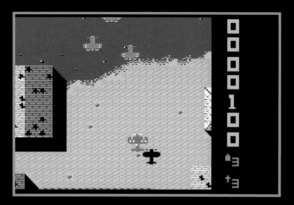

European publisher: Firebird (1987)

US publisher: Taito (1988)

Flying Shark – **Vertically scrolling shoot 'em up starring a biplane of some type**

Flying Shark was always a difficult game in the arcades, but both C64 versions push things a bit far, which ends in frustration for the player. The European version has disappointing graphics, and it's frequently impossible to see enemy bullets, which puts the US version (known as *Sky Shark*) well ahead. And the USA got better music too, which seals the deal.

**FIGHT OUTCOME: The US version dominates the fight, winning
by knock-out in the fourth round.
USA WINS!**

European publisher: Elite (1988)

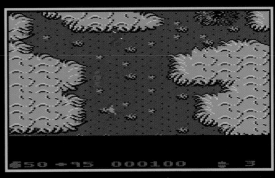

US publisher: Data East (1986)

Ikari Warriors - Vertically scrolling shoot 'em up starring shirtless soldiers

It's brutally difficult, but the European version is a great game. It's fast, responsive and exciting, with good graphics and superb music. The US version is like the same game written by a small child for a school project. An utterly appalling, semi-playable mess, and one of the worst games released for the Commodore 64.

FIGHT OUTCOME: The European version kills the US one with a single punch, then urinates on its twitching corpse.
EUROPE WINS!

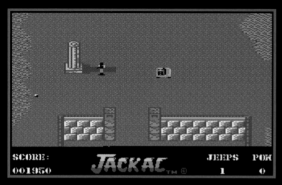

European publisher: Konami (1987)

US publisher: Imagine (1989)

Jackal – Vertically scrolling shoot 'em up starring a jeep that handles really oddly

This is a tight one, as although both versions are very different, neither is very good. The European version has very simple graphics and tiny sprites, but it runs smoothly. The US version has more detail, but it's messy and has a lower frame rate. It does, however, have more stuff happening on-screen. Both versions would pretty much be equal, but the USA got a two-player mode, which puts it ahead.

FIGHT OUTCOME: After strong initial display from the European version,
it tires in the fifth round and the US version wins by TKO.
USA WINS!

European publisher: Activision (1987)

US publisher: Activision (1989)

Rampage – Single-screen smash 'em down starring giant comedy monsters

The *Rampage* conversions take very different routes to each other. Europe got detailed graphics but slightly unresponsive controls, and the computer plays the other two monsters in single-player. The USA got blockier but more cartoony graphics and better controls, but you're on your own in single-player. The deciding factors here are that the European version lacks the backwards punch move, and a bug means you cannot restore your energy by eating bonus items.

FIGHT OUTCOME: After a long and bloody fight,
the European version collapses in the tenth round.
USA WINS!

European publisher: Go! (1988)

US publisher: Capcom (1988)

Street Fighter – **Early one-on-one fighting game starring a young, red-haired Ryu**

Let's face it: the first *Street Fighter* game wasn't really much fun in the arcades, unless you were playing with the pressure-sensitive punch buttons. The European port is fairly faithful, but it runs at a snail's pace with unresponsive controls and hideous, blocky graphics. It's absolutely dreadful. The US version wisely took a different approach and changed the game up entirely – it plays more like *Yie Ar Kung-Fu* than *Street Fighter*. The characters are tiny but nicely drawn, and they are better animated than the original arcade game! It's still not much of a game, really, but it's light years ahead of the Euro version.

**FIGHT OUTCOME: The European version dies of bubonic plague before
the match begins. The US version goes to the cinema instead.
USA WINS!**

OVERALL WINNER:
NOBODY CARES!

DIDN'T MAKE THE WEIGH-IN

Space Harrier and *Out Run* also had different American ports, but they were improved versions of the existing European games so didn't make the list. The US-specific versions of *Arkanoid* and *Operation Wolf* were identical except for added mouse support.

MINE'S A DOUBLE, THANKS

There are also two distinct versions of seminal beat 'em up *Double Dragon*, although they were both European releases and so don't qualify for this battle. The 1989 Melbourne House one is utterly awful, to the extent that the manual makes excuses for the poor quality of the sprites! The 1991 Ocean version is better but still not actually worth playing. There are two conversions of *Double Dragon* for the Amstrad CPC, which led to some confusion – one was distributed in the UK, the other in France. The French version is monstrously ugly, thanks mostly to terrible colour choices, but is otherwise far better than the UK one in every respect.

THE FLINTSTONES

BY LARRY BUNDY JR, GAMING HISTORIAN
AND COMEDY BLOKE

FORMAT: SPECTRUM, AMSTRAD, COMMODORE 64,
COMMODORE AMIGA, ATARI ST, MSX, SEGA MASTER SYSTEM
YEAR OF RELEASE: 1988
DEVELOPER: VARIOUS
PUBLISHER: GRANDSLAM
ORIGINAL PRICE: 8.95/29.99 POUNDS DEPENDING ON FORMAT

WHAT'S SURPRISING TO A LOT of our American friends is how we in the UK grew up playing UK-exclusive games based on their well-loved cartoons. We were treated to a huge bounty of titles, such as *ThunderCats* from Elite, *The Real Ghostbusters* by Activision and even *Inspector Gadget* courtesy of Australian publishers Melbourne House.

So it comes as no surprise that one of America's most famous cartoons of all, *The Flintstones*, would also receive an Anglo-adaptation courtesy of franchise peddlers Grandslam (aka Quicksilva), previously renowned for making home computer ports of *Pac-Land*, *Pac-Mania* and well... anything that had Pac-Man in it, really!

The Flintstones is Grandslam's sequel to their previous *Flintstones: Yabba Dabba Doo*, a Fred & Wilma escapade released two years previously in which Fred has to scavenge for boulders around a muddy field in order to build a home for Wilma. Then, once he'd collected enough, he'd go to work to earn enough money to hire a crane to put a roof on the thing, thus attaining Wilma's hand in marriage. So, the gameplay and Wilma's affection were about as shallow as each other.

But, with the sequel, Grandslam wanted to rein in the excitement of Mesozoic makeovers a notch by having Fred endure several dinosaur-era domestic disputes instead.

Now if this doesn't already sound thrilling enough, British publishers eschewed the console game route of loosely stringing the licence's plot around a platform game and sticking in the odd weird-looking secondary character as a boss. Instead they insisted on rigidly sticking to the

In the MSX version, Fred's face is a scowling mask of pure hatred, presumably mirroring the player.

storyline, using a series of usually nonsensical and rubbish mini-games to play out the scenes.

Essentially, most licences were like a particularly skinflint version of *WarioWare* that made you play the same segment over and over until you got it right... or you went around your friend's house and taped *The New Zealand Story* over the game's cassette using his dad's twin deck hi-fi.

For instance, the first level is a literal embodiment of watching paint dry as Fred is forced to decorate the living room using the arse end of a squirrel as a paintbrush before he's allowed to go bowling. All while looking after his daughter Pebbles, who manages to climb out of her easily escapable playpen every five nanoseconds to scribble all over his handiwork. He also has to constantly refill his squirrel from a paint tin in the middle of the room as he's too thick to carry it around the room with him.

The Sega Master System version helpfully points out how dull the game is before it starts. Also, why is the wall outside?

Pebbles gets dangerously near the paint in the Commodore 64 version. Fred silently looks on, his spirit broken.

Upon completing the torture of cretaceous childcare, Level 2 consists of the exhilarating odyssey of driving to said bowling alley. Now, one might assume this would be a great mini-game, dodging various traffic and hilarious dinosaur-related obstacles. But no. It's a side-on view of Fred and Barney in Fred's car, jumping over multiple boulders in fear of getting a punctured tyre, even though the tyres are made of solid rock. And a mistake means Track & Field-levels of frantic joystick waggling for the best part of 30 seconds to jack up the car and replace said tyre. So, if you're not very good at timing jumps, expect to come out of this level looking like a one-armed Popeye!

Level 3 has Barney and Fred finally at the bowling alley and – shock horror – actually bowling!

Surprisingly, it's a pretty decent bowling game for the late eighties. Why Grandslam didn't just base the entire game around them playing against other characters in a bowling tournament is beyond me, but they even managed to make this level pretty arduous thanks to them insisting Fred does his unskippable tip-toe throw every time it's your turn.

And Level 4 rounds up the game with Pebbles, who is now in mortal danger. Wilma left her alone in the paint-fume-filled room while Fred was bowling, and the youngling has fled to Fred's construction yard and climbed the biggest crane. So, Mr Flintstone's ultimate challenge is to navigate through eight platform screens of crane innards, scaling ropes and dodging giant floating

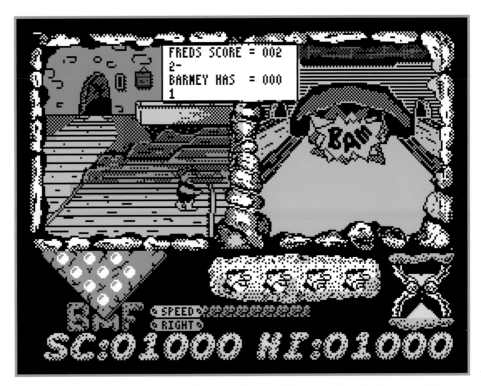

FREDS SCORE = 002
2-
BARNEY HAS = 000
1

BAM

BMF ◄ SPEED ► ◄ RIGHT ►

SC:01000 HI:01000

Barney bowls in the Spectrum version. The pins go 'BAM', which is coincidentally the name of his son.

nuts, bolts and... erm... clouds, before collecting Pebbles and making his way back through the whole level.

The original final level had Fred and Wilma desperately trying to justify their severe lack of parental competence to child services while Pebbles was put up for adoption, but it was sadly cut due to the memory constraints of eighties video-game technology. Well, that and I just made it up.

The Amiga and Atari ST versions are the prettiest. But which is this from? I'll never tell! Ahahaha!

Grandslam would go on to make further exciting licences, such as *Liverpool: The Computer Game,* and to port *Space Harrier II,* the Mega Drive game that no one liked, to home computers. They then moved to Croydon to develop Amiga CD32 games and promptly went bankrupt. A fitting punishment!

RECREATE THIS GAME IN REAL LIFE
Paint a room. Then go bowling. Hooray.

Larry **can be found on YouTube at www.youtube.com/larry and on twitter @LarryBundyJr**

PLAY THIS GAME INSTEAD

Oddly enough, wall-painting simulators never really caught on so there isn't much competition. Perhaps play the arcade game *Make Trax* (aka *Crush Roller*), where you have to paint a series of mazes?

REVIEW SCORES

Strangely, magazine reviews of *The Flintstones* at the time were polar opposites with their scores.

Issue 25 of *The Games Machine* awarded the PC version a princely 85%, as did 'every game ever is brilliant' brown-nosers *Computer and Video Games*, who rated it 30/40.

But on the other hand, *Commodore User* rated the Amiga port a lowly 3/10, and Spectrum magazine *Crash* awarded it just 52%, humorously quipping, 'Unfortunately, they can't stop Bedrock from approaching Rock-Bottom.'

Despite receiving mixed reviews, Grandslam thought it would be a great idea to port the game over to the Sega Master System three years later (courtesy of the Bizarro King Midas of eighties developers, Tiertex) and charge £30 for a game that you could get for £1.99 on other systems by then. However, the official Sega magazine *Sega Power* thought otherwise... and gave it 21%.

INTERCEPTOR SOFTWARE
PRESENTS
GALAXZIONS
BY A.BARTON
LOADING

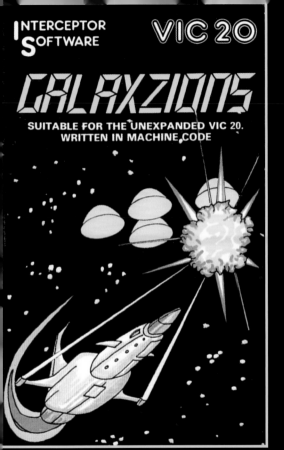

INTERCEPTOR SOFTWARE

VIC 20

GALAXZIONS

SUITABLE FOR THE UNEXPANDED VIC 20.
WRITTEN IN MACHINE CODE

*The cassette cover, showing an intergalactic space fighter
destroying some jelly tots.*

WHEN I FIRST SAID I was writing a book about terrible old games, a friend asked me if some of the games would be so bad there would be almost nothing to write about. I said I didn't think so, as I'd need to explain why the game is so awful even

if there's not much there. What does it look like? What does it sound like? What do you have to do? How does the game work? Are there any technical problems? There are plenty of questions to be answered in the pursuit of the very worst games ever excreted onto the public. There are always things to write about.

Then I found *Galaxzions*, an almost unplayable game that throws a seemingly random barrage of noise and images into your face then ends in about 30 seconds. There's almost nothing to it. But I'm going to write about it anyway, as that is my curse.

Using the rampant eighties scheme of attempting to avoid copyright issues by spelling the name of a popular game differently but keeping it phonetically similar, *Galaxzions* is a clone of the 1979 arcade hit *Galaxian*. Essentially an expanded version of *Space Invaders*, this time the aliens break formation to fly down in kamikaze-style attacks against the player. And that's what happens in *Galaxzions*... on a technical level, at least.

You know how grandparents could be quite sniffy about video games in the eighties? 'It's all just noise and flashing pictures!' Well... it turns out they were right in one instance. *Galaxzions* is literally just noise and flashing pictures, with the slight addition of being able to move a blue spaceship around ineffectually.

The game starts with a fanfare of beeps before you're thrust into the action. And by 'action', I mean 'enemies appearing and disappearing seemingly at random'. Instead of breaking formation and flying down the screen at your ship, they simply teleport to two random places on the

The deadly Galaxzion on the far right has broken formation. How thrilling.

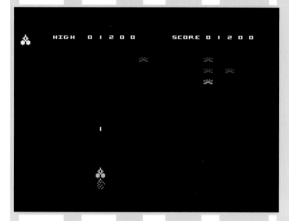

Notice that your spaceship has a constantly flatulent bum attached to the bottom.

screen and then go back. You can't follow them and shoot them because there is no way of knowing where they'll appear. And better still – the enemies' bullets just appear instantly out of nowhere and kill you! They have absolutely no movement, they just materialise on top of your ship. As a result it is totally impossible to dodge them.

As you've probably worked out, *Galaxzions* is almost entirely unplayable. You can jerkily move left and right and shoot, and the only possible strategy is to shoot at where the enemies sit in the formation in the hope that they'll be there when the bullet reaches them. It doesn't really matter what you do, as an enemy bullet will appear on your ship, and one of your three lives will be gone. Despite playing about 25 times, I never

beat the first wave of enemies. The longest game I had lasted 45 seconds, but many were considerably shorter.

And I haven't even mentioned the very worst thing yet – the sound! Oh my goodness, the sound. A shrieking series of four descending notes plays over and over on a permanent loop. And every time you fire, there's a weird screechy white noise sound overlaid on top of it. The only respite is a full two seconds of silence when you lose a life.

Galaxzions really is one of the feeblest excuses of a game to ever be copied onto a tape and flung into VIC-20 owners' faces. And this wasn't Interceptor Software's only gameplay-free title – their 1983 release *Jupiter Defender* can be played almost forever by moving to the bottom of the

GALAXZIONS

GALAXZIONS — MACHINE CODE
This is the most amazing alien game ever seen on the VIC 20. Galaxzions swarming in attack formation to destroy your planet. The nearest program to the real arcade game for the unexpanded VIC 20

....£7.00

As pointed out by programmer Jeff Minter on his blog, the advertisements for Galaxzions feature some astonishing lies.

screen and holding down the fire button. And you may remember from the first *Terrible Old Games You've Probably Never Heard Of* book that they also wrote *Crazy Kong*, so they really were the kings of tat in the early days of the Commodore VIC-20. They did release some decent games, but nothing can take away the lingering taste of *Galaxzions*.

REVIEW SCORES
No magazines reviewed *Galaxzions*. Perhaps they refused to, while hiding behind a sofa.

OTHER VERSIONS
There are many, many *Galaxian* clones for all the early eighties computers, but *Galaxzions* exists only for the VIC-20. It's a matter of opinion if it really exists as a game in any meaningful sense, but if it does, it's only for the VIC-20.

RECREATE THIS GAME IN REAL LIFE
Induce a migraine while attempting to sleep when you're suffering from a heavy fever.

SPELLING CORNER
Galaxzions isn't even the strangest spelling of Galaxian. That accolade goes to the consonant-mangling *Galakzions* from Mikro-Gen, released in 1983 for the ZX Spectrum.

PLAY THIS GAME INSTEAD
There's an excellent official conversion of *Galaxian* for the VIC-20 by Atarisoft – definitely play that instead.

HARERAISER: PRELUDE AND FINALE

When is a video game not a video game? How about when a puzzle uses the medium of video games to impart information? And what if that puzzle itself possibly doesn't exist and the information is meaningless?

Could these questions get any more confusing? Let's have a look into *Hareraiser* and see if we can dig up answers.

The rather lovely cover of the rather lovely Masquerade.

TO UNDERSTAND *HARERAISER* we have to go back to 1976 and the birth of the publishing phenomenon *Masquerade*. Artist Kit Williams had been approached by a publisher to produce a book of his paintings, but he wasn't keen on the idea as people just tend to flick through art books without paying attention like they would in a gallery. His clever idea was to make a visual puzzle book that would make people look closely at his paintings in order to solve it.

The result was *Masquerade*, an illustrated storybook that cryptically hid the location of a buried clay casket. Inside was the Golden Hare – a beautiful, five-inch-long pendant made of 18-carat gold and set with rubies and semiprecious stones, made by Williams himself.

The combination of sumptuous art and the possibility of winning an expensive item of jewellery caught the public's imagination, and *Masquerade* sold over 200,000 copies in the first week alone. It went on to sell well over a million copies worldwide and launched the concept of the armchair treasure hunt, where solving a puzzle in your house could provide a tangible reward.

The text of the book tells the story of Jack Hare, who is tasked to carry the pendant to the Sun as a token of the Moon's affection. He of course loses it, and it was up to the reader to solve the book's puzzle and dig it up for themselves. As ever, most people spent hours poring over the book then wrote in with an incorrect theory that was politely refuted.

The puzzle was not easy to solve. At all. No pointers or instructions were given, so armchair sleuths simply had the text and paintings to go on. Television personality and historian Bamber Gascoigne, the host of popular quiz programme *University Challenge*, had accompanied Williams when he buried the pendant, and even he couldn't work it out despite already knowing the location

The understated and powerful cover of Hareraiser: Prelude, *simply showing the Golden Hare itself. It's the only classy thing about* Hareraiser.

Painting number five from Masquerade, *featuring Tara Tree-Tops, who I really hope brought a parachute.*

and having the basis of the puzzle explained to him!

The difficulty was compounded by the huge number of false trails and red herrings Williams had woven into the book. For two and a half years

after publication, he received tens of thousands of letters suggesting solutions, but none of their methodologies were correct. The actual solution relies entirely on the pictures – the text pages are totally irrelevant – and involves drawing lines from the characters' eyes through visible fingers and toes. Most people had attempted to decode the text or use mathematics, but the key was observation and deduction.

Finally, on 19 February 1982, Kit Williams received the very first letter correctly identifying the Golden Hare's burial site as Ampthill Park in Bedfordshire. The writer, Ken Thomas, had not understood the puzzle and got there mostly by luck. A pair of physics teachers had dug almost in the right place but somehow missed the casket, and Thomas actually saw their badly filled holes and dug around them. Eventually, he found it in a pile of previously turned-over earth. But while the teachers may not have ended up with the Golden Hare, they were the only people to actually solve the puzzle properly. (Unfortunately, such accolades are not made of gold and set with gems.)

After the hare was found, Thomas did the publicity rounds (in disguise, no less) and the answer was published. And as with every game of this type, people wrote to Williams claiming that the actual solution was wrong and their patently incorrect ideas were the real truth. Bamber Gascoigne went on to write a book about the whole affair called *The Quest for the Golden Hare*, and in it he says, 'People are good at forming patterns and are good at self-deception.' I think that sums things up nicely.

Thomas now had possession of the Golden Hare, and he decided to capitalise on it by creating another puzzle offering it – or £30,000 in cash – as a prize. But this time, the puzzle would be in the form of a computer program rather than a book. He used the hare as collateral and set up

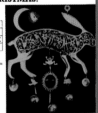

Hareraiser challenges you!

GOLDEN 30,000 PRIZE

IT'S NOT AN ARCADE GAME
IT'S NOT A BORING ADVENTURE TREK
IT'S A *GENUINE* PUZZLE THAT COULD BE SOLVED BY YOU!

HARERAISER THE **UNIQUE** COMPUTER TREASURE HUNT, A COMPUTER PUZZLE OF GRAPHICS AND TEXT IN 2 PARTS. EACH PART CONTAINS VITAL CLUES TO PLACES OR LOCATIONS WHICH WILL ENABLE YOU TO DISCOVER THE WHEREABOUTS OF THIS GOLDEN TREASURE. IT HAS NOT BEEN BURIED YOU JUST HAVE TO PINPOINT ITS LOCATION TO CLAIM THIS AMAZING PRIZE . . . THIS PUZZLE HAS BEEN SPECIFICALLY DESIGNED TO BREAK AWAY FROM INDIVIDUAL ARCADE AND ADVENTURE TYPE GAMES AND PROVIDE **FAMILY** INVOLVEMENT. A COMPETITION FOR ALL THE **FAMILY**. ONCE YOU'VE COLLECTED ALL THE CLUES YOU CAN WORK ON IT **ANYWHERE, INDIVIDUALLY** OR IN GROUPS.

YOU COULD SOLVE THIS...

PART 1 (PRELUDE) AVAILABLE NOW! @ **£8.95** each
PART 2 (FINALE) READY FOR CHRISTMAS.

AVAILABLE FOR *ALL* THESE MICROS

ELECTRON	BBC B	ORIC ATMOS
SPECTRUM	CBM 64	VIC 20 EX.
AMSTRAD	MSX	TANDY EXT COL 32K
ATARI 800 XL		

Available from W. H. SMITH, HARRODS, BOOTS, TANDY, CURRY'S, GRANADA, TV RENTALS, RUMBELOWS, LEWIS LTD, DEBENHAMS, LASKYS and good computer outlets or from Haresoft.

HARESOFT LTD,
P.O. Box 365
LONDON NW1 7JD
TEL 01 388 3910

An advertisement. Notice how it explains that you have to transcribe data from it, and thus there is no reason for it to be a computer program. Also note how it misspells 'puzzle'.

Haresoft, who released *Hareraiser: Prelude* in 1984 for all the major home computers of the time: the Acorn Electron, Amstrad CPC, BBC Micro, Commodore 64, Commodore VIC20, Dragon 32, MSX, Oric Atmos and ZX Spectrum. It was also

```
            Haresoft Ltd.

A HARE OF GOLD AND JEWELS WAS HID
 IT    LAY    BENEATH    THE    GROUND
A  SEEKER  SOLVED  THE RIDDLED CLUES
AND THE BEAUTIFUL TREASURE WAS FOUND
THE  HARE  AGAIN  A  NEW  OWNER SEEKS
 ONE   WHO   WILL   MAKE   HISTORY
SO GOOD  LUCK  WITH  YOUR  QUEST
 FOR   THE   HARE   IS   AT   REST
 TO AWAKE WHEN YOU FIND THE KEY
THOUGH  NO HOUNDS  WILL YOU NEED
  NOR   EVEN   A   STEED
 TO  FIND  THIS  HIDDEN  PRIZE
NO SPADE OR PICK OR COMPUTER TRICK
 JUST A PENCIL PAPER AND EYES
```

The only instructions you get. Notice the special squashed-up text characters that help to make the layout even more difficult to read!

advertised for the Tandy TRS-80 and Atari 8-bit systems, but I couldn't find any evidence that it was released for them.

Hareraiser: Prelude was heavily advertised in all the major magazines. It was extremely expensive, costing £8.95 at a time when even the most advanced games were £7.95. But no other game offered a prize, of course! Rather than digging something up, Haresoft wanted you to send in the location, the explanation of how you worked it out and the actual game cassette. Then the Golden Hare (or more likely the cash) would be yours! In theory, at least.

So, what do you get for your £8.95? The answer is almost nothing. *Hareraiser: Prelude* barely exists at all. All you get are 26 static screens that look like they were drawn by a distracted

five-year-old. And occasionally an ugly mess that represents the hare runs around a bit. There is no interaction beyond moving between the screens. Most of them have a platitude like 'The hare is golden' or 'Deep like an ocean' written in text at the bottom. The only audio of note is exclusive to the Spectrum and Dragon 32 versions, which play a bleepy version of 'You Are My Sunshine' on the title screen. And that's it.

Much like *Masquerade*, there are no instructions on how to interpret what the game shows. It can start on various different screens, and you can move between them using the cursor keys. (The Commodore 64 version also has the Z and X keys active for reasons unknown.) They appear in the same places each time but are not consistent with any sort of compass system or physical reality – going left into a screen does not mean you will necessarily return to the previous screen by going right. In that sense, it's not possible to make a traditional map. All the screens depict an outdoor scene made up of trees, grass and clouds. Some have the Sun visible and some have an appearance from the hare, who can hop either left or right before disappearing. The whole thing is entirely abstract and makes no actual sense.

As you'd expect for a single puzzle, the contents and position of each screen are consistent across the five formats I tested. (Annoyingly I couldn't find copies for the VIC20 or MSX, and I couldn't get the Oric version to work. The Electron and BBC versions are identical so I went with the BBC.) As an example, here are the screens titled

Amstrad CPC

BBC Micro

ZX Spectrum

Dragon 32

Commodore 64

'Help is here': As you can clearly see, each screen has a cloud, the Sun and three trees. The trees are generally in the same position except for one in the BBC Micro version. The Dragon 32 displays the text as a separate message before the graphics appear, which is why it's not visible in the screenshot.

So how do you go about solving the puzzle? Do you take note of the objects on each screen? Do you need to consider the hare when it appears? What significance does the text have? I have no idea whatsoever. And neither does anyone else except Ken Thomas himself, as the puzzle was never solved. There are no details or images to be studied and chewed over like there were in *Masquerade*; with *Hareraiser: Prelude* all anyone got for their £8.95 was confused.

Now, you may have noticed that I've been referring to the game as *Hareraiser: Prelude* since I got into specifics. It's an odd name for a release – what is it a prelude to? The answer, incredibly, is the other half of the puzzle that you had to buy separately!

Haresoft released *Hareraiser: Finale* in late 1984. It cost another £8.95 and was apparently required to actually find the location of the Golden Hare. So that's effectively an eye-watering £17.90 just to enter the contest! By comparison, the *Masquerade* book, full of beautiful art, cost £3.95 a few years earlier. *Finale* is extremely rare, as *Prelude* didn't sell well and the few people who

DRAGON

The cover for Hareraiser: Finale *is a bit less subtle about the prize on offer.*

FROM THEN PRESIDENT HILL MUST CURE

Hareraiser: Finale *for the Spectrum. WHY IS IT FULL OF SPIDERS?*

paid for it weren't keen on giving Haresoft more money. In fact it was only released in any serious capacity for the Spectrum, with the Dragon 32 and Commodore 64 versions being so scarce that only a couple of examples have ever been seen. I couldn't find evidence of any releases for other computers, so if you had an Amstrad, BBC Micro, Oric, MSX, VIC20 or Electron, you could never actually get the whole puzzle, and any money you spent on *Prelude* was wasted.

Finale itself is just another small set of crappy screens and text. The only major differences are that the title music has changed to 'Scarborough Fair', and a lot of the screens are full of spiders for some reason.

There was no technical reason for *Hareraiser* to be released in two halves. The game code is tiny, to the extent that both releases could easily fit simultaneously into the memory of even the 16k Oric-1. Haresoft themselves bizarrely claimed that they split the game to 'make it fun and enable competitors of all ages to participate'. Perhaps the greatest puzzle is how paying twice as much is more fun, or how making something insanely expensive opens it up to a wider age demographic.

113

The magazines of the time were generally un-impressed with *Hareraiser: Prelude*, viewing it as an expensive cash grab – if you were just supposed to note down what was on the screen, why did it have to be released as a video game at all? When *Finale* was released they ignored it entirely.

There was considerable backlash from people who purchased *Prelude*. The adventure column of *Popular Computing Weekly* received several letters from angry buyers wondering if anybody knew what on earth they were supposed to do. The only letter with anything positive to say about it came from a 'Mrs J Y Widdowson', who described the complainers as 'nerds' not intelligent enough to understand it. She offered no insight as to what she was doing with the game to actually enjoy it, and the letter reads like a particularly artless fake sent in by Haresoft in an attempt to save face. Or perhaps more accurately, stop losing sales.

Haresoft only gave – or claimed to give – one clue to the puzzle outside of the software. They issued a press release saying that Anneka Rice, co-presenter of the television show *Treasure Hunt*, had given a clue of some kind during an appearance at Harrods department store in London. As the event wasn't recorded, it was of little use to puzzle-solvers, and of course there was no actual proof that Rice had said anything relevant to *Hareraiser* at all.

Predictably, Haresoft went belly-up early on in 1985. The company was declared bankrupt, and

Talking of letters, here's one from a miffed *Hareraiser* fan: "Dear Tony, After reading about Hareraiser in PCW, I wonder who these nerds are who think this isn't any good. I am one of a group of six who have had immense fun from seeking clues on this treasure hunt, and furthermore, it's not meant to be like the book Masquerade. If one seeks to win the Golden Hare, the computer gives the clues, the rest is down to you — that is, if you're intelligent enough. Yours, Mrs J Y Widdowson."

From Popular Computing Weekly *in November 1984. Two words spring to mind: 'Sock' and 'Puppet'.*

in December 1988 the Golden Hare was auctioned off by the liquidators. It was sold to an anonymous buyer for £31,900 and disappeared from view.

'BUT WAIT!' you scream at me as you throw this book across the room. 'Surely it's unfair to say that *Hareraiser: Prelude* and *Finale* are terrible games merely because they are part of a puzzle? Surely you can't be saying that the entire *Hareraiser* puzzle is a terrible game in itself?' Well, I can and I do. In fact, here I go: THE WHOLE *HARERAISER* PUZZLE IS TERRIBLE. And now I shall attempt to show why, using information and reasoning, exactly the way people don't in modern political discourse.

Let's go back to Ken Thomas, the chap who won the Golden Hare and started Haresoft. It transpires that he has something in common with Sherlock Holmes! And it's not that they're both great detectives, it's that they're both fictional. Ken Thomas does not exist, and has never existed. It was a pseudonym of Dugald Thompson, the business partner of another man called John Guard. And John Guard lived with a lady called Veronica Robertson, who was Kit Williams' girlfriend at the time he thought up the *Masquerade* puzzle. According to a 1988 article from the London *Times*, she didn't know the precise location but was sure it had been buried at Ampthill. Thompson arranged seven separate metal detector searches in the hopes of finding it, but with no success.

The reason Thomas's – or indeed Thompson's – answer was so incomplete is that they had effectively cheated. It also explains why he cooperated with only the minimum of publicity for his win, and wore a disguise through it all. It seems that Veronica Robertson had been manipulated into giving up what she knew by promises that the hare would be sold in favour of animal rights groups. (As we know, it was actually used as collateral to set up Haresoft.)

When approached about this duplicity, John Guard denied knowing Thompson at all... until he was shown company documents featuring both their names. Then he changed his story and claimed to have never gone looking for the golden hare, despite having told a newspaper that he knew where the hare was and that he would be the one to find it. He had also offered the metal detector experts money to publicly claim they had found the hare after it was unearthed, which they

The Hareraiser: Prelude *title screen from the BBC Micro. I call it 'migraine nightmare'.*

declined. The whole affair was a mass of lies and deception, and Kit Williams himself admitted that he'd been 'conned'.

The common belief, which I share, is that the *Hareraiser* puzzle is either meaningless or the method of obtaining the answer is so wilfully obscure as to make it effectively impossible. That way there need never be a winner at all, and

The Golden Hare as rendered by the Spectrum, C64, BBC, Amstrad and Dragon. Odd how the Spectrum version has more effort put into it than the others combined.

Which Iron then me go

I got the Oric version of Finale *to work. Now I wish I hadn't.*

Haresoft's business model – based entirely around owning the Golden Hare – would get to continue. But in the event of a legal challenge, they would be able to claim some arbitrary answer existed. If this is true, then the whole *Hareraiser* puzzle effectively has no solution and is therefore monumentally terrible.

Of course, it's also possible that the puzzle is just extremely difficult or badly designed, but it's difficult not to assume there was some deceit present in the *Hareraiser* project. Whatever the truth, it's tragic that a puzzle as beautifully constructed and presented as *Masquerade* led to the creation of something as grasping and empty

as *Hareraiser*. For £17.90 you got a few lines of BASIC code, whereas a few years previously you could pay £3.50 for a book full of beautiful art.

But what happened to the Golden Hare? It transpires that the anonymous purchaser lives in Egypt and still owns the pendant to this day. They kindly allowed it to be sent back to England for the 30th anniversary of *Masquerade*'s publishing, where it was reunited with Kit Williams. It was also displayed at the Victoria & Albert Museum in 2012 as part of a retrospective on British design. So although *Hareraiser* may have been a huge bust, the Golden Hare itself lives on.

PLAY THIS INSTEAD
If you want an actual puzzle game, you can't beat Cliff Johnson's epic *The Fool's Errand*. It's a superb compendium of various brain-teasers with an overarching metapuzzle. I played the Amiga version many years ago, but now you can download a free emulated version for Windows or Mac directly from Johnson's website.

FURTHER READING
If you'd like to know more about *Masquerade*, try to track down Bamber Gascoigne's book *The Quest for the Golden Hare* – it's a fascinating read. Do bear in mind that it doesn't cover the later scandal as it was published before those details emerged. And of course you should get *Masquerade* itself.

KANSAS MUNCHMAN

PAC-MAN WAS AN absolute powerhouse of a game in the early eighties. It's still popular and widely known to this day, but back then every computer had multiple knock-offs of the game. Most were disappointing but *Munchman* really took the biscuit, ate it then vomited it back into the barrel.

Kansas City Systems (actually based in Chesterfield, UK) sold their games exclusively by mail-order. They seemed to be perpetually having a sale, much like those furniture shops that advertise on daytime television. Most of their games, *Munchman* included, claimed to have a 'catalogue price' of £8.95 each but were actually sold at £8.50 for three or £3.95 each. So everything looked like a heavily reduced bargain at all times!

Sadly, *Munchman* was less of a bargain and more the biggest waste of money imaginable, even for £3.95.

Munchman stars a more rounded, purple doppelgänger of the mighty *Pac-Man*. He is, of course, tasked with eating all the dots in a maze. Four dangerous red ghosts are haunting the place and there are four power-up dots that temporarily allow you to eat them. So far, so standard. The bonus fruit and side doors from the original are missing, as is any fun.

MICRO COMPUTER SOFTWARE

Kansas

The remarkably austere cover. Kansas used the same design in different colours, with the game's name on the spine.

You're first greeted by a series of annoying bleeps as the maze is slowly drawn. The game uses character blocks for the entire layout, which is a technical way of saying it looks ugly and there's no animation for any of the characters. They flick from one square to the next, forever trapped in the grid of Acorn Electron BASIC. And perhaps in an attempt to make the game look like less of an obvious knock-off, the background is bright cyan rather than black, which is a real pain in the retinas.

After a few seconds of play, another major problem rears its head. The game is just far too easy. The ghosts don't actively chase you but just meander around at random, and the design of the maze means there's always an easy way to get round them. And, incredibly, Munchman himself moves faster than the ghosts, so it's trivial to outrun them. It's a greater challenge to open a bag of crisps.

Eating one of the 'energiser' power pellets does the usual thing of making the ghosts flash and enabling you to eat them, but they don't actively run away and the effect only lasts about three seconds. Eating them is pointless anyway as they just teleport to another location on the map and it doesn't help your score. Points are awarded

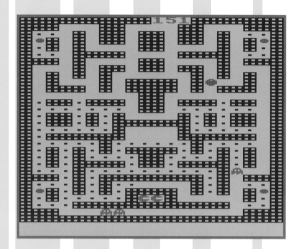

Munchman is the larger purple blob near the top right, because he curls into a foetal position when not moving. I know the feeling.

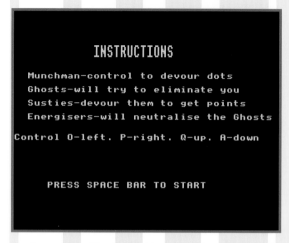

The instructions. 'Susties' and 'energisers' sound like something you could be arrested for possessing.

for eating dots, or 'susties' as they are called in the instructions, and nothing else.

Speaking of inexplicable teleportation, in the incredibly unlikely event you lose a life, you instantly teleport to another location on the map. A few weird red clones of Munchman – which can be eaten like dots – also appear at random on the map, which is both eerie and confusing.

And now we reach the real meat of Muchman's meal of crap: when you eat all the dots on the screen, nothing happens. Absolutely nothing. You're just trapped in the haunted maze forever because the game somehow doesn't know you've completed the level. I played it 12 times in the

hope that it might show me a second level at some point with no success.

But... on the 13th attempt I was so bored that I wasn't really paying attention and lost two lives. I was then somehow pushed through to Level 2 before I'd actually eaten all the dots! I can only assume the game seems to think you have to eat more dots than are actually present on the level, and eating the weird red clones pushes you above that limit. But as Level 2 is identical to Level 1, I don't think anyone is going to care.

Munchman is an absolute farce of a game. It's stupidly easy and totally broken, the graphics are ugly and the sound is mostly restricted to a distorted low beep when you eat a dot.

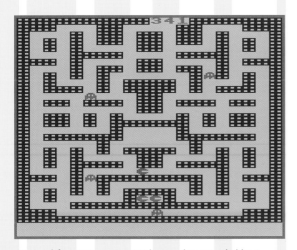

Trapped forever in an empty haunted maze. It's like a metaphor for working in insurance.

Kansas City Systems actually sold a number of decent games, but they really let quality slip with *Munchman*. In fact, it didn't just slip: it suddenly shot sideways at 800mph and smashed through a wall.

Is this worse than the notorious official *Pac-Man* for the Atari 2600? Yes. But only because you have to lose lives to finish the level.

PLAY THIS GAME INSTEAD

The go-to *Pac-Man* clone for the Acorn Electron is *Snapper*, which is an excellent version. In fact, it's one of my favourites for any 8-bit home computer.

RECREATE THIS GAME IN REAL LIFE

Lock yourself in an abandoned building and systemically clean the entire floor. Never, ever leave.

REVIEW SCORES

The *Electron User Group* pulled no punches, saying, 'It is the very worst Acorn Electron game ever commercially released.'

OTHER VERSIONS

There are several other games called *Munchman* or *Munch Man*, but there are no versions of this specific game for any other system.

Kieren can be found on YouTube at youtube.com/ LairdOfForsyth and on Twitter @RetroLaird.

HE'S THE MEANEST SON OF A SNAKE YOU'VE EVER SEEN!

HE'S THE ...

HKM

SPECTRUM 48/128K,+2, +3 Cassette

THE MOST DISAPPOINTING GAME I EVER BOUGHT

BY KIEREN HAWKEN, VIDEO GAME JOURNALIST

HUMAN KILLING MACHINE
FORMAT: ZX SPECTRUM
YEAR OF RELEASE: 1988
DEVELOPER: TIERTEX
PUBLISHER: US GOLD
ORIGINAL PRICE: 8.99 POUNDS CASSETTE,
12.99 POUNDS DISK

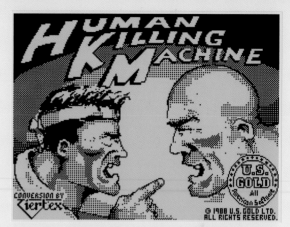

The title screen, apparently featuring an argument between a fitness instructor and a man with a giant head.

BEFORE WE GET gabbing about the game in question, I want to share another story with you that will not only bring back many memories for some of our readers but is also related to this very product. If you owned a home micro back in the day and lived in the UK, then you may well have been a member of, or just remember, something called the Home Computer Club. Now this isn't to be confused with those after-school clubs where you all met up to 'exchange games' (with a pack of TDK C90s and a double deck cassette recorder). This was a mail-order company that offered you special deals on all the latest games, as well as exclusive offerings, for a fairly small joining fee. The only catch was that you had to order at least one game per month; if you didn't, then they automatically sent you the 'Game of the Month' and charged you accordingly. More often than not, the so-called Game of the Month wasn't actually very good and was an obvious form of paid product placement. This is how I ended up with the rather substandard *Indiana Jones and the Last Crusade* (damn you, US Gold, you cursed me so many times!), but that's a story for another day.

Now as you have probably guessed already, *H.K.M.* (as it's commonly known) was one such title – the 'prestigious' Game of the Month at the Home Computer Club and one that came with a great deal of hype attached. I do have to confess, though, that I actually wanted *H.K.M.*; in fact, I wanted it badly, after all the magazines had been hyping it to death for months so it had to be good, right? I think you already know the answer

to that, otherwise it wouldn't be featured in this book, but in the history of home computers there are few games that came with so much enthusiastic publicity and then turned out to be so horrifically bad (possibly only *Rise of the Robots* beats it in that respect). Every single magazine out there swore that *H.K.M.* was going to be the next big thing, the game that would take fighting games to a new level and assert US Gold as the dominant force in home computer games. Now in hindsight it's quite obvious that said magazines were likely in receipt of bulky brown envelopes handed over to them in a dimly lit Birmingham car park, but as innocent children we were never aware that such things took place. However, the hype that followed *H.K.M.* was not without some sort of merit, which I will now endeavour to explain further.

If we rewind a bit through US Gold's illustrious past, we will find a key moment in their success, an exclusive contract with Japanese arcade giants Capcom to convert their many coin-ops to the

Our hero Kwon punches a man carrying a rifle outside Saint Basil's Cathedral. Hey, it's a hobby.

Kwon celebrates after pummelling a dog unconscious. He is no longer our hero.

humble home micros of the time. One of the first games to get this treatment was a new one-on-one fighting game called *Street Fighter*. Very much an evolution of another arcade title, Konami's *Yie Ar Kung-Fu*, *Street Fighter* was the first game to introduce us to the likes of Ryu, Sagat and Ken, although it wasn't until the far more successful sequel that these would become household names. As horrendously poor as US Gold's home conversions were, they sold like hot cakes, presumably riding off the back of the red hot licence. With these sales in mind, the Birmingham-based publisher was understandably desperate to follow up this success and produce a sequel. Without Capcom's consent they turned to developer Tiertex, who had previously handled

the original *Street Fighter* ports, to come up with a sequel, and the hype train began. Before long US Gold was promising us an amazing new sequel to *Street Fighter* that would take the game to the next level, but they hadn't counted on Capcom's objection. By this time the Japanese giants were working on a sequel of their own and didn't take too kindly to US Gold's own vision of *Street Fighter II*. Not wanting to risk their lucrative relationship, US Gold and Tiertex hastily came up with a new title: *Human Killing Machine*. This didn't stop them promoting it as a follow-up to *Street Fighter* behind Capcom's back, however.

Early images of the game were very promising. *H.K.M.* featured huge sprites, detailed backgrounds and a wide variety of different opponents

Meanwhile in Amsterdam, an impromptu dance number breaks out in front of a nightclub.

that would even see you fighting an angry bull! US Gold promised a wide variety of fighting styles, unique moves and fast, fluid gameplay. Unfortunately, Tiertex didn't deliver any of these promises, not even close. What we got was a jerky, broken mess that was about as fun to play with as your nan's cardigan collection. My first experience of *H.K.M.* was on the Sinclair ZX Spectrum, which was undoubtedly the weakest hardware the game was released on, but that doesn't always mean it gets the worst version, as we will find out. The Speccy iteration certainly looked great in screenshots, which definitely helped fool me in my Home Computer Club catalogue. Despite being in monochrome, it was detailed and well-drawn, and featured those big

arcade-like sprites we were promised. Unfortunately, it didn't play anywhere near as well as it initially looked and, to maintain those massive sprites, the animation was almost non-existent. The main problem was that each character could be easily beaten using a specific move or tactic repeatedly. Once you worked out what that was, you could breeze through the game in under 20 minutes. But until you figured out the tactics, you would get brutally beaten by the awful A.I.; there was no happy medium or any way to have properly competitive matches. The sound was also pathetic, even on the 128k machines where there was no excuse. Come review time, the magazines were strangely positive, with *Your Sinclair* awarding the game an incredible 7/10! I can only assume they liked brown envelopes too. This of course meant that my crushing disappointment was also felt by many others out there.

The only consolation for us Speccy owners was that the other 8-bit versions were even worse. First, we have the Amstrad CPC port, and port is the right word as Tiertex basically took the Spectrum version and dumped it on Alan Sugar's baby using the machine's four-colour mode, which has the same resolution as the Speccy. But rather than just leaving it in monochrome like so many other developers did with their lazy Spectrum to Amstrad ports, Tiertex thought it would be a good idea to add a splash of colour. But when you only have four available and you

The Atari ST version. More colours on screen; no more fun in the game.

choose blue, red, yellow and black, it looks like somebody swallowed half a pack of crayons and promptly threw up all over your monitor. It's also slower and jerkier than the Spectrum version, with even worse in-game sound effects! Amstrad *H.K.M.* is a horrendous mess in every regard, but still not as bad as the Commodore 64 version.

This is because the team behind C64 *H.K.M.* (not Tiertex) chose to make a few changes to the game to suit the hardware in question, alterations that actually manage to make it worse! First, the C64 version uses just half the screen, with a huge, rather obnoxious, status panel dominating the bottom half. The actual play area features sprites that are so small you would have been barely able to see them on that 14-inch TV in your bedroom. On the plus side the backgrounds are fairly good and there's some nice music too, but the tiny sprites and flawed gameplay that cursed the other versions ruin any enjoyment you might have got from it.

My next experience of *H.K.M.* came when I upgraded to an Atari ST. It wasn't a game I chose to purchase; it was one of the many included in Atari's now infamous Power Pack, a vast collection of titles that was both the ST's saviour and downfall, as while it certainly helped sell a lot of machines, it also upset a lot of publishers when ST owners didn't feel the need to buy new games thanks to their instant collection. Despite initially being very reluctant to put it in my disk drive, I did have some hope that Tiertex would have got it right in 16-bits with all that extra power at their disposal. Oh, how wrong I can be! The Atari ST version was barely much of an upgrade from the Speccy version I had loathed so greatly before it. Ok, so we now had lots of nice colours and there was some nice music too, but the game still absolutely sucked. There were still only five frames of animation for each character, the same broken A.I. and those stupid speech bubbles that pop up when you hit people. The Commodore Amiga version was no better really, the only real difference being in the music. It wasn't enough that *H.K.M.* had managed to punish me once; it was back for

revenge with my new computer. To this day, though, I am still baffled by how they thought it was ok to have both a dog and a bull as opponents – think what kind of outrage that would cause with animal activists these days!

You won't be surprised to hear that US Gold quickly forgot about *H.K.M.*, we never saw a *Human Killing Machine II* and before long they had the real *Street Fighter II* in their conversion queue. And, despite their former atrocities, Tiertex was handed the job once again, so I think that you can all guess just how well that turned out!

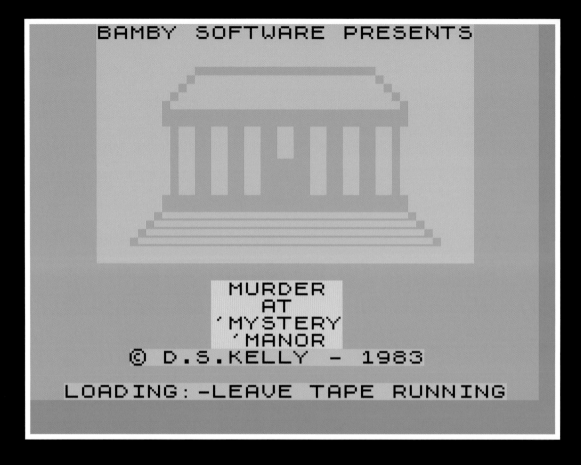

BAMBY SOFTWARE PRESENTS

MURDER
AT
'MYSTERY
'MANOR
© D.S.KELLY - 1983

LOADING:-LEAVE TAPE RUNNING

MYSTERY MANOR
AKA MURDER AT MYSTERY MANOR

FORMAT: ZX SPECTRUM
YEAR OF RELEASE: 1984
DEVELOPER: D. S. KELLY
PUBLISHER: BAMBY SOFTWARE
ORIGINAL PRICE: 6.50 POUNDS

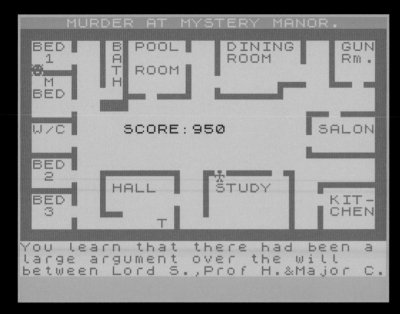

```
BED        B  POOL         DINING          GUN
 1         A               ROOM            Rm.
           T  ROOM
   M       H
BED

W/C           SCORE:950                    SALON

BED
 2
                                           KIT-
BED        HALL         STUDY              CHEN
 3
              T

You learn that there had been a
large argument over the will
between Lord S.,Prof H.&Major C.
```

Can you spot the characters? Inspector Solvitt is in the wall of the study; the murderer is in the wall between two bedrooms. Maybe they're fixing the wiring.

BAD NEWS EVERYONE: Lord Smedley is dead. And to make it worse, he was brutally murdered in his own home! And worse still, you're Inspector Solvitt, so it's your job to crack the crime as opposed to reading about it in the newspaper and saying, 'Tut! What is the world coming to?'

Solving the case involves deducing the murderer and murder weapon, much like the board game Cluedo except you don't need to worry about the room the crime occurred in. But you only get one guess, and your deductions are based on written clues rather than directly eliminating the possibilities.

Inspector Solvitt is represented by a tiny stick man who moves around the screen, which consists of a map of the manor. By walking into each different room, you are presented with a clue which may help you solve the murder. When you think you've worked out the murderer and the weapon used, you need to move to the telephone in the hallway, which allows you to make your accusation. If you are correct on both counts then you get a big score bonus and win the game, but make an error and you're stuck with the score you had when you made the call.

It sounds simple, and it is simple. Far too simple, in fact. The clues make things extremely obvious so there's no brain work, just wandering around the rooms to collect all the information. It's a very quick process to get round the map, so an average game of *Mystery Manor* lasts under two minutes. Not exactly great value for money.

And, due to the incredible technical shoddiness of the game, those two minutes will not be spent having fun. The single-game screen uses the Spectrum's character grid and effectively means the play area is made up of 30 by 16 squares, which your character flickers around since the screen only updates about twice a second. This makes the controls so unresponsive that you have to hold them down for almost a full second before they register.

To make matters worse, the controls themselves are stuck on the Spectrum cursors, which is never good as the machine lacked physical

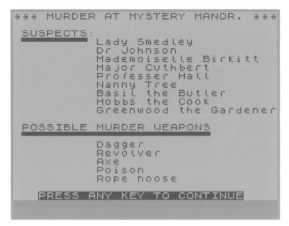

*** MURDER AT MYSTERY MANOR. ***
SUSPECTS:
           Lady Smedley
           Dr Johnson
           Mademoiselle Birkitt
           Major Cuthbert
           Professor Hall
           Nanny Tree
           Basil the Butler
           Hobbs the Cook
           Greenwood the Gardener
POSSIBLE MURDER WEAPONS
           Dagger
           Revolver
           Axe
           Poison
           Rope noose
PRESS ANY KEY TO CONTINUE

Those suspects and murder weapons in full. At the end of the game the revolver is referred to as the 'refolver', giving some idea of the game's quality.

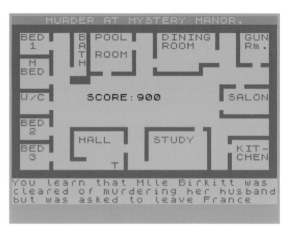

A French scandal! Notice that the characters are missing because this screen capture was taken on an off-frame.

buttons for them and the directions were mapped to the 5, 6, 7 and 8 keys. Only for owners of a relatively rare Cursor joystick would the inputs make any sense in relation to each other.

So you ram down the keys, watching your stick man disappear and reappear as the screen updates, and walk to each room in turn. Every single movement you make sets annoying beeps, which are the only sound in the whole game. You also start with 1,000 points which drop with each screen refresh. As you walk through the entrances, the game announces the room you're in, to remind you that you can now press the C key to get a short text clue. Here's an example of one: 'You

learn that Lord Smedley's will naming his daughter as his sole heir has disapeered.' Yes, that spelling mistake is present in the original text.

After getting a couple of clues, it quickly becomes apparent that there is no collision detection on the map, which means you can just walk through the walls to each room and grab the clues much faster. You can quickly run around the map in a circle as there's nothing to stop you. Or is there...?

Mystery Manor has an extra gameplay feature I haven't mentioned: the murderer is still in the manor and is out to get you! As you move around the map, the murderer moves around too, and if

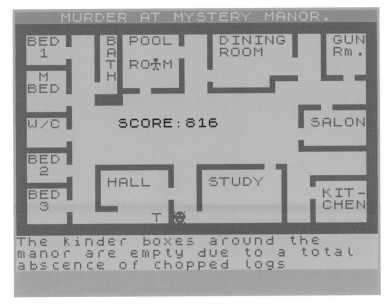

Kinder boxes? Do they mean 'kindling', or are there boxes of mystery toy eggs everywhere? (This is actually a not-so-subtle hint that the murder weapon is the axe.)

they catch you then it's instantly game over. I didn't mention it as it has no real bearing on the game – the murderer moves around at random, frequently teleporting several squares, and is never a threat. You have to deliberately chase them to get caught, and even then it can take a while. The murderer may actually be one of the least effective bad guys in history. And their presence breaks any logic behind the game's story – surely Inspector

Solvitt would immediately call for back-up for his own safety, rather than wandering about trying to work out who the person actively trying to kill him is?

Even the final part of the game, where you just have to pick a person and a weapon from a list, is a bit dodgy. Rather than reading your next key press, the game demands that you enter a number and press return, and it immediately crashes if you enter anything except the exact numbers listed. And crashing dumps you straight into the source code, because as you may well have predicted, the game is written entirely in the Spectrum's built-in BASIC language.

The program is so simple that I understood how the entire game worked from a cursory glance at the code, and I am far from being competent with Spectrum BASIC. This meant that not only could I change the potential murderers' names to things like 'Billy Poo' and 'Ezekial Flurbler', I could also see how many potential sets of clues there are. The answer is eight different murderer clues (despite there being nine potential murderers) and five different weapon clues, so you'll see everything the

game has to offer in a few plays.

It seems that somebody had an idea to make a Cluedo-based game but didn't really know how to program or design at all. As a result, *Mystery Manor* is something of an embarrassment – a glitchy, incompetent shambles that was released at the top price point at the time. Anyone who bought it must have been put off buying mail-order games for life.

Bamby Software released two other games, a serviceable clone of the board game Mastermind called *Master Code*, and *Free-Zone*, apparently a computerised board game, but no copies of it have ever been found so nobody knows for sure.

RECREATE THIS GAME IN REAL LIFE

Play Cluedo with over-excited five-year-olds and do not explain the rules or discipline them in any way. Before long they'll be pushing the pieces around the board, through all the walls, while pretending they're chasing each other. Perfect!

MYSTERY MANOR CHEATS

Go to the telephone and instead of entering a number, enter 'p' for the person and 'w' for the weapon. You will be correct every time, and have had no fun at all!

REVIEW SCORES

I thought this would be one of those mail-order-only games that magazines never bothered with, but *Crash* did actually give it a full review in their adventure section. They gave it 1/10 and said it was 'no better than most could achieve given a wet weekend'. A fair assessment, really.

OTHER VERSIONS

Mystery Manor was only available on the ZX Spectrum, which I imagine Commodore 64 and Amstrad CPC owners were thankful for.

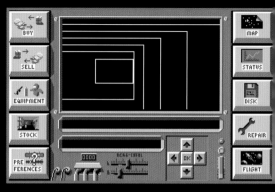

This is the flight sequence, not a lost Mondrian work.

LOWEST MAGAZINE SCORE CORNER

AMIGA COMPUTING MAGAZINE
Score: 11%
Game: *S.T.A.G.*
Format: Commodore Amiga

A very disappointing *Elite* clone where you fly around in a spaceship trading various inter-galactic commodities. The actual flight simulation part is very weak, mostly involving flying through a series of boxes. It also doesn't help that it's poorly translated from German, so a lot of the text is a grammatical nightmare. While *S.T.A.G.* is far from being a good game, it's not as bad as *Amiga Computing* claimed. I have no idea why they hated it so much – they only ever rated eight games below 25% in their 117-issue run. And they awarded the appalling Amiga version of *Street Fighter* 38%!

PLAY THIS GAME INSTEAD
Three years later US Gold published *Killed Until Dead*, an excellent game with a similar premise. There are versions for the Spectrum, Amstrad and Commodore 64 and they're all great.

MENTSKI'S ARCADE HALL OF SHAME

Hello, I'm Mentski. You may remember me from Ashen's previous book where I rambled on about the ZX Spectrum version of *Out Run*. You may remember me from other places. These other places are unimportant. I like arcade machines. In the early days they were the cutting edge of video game technology, and no home system could match what you played there. I can be found at youtube.com/user/mentski and on Twitter @mentski

We all wanted those games on our home computers, but big names such as Sega, Namco and Capcom probably didn't even know what a ZX Spectrum was, let alone how to port their latest masterpiece to it. So back in the beautiful, neon haze of the eighties, it would be up to software labels such as Ocean and US Gold to obtain a licence to make home computer versions of these games, usually with no help from the original developers, and often rushed to meet release dates in order to maximise profits. Sometimes, this did not go well.

Sometimes they were so desperate to profit on a licence they even made their own unofficial sequels. Unsurprisingly, this often wouldn't go well, either.

Join me as I take you on a journey through mediocre and sometimes outright bad versions of games that were originally rather excellent.

ZX Spectrum version: meet Linda and her loaf-of-bread head.

ZX Spectrum version: Jimmy Lee jumps to avoid the colour clash. He fails.

Double Dragon – Melbourne House/ Mastertronic, 1989

Never mind the apology for the C64 version's graphics in the manual – the C64 version fared far better than the others. We need to talk about the other 8-bit versions, published by Melbourne House.

Legend has it that in an attempt to accurately recreate the arcade game's graphics, they were digitised onto an Atari ST and then 'downgraded' for use on the ZX Spectrum and Amstrad CPC.

The problem is that any effort put into graphics comes to nought if you don't have the gameplay, and *Double Dragon* certainly doesn't. Part of this could be attributed to taking the original moves available using the joystick and three buttons and condensing them to the one-button controllers of your average computer.

I like to think that the fact that Billy and Jimmy Lee's kicks look more like the efforts of somebody with two left feet after a half-hour cancan lesson than the confident roundhouses of the arcade original might have a hand in it, too.

One thing can be sure: Ocean's unofficial sequel to *Double Dragon*'s arcade predecessor, *Renegade*, had already nailed simultaneous two-player beat-em-up gameplay a year before *Double Dragon* ever made it to shops.

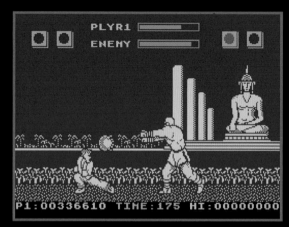

ZX Spectrum: Retsu is defeated by the ancient martial art of 'down-back and fire'.

ZX Spectrum: Hadou... Wait... This seems a little unfair.

Street Fighter – Go!/US Gold, 1988

'Never trust an arcade port by Tiertex' is a phrase you'll hear often in Mentski Towers, and this game is the reason why.

While the original *Street Fighter* wasn't the greatest game, the home conversion was highly anticipated on home formats as part of a newly formed partnership between US Gold and Capcom.

The arcade version was considered a technical achievement, with its initial arcade cabinets having hydraulic buttons and later versions introducing the iconic six-button layout.

The home port we got was a severely stripped representation of the original. Much like *Double Dragon*, there was always going to be a problem with accurately representing all the moves on a controller with one button, but to add insult to injury, all the players' special moves – which, due to the complexity, were usually performed with luck rather than judgement at that point – are entirely absent.

The question remains: were they removed due to memory restraints, or was Tiertex's staff so incompetent at researching the game they were converting that they didn't realise Ryu and Ken could do them?

... Because all your opponents can do their special moves. Just saying.

Tiertex went on to develop what was originally going to be marketed by US Gold as *Street Fighter 2: Human Killing Machine*. And if you don't know what happened with that, have a search on YouTube.

ZX Spectrum version: probably the only screen you'll ever see in Dragon's Lair.

ZX Spectrum version: probably the only screen you'll ever see in Singe's Castle.

Dragon's Lair – Software Projects, 1986

For the record, it took ReadySoft six 720KB floppy disks to (almost) accurately represent Don Bluth's laserdisk-based classic on an Amiga 1000 in 1989, so how well do you think Software Projects did, on tape, on a 48K ZX Spectrum in 1986? The answer is not well.

Split onto two tapes – named *Dragon's Lair* and *Dragon's Lair II: Escape from Singe's Castle* (not to be confused with the real sequel, *Dragon's Lair II: Time Warp*) – Software Projects' conversion featured multiple mini-games vaguely based on scenes from the arcade original, spread over both tapes, released a year apart.

Usually the home conversions are restricted in some way compared to the arcade original due to the confines of the computer hardware.

Not so in *Dragon's Lair*. The original arcade version is a laserdisk-based interactive movie where you tapped the joystick and button at predetermined points to advance the scene. The prototypical quick-time event. Software Projects' conversion (based on a US version of the game on the Coleco Adam) gave you far more control over Dirk the Daring at many points in the game, as he became a fully controllable sprite on screen.

Not that you're likely to ever get past the first screen to ever appreciate this, in *Dragon's Lair* or *Singe's Castle*. The initial screens have the type of difficulty rarely seen outside of the first screen of *Airwolf* on the ZX Spectrum.

Commodore Amiga version: it's Strider! *Or maybe* Strider II *... It's hard to tell.*

Commodore Amiga version: it's Strider II! *Or maybe* Strider *... It's hard to tell.*

Strider/Strider II – US Gold, 1989/1990

Strider is a beautiful-looking, beautiful-playing arcade game, so who did US Gold employ to make their home version? Tiertex, of course. After all they did such a good job converting *Rolling Thunder*.

Many of the shortcomings of Tiertex's 'interpretation' of *Strider* are similar to *Rolling Thunder*. Over a third of the screen is dedicated to a status window, leaving the gameplay in the top. This is evident in the 8- and 16-bit versions of the game, at a time when Sega's 16-Bit Mega Drive was about to have an almost arcade-perfect conversion of the game of its own in Japan.

The port was much slower, featured dumbed-down maps of the original stages, and some power-ups (such as Hiryu's robot tiger) were out right missing. Tiertex standard.

Regardless, it sold like hotcakes, and by the next year US Gold had decided they needed a sequel. Alas, Capcom wasn't to make one for another 10 years, so instead we got Tiertex's *Strider I*.

And holy asset reuse! The game is clearly based on a similar engine, but to Tiertex's credit, the game runs at a higher pace. *Strider* even has a new running animation on the Amiga, but for crying out loud... could you spare a few pennies to get somebody to make new music? It's exactly the same as the first!

Sadly, without having an initial Capcom design to base this game on, the level design is terrible and the enemies are dull and uninspiring. Oh... and Strider transforms into a robot-tank to fight

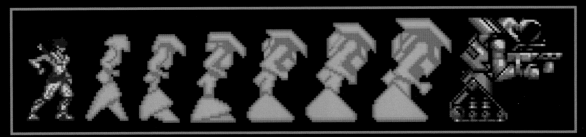

Commodore Amiga Version: Strider transforms and rolls out. Literally.

original arcade sprites. It's still terrible – and despite the increase in speed in the home versions, hideously slow – but at least they removed the tankbot.

By 1996, original lead designer Kouichi Yotsui and other members of the original *Strider* arcade development team had defected to Mitchell Corp to produce the spiritual sequel *Osman*, and in 1999 Capcom themselves produced the canonical sequel *Strider 2*. They're both brilliant games that allow us to try and forget that Tiertex's monstrosity ever existed at all. But nothing truly washes that Tiertex taste away.

the end-of-level boss. Yes... You heard that right. Because: reasons.

Three years later, *Strider II* got a slightly redesigned Mega Drive port using versions of the

ZX Spectrum version: playable but ugly.

Atari ST version: this is what playing in bullet-time looks like.

Rolling Thunder – US Gold, 1988

Rolling Thunder by Namco was a highly influential 'walk and gun' with a dual-level scrolling play-field, copied by many other arcade developers in later games such as Data East's *Sly Spy* and Sega's *Shinobi*.

Famed for its incredible animation and smooth, fast gameplay, *Rolling Thunder* was a highly antici-pated game for home computers. So how did US Gold manage to bum this one up? Welcome back to Tiertex country.

First, all the ports had a gigantic border, limit-ing the actual gameplay to roughly half the real estate of the entire screen. The beautiful anima-tions? All horribly redrawn. WCPO agent Albatross now looks like he's taking a casual stroll rather than infiltrating the evil GELDRA's base with any purpose.

And that smooth, fast gameplay? On most for-mats it's now a slow-paced, often jerky mess. Most notably on the Atari ST, which manages to be outperformed by a ZX Spectrum – probably the best port out of them all.

Compare with Namco's own conversion for the NES (developed by Arc System Works, no less) to see how to do this game justice on a low-powered home machine.

ZX Spectrum version: I'm afraid taking that power pill won't relieve you from the agony of this...

The three stages of Pac – original, preview and reality.

Pac-Land – Quicksilva/Grandslam, 1989

It's astonishing to think that a game like *Pac-Land*, a game considered by many to be an important forerunner in the scrolling platform game genre, took five whole years to get a home computer conversion. It's also astonishing what a total pig's ear Quicksilva made of it on many of the formats they released it on.

Early screenshots of the game showed a very different-looking *Pac-Land* to the one they released – the February 1988 edition of *Sinclair User*, for example, shows a screenshot that looks like quite an accurate representation of the original game, outside of being monochrome.

The final product looked totally different. Whether or not that original Speccy screenshot was a prototype or what we'd now consider a 'bullshot' is lost to time. The final graphics were a blocky mess, looked the same across the 8-bit formats, and featured a weird, squished Pac-Man sprite who, instead of jollily bounding through levels, had a walking animation that made it look like his feet were on tank tracks.

To add insult to injury, on every 8-bit format except the C64, this platform scrolling pioneer didn't even scroll, leading to cheap, frustrating deaths because you didn't know what you were going to find when the screen flipped.

The ST and Amiga ports fared far better, accurately simulating the graphics, sound and scrolling of the arcade. It should've been a shoo-in to accurately simulate the gameplay too, but with the power of hindsight, you can tell that it's a floaty, unresponsive mess compared to the original.

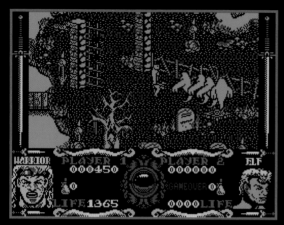

ZX Spectrum version: Gauntlet III *sees an unrecognisable warrior confront a conga line of ghosts on the green screen of doom.*

Commodore Amiga version: *not much happening here either.*

Gauntlet III: The Final Quest – US Gold, 1991

Gauntlet and *Gauntlet II* were incredible dungeon crawlers, allowing four simultaneous players in the arcade. While most of the home computer versions were only two-player, they were examples of a home conversion done right. It also helped that the tile-based map layout allowed the Speccy versions of the games to be accurate representations with little to no colour clash.

Sadly for us all, Atari Games did not seem interested in continuing the series. They slapped the name *Gauntlet: The Third Encounter* on an Epyx-developed Atari Lynx game that had a vague resemblance to the series, originally titled *Time Quests and Treasure Chests*, and that was their lot. So, US Gold, doing what US Gold did, decided

to make their own follow-up to the series.

Now, a third game with extra playable character classes, new monsters to kill, and maps featuring not only dungeons but external locales sounds great. On paper...

The problem is that US Gold and Software Creations thought they knew better than Ed Logg and the team at Atari Games and decided to create their game with an isometric perspective, which had its limitations compared to the top-down action of the original.

Instead of facing hordes of ghosts and grunts, enemies were limited to not much more than six on the screen at once. Lessening any type of real peril or panic in the game. The Spectrum and Amstrad versions also lacked any kind of colour, which meant you'd often not notice tentacles spawning under your character, sucking your health away.

Years later, Atari would continue the series with *Gauntlet Legends* using a similar isometric view. That wasn't much cop either.

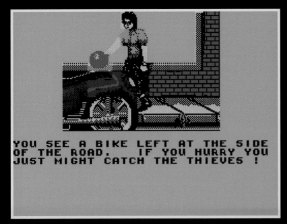

ZX Spectrum version: just what Out Run *needed – expository cutscenes.*

ZX Spectrum version: this was originally intended to have full-colour graphics, which can still be patched in. It looks terrible regardless.

Out Run Europa – US Gold, 1991

It rarely escapes anyone's attention that I'm a bit of an *Out Run* buff. Sega and AM2's game about a guy and his girlfriend speeding through beautiful locales in a Ferrari has left a mark in the minds of many gamers of my generation due to its sublime music, presentation and gameplay.

Despite all the home ports being utterly pants – particularly the Spectrum version – US Gold's conversions sold incredibly well, as did its sequel, *Turbo OutRun*, two years later in 1989. The problem is that by 1991, Sega hadn't made another arcade sequel, so US Gold decided they had to make their own to keep the gravy train running.

Developed by Probe Software (the people responsible for the somewhat mediocre ports of the previous two games), *Out Run Europa* attempts to mimic the pursuit-style gameplay of Taito's *Chase HQ*, and while admittedly it's technically superior to their previous attempts at *Out Run* on every format, it completely misses the point about why the original arcade games were fun.

Since the last game, somehow you've become some kind of super spy, but don't go expecting to be driving that shiny red Ferrari, oh no. That's been stolen by criminals. You spend 90% of the game driving motorbikes, jet skis and other vehicles through some pretty dull locales. Great.

If this game had been given an original title, it might've been remembered more fondly, but by giving it the *Out Run* name, they created expectations. Expectations that it could never possibly meet. Somehow, Sega allowed US Gold to port it to the Master System, too, giving it a kind of semi-legitimacy in *Out Run* canon. In my eyes, it can bog off.

Atari ST version: WHY DID I PAY £25 FOR THIS?

ZX Spectrum version: whoever converted the graphics had talent; whoever translated the gameplay is a lunatic.

Street Fighter II – US Gold, 1993

Street Fighter II. Eight playable characters and four bosses, each with a different fighting style (well, bar Ken and Ryu...) and special moves to match. That's a lot to squeeze into any home computer with not much RAM and without the hardware of a console that is far more suited to the purpose of replicating this game.

Oh, sweet criminy... What did you do, US Gold? What did you do? You couldn't do the original *Street Fighter* justice five years previously, how did you possibly think you'd ever be able to convert *Street Fighter II* to two computer formats that load off tape?

The SNES version had, by this point, been out for a year. The Mega Drive's Special Champion Edition was due at the end of 1993. Home computers were losing their lustre as the go-to platform for playing games in favour of consoles, yet US Gold, in a last-ditch attempt to feel relevant, released the game for C64, Spectrum, Amiga, ST and PC.

The Speccy version is uncredited but is allegedly by Tiertex – and is Tiertex standard. The others from Creative Materials fare better but not by much. All ports have missing animation, terrible collision detection and AI, and all but the Amiga version feature the same looping piece of music based on the character select tune over bloody everything!

One question remains: why on earth do I own a copy for the Atari ST?

STUART SAYS

I bought *Double Dragon*, *Street Fighter* and *Rolling Thunder* for the Spectrum. Some wounds never heal.

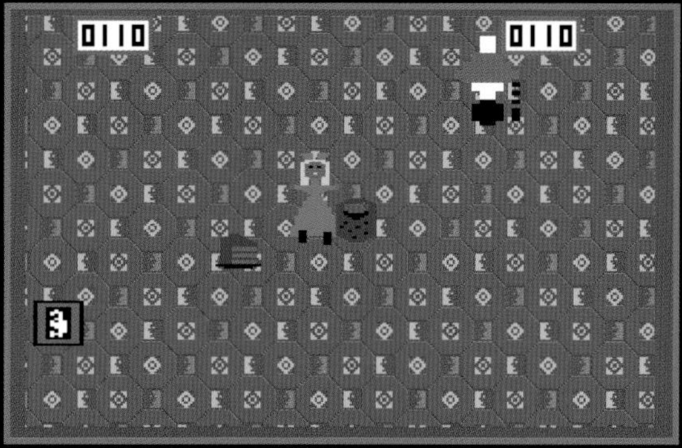

If you think Alice looks bad here, you should see it moving.

ARCADE CONVERSIONS THAT TIERTEX HAD A HAND IN

1943: The Battle of Midway
720 Degrees
Alien Storm
Black Tiger
Bonanza Bros.
Dynasty Wars
Last Duel
Mercs
Rolling Thunder
Street Fighter
Strider
Thunder Blade
UN Squadron

LOWEST MAGAZINE SCORE CORNER

ZZAP!64 MAGAZINE
Score: 3%
Games: *Robobolt* and *Alice's Adventures in Videoland*
Format: Commodore 64

Two utterly appalling titles share this dubious honour. *Robobolt* is covered in this very book, but *Alice's Adventures in Videoland* is a confusing mess of ugly pixels that's more like a headache simulator than a game. *Zzap!64* also reviewed Amiga games, the worst of which was *Willow* with 7%. It's a horrible set of mini-games based on the rather lovely children's film.

Laura is a co-founder of and regular contributor to letsplayvideogames.com, and can be found on Twitter at @Laurakbuzz.

THE MOST DISAPPOINTING GAME I EVER BOUGHT

BY LAURA KATE DALE, VIDEO GAMES JOURNALIST

BARBIE: GAME GIRL
FORMAT: NINTENDO GAME BOY
YEAR OF RELEASE: 1992
DEVELOPER: IMAGINEERING
PUBLISHER: HI TECH EXPRESSIONS
ORIGINAL PRICE: 19.99 POUNDS

AS SOMEONE WHOSE first introduction to video games was the original *Super Mario Bros.* on NES, I grew up heavily associating side-scrolling platformers with high-quality video games. That's why when I first got a Game Boy back in the early nineties, I decided I wanted a good handheld platformer to play alongside it.

Forget the Game Boy's *Super Mario Land*, I had already played *Mario* and knew what his deal was. I wanted something new, something exciting, something tailored to my own tastes. I wanted the exciting new 1992 platformer *Barbie: Game Girl*.

I can tell you now, this is not one of the prouder moments in my gaming life.

So, *Barbie: Game Girl* sees the titular heroine turn up for a date without having prepared in the slightest. She isn't dressed, she doesn't have a soundtrack ready for the date, she's totally unprepared. Thankfully, she starts on the bottom floor of a shopping centre, with her date conveniently taking place on the roof. Such a relief, she can prep for her date by running through seven different shops on her way to go impress that crotchless plastic man upstairs.

The game sees you visit such date-critical shops as The Atrium, The Soda Shoppe, Music Mania, The Fashion Boutique, the somehow-date-critical Mermaid World, the somehow-even-more-date-critical Mermaid World Too, and Toy City. Why a fully grown woman needs to visit two separate

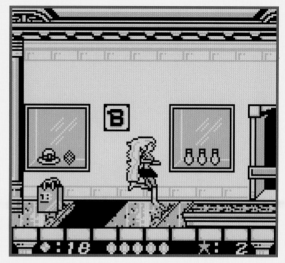
Is that Barbie's hair, or is an alien slug eating her head?

mermaid shops and a children's toy shop before her date with an adult man eludes me to this day. I'm not judging her life choices, but I feel like the game could certainly have better expanded on those specific store inclusions.

So, let's talk about the game itself. *Game Girl* is kind of like a Mario platformer, if everything was slowed down and imprecise, and Power Stars transformed Mario into cheerleader-hot-pants Mario who did needless flips every time he jumped. Oh, and the soundtrack was a terrible midi version of 'Everybody Dance Now' by C+C Music Factory.

Attempts to make small, precise movements were hampered by any tap of the controls, which

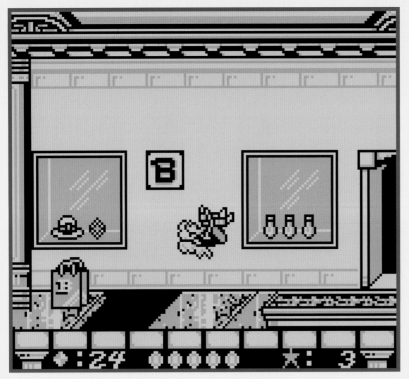

Barbie has ascended to her cheerleader form, which makes an annoying noise every time she somersaults. Which is all the time.

still struggle to place how it's simultaneously too easy and infuriatingly awkward to execute.

Still, what stuck with me more than anything, more than the terrible controls and the odd choice of level locations, were the enemies themselves. *Barbie: Game Girl*'s enemies are a weird mix of generic bouncing goblins with no narrative context, high-heeled shoes and paper cups of fizzy drink come to life, and on rare occasion actual vicious animals. There's no rhyme or reason to their inclusion, they just kind of exist in what is meant to be a real working shopping mall where Barbie has gone to prepare for a date.

would send Barbie moving a considerable distance. Jumps float forever before thudding down with a sudden limp fall; hit boxes on enemies are unpredictable; and the soundtrack notably glitches itself in odd ways for seemingly no reason. I've tried to play through *Game Girl* as an adult and I

Honestly, my lasting question 25 years on from the release of this game is why they felt the need to try and ground the game in reality with this plot about getting ready for a date with Ken. At one point you're an actual mermaid swimming underwater avoiding sharks. That is definitely not the interior of a

Barbie: Game Girl *is not the most intellectual of video game experiences.*

Mermaid Barbie confronts a fourth-wall-breaking scuba diver. Who may be naked.

shop. Why on earth the insistence we buy into this weird, grounded narrative?

Yeah, *Barbie: Game Girl* is one of those games I keep in my collection now just as a reminder that everyone has some mistakes in their past. Mine just happened to cost the price of a brand-new game.

FACT FACT FACT

Barbie: Game Girl was the third officially licensed Barbie video game to be made. To date there have been well over forty, with *Barbie: Dreamhouse Party* generally considered the worst.

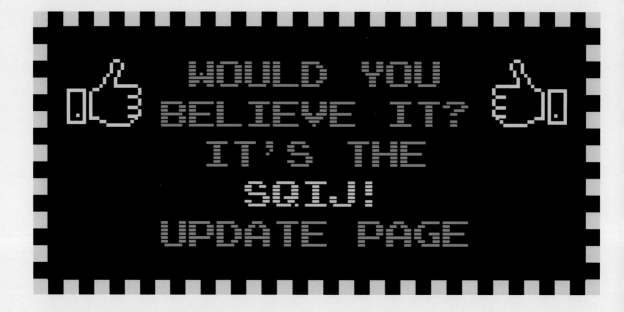

WOULD YOU BELIEVE IT? IT'S THE SQIJ! UPDATE PAGE

Readers of the first book in this series will recall the unending misery of the ZX Spectrum version of *SQIJ!*, a shockingly bad game that was literally uncontrollable unless you broke into the program and turned off Caps Lock by directly changing the value of a memory address. It also seemed to have no actual game attached, as it was impossible to leave the first room.

I said in the book that I was sure I had managed to escape from the room in the past, but had no idea how I did it. Now, thanks to ace reporter Kim Justice, we can tell the whole story.

The pigeon you control in *SQIJ!* is, according to the instructions, able to shoot projectiles of some type. However, the in-game key for activating it seems to do nothing. Intrepid Kim discovered that shooting does work, but only if you're aligned with a certain part of an enemy. The enemy then instantly disappears with no visual or audio feedback and you can leave the room.

And amazingly, there is actually a whole game in there that can be completed! It's an unbelievably badly programmed pile of hot garbage, but it does exist. You can move (farcically slowly) around the map and get to the end and everything. Admittedly, you often appear at the wrong entrance when you enter a room – enter it from the right and you'll appear at the bottom, etc. – but it does fundamentally work.

ENERGY : 90
LEVEL   :

SCORE;
127

So there ends the mystery of how I once got out of the first room of *SQIJ!*. Now if only
Kim can find out where I left my keys, everything will be well with the world.

*If you'd like to see Kim's comprehensive video on this subject,
search for 'kim justice sqij!' on YouTube.*

PROSOCCER 2190

FORMAT: ATARI ST
YEAR OF RELEASE: 1990
DEVELOPER: VIDEO VULTURE PRODUCTIONS
PUBLISHER: VULTURE PUBLISHING
ORIGINAL PRICE: 19.99 POUNDS

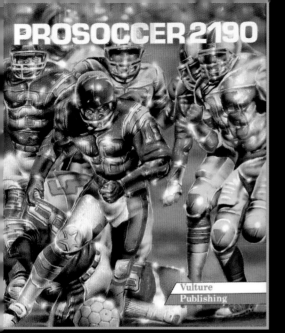

PROSOCCER 2190

Vulture Publishing

The cover shows American football players, who do not feature in the game at all. Amazing.

FUTURE SPORTS ARE an interesting genre of games. They're generally based on a contemporary sport, but with the added twist of unfettered violence being allowed by the rules. The most successful example before 1990 was *Speedball*, the Bitmap Brothers' brutal cyberpunk combination of ice hockey and handball. I also once paid money for a game called *Futuresport* for the Atari ST, which was rubbish, but considerably better than *ProSoccer 2190*.

Obviously based on association football, *ProSoccer 2190* posits that in 200 years the sport will have changed. It'll all take place indoors, the

players will dress in silly-looking outfits, and the pitch will be much narrower than it is now. And that's it really – the rules are similar, and there is none of the full-contact violence present in most future sports.

After suffering through the game's badly animated spinning globe logo, you're presented with a series of menus that have to be navigated through very slowly using the joystick. To slow things down further, it's not possible to move from the top of a menu straight to the bottom or vice versa. If you do feel like wasting a considerable amount of time menu-wrestling, you can give custom names to all the teams and their players.

Two options are extremely important. You need to change at least one of the teams away from computer control, something I didn't realise when I first played it, so I was just treated to an entire season of results screens and had no input into anything. The second is to change the length of a quarter, which defaults to a ludicrous 15 minutes, meaning that a single match would take an entire hour. Strangely there are only four options: 15 minutes, 5 minutes, 1 minute and an amazingly brief 20 seconds.

After dealing with some more menu misery to set up your team, you can jump into the game proper. This is where the true horror begins.

You see the appallingly animated, stiff-limbed players jolt their way out of the tunnel and get into position at a painfully shuddering eight frames a second. Then another menu appears to torment you, allowing you to set your players tactics, which ultimately make no difference

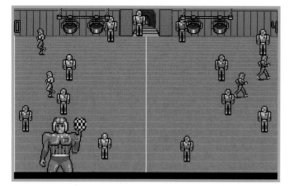

That's not a giant to the left – it's just an intro graphic.

Notice that none of the players seem to be putting much effort in.

whatsoever. Then the ball is thrown down from above and the action starts, and the urge to play something else quickly becomes overwhelming.

You control one player at a time, pressing fire to change to another when necessary. There are no sliding tackles or similar moves – to take possession of the ball you need to run into whoever has it, which will usually make it stick to your player's feet. Pressing fire when in possession brings up a little box that allows you to select the power, elevation and swerve of your subsequent kick. It also serves to stop the game dead in its tracks while you set it up, killing the flow of the gameplay.

However you set up the kick is irrelevant, as the ball tends to just bounce where it feels like. A lot of this is down to the low frame rate and the way the screen scrolls in huge chunks. This is a massive problem as the game is so fast-moving and jerky that you simply cannot keep an eye on where the ball is when the screen lurches along. And there's real joy to be had when the ball gets stuck bouncing

It looks like the blue player is being held at gunpoint, but that's actually a victory celebration.

Fans of boring, awkward menus will love this game! (Until they play the main part of it.)

between a wall and a player, as the screen violently flickers back and forth.

A goal being scored is something to avoid at all costs, as it forces a horrible replay which runs at about two frames a second. The goals themselves are odd – they're drawn as gaps in the pitch's walls, but the ball cannot pass through them and so just bounces off. Possibly it's some kind of force field, and thus the only actually futuristic thing in the game! It also takes the game a few seconds to tell you that a team has scored, which, coupled with the way you can't tell what's going on, means you frequently don't realise that there's been a goal until everything suddenly stops.

Sounds are few and far between, with the occasional crunch and bleep. There's also a little jingle that plays when the computer is working out the results of a league match between two computer teams, but any enjoyment you may get from the ditty is counteracted by having to watch the game's horrible jarring globe logo attempt to spin round.

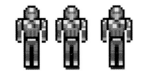

Each match allows you five time-outs to change tactics during the game. Expanding on this, there's also a 'coach mode' which enables you to get through an entire 22-week season without actually having to play the game, just issuing orders via the awkward system of interminable menus. It's unbelievably dull, but at least you don't have to try and work out where the ball is as the screen jolts around.

ProSoccer 2190 is a sickening mess. You never feel like you have any control over the action as you can never really tell what's happening due to the cripplingly jerky nature of the game. And it's not futuristic at all! It's just a bunch of Tron cosplayers kicking a ball around inside an elongated school gymnasium. It's only the costumes that stop it looking like it's set in 1957 rather than 2190.

This is without doubt the worst football game ever released for a 16-bit system. It manages to be worse than *Super Soccer* for the ZX Spectrum, which infamously has a bug that means that fouled players never get up again, so you can effectively kill most of the opposing team. And it's even less fun to play than *Amsoccer*, a bizarre pong/football hybrid for the Amstrad CPC in which the ball does not experience friction and keeps rolling at the same speed forever. Fortunately, the absolute classic *Speedball 2* came out at the same time as *ProSoccer 2190*, so even hardcore fans of future sport games looked past it completely.

But incredibly... *ProSoccer 2190* was released twice! Video Vulture themselves put copies out in 1990, and it was redistributed the following year by Active Distribution. Video Vulture ended up making four games for the Atari ST and none are very good. In fact, one of them is the execrable *Legend of the Lost*, which was on my shortlist for this book before being turned down in favour of *ProSoccer 2190*.

RECREATE THIS GAME IN REAL LIFE

Shout meaningless instructions at a bunch of kids playing indoor football while constantly opening and closing your eyes.

PLAY THESE GAMES INSTEAD

If you want to play a future sport game, play *Speedball 2*. If you want to play a football game, play *Sensible Soccer* or *Kick Off 2*. If you want to play a football management game, play *Championship Manager 93*. And that is my Atari ST advice.

REVIEW SCORES

ST Format magazine really hated this game, giving it 12% – the lowest score in the history of the magazine. The staff also voted for it as the worst ever Atari ST game in their 25th issue. And in a pan-European display of solidarity, German magazine *Power Play* also awarded it a measly 12%.

OTHER VERSIONS

As was common at the time, the Commodore Amiga version is essentially the same game with better sound. Although 'better' may not be strictly true in this case, as there's an annoying background hiss that's supposed to be the crowd cheering. Unsurprisingly, it was not well received – *Amiga Joker* magazine thought it was worth a measly 4%.

FIVE OTHER UTTERLY DREADFUL FOOTBALL GAMES

Kenny Dalglish Soccer (Commodore 64)
Five A Side Soccer (Amstrad CPC)
Indoor Soccer (BBC Micro)
Peter Beardsley's International Football (Commodore 64)
Penalty Soccer (Amstrad CPC)

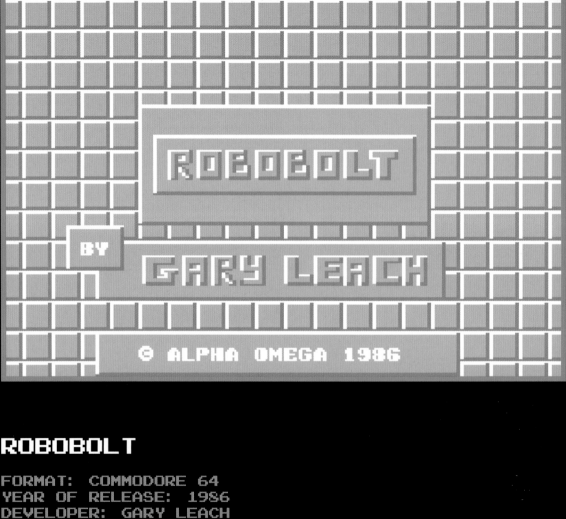

ROBOBOLT

FORMAT: COMMODORE 64
YEAR OF RELEASE: 1986
DEVELOPER: GARY LEACH
PUBLISHER: ALPHA OMEGA
ORIGINAL PRICE: 1.99 POUNDS

The cover's fairly accurate, except for the way something fun is happening.

CHEAP, SCI-FI STORYLINES were the bread and butter of eighties budget games. Made a game about a circle that goes around picking up squares and shooting other circles? Just claim they're robots on a spaceship and you've got yourself a backstory!

In *Robobolt* you control a robot that looks like a cross between a metal washer and a doughnut. Annoyingly, the spaceship it works on has been infected by some kind of radiation-causing space virus, and the robot is the only thing available to stop it. (When the fate of your ship lies with a robot that looks like two grey circles, it's probably time to eject and hope for the best...)

The ship consists of one long, bland corridor – made up of grey tiles and blocks – that loops back on itself. Combined with the grey protagonist robot, the game is about as colourful and charming as a concrete jail cell.

Four 'Death Pods' must be collected then placed in an 'Assembly Unit', which apparently kills off local infestations of the interstellar viral menace. The Death Pods may sound like a heavy metal band from Germany in the late seventies, but they are actually white squares dotted around the playing area. When you pick one up, the square goes black – this is the pinnacle of visual excitement in *Robobolt*. The graphics could be charitably described as 'minimalist' but more accurately described as 'bland'.

Filling your Assembly Unit full of Death Pods isn't quite as easy as it sounds. You can only pick up one Pod at a time, and they have to be deposited in a specific order for some reason. And because this game hates you and wants to punish you as much as possible for buying it, there is no way of knowing what that order is. All the Death Pods look identical so it's a case of just picking one up at random, taking it to the Assembly Unit and hoping that you happen to have the right one. And if you don't, it'll immediately teleport back to the place you found it, as that's apparently what Death Pods do.

This all combines into a tedious headache

158

Behold the grey glory of Robobolt. *None of the sprites are animated.*

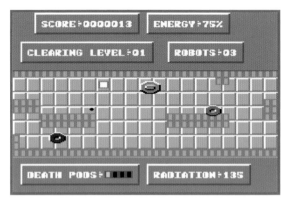

It's a Death Pod! Or a white square, as we call them in the trade.

when the time limit is taken into account. A number marked 'Radiation' counts down from 999 to 0, and when it hits the bottom it's instant death for our naff, round robot. It takes about 50 seconds to run out, and it takes about 35 seconds to travel far enough for the map to loop, so success really does depend on the random chance of picking up the correct Death Pods. And if you do succeed, then you have to do the same again on the next level, because this is a budget video game from the eighties.

Also, our geometric avatar isn't alone on the world's most boring spaceship. For reasons unknown, there are smaller, multicoloured washer-doughnut robots flying about that can drain our droid's energy by flying through it. Our

robo-hero's only defence is a small black rubber ball that bounces around the screen forever; this is apparently a 'laser'. (Light seems to work very oddly in the world of *Robobolt*.) This bouncy bullet and the enemy robots seem to exist in some kind of side-dimension, as they cheerfully glide straight through solid walls and are totally unaffected by the scrolling of the screen.

Gliding through walls would be a massive boon for the hero robot as it gets briefly stuck on any obstacle you encounter, leading to a serious case of the dreaded Sticky Controls. When you're having to speed around a maze against the clock, the last thing you need is to get attached to every single solid object like it's covered in a particularly irritating glue.

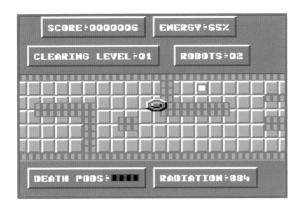

I'm stuck in a wall. The radiation timer is counting down. I want to play anything else.

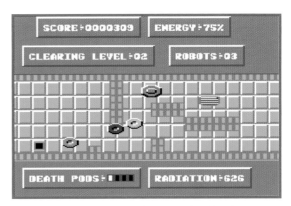

The awe-inspiring majesty of Level 2. That blue drain cover is the Assembly Unit.

In-game sound is limited to an annoying buzz sound effect when you unleash your bouncy bullet of doom and a blast of white noise when you die. However, the music on the title screen is actually half decent, and the only nice thing I can find to say about *Robobolt*.

If the gods of random item placement smile down and you manage to complete the first level, you're presented with the same corridor again in a different colour as a punishment. The only difference seems to be there's an extra enemy doughnut floating about, so the chances of losing a life due to energy loss are increased – the instructions claim that if you destroy an enemy, you get some energy back, but this is a filthy lie. And if you do manage to get on the high-score

table, it's painfully slow to enter your name, and you have to suffer a repeating flatulence sound as you do it.

Readers familiar with the Commodore 64 will have realised that *Robobolt* feels like an incompetent attempt to recreate Andrew Braybrook's superb arcade adventure *Paradroid*, one of the best games for the system. There might also be a hint of Braybrook's seminal shooter *Uridium* in the grey background and purely horizontal scrolling too. However, it does predate the movie *Robocop*, so the similar title is coincidental.

As you've probably realised by now, *Robobolt* is a horrible attempt at a game. With a storyline that sounds like the plot to *Silent Running* recounted by a heavily sedated toddler, and gameplay that manages to be simultaneously boring and frustrating, it's no wonder that it's considered one of the very worst commercially released Commodore 64 games by those unfortunate enough to have played it. The publisher Alpha Omega eventually seemed to realise this, as they stopped selling it a few months after release and instead gave it away free with their game *Gods & Heroes*.

Robobolt was made entirely by one-man army Gary Leach, who perhaps should have just stuck to composing title screen music. I can only trace one other Commodore 64 game by him – *Asteroid Lander*, a type-in listing from the March 1984 issue of *Your Commodore* magazine. It's a slow, clunky and simplistic *Lunar Lander* knock-off that's considerably more fun than *Robobolt*. Ten years later, Mr Leach was the director of *Rise 2: Resurrection*, the reviled sequel to the infamously disappointing *Rise of the Robots*, which seems a fitting punishment.

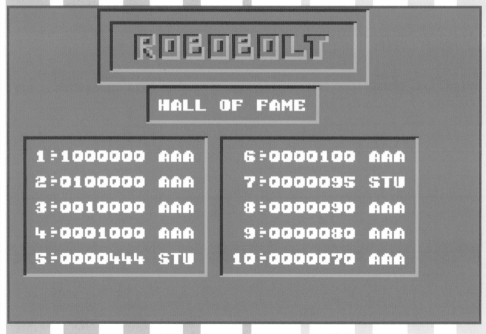

I got on the high-score table twice! The top three scores are not achievable by humans.

ROBOBOLT GAMEPLAY SEQUENCE

- Run around until you find a Death Pod.
- Take the Death Pod to the Assembly Unit.
- Discover it's the wrong one.
- Run around until you find another Death Pod.
- Take the Death Pod to the Assembly Unit.
- Discover it's the wrong one.
- Use the magnet from a speaker to wipe the tape.
- Take the tape back to the shop, pretending it's broken.

RECREATE THIS GAME IN REAL LIFE

Stand in a corridor and guess random numbers while someone throws doughnuts at you. Occasionally throw a small rubber bouncy ball at the ground as hard as you can.

PLAY THESE GAMES INSTEAD

Both *Paradroid* and its sequel *Heavy Metal Paradroid* are excellent games that work on the basic principle of rotund robots performing tasks on spaceships.

REVIEW SCORES

Commodore User gave it 2/10, describing it as 'painful to watch and boring to play'.
Your Commodore magazine was overly kind, to say the least. They thought it was 'a little mundane and uninteresting' and their score averaged out to 47.5%.

Zzap!64 were far more realistic, saying, 'Games can't get much worse than this.' They awarded it 3%, the joint lowest score they ever gave.

The reviewer from German magazine *ASM* was apparently suffering from a form of serious hallucinatory psychosis, claiming, 'The game is actually quite nice,' and awarding it the same 'Spielmotivation' score as *Sanxion*, an all-time C64 classic reviewed in the same issue!

OTHER VERSIONS

Robobolt was exclusive to the Commodore 64. Can't imagine it was much of a system seller.

TERRIBLE
OLD
GAME COVERS
THAT YOU'VE
PROBABLY NEVER
SEEN BEFORE

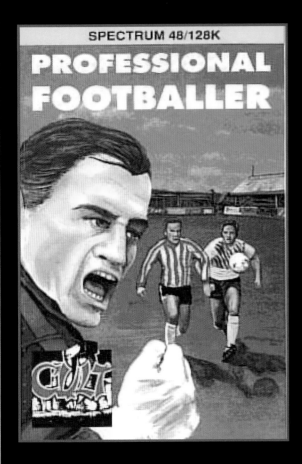

Professional Footballer

Format: ZX Spectrum, Commodore 64,
Amstrad CPC
Year of Release: 1991
Developer: Shaun McClure
Publisher: Cult Games
Original Price: 2.99 pounds

Nobody knows where the giant Ogre Lord
came from, but they have learned to fear his
dead eyes and alabaster fists. In order to
appease him, a ceremony is held once a year
where two men are forced to play football
against each other until a goal is scored. The
loser is eaten, then his bones are ground up
to make bread.

Timezone

Format: ZX Spectrum
Year of Release: 1985
Developer: G. Weight
Publisher: Atlantis Software
Original Price: 1.99 pounds

So... The idea here seems to have been a kind of robot dog, like the time-travelling Doctor Who companion K9. But instead of a cute robo-hound, we've ended up with a sickening abomination – a glowing sheepdog with metal boots shooting green beams out of its eyes. Or possibly it's a dead dog's skin stretched over a metal endoskeleton? Either way, I'm not sure if that's a broken sonic screwdriver or a high-tech spark plug in its mouth.

Vicky

Format: Commodore Amiga
Year of Release: 1994
Developer: L. K. Avalon
Publisher: L. K. Avalon
Original Price: Unknown

Getting models and props for photoshoots is an expensive business, so sometimes you just have to get your sister's boyfriend to put on a hairy vest and pretend to hold a hammer that you'll draw in badly on a computer later. Even the helmet is awful nineties CGI – could they really not find a cheap helmet from a dress-up shop? And did the Vikings really conquer Europe wearing purple socks? The inexplicable floating action shot will haunt my dreams forever, as it will now yours.

Krazy Kong

Format: Commodore VIC-20
Year of Release: 1983
Developer: Anirog Software
Publisher: Anirog Software
Original Price: 6.00 pounds

All great art makes us question ourselves. This cover makes me ask the following questions: Why isn't Kong looking at the barrel-smashing man? Why do the barrel pieces look like bananas? What is wrong with the man's nose? Why doesn't the lady care that she's been captured? Where is Kong's arm? What is the man standing on? Why was this deemed good enough to be used as a cover for both this game and Anirog's *Kong* for the ZX Spectrum? Who drew it and have they been tracked down and punished?

Metro-Cross

Format: Commodore 64, Atari ST
Year of Release: 1988
Developer: Probe
Publisher: US Gold
Original Price: 9.95/14.95 pounds
depending on the version

**The UK release of this game the previous year
got a dynamic airbrushed cover showing
a man in cybernetic armour racing down a
futuristic corridor. Then the USA got this: the
world's most gormless man bursting out of
what seems to be a cover of eighties magazine *Smash Hits*. Who did they think this
would appeal to? I remember posting this
to an online forum many years ago and one
of the members said it wasn't just the worst
game cover ever, but the world's crappest
image. They may well have been right, because in the intervening time I've yet to see
anything crapper. I wonder what the chap in
the photo is doing now, and if he ever lived
this down. There is one saving grace though:
the little prancing silhouette guy in the top
right is hilarious.**

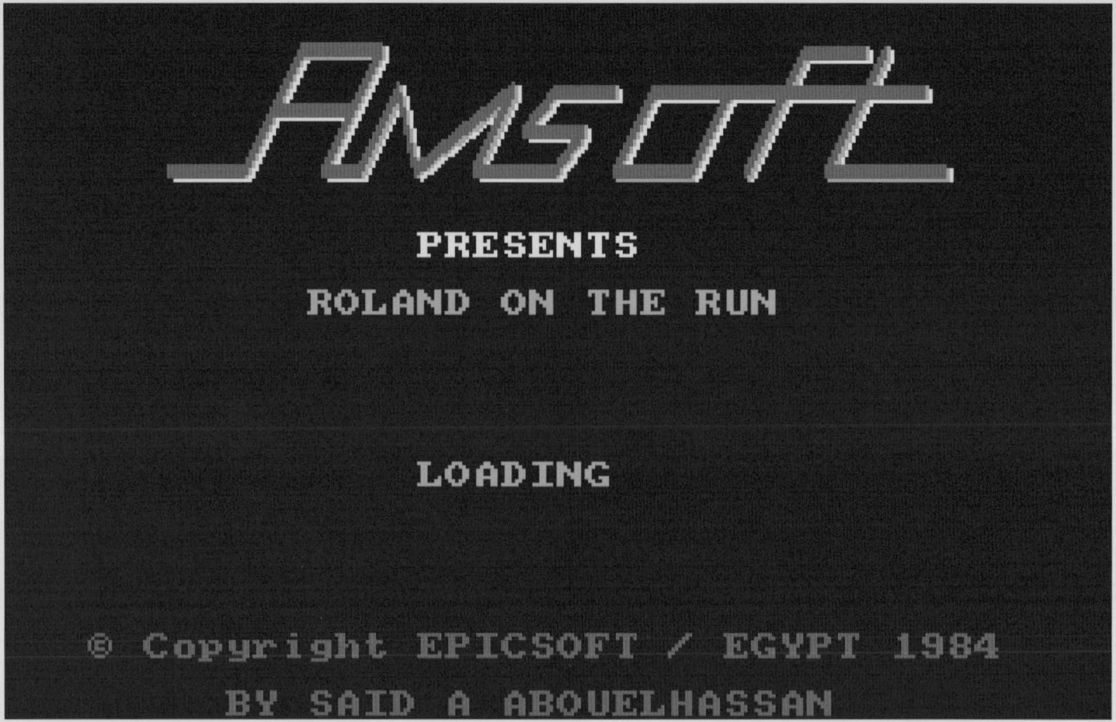

PRESENTS

ROLAND ON THE RUN

LOADING

© Copyright EPICSOFT / EGYPT 1984

BY SAID A ABOUELHASSAN

Roland on the Run

BY EPICSOFT

The cover shows Roland escaping with a screenshot of his own game. The two teardrop tattoos near his eye mean that he's murdered two people.

BRITISH COMPUTERS in the early eighties lacked popular mascot characters like Mario and Sonic the Hedgehog. The closest was Horace, a weird blue creature that appeared in three popular ZX Spectrum games before his creator suffered a collapsed lung and could no longer work on them.

In 1984, Amsoft, the game publishing arm of Amstrad, invented a character called Roland to promote sales for their new CPC range of computers. The plan was to release multiple titles featuring him, which they pulled off effectively – sadly, less effective was the character itself.

Roland was named after Roland Perry, an Amstrad engineer. And incredibly, the character's name is the only consistent thing. The whole idea of a mascot is to make a strong visual image which is easily recognised. But Roland is different in almost every game he appears in. And I don't just mean he wears a different hat – sometimes he is human, sometimes he is a little square robot, and sometimes he is a flea creature. I am not making this up.

This is because there was no unified design behind Roland. His games were made by different companies, and two of them were existing games that they just slapped the Roland label on. Also, most of them were pretty awful, which didn't help.

Roland may be the laziest, worst-thought-out attempt at a mascot in history. It's just a name that was slapped on eight games that appeared between 1984 and 1985. And the very worst of those games is *Roland on the Run*, a game so ineffective at being a game that playing it made my arms feel weird.

In this game, Roland is an unidentified member of a large group of stickmen, presumably because it was written as something else entirely and had the name slapped on it later. According to the

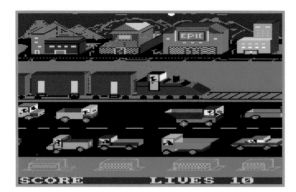

Since you can control the speed of the wedge-shaped train, why don't you just stop it and let everyone cross the road safely?

Look! It's the controls! Because all the screenshots of the actual game look the same!

bizarre plot, these people are being held against their will by Amsoft and are embarking on an escape attempt by hiding on a freight train.

Their ridiculously dangerous plan involves leaping from the moving train onto passing lorries, then jumping onto lorries travelling the other way, then finally throwing themselves into hideouts at the side of the road. The conditions at Amsoft must have been utterly inhumane to make such a suicidal escape plan an option!

Before starting the game, you're asked how many lives you want from 1 to 255, meaning that Amsoft had somehow imprisoned over 250 people in their offices. A lower number means the game is shorter so that's highly recommended. You can also select a difficulty level, which seems

to mean the trucks change speed more often.

The game starts with a pretty screen showing the train and the rows of lorries. And it's a good thing it's pretty as that's all there is! You can control the speed of the freight train, allowing it to synchronise with the first line of traffic. There are three separate buttons for making your little stickmen leap, depending on which row they're in. And that is the full extent of your control over the incredible action of *Roland on the Run.*

The train jerkily chugs along as the lorries flick and jolt across the screen. Any traffic that leaves the side of the screen loops round to the other side because they're trapped in a pocket dimension or something. Little stickmen start appearing in the three doors of the train. After a few seconds one of them starts to flash yellow, and it's go time.

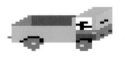
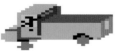

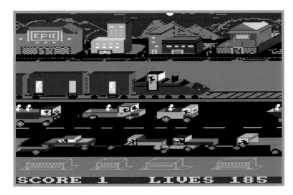

Proof that I did actually get at least one point. What a waste of my life.

The game-over screen. Only the Y button does anything, even though nobody in their right mind would press it.

You now have to press the first jump button when a truck is directly beneath your flashing person. This is relatively easy, as you can control the speed of the train and thus line things up. If you succeed, the stickman magically appears in the truck with no intervening animation whatsoever. If you fail, then there is no visual feedback of any kind. You just hear a beep and lose a life.

Jumping from the first line of traffic to the second is much harder, as the second is oncoming so the time window is tiny. But the real problem is that you have to wait for one of the stickmen in the trucks to flash yellow, which is seemingly random – it's far more likely that one of the train-bound people will flash.

In the unlikely event that you've put up with this dross long enough to get someone to the second row of traffic, you can now wait for an eternity before one of them starts to flash. Then you can finally press the third jump button and get them into one of the many hideouts at the bottom of the screen! Except it's never clear which area you're aiming for, so it's more luck than judgement.

Roland on the Run is one of the most incomprehensible excuses for a game I've ever encountered. It's a screen full of flickering, shuddering primary colours, where occasionally something flashes and then goes beep and you lose a life. It's almost impossible to play effectively and is less fun than fixing the computer of an elderly relative who constantly thinks you're somehow breaking it. Playing it actually made me feel slightly ill as well as annoyed.

Speaking of annoying, the sound consists entirely of a hideous, white-noise chugging effect that plays constantly, and a beep when you lose a life. Earplugs are strongly recommended.

Not content with making one of the worst games ever in both concept and execution, Epicsoft wrote two other games for the Amstrad, which were both released by Amsoft. One is *Bridge It*, another horrifying, single-screen failure of a game that some unlucky people actually got bundled with their computer. And the other is *Centre Court*, which may actually be the worst tennis game ever released commercially for any system. All hail Epicsoft!

Amsoft released a huge amount of dross in the early days of the Amstrad CPC, presumably to make sure early adopters weren't put off by a lack of software. But Epicsoft's trilogy of tat really scrapes the bottom of the barrel – to the extent that it goes through the barrel's bottom, all the way through the Earth's core and out the other side like that stupid lift in the *Total Recall* remake.

REVIEW SCORES
Amtix magazine awarded it a princely 19% and their review contained the words 'dull', 'boring' and 'terrible'.

The game didn't fare much better with *Amstrad Action*, which thought it was worth only 29% due to its 'boring, repetitive gameplay'.

But *CPC464 User* had a very different view, summarising the game with these falsehoods: 'Following the high standards of previous Roland games, this is no exception and will provide many hours of amusement.' I should point out that *CPC464 User* was the official Amstrad magazine and was run by the same people who published the game.

OTHER VERSIONS
Roland on the Run was never released for any other system. Because, of course, Roland was such a strong mascot associated solely with the Amstrad! Who could fail to recognise the strong image of... a man in a hat? A flea? A stickman? A square robot? Oh, forget it. (Just like everybody else did.)

THE ROLAND LEGACY
1. *Roland in the Caves* aka *Bugaboo: The Flea* – Poor
2. *Roland on the Ropes* aka *Fred* – Good
3. *Roland Ahoy!* – Okay
4. *Roland Goes Digging* aka *Diggerman* – Rubbish
5. *Roland Goes Square Bashing* – Dull
6. *Roland on the Run* – Abysmal
7. *Roland in Time* – Not too bad
8. *Roland in Space* – Also not too bad

PLAY THIS GAME INSTEAD
For train-based antics, try *Express Raider*, a fairly disappointing wild-west robbery game that's still at least 19,000 times better than this.

RECREATE THIS GAME IN REAL LIFE
DO NOT ATTEMPT TO RECREATE THIS GAME IN REAL LIFE. It will involve leaping from a moving train, and possibly human trafficking of some kind.

The soldiers have purple skin, and as such are likely to be night elves.

LOWEST MAGAZINE SCORE CORNER

AMTIX MAGAZINE
Score: 5%
Game: *Breakthru*
Format: Amstrad CPC

In the arcades, *Breakthru* was a fun little side-scrolling shoot 'em up where you controlled a jumping, bullet-spewing car. The Amstrad version is a horribly boring, mostly orange mess where your reward for completing it is to physically jump your car onto the Game Over screen. *Amtix* was understandably unimpressed, to the extent that they actually wrote, 'DON'T BUY THIS!!!!!!' in the review.

Nostalgia Nerd can be found on YouTube at youtube.com/NostalgiaNerd, and can be found on Twitter @nostalnerd.

THE MOST DISAPPOINTING GAME I EVER BOUGHT

BY NOSTALGIA NERD, YOUTUBER AND BUM BAG ADVOCATE

VIZ: THE COMPUTER GAME
FORMAT: ZX SPECTRUM
YEAR OF RELEASE: 1991
DEVELOPER: PROBE SOFTWARE
PUBLISHER: VIRGIN GAMES
ORIGINAL PRICE: 9.99 POUNDS

FOR MANY OF US, selecting a particularly disappointing game is easy. Even the mention of disappointment may create an instant flashback to pixels of such hideousness that you fall into a shaking mess on the floor. But for me, it's quite a difficult task. From the moment a ZX Spectrum was thrust into the hands of my brother and me, my mind was captivated by these little digital flashes of pixel light. How could all these interactive elements move around the screen like that?! How was I managing to actually participate in the television picture?! It's for this very reason that even when presented with a particularly terrible game, I still manage to find splendour in its bitterness.

As a small child, money was important, and like my friends I expected a reasonable return on hard-earned pocket money. During the latter part of the eighties, this usually involved some sort of split arrangement between me and my brother, in which I would provide a reasonable contribution for part ownership in a game title. However, given I was five years younger than him, the deal never seemed truly in my favour. Usually we'd be wise enough to consult magazines such as *Crash* and *Your Sinclair* and manage to pick out titles which would satisfy, even beyond the gorgeous cover art. If a game didn't meet expectations, but was a budget title, then it was no big deal. A couple of quid was no big loss even if getting past Level 1 of *Biggles* seemed damn near impossible. But when it was a big box game – which for the ZX Spectrum meant something roughly equivalent in size to a double cassette album – then the stakes were higher.

Viz was one particular game which came in this 'big box' format, and from the outside, everything seemed compelling. Usual *Viz* characters such as Buster Gonad and Roger Mellie were present, along with an array of screenshots representing various 8-bit systems on the back. This usually meant even better things, as if a game was truly crap, then you'd usually only find the screenshots of the best-looking version. However, something else on the box (possibly an afterthought) was Lord Kitchener, telling us, 'You'll never play a bigger load of crap!' Should have paid more attention to him really.

As a 10-year-old, the odd profanity appearing on screen after loading – in keeping with the *Viz* aesthetic – felt like we were definitely on to a winner. But this would, alas, prove to be the high point of proceedings. After the title screen, you quickly find yourself in the grand Fulchester fun run, pitted against two other opponents including Johnny Fartpants and our large-gonaded friend. Like that, the race begins, and... oh... my... good god. If you've never experienced bad collision detection, then please, fire up *Viz* and you'll quickly learn. You choppily fumble your way from left to right, desperately trying not to bump into anything which will send you flying to the ground. If this was a rare occurrence then it would be fine, but it happens a lot. Even in seemingly clear wide open spaces. Not only that, but it seems utterly impossible to get past the first race.

Even if by some fluke you managed to get an initial lead, one of the other characters would just

Left to right: Biffa Bacon, Johnny Fartpants and Buster Gonad. Mr Logic is also on the left, but is brutally concussed and not playable.

Johnny flatulates as high as he can to earn tokens for use in the main race game. This rarely happens at actual fun runs.

The race is on, and almost as much fun as it looks!

trot past at the end of the race and it would be game over. This left you with nothing but Roger Mellie's repeated commentary, over and over and over and over. Even with the profanities, it quickly wore thin.

In theory, this game filled with toilet humour should have been a small child's dream. But in practice, its bitterness hurt. It hurt deep. Not only with its bad gameplay, but the fact that you seemingly could not progress past the very first level. This became one of those Spectrum games which took far longer to load than it did to play. One of those games where you question whether the developers actually finished it before mastering to tape. One of those games where you absolutely question why in the name of all hell-spawn was it a full-priced, big-box game, with nothing more than a comic strip tie-in to keep you satisfied?!

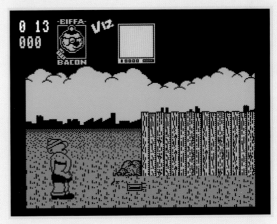

Biffa Bacon attempts to smash away bricks hurled at him by an unseen assailant. Do not try this at home.

THE WORST JOYSTICK EVER

THE CHEETAH TORTOISE JOYSTICK

Cheetah made a lot of different joysticks back in the eighties. Their most popular was the Cheetah 125+, a cheap stick that did the job and had a fairly comfortable design. Then they got into novelty controllers and lost their minds.

First came their awful licensed joysticks, where ergonomically designed grips were replaced with plastic statues of Batman, Bart Simpson, the Xenomorph from Alien and a T-800 skull from Terminator 2. They were almost unusable, mostly due to sharp plastic edges cutting into your hands and bizarre fire button placement. And then Cheetah thought it would be a good idea to replace an upright stick altogether. With a tortoise.

The Tortoise uses the base of a Cheetah Annihilator, one of their worst joysticks due to being exceptionally cheap and shoddy. Then it has a big lump of plastic slapped on it, leaving something that resembles a giant computer mouse... shaped like a tortoise.

The idea is to attach it to a surface using the suction cups under the unit, then push the tortoise's shell forward, backward and sideways to actually control games. If you think that sounds ridiculous and borderline unusable, then you're spot on. And to make matters worse, the shell has to be pushed with considerable force to get movements to register.

All three fire buttons perform the same function and really need to be jammed down hard to work. The only upside is that it's comfortable to hold in your hand – presuming you have large hands, because if not you'll end up with a cramp.

The Cheetah Tortoise Joystick is one of the strangest and worst-thought-out controller ideas ever. It totally fails on a practical level, but it does excel at looking like a tortoise with three buttons drilled into its shell.

TOP BANANA IS A GAME very much rooted in early nineties rave culture from design to execution. Its main character KT is dressed as a raver, and the entire aesthetic – both visuals and audio – is very much a product of its time. And it says, 'KICK IT TO EM,' when you start the game, which is the icing on the rave cake.

Originally released in 1991 for the Acorn Archimedes, *Top Banana* was a simple platform game clearly inspired by the arcade classic *Rainbow Islands*. It played smoothly but was overly simple, frustrating, and had a sub-psychedelic art style with backgrounds constructed out of gaudy blocks that made it difficult to see what was going on. Then it was ported to the Commodore Amiga and the colours on screen were reduced, which made everything look dreadful and it was almost impossible to make out what was happening. And then there was a conversion for the Atari ST, which looked slightly worse still and didn't move smoothly at all...

Firing up *Top Banana* on the ST kicks off a low-quality recording of a piece of generic rave music as some ugly, heavily dithered pictures flash obnoxiously. At least it does if you have one of the enhanced STe models – on a standard ST this sequence

is missing entirely, as are all the game's sampled sound effects.

Starting the game produces a sound effect taken from the TV gameshow *Catchphrase*, and you are launched into a nightmarish green mess of pixels. It's apparently supposed to be a rainforest, as the vaguely environmentally friendly plot of the game has KT defeating ecological disasters with the power of love. What this means in practice is that she can blow up evil chainsaws by firing hearts at them.

KT herself is not the cheery character shown on the title screen. Instead she's a bulbous-headed dead-eyed doll creature whose haircut makes her look a bit like nineties pop icon Betty Boop. (The first name in the high-score table is Betty so tha

That's a mechanical digger in the bottom right. Honestly.

Spot the two chainsaws on the left and win a prize!

It's the end of Level Giant Sugary Treat Geyser! I wouldn't eat any of those, you don't know where they came from.

may well be deliberate.) And you can't really make out anything else as the backgrounds, platforms, pickups and enemies are just a mess of coloured pixels.

Top Banana only scrolls vertically – the idea is to use the game's platforms to reach the top of each stage. On the way you can pick up various sugary treats for points, and destroy enemies who sometimes give up flashing hearts for you to collect. I don't know what happens if you get a full set as I never managed it. Much like *Rainbow Islands*, the stage slowly fills with water so you can't hang around too long. And if you make it to the top, you're rewarded with a load of giant, point-boosting treats that inexplicably fly up from below.

You've seen the screenshots by now, but I still

have to ram home just how bad the game's graphics are. They are an utterly indecipherable, garbled mess and the only reason you can actually pick out the enemies from the rest of the screen is because they move. The enemy roster is made of diggers, chainsaws and businessmen but I only know that because I've seen the Archimedes version; on the ST they are just indistinct lumps. It genuinely looks as if there's been a data error loading the graphics, and the screen is corrupt as a result.

The sound is also awful. There's a weird bubbling sound whenever you jump, and an incredibly irritating voice says, 'Eeh?' every time you pick up items – which are everywhere! The 'Eeh?' is actually an equally annoying mooing effect on the Archimedes, but it's been reduced in quality

Welcome to Stage 4 of the Amiga version. There is no life in the void.

so much for the ST that it sounds like something else entirely. As I mentioned earlier all these sounds are missing if you play the game on a standard non-STe machine, and they are replaced with uninspired sound chip effects. It's actually much less aggravating and improves the game slightly! It is odd that no version of *Top Banana* has in-game music, as you'd think that would be a high priority for a game based around music culture.

Setting aside the repugnantly muddy visuals, the game would be utter tosh even if you could see what's going on. The chunky enemies don't move far and take up large areas of the screen, making them hard to avoid when jumping up. And if you get hit by one, you not only lose energy, but immediately fall straight through the floor

you're standing on – often straight onto another enemy. Some of them require such precise timing to get past that it's almost impossible to avoid them on the ST version as it runs so much slower and jerkier than the original. There's also a slight pause before KT fires one of her hearts, which makes things worse.

Factor in the way you can barely see what's going on and some other minor annoyances, like the green star which makes the background scroll when you pick it up, and *Top Banana* is one of the most aggravating gameplay experiences I've ever had. Nearly every loss of energy is down to something you couldn't see or because the controls didn't react in time.

There are four areas in the game, with three stages for each. I found it impossible to progress beyond a certain point on the second stage of Area 1, even with an infinite lives cheat. I had to resort to a specific version of the Amiga port with a level skip cheat so I could report on the horrors beyond the rainforest.

As hard as this is to believe, each area gets progressively uglier and even more muddled. The second is some kind of industrial mess, like the remains of an exploded factory. Area 3 is some kind of bright-yellow palace or mansion or something. And as for Area 4, I have no idea – I think the enemies are mostly toys, but the background mostly looks like ripped-up intestines. Haunted toy box rammed with viscera, perhaps?

If you complete Top Banana, *you are presented with this screen. A creepy laugh plays in the background. Frankly it's better to lose.*

There is one good thing about *Top Banana*, and that is it actually kept true to its environmentally conscious message of sharing. It came packaged in a tiny box made from recycled paper, and all the samples and sprites are stored on the disc in an easily editable format so you can remix the game to your heart's content. Or, y'know, maybe just change the graphics so you can see what's going on.

Top Banana is a frustrating, semi-playable shambles. It looks like vomit and plays like excrement. The core of the game is an incredibly simple and badly executed platformer, but add the ludicrously indistinct graphics into the mix and you end up with something monumentally nasty. Especially for £25.99 in 1992!

Hex released no other games, although they did put out a disk for Commodore's super-flop CDTV system called *Global Chaos*. It contained a few computer-generated music videos and, tragically, *Top Banana*. Hex itself was an interesting group – it was made up of an artist, a programmer and the super successful electronica duo Coldcut. They produced a lot of interactive works across a wide range of media using the cutting-edge technology of the time. Sadly, when it came to *Top Banana* their heart was in the right place, but the rest of their internal organs were shoved down in their legs.

PLAY THIS GAME INSTEAD

Play *Rainbow Islands* instead. Without question.

RECREATE THIS GAME IN REAL LIFE

Go to a noisy club, drink too much, get really sick and go out into a back alley and throw up everywhere. The resultant mess will be a level design from *Top Banana*!

REVIEW SCORES

ST Format could find no positive points whatsoever, saying, 'Hex have tried hard to make a game that's fun, young, trendy and interesting to play, and failed dismally on all counts.' Yet they still awarded it 48%.

OTHER VERSIONS

The Amiga version is noticeably better – though the graphics are just as ugly and confusing, it's far smoother than the ST version so is less of an awkward chore to play. *Amiga Joker* still only gave it 14%, however. The original Acorn Archimedes version is far and away the best. Smoother still than the Amiga conversion, the 256-colour graphics are far clearer too. It's still not a great game by any means but you could actually have some fun with it. And it came with a free T-shirt.

FIVE EIGHTIES GAMES BASED ON MUSICAL ACTS

Journey – *Journey Escape* (1982, Atari 2600)
Shakin' Stevens – *The Shaky Game* (1983, ZX Spectrum)
Thompson Twins – *The Thompson Twins Adventure* (1984, ZX Spectrum, Commodore 64)
The Beatles – *Beatle Quest* (1985, ZX Spectrum)
Frankie Goes to Hollywood – *Frankie Goes to Hollywood* (1985, Various)

Kim is a 'taste influencer' who supposedly 'creates content' on YouTube. She does this through making videos that cover old computers and games that are usually of the licensed and/or sports variety. While she does like good games, she'd probably rather play Chris Kamara's *Street Soccer* over almost any of them. She can be found on YouTube at youtube.com/elmyrdehory and on Twitter at @KimxxxJustice.

THE MOST DISAPPOINTING GAME I EVER BOUGHT

BY KIM JUSTICE, VIDEO PRODUCER

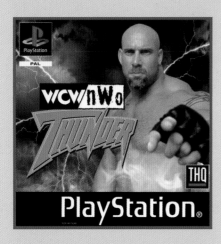

WCW/NWO THUNDER
FORMAT: SONY PLAYSTATION
YEAR OF RELEASE: 1998
DEVELOPER: INLAND SOFTWARE
PUBLISHER: THQ
ORIGINAL PRICE: 39.99 POUNDS

ULTIMO DRAGON   MACHO MAN

Randy Savage's over-enthusiastic Morris dance scares off Ultimo Dragon.

AS A LONG-TIME FAN of wrestling games, and wrestling in general, I've gotten pretty used to disappointment – buying a game every year only to find it's exactly the same as the last one, which was already outdated in the last generation, tends to do that to you. But as far as disappointment goes, nothing comes close to *WCW/NWO Thunder* on the PS1

– which, for some completely unknown reason, I bought for a not inconsiderable chunk of change... was it just because it wasn't a WWF game and therefore a promising alternative? Was it the promise of hundreds of wrestlers being included, all oiled up and ready to go? I simply can't put my finger on it.

One particular reason why it's so hard for me to think about why I bought this game is because I already knew, without a shadow of a doubt, that it was terrible. I'd already seen it reviewed in the *Official PlayStation Mag*, where it scored 3/10. It was clearly the same game as the earlier *WCW Nitro*, which I'd played on a demo disk and hated. I knew all of this going in. I knew exactly what I was letting myself in for – but all of these smoking guns weren't enough to stop me from somehow convincing myself I should buy it, because a snarling Bill Goldberg was on the front; it was a game about wrestling and therefore something I should

I have no idea what's going on here, but it looks painful.

like. So I bought it. And shockingly enough, it was awful in every way – the graphics and animation were among the worst I'd seen in any game up to that point, and short of slightly different hues and textures, every one of the hundreds of wrestlers that were advertised on the box were basically identical to each other. But truthfully, I couldn't put down here that the game itself was disappointing; all the evidence was there, so how could I? No, the disappointment I felt was entirely in

ULTIMO DRAGON   MACHO MAN

Worst salsa dancing ever.

– sometimes you've really got to lean into your disappointment and pretend that you're enjoying the drudgery of matching Hollywood Hogan up against some no-name programmer that's only accessible via the cheat codes for a match that plays out exactly the same as the last 40 or so you've played. Fortunately, these days you can easily capture the true essence of *WCW/NWO Thunder* by watching Roddy Piper's video on YouTube and then forgetting that the actual game exists at all.

myself, for ignoring all the evidence that was there and still buying a game just because it had the face of an angry wrestler on the front. Clearly I was not as smart as my parents had always said I was.

Mind you, the game did allow you to watch little promo videos of every wrestler urging you to pick them for a match, and 'Rowdy' Roddy Piper's crazed and snarling pitch was undoubtedly worth the £39.99 on its own. If I hadn't bought the game, how would I have become aware of such a glorious thing? And because it was a wrestling game, I still put a silly number of hours into it

FACT FACT FACT FACT

WCW/NWO Thunder is one of the worst-received wrestling games in history, and for good reason. Due to the strange way grappling in the game works, you can effectively drain an opponent of all their strength and pin them in about half a minute.

WEC LE MANS

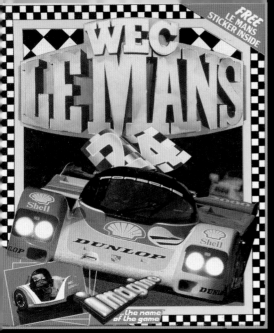

Exciting! Dynamic! Unrepresentative!

IT'S TIME TO DON our hazardous environment suits, as we're revisiting the worst of all possible worlds: that of Commodore 64 racing games. Please remain behind the safety rail at all times and do not make direct eye contact with any of the software.

WEC Le Mans was an arcade game based around the famously gruelling 24-hour endurance race that takes place each year in France. It was a big success, guzzling many 10 pence pieces in the days before the arcades became filled with nothing but cheating prize machines. And as with

all successful arcade games of the time, it was duly converted to the 8-bit home formats, with varying degrees of success.

The Commodore 64 version begins well enough, with a pretty title screen – although it looks like a large, fibreglass, modern art sculpture has been attached to the back of the car – and a nice little music loop from acclaimed musician Jonathan Dunn. Then the game starts, and the quality falls off a cliff quicker than Wile E Coyote when you're watching a Road Runner cartoon on fast forward.

As the lights count down for the race to begin, it becomes obvious just how grey this game is. There is no colour at the sides of the road at all, as if the race is taking place in a giant, empty car park. This feeling is exacerbated when the race actually starts and you notice how few roadside objects there are. You're in a drab expanse racing towards nothing, which is a perfect metaphor for a career in a call centre.

Most of the sense of movement comes from the alternating grey stripes of the road, which is where this game really falls down. The programmer's attempt to convey speed using the stripes simply does not work – they flicker back and forth and have little relation to how fast your car is supposed to be going. A lot of the time they actually appear to be moving backwards, as if you're speeding round the track in reverse – a manoeuvre only used in real life when trying to take a supermarket car park space before someone else. Sometimes they reach a kind of stasis and it looks like your car is stuck on the spot. For large parts of the game, the only impression of

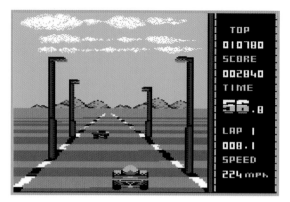

TOP
010780
SCORE
002840
TIME
56.8
LAP 1
008.1
SPEED
224 mph

Roadside objects and a rival car together! This is sadly as exciting as it gets.

TOP
018340
SCORE
007650
TIME
52.3
LAP 1
012.6
SPEED
114 mph

In a depressingly common scene, your car flips in the air as the screen empties.

forward momentum you get at all is when one of the sparse roadside objects appears and shoots past you, as if it's a vehicle itself floating above the road.

This feeling of detachment isn't just reserved for the roadside objects. The car is rendered as a sprite on a layer above the track, which means it moves left and right very smoothly but it never quite feels as if it's on the road. And as the road is a crazy, flickering mess that seems to move in random directions, you never really get any impression of speed at all. And that's pretty much a fatal flaw in a racing game.

And things get much worse! You know how in racing games the car tends to remain mostly centred in the middle of the screen and the track

moves around it? Well, in this game the track remains central and the car slides left and right, like one of those old LCD games where you had to dodge objects jerking down the screen. And the car slips left and right as if friction is fiction, moving exactly the same regardless of the speed you're supposedly travelling. Both of these points further increase the weird, detached feel, meaning at this point it's less of a game and more of an out-of-body gameplay experience.

The computer-controlled cars you race against provide another method for sucking any potential joy out of the game. For starters, they look more like palette boxes full of paint cans than they do cars. They have a tendency to suddenly ram you when you get close to them, which they do at

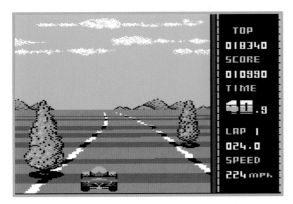

A rare sighting of some scenery! Scenery that will destroy you, of course.

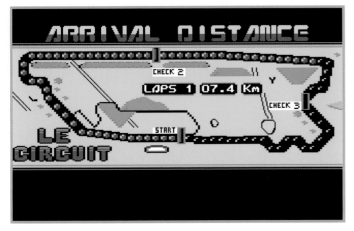

You're shown this map after you lose so you can work out how much time you've wasted.

such speed that it's seemingly impossible to avoid. And sometimes unseen cars will appear from off the screen and hit you from behind, which is literally impossible to avoid unless you have the ability to psychically predict future events. Getting hit by a car is not a minor problem, as the slightest touch sends your vehicle flying 20 feet into the air while the other party is totally unaffected, although sometimes you can pass straight through other cars, possibly as a sympathy move from the collision detection routine.

I shall now mention the in-game sound. There is only engine noise, which is an irritating whine that sounds like a demented wasp stuck in a kazoo. Let us never mention the sound again.

And those are all the problems with *WEC Le Mans*. Except that the corners come out of nowhere as you don't see the track bend in front of you and there are no warning signs. And your car is weirdly sucked into bends as a failed attempt to simulate its place on the road. And the roadside objects sometimes creep onto the road itself. And there's no indication of which of the two gears you're in, which is confusing as you switch back to low if you crash. And the entire game has

194

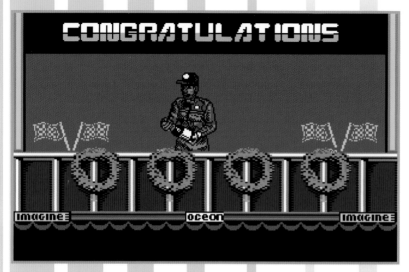

This man appears to be covered in burnt flesh. He looks better in motion, honest.

the same dull grey track with only the sky eventually getting darker. And sometimes when you crash, the roadside objects stop but the road itself keeps moving. And it's more fun to chew on cardboard than play this game.

There's also a weird visual glitch that shows up on later revisions of the Commodore 64 hardware. A problem with changes to the screen's colour register makes random white pixels appear all over the track, as if the road itself is sparkling like a vampire from *Twilight*.

But there is one positive thing about this game! If you somehow manage to play through it, you're

treated to a two-scene animated end sequence that's actually better than the original arcade version. Pity you'll have gone mad by that time.

WEC Le Mans for the Commodore 64 is a dismal technical failure. It's buggy, boring, annoying, almost uncontrollable and there's no sense of speed or excitement. Your car is so weirdly detached from the action that it feels more like a journey to the astral plane than a racing game. It's just as bad as the infamously awful *Crazy Cars*, but it is still a step above the distressingly terrible *Cisco Heat*. But then so is cholera.

RECREATE THIS GAME IN REAL LIFE
Get horribly drunk, then stand on a greasy tarpaulin in a striped tent that's being spun around you at high speed. The game is over when you vomit.

PLAY THESE GAMES INSTEAD
Pitstop II, despite being released four years before this game, is infinitely better and has an extremely fun two-player split-screen mode.

WHAT DOES THE TITLE MEAN?

WEC stands for World Endurance Championship, and Le Mans is the French city the race takes place in. The game is not endorsed by the World Energy Council or the Westinghouse Electric Company.

REVIEW SCORES

ACE gave it 586/1000 and claimed it's better than the horrible C64 conversion of *Out Run*. It's not.

Computer & Video Games described it as 'laughable' and awarded it 32%.

Commodore Force went two points lower at 30%, calling it 'shoddy'.

No punches were pulled by *Commodore Format*, who deemed it only worthy of 20% and said it was 'a pile of old poop'.

Commodore User flat out called it 'one of the worst full-price releases I've seen for a while' and gave it 31%.

But the lowest score came from *The Games Machine*, who said it was 'awful' and worthy of just 14%.

Zzap!64 reviewed the game three times due to it being re-released at a lower price. They first decided it was 'very disappointing' and worth 40% in March 1989, then inexplicably increased the rating to a ludicrously overblown 60% in February 1991, then finally settled on 'flippin' awful' in October 1992 with 18%.

OTHER VERSIONS

The ZX Spectrum is a far better conversion. It's fast, fun and fairly smooth. The main weakness is that there's no variation in the visuals as you progress through the game.

The Amstrad CPC version plays well but has a very limited (and oddly dim) colour palette, due to using the Amstrad's medium resolution mode. It was later reworked into *Burnin' Rubber*, a more impressive title that shipped with every Amstrad Plus and GX4000 system.

Sadly, the MSX only received a port of the Spectrum version, as was so common at the time. However, it was better optimised than usual, running only slightly slower than the original. There is a potentially serious problem, however – it deviated from the MSX standard for using the machine's Portable Sound Generator chip, and it could actually damage the hardware of certain models as a result.

ACKNOWLEDGEMENTS

I would like to offer thanks and appreciation to:

■ The team at Unbound for putting up with my inability to stop double-spacing before a new sentence.

■ The unknown army of people who scan old video-game magazines and upload them to the internet, and the heroes who cross-reference the contents.

■ All the guest contributors, who without exception delivered their pieces when asked.

■ Everyone who came to see my *Hareraiser* presentation at the 2017 Norwich Gaming Festival, as it proved the chapter makes sense.

■ Daniel Hardcastle for introducing me to the cover of *Timezone*.

■ Mentski for going above and beyond the call of duty.

■ Tip o' the hat to Evan Amos for taking the photo of the Commodore 64GS (p.49) as part of his excellent Vanamo Online Game Museum project, a collection of public domain images of video game consoles.

■ People who watch my YouTube videos. I love you all.

HORSENBURGER
APPRECIATION PAGE

Massive thanks to Steve Horsley, who
combined the powers of art and
3-bit technology to create all the teletext
portraits used in this book.

*His work can be seen at horsenburger.com
and he can be found on Twitter
@horsenburger*

TERRIBLE OLD NAMES YOU'VE PROBABLY NEVER HEARD OF

UNBOUND is a new kind of publishing house. Our books are funded directly by readers. This was a very popular idea during the late eighteenth and early nineteenth centuries. Now we have revived it for the internet age. It allows authors to write the books they really want to write and readers to support the books they would most like to see published.

The names listed below are of readers who have pledged their support and made this book happen. If you'd like to join them, visit www.unbound.com.

Claire A
Dominic Jenson Abbey
Carlo Abbona
Billy Abbott
Loren Abbott
Peter Abbott
Richard Abbott
Shakir Abdulaziz
Shehzad Abdulcadir
Roy Ackermans
Edward Adam
Jhon Adams
Terry Adams
Esme Adams-Walsh
John Adlington
Salmir Aeon
Michael Agostinelli
Dave Ahern
Jim Aitken
Neil Aitken
Simon Aitken
Kim Akerø
Akwa
Jaber Al-Eidan
Haider Al-Rekabi
Atte Ala-Välkkilä
Anton Alaküla
David Alasow

Robert Alavoine
Kenneth Albanowski
Oskar Albinsson
António Albuquerque
Adam Alby
Cody Alcina
Phil Alderton
Shea Aldridge
Rusu Alexandru
Brian Allan
James Allan
Jim Alm
Robert Altoft
Ian Alty
Saul Alvarez
Vasco Alves
Mike Amos
Martyn Anderson
Matthew Anderson
Sam Anderson
Virginia Anderson
George Andrew
Alex Andrews
Cayden Andrews
Matthew Andrews
Fabian Angel
Meaghen Angel
Christian Ankerstjerne

Joseph Ansell
Jacob Antholz
Austin Anthony
Jayvian Antunes
Nathan Applegarth
Luciano Aque
Phil Arber
Peter Arbuthnot
Eyal Arditi
Ernesto Arias
John Aridi
Kristen Arnesen
Bernard J. Arnest
Dan Arries
Aislinn Arthey
Elliot Ash
Chris Ashford
Elizabeth Ashford
Dominic Ashman
Tharglet Asimis
Magnus Asplund
Hannah Atkins
Nick Atkins
Michael Atkinson
Rik Attrill
Brandon Attwood
Anna Ault
Katherine Aurelia

Paul Austin
Paul Auton
John Awdish
Michael Ayling
James Ayre-Anderson
Martin B
Samuel B.
Richard Babb
Nicholas Backhouse
Ashton Bacon
Bad Game Hall of Fame
James Bagg
Richard Baggaley
Michael Baggett
Adrian Bailey
Michael Bailey
Michael Bailey
Richard J Bailey
Rob Bailey
Graeme Bailey-Lewis
Emerson Baillie
Heather Bain
Michael Bainbridge
Richard Bairwell
Richard Baister
James Baker
Matthew Baker
Mike Baker
Paul Baker
Vyvyen Baker
Richard A Baker Jr.
Hynek Bakstein
Dustin Baldus
Neil Baldwin
Stephen Baldwin
Christopher Ball
Curtis Ball
Holly Ball
Jon Ball (Tidmouth)
Arex Ballantino
Duncan Ballantyne
Robin Ballard

Tom Balzer
Andrew Rafael Bañas
Jacob Bang
Broderic Banta
Layla Baptiste
Robert Barbee
Doru Barbu
Andrius Barkauskas
Ben Barker
Ben Barker
Michael Barker
Karl Henrik Elg Barlinn
Daniel Barlow
Riyad Barmania
Jonathan Barnes
Patrick Barnes
Jakob Barnstorf
Joe Barrett
Victoria Barton
Jeremy Baruffa
Zoran Basic
Paul Bastin
Leroy Baum
Jens Baumann
Megan Baumann
Chelsi Beale
James Beale
Brandon 'DemolisherB-PB' Beardsall
Fraser Beattie
Travis Beaudette
Dallas Bechard
Brent M. Bechtold
Connor Beck
Greg Beck
Joseph F. Becker
Richard Beckett
Sam Beddoes
Lewis Bedford
Daniel Beer
Tom Beers
James Begley

Chad Behr
Ole Bekkelund
Adrian Belcher
Alex Belcher
David Bell
Erik Bell
Mark Bell
Max Bell
Jon Benard
Charles Bennett
Daniel Bennett
Matthew Bennion
Boris Bentley
Joe Bentley
Jon Bentley
Jake Berg
Melissa Bernhardt
Michael Berry
Patrick Berry
Simon, Rachel, Eleanor, Isabelle and Abigail Berry
Tim Berry
Ruth Bertram
Sundae Best
Susan Bevins
Eric Bickerdyke
Marcel Bienert
Jordan Bigness
Sophie Billing
David Bilous
Matthew Bilverstone
Charlotte Birch
Chris Birch
Bird Flu Czar
Alexander Birk
Nicholas Birlie
Scott Bishop
Aastha Bist
Josh Bitzer
Lars Bjarby
Andy Black

Guy Black
Jennifer Black
Stacey Blackburn
Alex Blackmon
Melanie Blagg
Graeme Blake
Jonathan Blake
Andrew Blane
Thomas Blindbaek
Blobbem
Stephen Bloom
Jason Ray Bloomer
Jamie Boden-Johnson
Tabitha Bodin
Philipp Boehme
Ed Boff
Franklyn Boiling
Stephen Boisvert
Bartek Bok
Sarah Bolinger
Steve Bolsover
David Bond
Wilf Bond
Anthony Booth
James Booth
Robert Booth
Peter Boräng
David Bordicott
Sebastiaan Borghstijn
James Borrett
Neal Boser
Johanna Böttcher
sam Botwright
Brian Boucher
Hakim Boukellif
Alan Boulais
Jonathan Boulton
Joel Bourassa
William Bourgeois
Adam Boutcher
Ross Bowater
Mackinnon Bowden
Drew Bower
Joth Bowgett
Richard Boyd
Elliott Boyko
J. M. Bradbrook

Adam Bradley
Douglas Bradley
Michael Bradshaw
Owen Brady
Paul Braiden
Christopher Brailsford
Dave Brain
James Bralant
Kristen Brand
Asbjørn Brask
Steve Brassard
Matthew Bratrsovsky
Alex Breach
Derek Brealey
Martin Brear
Ben Breen
Corwin Brence
Mike Brent
Jackie Brewster
Stephen Bride
Ian Bridge
Laurence Bridge
Jakob J. Brink
William Brittain
Alice Broadribb
Anthony Broccoli
Khaymen Brock
Christopher Brockman
Sam Brookes
Gareth Brooks
Owain Brooks
Ryan Browell
Andrew Brown
Antony Brown
Justin Brown
Mark Brown
Mark Brown
Nigel Brown
Thomas Brown
Zachary Brown
Brown Software - Purveyor of Crap Games since 1982
Jason Browne
Mike Bruce
Max Bruton
Steve Bryce

Robert Bryden
Michael Buchan
Keef Buckley
Kevin Bucknall
Steven Buijser
James Bull
Lars Bull
Matthew Bull
Sam Bull
Kirk Bunston
Shawn Bupp
Ian Matthew Burch
Wes Burden
Jesse Burgess
Wayne Burgess
Brian Burke
Kyle Burke
Andrew Burnett
Casey Burnett
Thomas Burnip
Joshua Burns-Marsh
Ryan Burrage
Daniel Burridge
Edward Burrows
Peter Burrows
keith burton
Karl Busby
Ben Bussell
Alicia Butteriss
Oliver Byers-Jones
Elizabeth Byrne
Scott Byrnes
Simon Cadman
Richard Cadwell
Stephen Caile
Ryan Cain
Captain Cakewalk
Cameron Calderwood
Dustine Camacho
Craig Cameron
Gregor Cameron
Timmy Cameron
Oliver Camilleri
Erik Campbell
Gideon Canales
Brandon Canty
Donald Caple

Rob Caporetto
Michael Carabine
Matthew Caravello
Mark Carbonaro
Chris Cardus
Dane Carless
Philip Carlson
Rachel Carn
Drew Carpenter
Gavin Carpenter
Kyle Carr
Nicholas Carr
%N0 CARR13R
David Carreiro
Tom Carrick
Joe Carroll
Thomas Carroll
Tom Carroll
David Carruthers
Laurie Carter
Alex Cartwright
James Carver
Alexander Cassidy
Keith Cassidy
Stephen Cassidy
Corey Catalano
Dan Catt
Richard Caywood
Jani Cederqvist
Rosie and Nathan Chalam-Judge
Claire Chaplin
Chris Chapman
Ben Charlesworth
Shelly Woo Chatterton
Anu Chauhan
James Chavis
Check the PO Box
Hendrickson Cheong
Alex Chernogaev
Pavel Chernov (SirenQ)
Guillaume Chetard
Dalton Chew
Jordan 'Chewy' Chew
Artyom Chichkovskiy
David Chipres
Oscar Chrin

Andrew Christoffersen
Anthony Chung
Tom Churcher
Richard Churchill
Anthony Cid
Louis Cifelli
Daniel Clackson
Charlotte Clark
Em Clark
Lewis Clark
Alanna Clarke
Iwan Clarke
Matthew Clarke
Rachel Clarke
Toby Claus
Adrian Clay
Daniel Clements
Jordan Cleverley
Daniel Clymer
Garrett Coakley
Nick Coakley
Christopher Cobb
Jay Cochran
Larissy Cockblock
Ben Cockerill
Jurgen Coenegrachts
Macauley Coggins
Robert Coggle
Kyle Coghill
Richard Cohen
Maxime Cohin
Jakob Dittmayer Colarič
Samuel Colborn
Darren Colclough
Catherine Cole
Liam G Cole
Christian Colella
Jacob Coleman
Ryan Coleman
Stephen 'Zee' Coleman. GIVE SLEPP YOUR BONES!
Elliot Coll
Finnley Collett: Magnificent Skelly Bastard
Christopher Collingridge

Adrian Collins
Aodhán Collins
Joshua Collins
Robert Collins
Arthur Colombo
Murray Colpman
Ben Combee
Aengus Concannon
Rory Conneely
Cian Connellan
Christopher Connor
Kurt Connor
M. Conrace
Roger Civit Contra
Cody 'ganbarabbo' Cook
Hannah Cook
Ollie Cook
Sam Cook
Andrew Cooke
Cool
Carys Cooper
Christian Cooper
David R Cooper
Mathew Cooper
Neil Cooper
Steve Cooper
Zachary Cooper
Tay Coopz
Michael Coppolino
B Corbett
Jessika Leigh Corbett
Larry Cordner
Paul Corkindale
Philip Corner
CorranJP
Luke Lalor Corrigan
Jack Cossens
Damian Costales
Brenton Costan
Michael J Cotton
Gavin Coull
Ieuan Courtney
Matthew Cowan
Leon Cox
Lewis Cox
Matthew Alexander Cox
Sam Cox

Tom Cox
Jessica Coyle
Kit Coyne
Ryan Cozzubbo
Sean Craig
Danielle Crain
Elizabeth Crampin
Jacob Crane
Kevin Crane
Matthew Crane
James Cranwell
Mike Crawford
Sorcha Creighton
Adam Cresser
Chloe Cresswell
Bram Crielaard
Magnus Criwall
Kyle Crocker
Oscar Crocker
Brian Crockett
Deborah Crook
Mark Crook
Sapphire Crook
Mark Crosby
Mitch Crosby
Terry Crosher
Alex Crossley
Neil Croucher
Ben Crowe (who is
    secretly a fox in
    disguise)
Richard Crowther
Malte Crüsemann
Aaron Crutchley
Christopher Cryer
Joey Csobonas
Shaun Culkin
Michael Cullipher
Sanya Culp
Simon Curry
Matthew Curtis
Isabel Cushey
Kelsey Custodio
Taha Cutchi
Fox Cutter
Evan Cygnor
Daniel D'Abate

Claire D'Angelo
Rikki 'Marphy Black'
    D'Angelo
Nic D'Herde
Lewis Dachey-Jenkins
Dennis Dahlén
Brian Daji
Katie 'Kateish' Dale
Joseph Damiano
Jacqui, Daniel &
    James Etches
Julian Daugaard
Michelle Dauray
John Davidson
Matthew Davies
Tony Davies
Adam Davis
Alex Davis
Finlay Davis
Michael Davis
Geoffry Davis &
    Morgan Davis
Allan Davison
Richard Davison
Graham Dawes
Drew Dawkins
Mark Dawson
Dik de Jong
Cas de Rooij
Kevin De Wachter
John Deakin
Alice Dean
Benjamin Dean
Logan Dean
Shaban Jonathan Dean
Elliot Deans
Zachary Dearing
Dan Debling
Matthew Deeprose
Klaas Deforche
Aaron Deicmanis
Joao DeJesus
Niall Delaney
Lee Dellbridge
Sophia & Joe Dempsey
Mark Dempster
Christopher Denk

Pierre Dennert
Paul Dennett
Hamish Dennis
Kyle Dennis
Jonathan Denton
Shawn Depoe
Ian Derrick
Sebastian Deußer
Adam Devlin
Elizabeth Dewsnap
Nick DiCesare
Alexander Dickinson
Stuart Dickinson
Monika Dieker
McKenzie Dietrich
Gabriel DiGennaro
Matthew Dimmick
Simon Dimmock
Alex Dina
Marc Dinnsd
Ben Divers
Nick Divoky
Adam Charles Dixon
Samuel Dixon
Calum Dobb
James Dobson
Levi Dodd
Chris Doig
Jeroen Domburg
Jack Domenici
Leonardo Domingues
Tom Dongolo
Amy Donnelly
Claire Baker Donnelly
James Donnelly
Robert Donovan
Wayne Dorrington
Jack Dorris
Christopher Dostal
Simon Douglass
Catie Dow
Stephen Dowson
Andrew Doyle
Marius Dragomir
Ashton Drake
Thomas Drake
Laurent Dreikaus

Kevin Dring
Lee Anthony Dröge
Kirill Dronov
Mikey Druce
Colin Drum
Alexander Drury
Phoebe Dua
Sebastian Dubke
Edmund Dubois
Kristian Duckworth
Christopher Dudley
Alan Duhamel
J.J. Dumlao
Krzysztof Dunajewski
    (Dunażyd Xyztof
    bottom tile)
Steph Dunbar
John Duncan
Alex Dunn
Michael Dunn
Richard Dunn
Mark Dunsmore
Vivienne Dunstan
Barnaby Durell
Brad Durkin
William M. Durkin III
Andrew Durney
Neil Dutton
Gary DuVall
Martin Dvořák
Eleanor and Larry Dyde
Rhys Dyer
Bartosz Dzidowski
Earfolds
PJ Eastabrook
Tom Eatwell
Ben Eaves
Davis Eckardt
Richard Eckley
Gregory Edgar
Pete 'Totes-Not-a-Flick-
    ering-Skeleton-Honest'
    Edge
Thomas Edge
Chris Edis
Nikki Edmiston
Steven C. Edmonds

Timothy Edmonds
Andrew Edwards
John Edwards
John 'I'd no idea it'd be
    full of spiders' Edwards
Kelman Edwards
Stephen Edwards
Daniel Efird
Karl Egerton
David Eggleton
Adrian Eiffe
Jens Eiming
Connor Eliffe
Jacob Elkin
Lady Sarah
    Ellington-McTude
Thomas Ellinson
Dan Ellis
Paul Ellis
Scott Elrick
Rob Wagner Else
Dave Ely
Kate Emily
Sean Emmett
Harry Emmott
Addie Empson
Marshall Eng
Paul England
Ashretro Epic
Zach Ernst
Midi Error
Wolfgang Ervin
Adan España
Joel Esson
Matthew Etherington
Cameron Evans
Graham Evans
Jarvellis Evans
Daymara Excel
Harley Falkoff
Edwin Falter
Antoine Fantys
Rachel Farguson
Kit Farman
Joseph Faulkner
Matthew Faulkner
Steven Feary

Allison Feinman
Jacob Felger
Paddy Fellows
Mark Felton
Andrew Feneck
Mark Ferguson
Ángel Fernández
Samuel J. Ferry
Thomas Ferry
Robert Fiddis
Mark Fieldhouse
Bret Finley
Kieran Finneran
Nick Firth
Andrew Fisher
Thomas Fitch
Sarah Fitzgerald
Richard Fitzjohn
Angus Fitzsimons
Andreas Fjärrwall
Fjimbob
Harvey Flage
Adam Flagg
Neil Flannery
Katya Maria Rogowsky
    Preo Fleming
Jack Fletcher
Richard Fletcher
Joseph Flint
Todd Flitton
Chris Floof
Denis Fogarty
Toby Foot
David Foote
Stephen Ford
Alan Foreman
Nils Forsberg
Mikael Forscythe
Joe Forster
Helge Förster
Jamie Forsyth
Tom Forsyth
William Forsyth
Delilah Rose
    Forzani-Fawcett
Paul Foster
Rus Foster

Simon Foster
Stacey Foster
William Foster
Stefan Fouracre-Smith
Luke Fox
Mia Fox
Simon Fox
Sebastian Fraatz
Dan France
Lucian Francis
Kimberley Fraser
Robert Fraser
Stuart 'Felix' Fraser
Cameron Fray
D. M. Ray Frazee
Thomas Alexander
  Frederiksen
John Fredriksson
Max Freshour
Carl Frill
Steve Frost
Torey Frost
James Fry
Ian Fuller
Jackson Funiciello
Bernie Furlong
Justin Furlong
Peter G
Cameron Gable
Matthias Gaebel
Thor Gaffney
David Gagnon
Sam Gain
James Gale
Jake Gallagher
Róisín Gallagher
Adam Gallant
Rachael Galley
Arran Gallon
Tyler Galvao
Liam Gannon
Barry Gardiner
Robert Gardiner
Russell William Gardiner
Brooklyn Gardner
Elliott Gardner
Robert Gardner

Dave Garnar
William Garrard
Michael 'Mikki' Garry
Daniel 'Lord-Ashford'
  Garton
Christopher Gateley
Edward Gaudion
Gavlar & Cazzlar of GCIP
Dmitriy Gavryushkin
Tianyu Ge
Ross Geach
Tim Geens
Pete Geer
Mariah Geiger
Alexander Geissler
Nick Gelaudie
Daniel Geoghegan
Dimitrios Georgako-
  poulos
Harry George
Jack George
Nils Georgii
Rick Geraedts
Michael Gernoth
Sebastian 'The Marshal'
  Gerstl
Jan Geselle
Victoria Gibbens
Douglas Gibbons
Mark Gibbons
Frederick Gibson
GigerPunk
Jonathon Gilbert
Neil Gilbert
Ash Gilbody
Peter Thomas Gildersleve
Ben Gill
Freya Gill
Tom Gillespy
Lewis Gillingwater
Nat Gilson
Adam Girling
Nigel Henryk Girouard
Joseph Giurintano
Edward John Gizzi
Lewis Glaister
Ed Glaser

Jordan Glen
Allison Glover
C. J. Glover
David Glover-Aoki
Adam Glynn
Danny Godál
Bartosz Godlewski
Jose Godoi
Eduardo Godoy
Killian Goetowski
Goggz
Christopher Goldasz
Felix Goldberg
Alex Golder
Leo Goldsmith
Juan Gomez
Facoochy Gonzalez
George Goodfellow
Sean Goodliffe
Clayton Goodman
Dan Goodwin
Sam Goodwin
LJ Goody
Alun Gordon
Keegan Gordon
Scott Gordon
Matt Gorner
Megan Gorski
Andrew Gossen
Chris 'Chairs' Gough
Ben Gough (Terrum)
Bill Gould
Andrew Goulding
Mike Grace
Daithi Ó Grádaigh
Billy Gradwell
Aaron Graham
Jamie Graham
Joe Grant
Dustin Grau
George Graumlich
Adam Gray
Matt Greaves
Andy Green
Asher Green
David Green
Jessica Green

Mark Green
Paul Green
Timothy Green
Tom Greenaway
Damien Marc Greenhalgh
Daniel Greenley
Andrew Greenwood
David Gregg
Daniel Gregory
Harry Gregory
Jay Gregory
John Griffin
Gethin Griffith
Mike Griffiths
Ryon Griffiths
Christopher Grimshaw
Lars Groeber
Jack Gross
Claus-Tristan Grossnick
Peter Guess
David Guevara
Chris Guler
Andrew Gurcsik
Izzy Guthrie
Andy Guy
Benjamin Guy
Carl Guyton
Josh Haas
Alastair Hackett
Gary Hadfield
Kevin Hague
Alastair Haig
Chris Haimson
Harrison Hake
Ilja Häkkinen
Thomas Hale
Calvin Hall
James Hall
Matt Hall
Matthew Hall
Shannon May Hall
Fredrik Hallenberg
Alex Halstead
Andy Hamilton
Katie Hammer
Alan Hammerton
Jackson Hammond

Sam Hampshire
Stephen Hampshire
Emma Hancock
Matthew Hancock
Richard Hancock
Robert Hancock
Doug 'TestZero' Hancox
Alex Handley
Matthew Hanley
Jared Hanna
Mads Frederik Hansen
Morten Hansen
Jan E Hanssen
Matthew 'Zoidberg'
  Harbin
Matthew Harbour
Will Harding
Farran Hardisty
Alan Hardman
Tobias Hardt
Stephen Hardy
Jason Hargrave
Jake Hargreaves
Daniel Harman
Ryan Harms
Sinead Harold
Jake Harrand
Kiean Harratt
Brad Thrustmaster
  Harriger
Kyle Harris
Breffni Harrison
Gareth Hart
Jonny Hart
Liam Hart
Stewart Hart
Adam Hartley
Sam Harvey
Symi Harvey
Oliver Haslinger
Irene Hast
Jamie Hasted
Aaron Hastings
Moshe Hai Hatan
Campbell D Hatfield
Richard 'dragonridley'
  Hatton

Ådne Haugen & Victoria
  Haugen
Bryan 'VmKid' Hauser
Adam Hawkes
Geba Hawkins
Luke Hawkins
Logan Hawley
Anthony Hayes
Thomas Haynes
Tony 'Facey' Heald
Benjamin Heap-Webster
Andrew Heaton
Ben Heaton
Cameron Heide
Ville Heikkilä
Michael Heikkilae
Daniel Heinrich
Heikki Heiska
Olli Heiskanen
Ylva Hellstrand
Patrick David Helm
J Hemphill
Ryan Hemsley
Thomas Henderson
Maick Hendrick
Mario Hendriks
Oliver Henkel
Fin Hennigan
Andrew Henry
Paul Henry
Ryan Henry
Heather Henschel
Freddy Heppell
Abe Herbert
Qynn Herd
Keegan Hereygers-Bell
Craig Heritage
Robert Hermann
Marius Herrmann
Alex Hesford
Elizabeth Hesketh
Robbie Hess
Andy Hewitt
Joe Hewitt
James Heydecker
Alex Hickey
Adam Hicks

Riku Hietalahti
Alex Higgins
Marlon Montel Higgins
Anthony Highton
Carly Hill
Samuel Hill
Tony Hills-Duty
Stephan 'The Game Chaser' Hilzendegen
Daniel Hinchcliffe
Matthew Hine
Adam Hirst
Kyla Hislop
Bethany Hitchen-Grant
Isabelle Ho
Adam Hobson
Martin Hodgson
John Hoelzle
Alex Hoffman
Gunnar 'Crazy_Borg' Hoffmann
Patrick Hogan
Sam Hogg
Harrison Hoggarth
Jacob Holdcroft
Scott Holder
Jamie Holdroyd
Dan Holmes
Liam Holmes
Justin Holt
Logan Holterman
Steven Holtz
Calvin Holtzclaw
Sam Homand
Matt Honeyball
Mark Honeyborne
Hoodo Hoodlum
Mark Hooton
Liam Hope
Simon Hopley
Austin Hoppes
Jeffrey Hordon
Zander Horn
Rachele Horsfield
Steve Horsley
Benjamin Hoskins
Jonty Hourn

David Howard
Ralph Howard
Tony Howe
Adam Howes
Paul Howes
Adam Howie
Samuel Howitt
Bryan Hoyle
Rhiannon Hubbard
Jett Hudjik
Charlie Hudson
Steven Hudson
Folko Huelsebusch
Matthew Huffman
Brian Hughes
Cian Hughes
Daniel Hughes
Dave Hughes
David Hughes
Susan Hultquist
Bryan Hunt
Elisha Hunt
Walter Hunt
Andy Hunter
Jeremy Huntink
Calvin Hurndell
Michael Hutchinson
Rob Hutchinson
Sebastian Hutter
John Huxley
James Hynes
Heikki Hyppänen
Jack Iball
Lauri Ilvas
William Immendorf
Karl Inglott
William Irvine
Jason Irving
Sara Isakova
Hanne Isaksen
Biliby Iwai
Yappa Pie Jack
James Jackman
Ben Jackson
Brian Jackson
Connor Jackson
Rob Jackson

Joe Jackson aka UncleYuu
Oli Jacobs
Rowan Jacobs
Paul Jacobson
Justen Jagger
Alec Jahn
Ben Jakobek
Ashley James
Edward James
Greg James
Jason James
Marcus James
Nicole James
Sam James
Kyle Jameson
Lewis Jamieson
Grace Jardine
Mason Jarrell
Chris Jarrett
Paul Jarrow
Tavorie Jarrow
Daniel Jarvis
Russell Jarvis
Chris JC
Mike Jeavons
Andrew Jefferies
Josh Jefferies
Rob Jenkins
Andy Jennings
Damien Jennison
Parker Jensen
Cristiano Jepson
William Jewitt
Boxuan Jiang
Jimpan666
Tom Jinks
Runa Johannsdottir
Andreas Johansson
Kim Johansson
Sebastian Johansson
Amber 'tooly' Johnson
Chris 'Chika' Johnson
Edward Johnson
Eric Johnson
Gram Johnson
Hayley Johnson
Jamie Johnson

Kitty Johnson
Nigel Johnson
Richard Johnson
Leeha Johnston
Scott Johnston
Arfon Jones
Ashley Jones
Ashley Jones
Jonathan Jones
Lauren 'Frog' Jones
Michael Jones
Phoenix Jones
Rachael Jones
Samuel M. Jones
Will Jones
William Jones
Viktor Jönsson
Chris 'DeADbyDaYiN-blAcK' Jordan
Stephen Joyce
Mark Joynes
James Judd
Spencer Julian
Tara Jurhs
Jürgen Kadlec (DC the cyBerfoxy)
Sarah Kage
Geoffrey Kahler
Markus Kakko
Lauren Kalma
Michele Kalva
Robert 'Ironleg' Kampas
ZH Kane
Jason Kapalka
Kevin Karan
Jussi Karjalainen
Jesse Kärkkäinen
Jonny Karlsson
Dennis Karm
Alexander 'Xan' Kashev
Alex Kassa
Peter Kaszynski
Søren Katborg-Vester-gaard
Adam Kavan
Aaron Kavanagh
Ian Kavanagh

Stephen Kay
Kathleen Keating
Sam Keen
Jonathan Keimig
Michael Keith
Tobias Kelle
Chris Kelley
Ben Kelly
Caitlin Kelly
Declan Kelly
Ryan Kelly
Ryan-John Kemp
Paul Kendall
Euan Kennedy
Sean Kennedy & Katharine Huseby
Nick Kenny
Nick Kent
Jonathan Kenworthy
John Keogh
Nicholas Kerins
Fraser Kerr (OfficialPirateFraser)
Jae Kerwood
Adam Kieffer & Lisa Tonkinson
Thomas Kieninger
Dan Kieran
Richard Kiernan
Brandon Kiesling
Joanne Kilgour
Ryan Killey
Mike Kilroy
Thomas D. Kim
Adrian Kind
David King
David King
Rachel King
Robert Kinns
Chris Kirman
Andre Kishimoto
Wesley Kitchens
Tomi Kivimäki
Alex Klammer
Adam Klassen
Michal Klaus
Stefan Klingenberg

Sebastiaan Klippert
Christine Klokow
Simon Klotz
Brian Kmak
Kristian Knarvik
Howard Knibbs
Paul Knibbs
Neil Knight
Julian Knight MP
Alicia Knightly
Matthew Knights
Valentinas Knyva
Kymo Misenica Kobayashi
Richard Koewer
Robert Kondrk
Christian Konglund
Petra Königstorfer
Konstantinos Kontochristos
Lars Koppens
Janne Mikael Korhonen
Aaron Korytkowski
Tim Kowalik
Lindsay Kozak
Julian Kragset
Jan Krause
Remy Krause
Tjalfe Krause
Thomas Krolikowski
Zach Kromer
Stephen Kruger
Matthew Kubicki
Paul Kujawa
Rick Kulacki Jr.
Mart Kuldkepp
Michael Kuligowski
Satu Kumpulainen
Rene Kuntkes
John Kunze
Robert Kupper
Teemu Kurki
Sascha Kutzmann
Ryan Kuzupas
Lukasz Kwasek
Joshua Laber
Simon Lacey

Eric Lacoste
Harmohn Laehri
Jamal Lahmar
Henri Lähteenkorva
Ville 'jipostus' Lahtinen
Josh Lake
Oliver Lake
Ionuţ Lala
Tommy Lambert
Nick Lamestain
Keith Lane
Miranda Lane
George Langdon
Dominic
 Laoutaris-Brown
Evan Lapensee
Nick LaPointe
Charlotte Larson
David Larsson
Rowena Lashley
Jed Lath
Michael Latoski
Zachariah Laurano
Gennady Lavrov
David Lawrence
Lindsey Lawrence
Ashley Lawrenson
Jacob Lawrie
Kris Lawton
Ben Leach
Katie Leach
Dan Leader
Kevin Leah
Alexander Leake
Darren Lean
Joseph Lear
Daniel Learmouth
Ronan O Leary
Daniel Leask, King of
 Scunthorpe
Michel LeBlanc
Adrian Cedira Lee
Andy Lee
Darren Lee
Kris Lee
Neil Lee
Rhys Leeke

Leelahsboots
Stephen Leeson
Joe Legget
Carl and Ryan LeGrand
Ryan LeGrand
Petri Lehtinen
Keith Lehwald
Steven Leicester
Ian Leighly
Pentti Leino
Eric Leitl
Hannah Lenard
Matthew Lennon
Stefan Lenschow
Brad Leonard
Daniel Leonard
Janne Lepistö
Serena Leppanen
Alyssa Lerner
Samuel Lessiter
Jonathan Lester
David Lever
James Lewandowski
Bex Lewis
Bob Lewis
Christopher Lewis
Dan Lewis
Kaleb Lewis
Owen Lewis
William Lewis
GlenDisney Leysen
Francesco Lezi
Simon Li
Libbey the O.G.
Tuomas Lietepohja
Alex Lightfoot
James Lilley
Duncan Lilly
Rolf Lindbom
Daan Lindeman
Steven Lindquist
Jamie Lines
Alex Linton
Joshua Linton
Mark Liptrot
Joe Listman
Reece Litchfield

Monty Livesay
Ian Livingstone
James Llama
Dan Lloyd
James Lloyd
Josh Lloyd
Kingston Lo
Jamie Lockyer
Daz Lodge
Aaron Loessberg-Zahl
Todd Lofthouse
LoganWhal LoganWhal
Logi8ear
Karl Johan Lõhmus
Lucy Lole
Frank Lopes
Dillon Loranger
Reginald Lorenzo
Thorbjørn Lotsberg
Norman Love
James Loveridge
Ryan Low
Jim Lowe (Lowey)
Rhys Lowen
Matt Lowery
Alexander Lowson
Alison Lucas
Peter Lucas
Ed Luck
Louis Luck
Andy Lundell
Andreas Lundgren
Alice Lunell
Hayleigh Lynch
Michael Lynch
Rachel Lynch
David Lyons
Tamara Macadam
John Macaulay
Sean MacBean
Angus Donald
 Macdonald
Myles MacDonald
Rhianan MacDonald
Nick Macey
Povilas Mačiulis
Martin Macken

Katlin Maddox
John Madigan
Alexis Maes
Patrick Magee
Kassandra Magnusson
Alex Maillot
David Mair
Mathew Major
Jacek Maksymowicz
Neil Malcolm
G Maldoven
Christopher 'Chris' Man
Will Manning
Marko Mannonen
Thomas Manship
Barry Marcel
Ian Marchant
Philip Marien
Scarlett Markham
Richard Marklew
Daniel Maros
Richard Marr
Alan Marriott
Warren Marris
Chris Marsden
Andrew Marsh
Benjamin Jac Marshall
Ethan Marshall
Mark Marshall
Rhys Marshall
Bryan Martin
Graeme Martin
Robert S Martin
Steven Martin
Thomas Martin
Tom Martin
Jami Martinez
Stephen Martyn-Johns
Rachel Maslona
Christopher Mason
Kyle Mason
Timothy Mason
Zak Mason
Michael Massey
Samantha Massey
Richee Mathwin
Lizzy Matterson

Colin Matthews
Stephen Matthews
Christopher Mauro
Matthew Mawson
Maxamorph
Jonathan May
Nick May
Paige May 316
Andreas Mayerhofer
Bryan Mayes
Jessica Mayes
MBedd
Shaun McAlister
Chris McBride
Jim McBride
Daniel McCabe
Brian McCafferty
Melissa Mccafferty
Connor McCallum
Alistair McCann
Paul McCarron
Matthew McClane
Phillip McCloughan
Ashley Mccolvin-
 Dodsworth
Joey McConnell-Farber
Jonni McConville
Matthew McCoy
Richard McCreadie
Kevin McCullagh
Robert McDaniel
David McDermott
Charlotte McDonald
Thomas McDonald
Jeffrey McDonnell
Richard McDuffie
Doug McGarvey
Ross McGarvey
Conor McGhee
Thomas Mcgrady
Andrew McGregor
Niall McGuinness
Nicholas McHale
Sean McIntosh
Andrew McIntyre
Ian McIvor
Lewis McKaig

Dean McKay
Jonathan McKendry
Connor McKenzie
Neil McKenzie
Richard McKeon
John McLean
Bruce McLennan
Lachlan McLeod
Jennifer McLester
David McLintock
Matt McMahon
Willum McMillan
Alex McNair
Oscar McNaughton
Kelly McNeil
Alan McNeill
Cameron McPherson
Jason McPherson
Craig McSeveney
Eric Meadows
Dana Meddings
David Medina
Chris Meeder
Alexander Meijs
Francisco Mejia
Nick Mellish
Carly Mendoza
Michael Merz
Vlad Meşco
Andrew Middlemas
Emmie Midona-Mole
Alex Mileham
David Miller
Douglas L. Miller
Ian Miller
Isaac Miller
Jack Miller
Jamie Miller
Justin Miller
Kay Miller
Scott Miller
The Twins Mills
Alexander Milner
Daniel Milnes
Zxin Mine
Liam Minshull
Maria Mira

Owen Misik
Tom Miskin
Bryan Mitchell
Chris Mitchell
Matthew Mitchell
Ross Mitchell
John Mitchinson
Hayley Mitrano
Matthew Mitstifer
Harrison Moenster
Tom Moffat
Aleksandr Mokhnar
Jamie Moloney
Nathan Monaghan
David Monid
Robert Montgomery
Monty & Bex
Dimitri Moore
Dom Moore
James Moore
Lottie Moore
Robert Moore
William Moore
Finian Moran
Jonathon Moran
Rachel Moran
Alexander Morley
Vince Morley
Adam Morris
Chris Morris
Mason Morris
Drew Morrison
Andrew Morrow
Jacob Mortensen
The Mother
Sarah Mouhajer
Jacob Mould
William Mower
Laura Muehlbauer
Wayne Muff
Toshiro Mühlfeld
Alfie Walker Muir
Ian Muirhead
Michael Mullins
Trisha Mulvahill
Jason Mumford
William Murbach

Mark André Murphy
Patrick and Zana Murphy
Rory Murphy
Devin Murray
Ewen Murray
Andy Murrell
Ben Musgrave
John Mylan
Uncle Travelling Nack
Benoit Nadeau
Victoria Nafziger
Billy Naing
Josef Narkowicz
John Nash
Sven Naudts-Haemels
Carlo Navato
Luke Neal
Marcus Neal
Christopher Neale
Chuck Neely
Jason Neifeld
Zane Neill
Edward Nekoliczak
Dylan Nelson
Michael Nelson
Jamie Newall
Benjamin Newman
Elliot Newman
Josh Newman
Kate Newman ☺
Stu Newnham
Carrie Niamh
Natalie Nicholas
Hunter Nichols
ryan nichols
Robert Nicholson
Ed Nickel
Chris Nicklin
Max Nicoll
Cameron Nicolson
Derek Nielsen
Krzysztof Nierodziński
Mike Nieskes
Alice Nietgen
Marie-Jose Nieuwkoop
Michael Niklasson
Nathaniel Noda

Matti Nordström
Matt North
Carsten Nottebohm
Patrick Novak
Ben O'Brien
Kevin O'Brien
Eileen O'Byrne-Hudson
Rob O'Donnell
Aoife O'Donovan
Joseph O'Donovan
Josh O'Leary
Mark O'Neill
Ted O'Quilley
Ariel & Sarah Oak
Andy Oakley
Paul Oakley
Robert Oberlies
Mike OBrien
Jarosław Ochociński
Oliver Ockenden
Paul OConnor
Azriel Odin
Travis Odinzoff
IG Oertel
Andrew Ogden
Ogihci
Rose Oldershaw
Luke Oliver
Brian K. Olsen
Ben Olson
Cameron Olson
Ella Olson
Erik Olson
Par Olsson
Alpharius Omegon
Lee Orchard
Harry Orsmond
Ryne Ortega and Colton Vosburg
Paul Osman
Maciej Ostaszewski
Daniel Österby
Andreas Filskov Kirk Østergaard
Bas Otting
Alwyn Owen
Danny Owen

Donald Owen
Aaron Owens
Tyler Owens
Alastair Oxby
David Oxley
Hakan Özalp
HiP P
Nick P
Frank P.
Will Padgett
Bob Page
Nicholas Page
Steven Page
Tony Palka
Alan Palmer
Matthew Palmer
Ty Palmer
Zoey Palmer
Gunnar Pálsson
Arjen Pander
Nep Pangilinan
Pantheria & Anton
Iván Francisco Sánchez Pantoja
Kostas Papadakis
Stelios Papanastasiou
Themistocles Papas-silekas
Jacob Papenfuss
David Paperin
Aaron Parker
Allan Parker
Jamie Parker
Jonathon Parker
Josh Parker
Robert Parker
Letitia Parkes
Sam Parkinson
Jacob Parley
Dev Parmar
David Parr
Jon Parry
Karl Parry
PartyMarty
Neil Passfield
Mark Patelunas
John Paterson

Mark Paterson
Michelle Paterson
Sarah Patmore
Justin Patrin
Tanja 'Tikal' Pattberg
Jacob Paulsen
Tom Pawinski
Jonny Paylor
PeachyPixel8
PeachyPixel8
Alex Pearce
Lewis 'Lara' Pearce
Nick Pearce
Iain Pearson
Jordan Pearson
William Peckham
Mads M. Pedersen
Erica Pegg
Riccardo Pellico
Ruben Pender
Griffin Percy
Elena Pereira
Leo Peretz
Richard Perrins
Nancy Persson
Fokko Perton
Peskeh
Carl Peters
Dan Peters
Thomas Petersen
Autumn Peterson
Christopher Peterson
Eric Peterson
Michael Peterson
Simon Peterson
Robert Petrie
Luke Petrie-Hay
Scott Petrilli
Jon Petrusev
Roger Pettersson
Tau Phi
Jack Philipson
Dale Phillips
Eric Phillips
Frederick Phillips
Jacob Phillips
Martin Brett Philo

Connor Philpott
Brian Phipps
Severin Pick
Steven Pickard
Alex Pickett
Dixie Pickles
Robbie Pierce
Mateusz Pikora
Adam Pilborough
Holly Pilgrim
Thomas Pilkington
Asher Pinson
William Pitts
Mike Plant
John Plasket
Michael Plasket
Mark Pocock
Michael Polcari Daniel Polcari
Ford Polia
Justin Pollard
Matthew Pont
Amir Porat
Thomas Porter
Jake Posner
Jorg Pot
Daniel Potter
Andrew Potts
Matt Powell
Alex Powers
Mats Powlowski
Brian Pratt
Andrew Premovich
David Presnell
Jake Preston
Martin Preston
Richard Preston
Bobby Lee Price
Ian Price
Lee Price
Alex Pringle
Daniel Proença
Patrick Prudlik
Kevin Pryke
Michael Cody Przeslica
Brent Puet
Alex Pugh

Justin Puopolo
Edward Purkis
Tyler Puryear
Aaron Puzey
Oliver Quade
Laura Quin
Jamie Quinlan
Joe Quirk
Shaun R
Kayam Raaphorst
Luca Rabaiotti
Kevin Rademacher
Sean Radford
Angus Rae
Graeme Ralph
Niko Ramdorf
Eric Ramirez
Sarah Ramsay
Jonathan Ramsaywack
Bernard F Randall
  (@bfrposh)
Timbo Randomraver
Bobby Rank
Alex Rankin
Leo Ratner
Dylan Raucci
Rasmus Ravantti
Raccoon Raver
Rhys Rawcliffe
Cameron Rawle
Stephen Rawlings
William Elliot Rayner
Phill Raynsford
Devin Read
Gordon Ream
Jasper 'Fox' Rebane :)
Jeff Reed
Gaz Rees
Joe Rees-Jones
Michael Paul Reeve
Wade Reich
Jay Reichman
Craig S. Reid
Craig Reilly
Steffen Reinbold
Martin Christian Reincke
Matti Reinikka

Thibaut Renaux
Dom 'Doge' Render
Ian Reynolds
Jennifer Reynolds
Martin Reynolds
Quinton Rhinehart
Shawn Ricci
Troy Gordon Rich
Craig Richards
Dan Richards
Stephen Richards
  (RetroUnlim.com)
Ashley Richardson
Ian Richardson
Justin Richardson
James E Richmond
Owen Rickard
Theo Rickman
Liam Riddell
Sam Riddell
Brett Riddle
Chris Rider
Jonathan Rigby
Michael Rigney
Maxwell Schladetzky Rile
Aidan Riley
Mikael Riltoft
Patrick Rimdzevicius
Nicholas Ring
Darleen Ringe
Tom Rini
Anthony Rippin
Jess M. Rivera
Jon-Carlos Rivera
Jack Rix
Martin Rix
Ashley Roach
Ian Robb
Anthony Roberts
Christopher Roberts
Iain 'chumpyman'
  Roberts
Patrick Roberts
Russell Roberts
Stacy Roberts
Brandon Robinson
Dan Robinson

Oliver Robinson
Paul Robinson
Zachary Robinson
Samantha Jane
  Robinson :-)
Luis Robles Jr.
John Roblin
Thomas Robson
Hannah Rocha-Leite
Iain Rockliffe
Andrew Rodland
Stian Rødland
Pablo Rodriguez
Kenn Roessler
Marek Rogalski
Sophie Rogerson
Przemysław Rogowski
Lola Rol
James Rollauer
Codie Rome
Andrew Rose
David Rose
Paul Rose
Phoebe Rose
Rose
Scott Rosevear
Khairuddin Rosnan
Anthony Ross
Rossco :)
Brendan Rossignol
Guido Rößling
Aidan Rothnie
Kameron Rougeou
Stephen Rowley
Maxi Rüdiger
Robin Ruewell
James Ruggles
Jacob Ruscetta
Oliver and James
  Rushmer
Andre Russell
Polly Alice Russell
Phil Ruston
Alex Ryan
Kian Ryan
Meg ('non famous') Ryan
Autumn 'Darian' Sabisch

Joshua Sacco
Oscar Sadler
Phil Sadler
Aaron Saine
Sarah Sale
Frank Sales
Matthew Salisbury
Chris Salomon
Colin Salvona
Thomas Salvucci
Michael Sanders
Luke Sanderson
Scott Sanderson
Mara Sankey
Sarah & Alex
Luke Sargent
Michael Sargent
Alex Sarll
Alexander Saunders
Nigel Saunders
Joseph Saxton
Perry Scalfano
Dave Scammell
Marc Scattolin
Matthew Schacht
Brent Schaffhauser
Jonathan Scheiner
Michael Schlechta
Daniel Schmitt
Harry Schmitt
Daniel Schnabel
Austin Scholl
Jason Schooley
Rod Schouteden
Alexander Schraff
Colin Schulte
Frank Schulz
Jan Ruud Schutrups
Jakob Schwarzwälder
Alex Scott
Anthony Scott
Mitchell Scott
Philip Scott
Tony Scott
Tim Scott (@phlum)
Paul Scullion
Seagull

Tim Seaholm
Jack Seaton
Robbie Seatter
Andrew Seidl
Jochen Seidler
Claudiu Selar
Liam Self
Terho Selin
Mica Sellers
David Sellinger
Dell Selter
Alexander Scott Sequeira
Guy Sercu
Steven Serzant
Matthias Seul
Tiffany Seymour
Mehdi Shah
Mahmood Shaikh
Kevin Shales
Evan Shallcross
Zane Shands
Bill Shapkauski
Graham Shapley
Ethan Sharon
Christopher Sharp
Paul Sharp
Stephen Sharp
Zeki Shaw
Matthew Shedlock
Brendan Shepherd
Cheryl Shepherd
Josh Shepherd
Matt Shepherd
William Shepherd
Kelvin Sherman
Michael Shield
Daniel Shinks
Grant Shipcott
Graham Shirling
Stephen Shiu
Emily Shor
Adam Shorting
Jon Shute
James Shuter
Jonathan Siddle
Matthew Sigmond
Silatham

SilentS (JGW)
Aiden Silk
Joonas Siltanen
Dan Silvester
Silvia (DoubleSNL)
Luke Simmonds
David Simmonite
James Simon
Ville-Veikko Simonen
Ben Simons
Brandon Simonson
Alan Simpson
Alex Simpson
Lauren Simpson
Louise Simpson
Michael Simpson
Iain Sinclair
Nathan Kerns Sinclair
Lauri Sinivaara
Lauris Sinka
Antti Sirviö
Charles Skeavington
Timothy Skeavington
Jack Skellington
Anders Sköld
Søren Skov
Misty Skylight
Alex Slade
Ben Slee
Mike Sleeman
Jamie Slowgrove
Eva Slusher
Alexander Smakman
Matthew Smalley
Ash Smart
Ricky Smart
Adrian Smith
Alexander Smith
Amy Smith
Anthony Smith
Chloe-Elise Smith
Chris Smith
Christopher Smith
colin smith
Daniel Smith
Ian Smith
Jessica Smith

Joel Smith
Josh 'SilentChain' Smith
Julie Smith
Mathew Smith
Michael 'Kyurem' Smith
Richard Smith
Ryan Smith
Simon Smith
Steve Smith
Will Smith
Zaq Smith
Caleb Smith-swab
Tim Smulders
Michael Smythe
Natalie May Snook
Oliver Snowden
Alexander Sofras
Victoria Solli
Alexandra Solomon
Kevin Somerville
Matthew Soovajian
Morten Sørensen
Mario Sorgente
Audun Sørlie
alex soutar
Thomas Sparey
Brad Sparks
Mr Spatula
Tyler Speakman
Michael Speare
Benjamin Spence
Chloe Spencer
Gareth Spencer
John Paul Spencer
Sam Spencer
Samuel Spencer
Will Spencer
Ellis Spice
Joel Spicer
Spiderish and SilentBob
Austin Spinks
Joe Spivey
Jamie Spong
Marcus Spry
William Squires
Matt 'Grim...' Squirrell
John Squyers

Matt St. John
Daniel Stalter
Michal Nikisaku Stan
Louise Stanley SFX
Dan Stanton
Edward Stapleton
The Star
Ebony Stark
Nicola Staub
Matt Staubin
Tom Stebbing
Alex Steckly
Teraunce Steeldragon
Sam Steele
Matvei Stefarov
Matt Steinam
Emily Stell
Thomas Peter Sartov Stelmach
Anders Stensson
Jens-Ejnar Stephansen
Robert E. Stephenson
Steven Stephenson-Taylor
Alec Stevens
Carrie Stevens
Hannah Stevens
Oliver Stevens
Sage Stevens
Sam Stevens
Thomas A Stevens
Dominic Stevenson
Perry Steward
Collin Steward
Michael Still
Anthony Stiller
Matthew Stockdale
Sam Stockdale
Paul Stocker
Dennis Stolarek
Micky Stone
Elsa Storlind
Dan Stott
Joshua Stough
Patrick Strahm
George Strange
Jonathan Strange

Lily Stranger
Antonio Strappini
Kevin Street
Stuart Stretch
Matthew Streuli
S Strickland
Ulf Strömberg
Graham Strong
Kurtis Stryker
Billy Strzyz
Will Stubbs
Jamison Sullivan
Benjamin Suminsby
Tim Suter
James Sutton
Lee Sutton
Matt 'Echo' Sutton
Vivian Sutton
Suwa
Wilhelm Svenselius
John Swanson
Jeanne Sweeney
Lewis Sweeney
Gabriel Swetman
Mark Swickard
Nathan Swickard
Lyndon Swift
Rik Swift
Jenny Swindells
Ian Synge
Jorma Syrjä
Mark Szymanski
Nulani t'Acraya
Taizou the Lion
Timo Takalo
Toni Tammisalo
James Tanner
Ian Tanswell
Ashley Tasker
Ezra Tassone
Kuba Tatarski
Kayleigh Tate (Wonderful Sound, Strange Shape)
Schwulian Maria Tatütata
Chris Taylor
David Taylor
David Taylor

Hannah Taylor
James Taylor
Justin C. Taylor
Lee D Taylor
Ray Taylor
Richard Taylor
Robin Taylor
Ross Taylor
Jade Ebony Taylor,
Leigh Sears
Matthew Taylor"); DROP TABLE Names; --
Stuart Teasdale
Nick Tebbs
Glyn Tebbutt
Andrew Tees
Jeffrey Teipe
Josh Tellez
Robert Temple
Rathe Temple-Green
Ben Thacker
Andrew Thackray
Jimmy the Eyes
The return of the Rt Hon Sir James Rich Esq
Daniela Thelen
Thrasyvoulos Theologou
Richard Thistlethwaite
William Thode
Dan Thomas
James Thomas
Max Thomas
Paul Thomas
Leivur Thomassen
Randy Thomet
Elise Thompson
Derek Thomson
Shaun Thomson
Tim Thomson
Renzo Thönen
Kody Thorgerson
Christopher (Hectobar) Thorne
Raphael Thoulouze
Kyle Thurman
Alex M. Thurman
'Flaming Spider Cyclone'

Michael Tickle
Valerie Tierney
Owen Tilling
Bas Timmerman
Jamy Timmermans
Hans Timmers
Alastair Tipping
Morgan Tippings
Douglas Titchmarsh
Brian Todd
Jake Todd
Alastair Toft
Ville Toivanen
Lovro Tokić
C Toler
Mark Tolladay
King Tom the Great
Goran Tomasic
Paul Tomlin
Dan Tootill
Tommy Törnqvist :)
Dylan Towers
Adam Towsey
Rachael Trace
Brandon Trafton
Richard Tranter
Trashbird
Stefan Trautvetter
Ross Tregaskis
Daniel Tribe
Joe Trigg
John Trigonis
Jamie Tripp
Joshua Trober
Stijn 'Zeehond' Tromp
Jason 'Vamped' True
Justin Trueland
Paul Truelove
God Emperor Donald J. Trump
D Tryba
Robert Tucker
Will Tucker
James Tudhope
Peter Malcolm Tullett
Izaak Tunmore
Faye Tunnicliff

Andrew Turcich
Foone Turing
Marcin Turkiewicz
Dylan Turnbull
Kevin Turner
Shareef Turner
Stefan Turner
Alex Turnpenny
Twilight the Pony
Joshua Tyndall
Jake Tysome
Jeffrey Tyson
Tim Uddh
Frank Uebel
Uedn
Joseph Ullmann
Kay Are Ulvestad
Josh Underdown
Alan Unger
Lloyd Unruh
Ryan Unruh
David Unso
Juha Uusitalo
Christopher Valentine
Martijn van Antwerpen
Peter van Beek
Patrick van der Ende
Anthoinette van der Hurk
Erwin van der Meulen
Jeroen van der Velden
Frank van Dijk
Mitchel van Ham
Tom van Heel
Yves Van Hoof
Jan Van Hooijdonk
Henry Van Le
Gunnar van Lit
Davy Van Obbergen
Patrick 'paardezak' van Oostrum
Garrett Van Tiem
Jukka Varsaluoma
Daven Vasishtan
Alex Vaughan
Matt Vaughan
Daniel Veal
Mark Vent

207

Colin Venters
Jacob Ventresca
Leonardo Venturelli
BjøRn Vermöhlen
Robin Verschoren
Adam Vertigan
Lane Vick
Vicky and Craig
Pere Lluís Vidal
Nick Vincent
Parminder Virdi
Kimmo Virkkilä
Virtually Reality Gaming
Philipp Visintainer
Antje Wachtmann
Neil Wadley
Bradley Wainwright
Daniel Wakefield
Dave Wakefield
Simon Wakefield
Martin (White Gold) Wakenell
Barry Wakenshaw
Thomas Waldo
Andrew Wales
David Walford
Joshua Walhane
Ash Walker
C.M. Walker
Chris 'Woodstock' Walker
Colin Walker
Kailan Walker
Mike Walker
Paul Walker
Thomas Walker
Trevor Walker
Matthew 'J Wall' Wallace
Jono Wallcraft
Nicholas Waller
Simon Walliams
Adam Wallington
David Wallis
Bracken Walsh
Jorge Walsh
Kieran Walsh
David Walter
Jesse Walters

Andrew Waltman
Christopher Walton
Daren Walz
Mark Wane
Sanwei Wang
Michael A. Ward
Niall Ward
Steven Ward
Alex Wareham
Timmo Warner
David Warren
David Warrington
Joshua Washburn
Justin Waskiewicz
Peter Wass
Kevin Waters
Stacey Watkins
Griffin Watson
Stewart Watters
Ryan Watts
Susan Watts
Cameron Wattson
★ Adam J Waugh ★
Michal Wawer
Marcus John Martin Weaver
Bethany Webb
Duncan Webb
Ben Webster
Thomas Webster
Ben Wedlake
Michael Weeks
Max Wegner
Stewart Weir
Jeff Weiss
Paul Welbourn
Russell Welfare
Sheldon Wellborn
Kyle Wells
Reese Wells
Tom Wells
Alexandra Welsby
A Very Proud Sean Welsh
Stephen Welsh
Roswell Wendel
David Wendt Jr.
Clemens Wenners

Magnus Wersén
Mark West
Chris Weston
Graham Marc Westrope
Mark Wheeler
Phoebe Wheeler
Matthew Whelan
Nathan Whelan
Craig Whilding
Steve Whipp
Marc Whitcombe
Billy White
Colin White
Collin White
James White
Jason White
Richard Whitechest
Anthony Whiteley
Tom Whitfield
Dani Whitford
Ben Whiting
Andrew Whitman
David Whitney
Lisa Whittingham
James Whittle
Luke Wholey
William Whyatt
Dave Wickham
Matt and Lizzie Wieker
Callum Wigley
Wout Wijker
Ernest Wike
Gavin Wilcock
Nicola Wilcox
Samuel Wildboar
Marty Wilding
Oliver Wiles
Ben Wilkinson
Christian Wilkinson
Dan Wilkinson
Jack Wilkinson
Abigail Williams
Andrew Williams
Caylen 'Lepecard' Williams
Clara Williams
Dafydd Williams

Flyss Williams
Giles Williams
Glyn Williams
Hollie Williams
Jamie Williams
Jonathan Williams
Matt Williams
Simon Williams
Lowri Wyn Williams-Jarvis
Jonathan Williamson
Katie Williamson
Nikolas Willingham
Martyn Willis
Edward Wilmers
Bob Wilson
Frank Wilson
Iain Wilson
James Wilson
Justin Wilson
Martin Wilson
Nicholas Wilson
Robert Wilson
Steven Wilson
Joe Wilson-Palmer
Michael Wincott
James Winder
Matthew C H Winder
Edward Windows
Dean Winger
Elias Winkelmaier
Michael Winn
Jason 'Termy' Winstanley
Philipp Winter
Karl Wiseman
Alex Witney
Shåd Witt
Hailey Wolf
Matthias Woltmann
Dave Wood
Emily Wood
Joshua Wood
Josh Woodard
David Woodley
Stephen Woodley
Connor Woodman
Tommy Woodward

Eddy Worthington
Thomas Wren
Chris Wright
Harry Wright
Philip Wright
Steve Wright
Zak Wyeth
Jonathan Wynter
Che Wys
Yuyang Xu
John Yaeger
David Yarnold
Ben Yates
Peter Yates
William Yates
Mykola Yeromin
Timo Yli-Rosti
Jarno Yltävä
Brian Yocupicio-Bolanos
Jason You
David Young
Peter Young
Scott Young
Thomas Young
Tim Young
Zac Youngdale
Tarik Youssef
youtube.com/iamthe-bestmang
David Yuill-Kirkwood
Daniil Yunanov
Snykier Zaerthaun
Steven Zeffield
Toncho Zhelev
Lam Zhou
Luca Ziane
Greg Ziegler
Nick Zignauskas
Sam Zimmer
Trey Zimmerman
Janez Zonta
Evan Zucker
Elric Zufan
Bart Zuidgeest, O they added a name size limit now

INDEX